LOOSED HEARTS

KELLY MCKERRAS

COPYRIGHT

Cover design by
The Red Leaf Book Design
www.redleafbookdesign.com

www.kellymckerras.com

❀ Created with Vellum

DEDICATION

For Joshua. I apologize for being your greatest management failure.
Also, sorry about the cats.

And the skunk.

CHAPTER 1

G reta Tremaine didn't usually put much—okay, any—
stock in horoscopes. That said, when her mother
emailed her a link to an online horoscope that promised
amazing things were going to happen to her that day, she decided
that it wouldn't hurt to believe that particular prediction.

Of course, whatever happened would have to be pretty
amazing to stand out in her already perfect life. As a copywriter
for the prestigious Prescott Agency, she had the perfect job. She
had a perfect circle of friends, people who were well-traveled and
owned furniture pieces with interesting stories behind them,
who held dinner parties where they ate a lot of ancient grains—
the more obscure, the better—and discussed articles they'd read
in *The Economist*. And she had the perfect apartment, a lovely
one-bedroom in Chicago's River North neighborhood.

None of this was due to some mystical arrangement of the
stars, or even luck for that matter. It was all the result of careful
planning, hard work, and a refusal to accept failure as an option.

Oh, and a lot of time on Pinterest.

It wasn't as if she had no idea how to dress or what appetizers to serve at a cocktail party. She'd gleaned some of that over the years from her stepfather's family, and she'd picked up some things from her college classmates. But when it came to projecting a certain image, specifically "understated elegance," she found Pinterest to be incredibly helpful.

That was how she'd decorated her apartment, layering textures and neutrals the way several blogs instructed her to do. Her living room was like a math formula: one midcentury-modern couch in tweedy gray + one chunky knit blanket in ivory wool + decorative woven basket + bookshelf full of books, their hodge-podgy covers all hidden behind cream-colored paper so Greta could no longer tell what the books were without opening them = effortless sophistication.

Okay—"effortless."

For a more personal touch, she added a circular wall hanging made from white faux fur. She wasn't completely sure what it was, but the salesperson, a sleek, dark-haired woman named Esme who looked like all she'd eaten in the last three days was a handful of Tic-Tacs, said it was timeless and very chic, and since those words fit into Greta's whole "understated elegance" theme and the piece fit into her budget, she bought it. Esme was also responsible for Greta's collection of décor balls, something she had no idea existed until the woman showed her the various ball options.

"What do I do with them?" Greta asked as she surveyed the variety of sizes and colors and materials available.

"Just keep them in a bowl on your coffee table," Esme said. "You'll be amazed at how they pull a room together."

And so Greta had purchased a shallow wooden bowl and more balls than she thought it possible for one person to need. But when she said she only wanted a couple, Esme had looked horrified. "Oh, you need more than that. That way, you can rearrange the balls in the bowl every so often and it will give your room a whole new look."

Privately, Greta worried that one day someone would walk into her apartment and ask, "Why do you have a bowl of balls?" and she would have no idea what to say. But everyone who came over complimented her on her taste, so she figured the balls were doing what they were supposed to do.

Apparently, understated elegance encompassed far more faux fur and balls than she had first assumed.

That wasn't the kind of story her friends had about their home décor, but Greta knew that one day she, too, would smile when someone complimented her on a wooden hippo the size of a lapdog and say, "Oh, thank you. I got that when I was back-packing through Uganda."

Once she actually got around to backpacking through Uganda, that is.

And on that Monday morning she felt well on her way to wooden-hippo status as she sat in her perfectly decorated cubicle thinking about how her horoscope had said amazing things were going to happen.

She hoped they happened soon, because she was working on some ad copy for a luxury vehicle and had already run out of synonyms for *fast* and *smooth*, which did not bode well for the rest of the ad.

And that was when her office phone beeped. "Greta?" a crisp voice said. It was her boss and mentor, Tamsin Chance.

Greta scrambled to grab the receiver. "Good morning, Tamsin," she said. She would have asked her boss how her morning was going, but Tamsin was always too busy for small talk.

And if the boss was too busy for small talk, then Greta should be, too.

"Do you have a moment to chat in my office?"

"Of course." She smoothed one hand over the sleek French twist she'd battled her hair into that morning and did her best to tamp down the wave of excitement that threatened to swamp her. Although she had worked at Prescott for six years, she could count on one hand the number of times she'd been in Tamsin's office. Either something very good was going to happen, or something very bad.

Amazing things will happen to you today...

"Perfect." The line went dead as Tamsin clicked off.

She wasn't exactly into goodbyes, either.

Taking a deep breath, Greta glanced around her perfectly decorated cubicle. Many of her coworkers had photos on their desks, maybe a knickknack or two lying around to spruce up their space. Not Greta.

She'd Pinterested the crap out of her cubicle.

She'd done a mood board, selected a color palette, the whole nine yards. And maybe—just maybe—when she was visiting the seventeenth antique shop in search of just the right pewter jug to fill with fresh-cut apricot roses, the process might have seemed a little...intense. But it was all worth it. Because now her horoscope said amazing things were going to happen and Tamsin wanted to see her, and soon she would be decorating a corner office instead of just a cubicle.

She grabbed her notebook and pen, then made her way through the maze of cubicles. Stepping into Tamsin's office, she took a deep breath. With its modern Scandinavian vibe and generous natural light, the room was a reminder of what Greta worked so hard for. As Prescott's vice president of creative, Tamsin was the only woman on the agency's executive team.

Someday, Greta would join her.

Tamsin sat behind the desk, straight-backed and regal. Other women might have looked like Crayola crayons in the bold colors she favored, but Tamsin, with her glittering eyes and refined but strong features, reminded Greta of granita—tart and icy and just gritty enough that you would never confuse it with ice cream. Today her suit was a rich strawberry red, her only accessory a small golden key dangling from a delicate chain around her neck.

Greta's blood hummed through her veins as she took a seat.

"Anita Lane has decided she will not be returning to work once she goes out on maternity leave," Tamsin announced, the stiff set of her lips revealing exactly what she thought of Anita's decision to quit her job to stay home with a baby. "That means we're going to be short a creative director."

Greta's heart thudded heavily in her chest. If the agency decided to promote from within, one of the associate creative directors would be moving up.

And that would leave a spot open for a hard-working copy-writer to advance.

Amazing things are going to happen to you today.

"I really liked what you did with the Revelment campaign," Tamsin said. "Your suggestions were inspired."

Inspired! Greta had to press her palms together to keep from squealing in a very overstated and inelegant kind of way. "Thank you."

Her boss made a quick motion with one hand as if brushing aside her thanks. "Brandon has asked me to come up with a short list for the position, and I am going to put your name on it."

It took a moment for the words to sink in.

"But..." Greta stopped herself before she could protest her way out of her dream job.

"I know you don't have as much experience as Jim and Reed, but you have that 'it factor' we're looking for." Tamsin smiled. "In fact, you remind me a little of myself when I first started."

Amazing things...

It was right there. The brass ring. Everything she'd been working for since she was a teenager, the culmination of years of hard work, the long hours she put in every day, the fact that she refused to let anything get between herself and success. If she reached out her hand she could practically touch it.

It took every ounce of restraint not to leap to her feet and throw her arms around Tamsin. "I'm so…Thank you."

"Don't thank me yet. You're going to need to prove yourself if you want Brandon to take a chance on you. We just got a request for a proposal from Stella Fragrances. Jim and Reed are both currently working on projects, so this is your chance to wow us."

No pressure there, Greta thought. But as her mother always said, pressure was what turned coal into diamonds. Over the course of a few million years, but still.

"Stella's director of marketing will be flying in next month to hear proposals from Prescott and a couple other agencies. They're looking for a campaign for their new Coeurs Sauvages fragrance."

Greta began jotting down notes. *Creative director.* Just being considered for the position was a tremendous honor, especially given the talent and experience Jim Carroll and Reed Pearson had to offer.

Ridiculous as it was, her horoscope had been right. This was a day of limitless possibilities.

Just then the door opened and Marion Grimes, one of the Prescott Agency's receptionists, opened the door, looking nervously from Tamsin to Greta.

"There you are, Greta. I've been looking all over for you. There's a Helen Anderson on the phone."

Keenly aware of Tamsin's gaze on her, Greta pressed her lips together in an approximation of a patient smile and shook her head. She had no idea who Helen Anderson was, and, given the nature of her meeting with Tamsin, she really didn't care.

And then Marion added in a rush, "It's your father. He had a heart attack."

For a moment, her vision went dark. From somewhere very far away she could hear Tamsin making sympathetic sounds, and Marion was apologizing over and over—whether for interrupting them or for having to deliver the news or for the heart attack itself, Greta wasn't sure.

Under it all, beneath the shock and sharp-edged grief, one word stood out: *Daddy*. She'd always called him Dad or, when she'd been a teenager and really wanted to piss him off, Paul. She couldn't remember ever calling him Daddy. But just then she thought maybe she remembered the feeling of calling him Daddy, maybe when she was very young and her parents still lived together and her father came home to her every night.

And then, through the pixelated twilight that had for an instant become her reality, she saw a red light blinking. Tamsin's office phone. A waiting call. Helen Anderson. Had she even heard that name before? "Excuse me," she said to Tamsin through numb lips. Lifting the phone to her ear, she pressed the blinking line and steeled herself for whatever this stranger had to tell her. "Hello?"

"Greta?" The voice on the other end of the phone was thin, nearly a whisper. Greta's hand tightened on the phone.

"Yes."

"I'm so sorry to have to tell you this, honey, but your father had a heart attack. He's going to be okay," she added hurriedly, and Greta let out a long breath she hadn't realized she'd been holding.

He wasn't dead.

And wasn't it just like her father to not be dead after scaring her half to death?

"The thing is," Helen continued, "he's going to need some help."

Greta blinked, her brain struggling to comprehend what this woman was telling her. Across the desk, Tamsin's brow wrinkled and she reached out a hand as if to offer some comfort. She must have thought better of it, though, because she stopped, her hand resting awkwardly on the desk halfway between them. Greta stared at it. "Need some help with what?"

"With everything." Helen's breath hitched. "He can't go home alone. He needs someone to take care of him."

Pressure was beginning to build in her temples. "I'm sorry. Who are you?"

"Oh." There was a pause. "I'm Helen. Your father's never mentioned me? I work with him. I'm the receptionist at King—"

"Right," Greta said quickly. She knew her boss probably couldn't hear Helen's side of the conversation, but she absolutely did not want to take the chance that anyone from Prescott might find out about her father's company. "Yes. He's mentioned you."

He hadn't, but then they rarely spoke. His receptionist? She'd been hoping Helen was a girlfriend, someone who would feel obligated to step up and care for her father while he was recovering. If he didn't have a girlfriend, who was going to take care of him? Greta briefly thought about her mother, but there was no way Miranda Tremaine would sacrifice a minute to help out her ex-husband, especially considering that would mean going back to her small Kentucky hometown. Who else was there?

"We'll get him a nurse," she decided. "I'll see about hiring one today."

"He can't afford a nurse," Helen said. "Besides, your father wants *you*."

Greta didn't believe that she'd ever heard that before. Ever since she was little, she'd known she wasn't the child he wanted. And even though she was an adult who no longer needed his approval, she felt herself softening.

Her father wanted her.

"So, will you come down?" Helen's reedy voice sounded so hopeful that Greta already knew, despite her dawning horror, what she was going to do.

She squeezed her eyes shut and rubbed her temples. As it turned out, horoscopes were every bit as worthless as she had thought.

* * *

IT WAS ONLY when she was standing in her bedroom staring numbly at the open suitcase on her bed that she could appreciate the reality of the situation.

Her father had had a heart attack. The indomitable Paul King. It didn't seem possible that something as mundane as a heart attack could fell a man like that. She'd always believed that it would take a mountain lion or a grizzly bear somewhere in the mountains to bring down her father.

And it probably would, she thought as she walked to her closet and grabbed an armful of clothes at random. After all, the heart attack hadn't killed him. But his non-death had its own set of complications.

She was going back to Bartlett.

Dumping the clothes into her suitcase, she sank down onto the bed. Her father was the reason why she'd worked so hard to get where she was. She knew it was completely illogical, knew that if she weren't a copywriter at the Prescott Agency she would be doing something else in advertising. Failing that, she could work in PR. She could be a receptionist if she had to. Hell, she could even be a waitress. She had plenty of options.

But deep down she was terrified that if she didn't succeed at what she was doing, somehow she would end up in tiny Bartlett, Kentucky. Working for her father.

At his deer pee company.

Some people came from old money. Some people were new money. Not Greta.

Greta came from deer pee money.

It was her grandfather who started King Lures decades ago, selling deer urine to local hunters. Paul joined his father right out of high school, around the same time he'd married Miranda. Their marriage had lasted all of four years, by which time

Miranda had managed to earn a college degree and was well on her way to becoming a CPA.

Not that she'd needed to work for very long. Paul King proved to be a savvy businessman, and the child support payments he sent covered far more than the essentials. In fact, they allowed Miranda to sign Greta up for piano lessons and ballet classes and a fancy private school in the suburbs of Chicago.

As much as it pained Greta to admit it, King Lures was pretty much the goose that laid the golden egg.

Or, perhaps more appropriately, the golden showers.

It was also the stuff of nightmares. The summer she was fifteen, her mother and her stepfather, Don, had decided to spend a month in Italy. Greta had sworn up and down that she was old enough and responsible enough to stay by herself, but they insisted on sending her down to her father's house in Bartlett for four miserable weeks. And because her father also believed she was too young to stay home alone, she'd had to go to work with him every day.

"Oh, look," his employees would say as she trailed big Paul King through the front door. "It's the Deer Pee Princess."

It wasn't intended to be cruel. She'd understood that even then. After all, her father had started calling himself the Deer Pee King in the advertisements that ran in various hunting magazines—a fact Greta had discovered about the same time she learned hunting magazines were just about the only reading material to be found in her father's house.

The Deer Pee Princess. It made Greta sick just to think about returning to Bartlett. Especially with the possibility of a promotion on the line. But she wasn't going to lose this opportunity. She closed her eyes and remembered the moments after the phone call.

"Well," Tamsin had said after Greta had hung up the phone. "You have the right to take FMLA leave. That's what it's for." But her tone implied that FMLA leave was actually for weak-stomached people who couldn't leave their fathers to die alone and uncared for.

Greta stared down at the notes she'd made in her little notebook. Stella. Coeurs Sauvages. Next month.

"I can give the Stella proposal to Reed," Tamsin said, tapping her index finger against the surface of her desk. "We can shuffle some of the work around, maybe get that new girl more involved on some of the lower-priority projects. What's her name?"

"Angelique," Greta said tonelessly. Angelique had been hired as a copywriter less than two months ago, and now she was going to get a chance to show what she could do.

Perhaps Angelique was also an Aquarius, and that horoscope had been meant for her.

Greta watched Tamsin's lips move as she silently reassigned work to all the people whose fathers had not had a heart attack that day. It's okay, she told herself, even though she was squeezing her pen in one hand so hard it felt like it might pop out of her sweaty fist and land in a very unsophisticated clatter on the desk. There was, after all, still the chance at an associate creative director position if Reed got promoted.

Unless Angelique blew everyone away while Greta was gone.

Bad news, especially bad news that's actually good news for everyone else, travels fast, and Greta wasn't surprised when there was a soft knock on her door. It was Reed, an expression of exaggerated sympathy on his face. "Greta, I just heard," he said, one hand still on the doorknob. "How you doing?"

"Fine. I'm fine."

Reed offered a small, skeptical smile that did nothing to dull the gleam in his eyes. She was dimly aware of Tamsin filling him in on the Stella campaign, of his smile shedding some of its fake sympathy, becoming ever so slightly self-satisfied. Greta wasn't sure how Reed had known that she was a threat, but he had. Now he saw an opportunity, and he was seizing it.

She couldn't believe that she was going to lose this chance at a promotion because of her father. And to Reed, of all people. Reed, a man who, when she'd asked him why he always insisted on using young, incredibly attractive female models even in ads directed at women, had said, slowly and with mock patience, "All women are bisexual, Greta. Some just won't admit it to themselves."

No. Not Reed. This wasn't his opportunity. It was Greta's.

"I can still do it," she heard herself say.

Tamsin stopped speaking in mid-sentence and turned back to face her. "What was that?"

"I can still work on the Stella proposal." Her mind raced, rapidly throwing together the barest sketch of a plan. "I could do it from my father's house. There's no reason why I have to be in the office to do it, right?"

Reed's smile tightened. "That sounds like a lot on your plate. Wouldn't it be best to just focus on your family for the time being?"

"Are you sure? That does sound like a lot to take on," Tamsin cautioned. But she was leaning back in her chair now, her shoulders relaxing for the first time since Greta had taken Helen Anderson's call, and Greta knew she was on the right track.

"Of course," she said. "I'm just going to be sitting around watching my father sleep most of the day." That was true, wasn't it? People who had heart attacks must need a lot of sleep, right? "I'll have plenty of time to work on the proposal."

And that was that. She'd spent a few more minutes with Tamsin hashing out the details, and then she'd come home to pack.

For Bartlett.

The heap of clothes in her suitcase was making her edgy, so she grabbed a pair of slacks and folded them into a neat rectangle, fitting them into one corner of the suitcase. Slipping a taupe blouse off one of her wooden clothes hangers, she told herself everything was going to work out just fine.

She'd saved her shot at the promotion. And while she had to go back to Bartlett, it would just be for a little while. How long did it take someone to recover from a heart attack? One week? Two? All she had to do was get her father on his feet again and she would be back in Chicago in no time.

CHAPTER 2

*G*reta pulled into the hospital parking lot, nosing her
silver Civic between a pickup truck and a minivan and
taking a deep breath. She'd made the drive on adrenalin,
a single Luna bar, and three cups of coffee, and now that she was
there she realized that perhaps all that caffeine on a mostly
empty stomach had been a bad idea. Her hand, when she reached
up to make sure her French twist was still intact, shook so much
that she knocked a hairpin loose. A wispy lock of dark hair
drooped lazily over one eye.

Great. Just great. Instead of sweeping into the hospital
looking cool and unruffled, which was how she preferred to look
when dealing with difficult situations, she would be tottering in
on quivery legs, her linen sheath dress impressively wrinkled and
her hair a rumpled disaster.

Well, there was no help for it. She tugged whatever hairpins
she could find out of her hair, letting it spill over the tops of her
shoulders. Grabbing her purse, she slid out of the car, snagging
one heel on her pantyhose in the process. And why not? It was
that kind of day.

At the information desk, she learned her father was on the

third floor and took off briskly for the elevators. But the closer she got to them, the slower her feet seemed to go. Now that she was there, the thought of seeing her father again made her feel queasy. She hadn't seen him in almost a decade, their only communication the occasional awkward phone call in which they both did their best to pretend they weren't desperate to wrap up the conversation as quickly as possible.

She paused outside the gift shop, peering in at the bouquets of flowers, the brightly colored teddy bears, and a little display of Get Well Soon cards. Her eyes fell on a large stuffed pink rabbit with heavily lashed blue eyes and a stitched black mouth stretched in an almost maniacal smile. For some reason it reminded her of her father. Without thinking, she slipped into the tiny shop and carried the rabbit to the register.

She hugged the rabbit to her chest as she made her way to the elevators. It was cheaply made, of the quality she associated with shady carnival games, deceptively light and stiff in her hands. The stitching at the back of his head strained to keep the stuffing inside, and the fur was so fine as to be nearly translucent. She shifted her thumb, and a dozen barely there fibers came away, clinging to her clammy skin.

One of the eyes was crooked, and, as she stepped onto the elevator, Greta worried at the eyeball absently with her index finger, thinking of the last time she'd seen her father. She'd been nineteen, and Miranda had guilted her into spending Christmas with Paul. He hadn't called to invite her himself, of course. Looking back, Greta was fairly certain that Miranda wasn't as concerned about strengthening the father-daughter relationship as she was about the invitation she and Don had received from one of his clients to spend the holidays at his chalet in Aspen.

The visit hadn't gone well.

It takes more than just sending checks every month to be a father.

Yeah? Well, it takes more than just cashing those checks to be a daughter.

She'd gotten in her car and left, driving back to her mother's empty house, where she spent a quiet Christmas alone.

The plastic eye she was wiggling suddenly popped out, flying through the air and landing with a thin clatter on the elevator floor. Swearing under her breath, Greta snatched it up and shoved it back into the woolly hole it had left behind.

The elevator finally creaked to a halt and, still trying to push the eye into place, she stepped out onto the third floor. The hallway smelled of antiseptic and roast turkey. Reaching her father's room, she stood just outside the door for a full minute, thinking.

If she was going to turn around, she needed to do it now. Once she opened that door, it would be too late.

But she wasn't going to turn around. Her father needed help, and there was no one else to help him. She turned the doorknob and stepped into his room, bracing herself for whatever she found there.

And there he was. The mighty Paul King, propped up in his hospital bed with umpteen pillows, glaring down at the tray in front of him. He had a fork in one hand, which he was using to poke at a grayish lump of turkey.

At the sound of the door opening, he looked up and their eyes met. Greta felt a rush of relief followed quickly by resentment; he really was okay. His shoulders were still as broad as she remembered, although even under the voluminous hospital gown it was obvious that he'd thickened around the middle. His hair had started going gray, but it was a distinguished steel gray and still as thick as ever, and though the bitter-chocolate eyes that locked on hers were a bit bloodshot, they still glittered with the keen intelligence that made him such a successful businessman.

They were, she remembered, her eyes, too.

His mouth moved silently, and for a moment Greta wondered if the heart attack had somehow affected his mind. But then he spoke, his voice just as gruff and gravelly as it had always been.

"So you came," he said, setting down his fork. "Wasn't sure you would."

"Of course I did." She'd meant it to sound soothing, but it came out snippier than she'd intended.

Her father started to respond, but then his eyes narrowed. "What the hell is that?"

She realized he was staring at the rabbit, which looked suddenly ridiculous.

Too late she realized why the rabbit had reminded her of her father: it was the kind of thing he would have sent her for Christmas and birthdays, long after she outgrew stuffed animals, every professionally wrapped package that arrived in the mail just another reminder that he didn't know her at all.

Resisting the urge to dump the rabbit in the closest trash can, she forced herself to move toward him and set the rabbit on the side of his bed. "It's a rabbit, Dad. I thought it would cheer you up."

His brows drew together. "You shouldn't have wasted your money."

"You're right." Up close, Greta could see the toll that the heart attack—and perhaps the years that had passed since she last saw him—had taken. In the bright wash of the hospital lights, his leathery tanned skin had a gray cast, and there were lines around his mouth.

The sound of the door opening startled them both. "Sorry that took so long," a man's voice said from behind Greta. "Rally's was crazy."

She turned, a polite smile fixed on her face. And froze.

Years ago when she'd interned at a small ad agency, Greta had worked on a campaign for a cologne by Minot Fragrances. It was an outdoorsy scent, Minot insisted, with bergamot and bitter orange and musk and several other notes that Greta could no longer remember. For several days, Greta and the art director had reviewed headshots of male models looking for someone who could pull off both rugged and brooding. They'd eventually found the perfect candidate, a model with a thin face, razor-sharp cheekbones, sable eyes, an almost feminine mouth, and a close-cropped black beard. All he needed was a dark waffle Henley, and he was the outdoorsman of every woman's fantasies.

Except, as Greta gazed at the man who'd just stepped into her father's hospital room, she realized how completely wrong she'd been.

She owed America's female population an apology for trying to pass off that pretty model as an outdoorsman. *This* man was what she'd been looking for, and she'd had no idea.

He wasn't as pretty as the model, of course—not that Greta could imagine the word "pretty" applying to him at all. He was long and lean, packaged unremarkably in a white T-shirt and hard-worn jeans, but he moved with a kind of steely grace, an unconscious confidence that put her in mind of a predator. His dark blond hair was tousled in a way she'd seen plenty of men try to replicate with hair gel, but she was quite sure there were no hair products in this man's bathroom. He had a strong nose beneath cool, assessing blue-gray eyes, and his jaw was darkened with stubble gilded by the overhead lights.

This was the kind of man who'd ensured the human race's survival, the kind who'd brought down woolly mammoths with nothing more than a stone-tipped spear, who'd stood with a hand on his sword as he watched the Roman army advancing, who'd stared off at the ocean disappearing on the horizon from the prow of his tiny boat and thought, "Why not?"

He probably didn't even have to pick up a weapon to kill a deer, she thought. He simply gave the deer a stern look, and it obediently toppled over, dead.

"Nick," her father said. "I'd like you to meet my daughter, Greta. She came all the way from Chicago. Greta, this is Nick Campbell, King's vice president and my right-hand man."

Nick smiled, and Greta's heart fluttered as the slightest hint of a dimple appeared in one honed cheek. "Nice to meet you," he said.

"You, too," Greta said, one hand smoothing her rumpled dress, the other involuntarily trying to pat her hair into submission. He wasn't her type. At all. She preferred a man who knew his way around a library to one who knew, well, anything about deer pee. Any interest she might have in a man like this was strictly professional. Sure, many women might find him appealing, but those were women who liked to eat their steaks rare and have sex outdoors, the dark sky above them pierced all over by starlight, a campfire glimmering amber and scarlet as it died beside them, the taste of burned sugar from s'mores sharp on their lips...

Obviously, that was not at all appealing to Greta.

If she found that she couldn't tear her eyes from him, it was only to get a better feel for his look. It might come in handy if she ever needed to come up with an idea to sell plaid shirts or hatchets.

She ran an eye over the solid length of his legs. Sleeping bags came to mind, too.

She was still patting her hair when Nick handed the Rally's bag to her father. With a deep sigh of appreciation, Paul unfolding the top of the bag. The thick scent of grease filled the air.

"Wait. What is *that?*" Greta asked as she watched her father peel the wrapper from what appeared to be half a cow cradled by a greasy bun.

"Bacon Roadhouse," Paul said, his eyes fixed on the double burger in his hands. "I've been craving one of these since they brought me in here."

"You're eating a burger?"

"With bacon. And onion tanglers." Paul licked his lips. As he brought the burger to his mouth for a bite, Greta had a sudden flash of Reed. Had he left for the day, or was he working late, ordering takeout so he could be seen eating at his desk? Greta may have agreed to handle the Stella proposal from Bartlett, but that didn't mean Reed was going to give up. He'd be working even harder now that Greta was out of the office, showing Tamsin and everyone else he was totally committed to his career.

And Greta was in Kentucky, babysitting a man bent on indulging in bacon cheeseburgers from his hospital bed.

Right after a heart attack.

Moving faster than even she would have thought possible, she flung herself at her father, grabbing the burger from his hands. He was left clutching two pinches of bread and melted cheese. A lone onion tangler rolled down the slope of his chest to his lap.

"Hey!" Paul's mouth slackened. "That's my dinner."

"No." Greta pointed at what she doubted was actual turkey. "*That's* your dinner."

"What the hell are you doing?" Nick said, wedging himself between Greta and Paul. He towered over her, and only her own self-righteous anger kept her from retreating.

"Saving his life. Do you know how much fat is in one of these things? Sodium? Cholesterol?" She snatched the Rally's bag from her father's lap and shoved the mangled burger in. "The American Heart Association clearly says that too much fast food significantly increases your risk of heart disease."

Nick lifted an eyebrow. "The American Heart Association sounds like a lot of fun."

"I think my father would agree that it's more fun not to be stuck in a hospital bed after a heart attack."

Greta wadded the greasy bag into a ball and chucked it toward the trash can. It hit the rim, bounced off, and rolled under Paul's bed.

Nick's gaze followed the errant shot, his hands on his hips. "Impressive," he drawled when the bag finally came to a stop.

Shooting him a glare, Greta knelt down and peered under the bed. The bag had rolled quite a ways toward the head of the bed. Gritting her teeth, she ducked down and crawled a few feet, one hand outstretched to grab the bag. Conscious of a pair of cool blue eyes on her legs, which, she imagined, stuck awkwardly out from beneath the bed, she pitched forward, lunging at the bag. But her fingertips bumped against it, sending it shooting out from under the bed just as a pair of well-loved brown boots moved to intercept it.

"Let me get that for you." Nick's head appeared as he bent down to grab the miserable bag, his eyes gleaming with amusement. She squeezed out from under the bed, her hip brushing against one of the wheels in the process. As she stood, she noticed a smear of some kind of grease on the waist of her light-colored dress.

In a move that, thanks to her own failed shot, seemed impossibly graceful, Nick sent the balled-up fast food bag sailing over the bed. Greta watched it fall perfectly into the trash can, along with what remained of her dignity.

"I'm here to take care of my father," she said, drawing herself up to her full, admittedly unimpressive height. "I'm not about to let him have a second heart attack on my watch."

That's when the rabbit's eye popped out again.

Nick's lips twitched. "Cute rabbit."

Greta fought the urge to drop her head into her hands.

Eying the plush animal with suspicion, Paul cleared his throat. "Well," he said. "I actually have something I need to talk to you about. Both of you."

"Sure, Paul." Nick folded his arms across his chest and leaned against the wall. When he moved his arms, his bicep muscles shifted beneath the sleeves of his T-shirt. Those weren't gym muscles. They were muscles forged through sheer hard work.

Paul looked from Greta to Nick. "The company isn't doing very well."

Greta blinked. King Lures not doing well? As embarrassing as it was to come from deer pee money, Greta had never once doubted her father's ability to make good money from urine.

"You don't need to worry about that, Paul," Nick said. "I've got everything under control until you get back."

"I know you do, Nick," her father said. "But I think we've needed help for a long time. We need a new perspective." He leaned his head back against the pile of pillows and closed his eyes for a moment. When he opened them again, he looked about five years older. "That's why I want Greta to run the company in my absence."

CHAPTER 3

"*W*hat?" Greta yelped.

"What?" Nick couldn't believe his ears. Paul wanted to hand his company over to this woman to run? He ran his eyes over her, taking in her stockinged legs, the heels that were too high to be comfortable and not high enough to be sexy, the short but neat fingernails all shiny with clear nail polish. Her dress was the exact color of the inside of a Three Musketeers bar, which was a delicious color for whipped chocolate filling but was just about the wishy-washiest color for a dress he'd ever seen.

Altogether she was too fragile and too pale to be attractive. Even if Paul hadn't mentioned she was from Chicago, Nick would have known in an instant that she lived in a city. She had the look of someone who'd spent a lifetime in a climate-controlled environment, the only light she knew coming from humming fluorescent overheads.

This woman knew as much about deer hunting as he knew about the company that made her shoes. Which was exactly nothing. Clearly, the heart attack had addled Paul's brains a little. "I think we'll be just fine without any outside help," Nick said.

Paul's daughter didn't look any more excited about being put in charge of the company than he was at the prospect. "Dad, I really don't think I can help you with the business."

"Nonsense. You're good at what you do, aren't you?"

She flicked a glance in Nick's direction. "I'm a copywriter, Dad. Yes, I'm good at what I do, but I don't know the first thing about deer urine."

"You'll figure it out. It's in your blood."

Nick's jaw clenched. Was Paul seriously suggesting a copywriter could "figure out" how to run King Lures—and do it better than he could?

Paul's face was growing more haggard by the second, and Nick pushed aside his feelings about the company. "I don't want you to worry about King right now," he said, offering what he hoped was a reassuring smile. He hated seeing Paul like this. This was, after all, the man who prepared for elk season by waking up at six every morning and walking five miles with a weighted pack on his back. This was the man who loved bivy hunting, who refused to use horses to pack out his elk even if that meant packing 200-plus pounds of meat out over the course of several days, over miles of mountainous trails and pure wilderness. Paul King was larger than life, the most vital man Nick knew.

And now he looked sicker and more tired than Nick would have ever believed possible.

"We'll be fine," he continued. "Auggie's feeling optimistic about fourth-quarter sales, and Ben and I are working on a whole new advertising campaign in time for the trade show."

"But that's what Greta does. Advertising. She can help you with the new campaign."

Greta chewed on her bottom lip. "Dad, I don't have the experience you're looking for."

"If you're too scared to try, just tell me." Paul picked up his fork and began spearing individual peas on the wide plastic tines.

The effect of that statement on Greta was remarkable. She

drew herself up, her shoulders stiffening as she lifted her chin. Color stained her cheekbones, and her dark eyes burned with an all-too-familiar fire. If this weren't such a serious matter, Nick would have found her response intriguing.

It was exactly how Paul would have responded to such a statement.

"I'm not scared."

Paul shoved the fork of impaled peas into his mouth and closed his lips around it. He chewed slowly, thoughtfully, his gaze fixed on Greta's face. "Could have fooled me."

As amusing as it was to watch Paul push his daughter's buttons, Nick couldn't just stand by and let him make a huge mistake. "With all due respect—"

"I'll do it." Greta's voice was low but firm. She looked up at Nick and he read the challenge in her eyes. She was waiting for him to argue more, he realized. But then he looked at Paul, and the fight went out of him.

This wasn't the time or the place.

"Good." Scowling, Paul cut off a bite of turkey and dredged it through a heap of mashed potatoes before popping it into his mouth. "You'll be working quite a bit with Nick."

"Great." She smiled at Nick. Or bared her teeth.

It was too close to call.

"Glad we got that settled. Now I can get some rest." He shoved the tray away, his dinner not even half-eaten. "Nick, can you grab my keys from that bag in the corner? She'll need them. My house keys and the keys to the office are there."

Greta brought one hand up as if to ward the keys away. "I was going to just get a room at the Super 8 until you were released from the hospital."

Paul's brows snapped together. "You can't stay at a hotel when there's a perfectly good house sitting empty. You'll stay at the house."

There was no point in arguing with him, and Greta must have known that, too. Her hand dropped, and she nodded. "Fine."

Nick watched Paul and Greta say their awkward goodbyes. Normally, he would have offered to walk her to her car, but he was afraid that if he left Paul alone, the older man would fall asleep before he got back to the room.

"Want me to get you another Bacon Roadhouse?" he asked as soon as the door closed behind Greta.

Paul waved one massive hand. "No, she's right. I probably should eat better."

"We don't need her."

Paul closed his eyes, and the fear Nick had pushed aside came back with a vengeance. Without those alert eyes, his face looked pale and thin. "We do, Nick. Trust me."

"Paul—"

"If King Lures is going to survive, we're going to have to do something different. You know it, and I know it." Paul opened his eyes, but it wasn't as comforting as Nick had hoped; they were flat and dark. "She's something different."

Nick pressed his lips together. There wasn't much to say to that. Paul was right; King Lures didn't have much longer left if things didn't turn around in a big way, and there was no sugar-coating it. And while he failed to see how a non-hunter from Chicago would be able to help sell premium deer lures, arguing with Paul about it wasn't going to speed his recovery or do much to save the company.

"Right," he said. Then he sank down into one of the visitor's chairs and propped his ankle on one knee. "The important thing is you get better in time for whitetail season. I finally got permission to hunt that big farm behind my house, and you should see the buck I got on my trail cam the other night."

Paul settled back against the pillows, a small smile creasing his face as his eyes closed. Nick kept talking, describing the stand setup he was considering, the plans he was making for a

Wyoming elk hunt with Ben in September, the status of the food plot growing behind the King Lures office.

Only when Paul's breathing deepened in sleep, the monitors counting his heartbeats with reassuring regularity, did Nick get to his feet to leave.

he sun had sunk below the horizon by the time she emerged from the hospital, leaving behind a mellow golden light that reminded Greta of old movies about summer and small towns and kids playing baseball in dusty playgrounds.

Bartlett would be the perfect setting for just that kind of movie. In fact, a few years ago the Sutton County Little League team had made it all the way to the Little League finals. They'd lost in the end, but the team was obviously still a point of pride for Bartlett; a banner that read "Bartlett: Home of the 2013 Little League Finalists" hung over the intersection of Lafayette Avenue and Main Street.

Greta turned right on Main Street, her tires bumping over the railroad tracks that ran right down the street. It was as if Bartlett prided itself on its inefficiency; trains chugged through town multiple times a day, stopping traffic on both Lafayette and Main Street and freaking out tourists who glanced in their rearview mirrors to find a train slowly but inexorably bearing down on them.

She wouldn't have expected to remember where the turnoff to her father's neighborhood was, but the route seemed to be ingrained in her muscles. Her right hand turned on her blinker before she realized she was coming up on the little road, and she pulled into his driveway just as she was beginning to wonder how she'd recognize the house. A monstrous black pickup truck with a license plate that read PEEKING sat beneath the carport. Greta wondered if her father had really thought about how that would look written as one word.

At least she had gotten out of Bartlett before she ended up with her own vanity plate: PEEPRNZS.

She slid out of the car and stood for a moment, staring at that loathsome house. It was as ugly as she had remembered it, a squat little ranch with a weirdly proportioned mix of brick and tan siding, the door painted a disturbing shade of brown. She would never admit it to anyone, but the house's façade looked like a face, one with a faintly disapproving air. If you cared about appearances, the place was an eyesore.

Of course, her father had always made it very clear that he did not care about appearances.

It wouldn't be so bad this time, she thought. She was an adult, not a child. And her father wasn't even going to be there.

With that reassuring thought, Greta unlocked the front door. She had just started to push it open when the interior of the house seemed to explode. Something huge and dark rushed toward her, growling and snarling.

Greta let out something between a shriek and a squeal and slammed the door closed just in time. Claws scrabbled at the base of the door, and frantic barks practically shook the posts that held up what passed for a porch roof.

A dog. Her father had a dog.

Either that or a bear that barked.

She took a few deep breaths to collect herself. It was just a dog. Of course, knowing her father, it would be some immense breed of dog designed to tear the throat out of a wild boar.

After a few minutes, the dog settled down. Greta crept closer to the door, cocking her head to catch any sounds from inside the house. Was that the dog breathing or just her own blood pumping through her veins?

Gingerly, she touched the doorknob, the pressure rattling it ever so slightly.

The beast inside surged at the door, barking its head off and snapping at the doorknob as if it could, by tearing the knob off, get at Greta's hand.

At least, that was Greta's impression. She couldn't actually see the dog snapping, but it sounded like that was what it was doing.

She stepped back. What was she going to do about this? Obviously, the only sensible thing to do was get a hotel room for the night and then see if it was possible to order a rhino-sized tranquilizer gun on Amazon. Then she could come back.

But as she turned to leave, she heard the dog snuffling at the bottom of the door. There was a dog in there, and since her father thought she was staying at the house overnight, he probably assumed she would take care of it. That meant she had two choices: buck up and find a way to deal with the situation, or heartlessly abandon a dog without food, water, or access to the yard.

It was a tough choice.

Sitting down on the front porch, she mulled over her options. She definitely didn't want to go inside the house, not with that dog there. But she couldn't see herself just leaving an animal alone all night.

It seemed to be a day of tough choices.

Behind the thankfully solid door, the dog let out a long, low whine. Greta wasn't sure if that meant the dog was hungry and lonely, or if it was whining because it was hungry and wanted to eat her.

Either way, it was probably hungry.

With a sigh, she realized that she was going to have to figure out a way to get into the house. And as long as she was willing to compromise one of her most cherished principles, she had a good idea of what might work.

At least, it had worked in a movie she'd seen.

Or she was misremembering the movie, and the plan had gone horribly, gruesomely wrong. She really needed to start paying more attention to movie plots.

* * *

As she had hoped, the old Shell station was still on Lafayette. A gangly teenaged boy with a Shell logo on his stained polo shirt crouched a few feet from the front door, leaning back against the building and smoking a cigarette with the world-weary air of someone three times his age. A faded sign on the window promised that she was never too old to enjoy some multi-colored slushy drink she would have found far too sweet even as a six-year-old.

Inside the gas station, Greta found what she was looking for: hot dogs basking beneath a heat lamp, their skins glistening like oiled-up models in the *Sports Illustrated* Swimsuit Edition. As a vegetarian, she had never purchased a hot dog before, and she stopped dead in front of the glowing hot dog display.

Now what should she do? There were the hot dogs, bumping along on their rollers. She saw a set of tongs, but what did she do with the hot dog once she picked it up? She looked around for some sort of packaging to place it into and came up empty.

There was no one at the front counter. A middle-aged man, his dirty jeans sagging around his hips, stood at the back of the store surveying the selection of energy drinks in the beverage case. Greta considered asking him if he knew anything about purchasing hot dogs from gas stations, but as she played out the rest of that conversation in her head, she cringed. Telling a man she needed help figuring out how to get a hot dog home was a recipe for an awkward conversation at best.

This was, she decided, exactly the kind of situation smartphones were made for.

As she scrolled through some fairly disappointing search results—why were there no step-by-step tutorials on buying hot dogs at gas stations?—the bell above the door jingled.

"Need some help?"

She knew that voice. She hadn't known it for long, but apparently it didn't take much time for Nick Campbell's voice to get under her skin in ways she did not want to examine too closely.

One finger touching her phone screen, she contemplated the situation. She had just been charged with running her father's company, and she wanted—no, *needed*—to appear capable, adaptable, and intelligent. Instead, she felt tired and frayed. The fabric of her dress, once crisp and elegant, now sagged against her skin, accentuating the fact that her body—which ran to curves instead of the slim shape she desperately wished she had—had never been meant for this style. Her makeup was long gone, and her hair—well, she couldn't see it, but she imagined it had taken on the general shape and texture of cotton candy.

And now the man who most doubted her abilities had caught her Googling "how to buy a gas station hot dog."

"I'm good. Thank you," she said. She didn't look at him, but it was impossible not to notice him out of the corner of her eye.

He didn't move.

"What are you doing?" she asked.

"I was just about to ask you the same thing."

"I'm buying a hot dog." She glanced over at him. His perfectly formed mouth quirked up in amusement.

"I've never seen someone buy a gas station hot dog with their phone before," he said, sliding his hands into the pockets of his jeans and rocking back on his heels like he was settling in for the long haul.

Trying to look as unruffled a possible, Greta hit the Home button on her phone and shoved it back into her purse. "I was just dealing with some work stuff." She didn't miss the way his eyes narrowed. "My work. In Chicago."

"It looked to me like you were reading about hot dogs." His lips curved into a mocking smile, which had the unfortunate effect of somehow making him look even more attractive. "You don't know what you're doing, do you?"

If this weren't her first day in Bartlett and she knew somewhere else to buy hot dogs, she would have walked out. But she had the spawn of Satan to contend with at her dad's house and she had no idea where else to go and she was so tired. "Fine. I've never done this before."

"You don't say."

She waited for him to move to the hot dog machine (roaster? heater? roller thingy?), but he stayed where he was, hands still in his pockets, watching her with an expectant expression. "Now what are you doing?"

"Waiting for you to ask nicely for my help."

She was beginning to regret not asking the man in the dirty jeans to help her. Who cared if it somehow came out like a come on? At least she could have avoided this. Gritting her teeth, she said, "Will you show me how to get a hot dog?" He cocked an eyebrow at her, and she sighed. "*Please.*"

"Of course." He moved closer and reached down, pulling open a drawer beneath the hot dog warmer that, now that she saw it, suddenly seemed completely obvious. Inside the drawer were clear plastic clamshells, each one holding a bun.

As Nick picked up one of the clamshells, she said, "I don't need the bun."

His eyes flicked over her as if she had just said she kind of enjoyed torturing puppies in her free time. "Let me guess: The Paleo Diet?"

"No, I'm actually a vegetarian."

"Of course you are."

"What's that supposed to mean?"

"Nothing." He looked down at the clamshell in his bronzed hand. "You're getting a hot dog."

"Yes."

"But not the bun."

"Right."

"And you're a vegetarian."

A young couple, maybe fourteen or fifteen, entered the store, holding hands and walking so close together that their shoulders kept bumping into each other. The girl's cutoff shorts barely hit the tops of her thighs, and the ties of her purple haltertop hung limply over her shoulders like droopy dog ears. The boy had finely carved features that would make him an Adonis in his youth but that wouldn't age well.

"It's not for me," she snapped.

"I assume it's not for Paul."

She almost explained that the hot dog was for Paul's dog but thought better of it. It was embarrassing enough that she didn't know how to buy said hot dog. She didn't need Nick to know she was having trouble with a dog, too. "Of course not."

He studied her, his face unreadable. Then his mouth curved into a feral smile. "I know this isn't any of my business—"

"It definitely is not."

"—but if the guy you're with sends you out to buy him a gas station hot dog, you can probably do better."

She didn't miss the *probably*. Shifting the strap of her handbag higher on her shoulder, she said, "I guess we all have to have standards."

He looked meaningfully at the slowly rotating hot dogs and then back at her. "Apparently not."

"I think I can figure it out from here." She grabbed the clamshell from him, her fingertips just barely grazing the side of his hand. Even that slight contact sent a shiver up her arm.

From the air-conditioning, of course.

"I would think so," Nick said, walking toward the beverage case at the back of the store. "I did the hard part for you."

"I fail to see what's so hard about grabbing a bun," she called after him, remembering the teenagers too late. The girl giggled and stood on tiptoes to whisper something to the boy.

Desperate to get out of the gas station without further embarrassment, Greta picked up the tongs and gingerly closed them around one of the hot dogs. Then she looked down at the bun in the clamshell, its edges a bright white against the toasted brown exterior. Dogs ate bread, too, right? She might as well just take the bun, too.

She shoved the hot dog into the bun, snapping the clamshell closed. Thinking back to the massive dark shape that had thrown itself at the door, she decided to buy another hot dog. No—two more.

Sorry, pigs, she thought. At least she could take comfort in knowing that she was using up parts of the animal that would otherwise go to waste, because surely gas station hot dogs were the last place edible bits of the animal found themselves.

Balancing three steaming clamshells, she got into the short line waiting at the register. The young man from outside had come in and now stood behind the counter listening to the dirty-jeans guy run through the lottery tickets he wanted to purchase.

Greta turned her head a little, trying to keep from breathing in the sweet, meaty smell of the hot dogs.

"Three, huh?" a voice said just over her shoulder. "Your boyfriend must have an iron stomach."

She glanced behind her. Nick lounged there, one elbow propped on the edge of a rack of Twinkies, a 20-ounce bottle of Coke in one hand. Of course he would drink soda. And at night, too. How would he be able to fall asleep after drinking that much caffeine? "You don't need to worry about my hypothetical boyfriend's stomach," she said, turning her head back toward the register.

That was a mistake. Warm, hot-dog-scented steam bathed her face.

"Hypothetical, huh?"

Greta pretended not to hear him.

"You know," he said, "around here, most people would say 'thank you' to someone who'd just helped them out."

"Really?" She angled her body so she could look up at him and smiled sweetly. "Where I come from, we have another expression we might use in a situation like this."

His eyes glinted like a knife's edge, and his lips formed the ghost of a smile. Then he inclined his head toward the register. "You're up."

Greta realized the dirty-jeans guy had left, and the boy at the register was waiting dispassionately for her to step forward. She dropped the hot dogs onto the counter, relieved to get some distance from the smell.

"You need a bag?" the boy asked without looking at her.

She'd left her reusable grocery bags in Chicago, and normally she would do whatever was necessary to avoid using a disposable plastic bag. But the thought of being able to contain that awful smell inside a plastic bag was so tempting that she found herself nodding. "Yes, please."

What did it matter? She was buying hot dogs, which had to be a worse crime than using a single plastic bag.

After she paid, she slid down the counter a little ways, taking a minute to tie the handles of the bag together, effectively trapping the smell inside. She felt Nick's presence just a few feet away, and when she glanced up she found him looking at her.

"You might as well get used to saying it," he said as he handed a five-dollar bill to the kid behind the counter.

"Saying what?"

"'Thanks for your help, Nick.' Looks like you're going to be saying it plenty." And, stuffing his change into his pocket, he grabbed his Coke and left the store.

Greta fished her keys from her purse and hefted the bag of hot dogs. Yes, if this encounter was any indication, she *was* going to be getting a lot of use out of a certain expression.

But she had a feeling it wasn't "thank you."

$\mathcal{B}$ack at her father's house, Greta tiptoed up to the door with her house key in one hand and a hot dog in the other. She was glad now that she'd decided to get the bun, too, because the thought of touching the greasy skin of the hot dog with her bare hand made her stomach churn.

As quietly as she could, she slid the key into the lock and turned the doorknob. This time, the frantic barking and sound of heavy feet galumphing toward the door didn't come as a surprise, but her heart pounded as she pushed the door open a crack and chucked the hot dog as far into the house as she could.

Snuffling, the beast made an abrupt U-turn, disappearing into the gloomy twilight of the house's interior.

With a sigh of relief, Greta grabbed the bag of hot dogs from the front step and stepped cautiously inside.

It was freezing, the air conditioner groaning as it pumped frigid air through the vents in the living room. With the heavy front curtains closed, it was also dark, with just the last vestiges of evening light slanting through the open front door.

And from the darkest corner came the sounds of some terrible monster mangling a hot dog.

Fumbling around in the bag to get another hot dog ready, Greta took a step closer to the wall and found a switch. Light flooded the room from the overhead fixture, revealing the beast in all his horrific glory.

It wasn't a dog at all. It was, in fact, an actual bear. A massive brown bear, standing on two legs in the far corner, his mouth twisted in a terrible roar.

A soundless roar, apparently. A scream froze in Greta's throat as she felt something warm and wet on her hand. Tearing her eyes away from the hulking bear across the room, she discovered a small gray dog with bushy white eyebrows and a white beard licking her hand and nosing hopefully at the bag of hot dogs.

It was a schnauzer.

A miniature schnauzer. Not even remotely beast-like and terrifying.

And the bear, fortunately for her—although unfortunately for him—was dead. Dead and stuffed and terrible, but at least not an immediate threat.

"Well," she said to the dog. "This is embarrassing."

Closing the front door, Greta handed the dog a second hot dog and then paused to take in the horror of her father's living room, with its excessive wood paneling, lifeless deer heads, and scattered Mountain Dew bottles, the whole thing smelling faintly of some sickly sweet tropical air freshener.

Not a décor ball to be seen, which, Greta decided, was a good thing. If décor balls had trickled down to her father's living room, it would have been a sure sign that the trend was over.

The dog finished snarfing down the hot dog and rose to its haunches, soulful brown eyes fixed on Greta as it tapped its front feet impatiently. "I'm sorry. I don't think another hot dog would be good for you," Greta said. The dog gave a low whine. "Oh, fine." She opened the final clamshell and let the dog have the last hot dog.

She sank onto the couch—a monstrosity in worn red, blue,

and yellow plaid—and rubbed her temples. It had been a hell of a day.

She'd been outwitted by a gas station hot dog cart.

Her phone dinged, notifying her that she'd gotten email. Pulling it up, she saw that Reed was still trying to press his advantage: "Hope things are going well. Let me know if the Stella proposal gets to be too much."

Jerk.

But Reed's email was a reminder that not everything had gone badly that day. She punched a number on her phone and was gratified when Andi Molina, her favorite graphic designer at Prescott, picked up on the first ring. "OMG, Greta!" Andi squealed. "Where are you? Reed has been storming around the office all day, and Marion said you and Tamsin were in her office for, like, an hour. What's going on?"

Trying to be professionally above feeling smug that Reed was grouchy, Greta filled Andi in on the events of the day, leaving out her exact whereabouts and the fact that she'd be peddling deer urine for a few weeks. "So I'll be developing the Stella campaign from here. Want to work with me on it?"

"Hell, yeah. I'm in. Got any of your brilliant ideas yet?"

No. She had nothing. "I have some thoughts I'm kicking around, but nothing ready for you just yet."

After she got off the phone with Andi, she opened her notebook to a blank page and spent several minutes brainstorming initial concepts. Coeurs Sauvages. Wild hearts—not the most original name, but at least it lent itself to a number of different interpretations. What was wild? Tigers, for one thing. The jungle. A man dressed all in black with a sleek, red—no, big, black—motorcycle. Heathcliff on the moors, although Greta was having trouble picturing what that might look like. "Windswept," she jotted down. "Craggy. Something about heather?"

Leaning back, Greta surveyed her list. It wasn't much of a start, but she'd be sharper in the morning after a decent night's rest. Dinner would be far too much trouble at the moment, and, besides, watching the dog scarf down those hot dogs had done away with her appetite. She stuck her notebook back into her purse and grabbed her last Luna bar, nibbling on it as she wandered through her father's house.

She'd assumed it would be easier to be there without her father, but it still wasn't easy to walk down the hallway to the guest room—her room, although it had never felt like her room at all. Maybe it had once been decorated for her; knowing her mother, before the divorce the room would have been painted bubble-gum pink with pink-and-white gingham everything. But then Miranda and Greta had moved to Chicago, and Greta was in Bartlett so infrequently, Paul explained, that it didn't make sense to keep a room just for her. Not when he had hunting buddies coming in regularly to hunt turkeys or deer or squirrels or what-ever furry animal was legal to kill at that time. After all, he said, it made a man uncomfortable to sleep in a room meant for a little girl.

And so, in order to make sure his friends weren't made to feel uncomfortable, Paul had painted the walls beige and thrown a camouflage bedspread on the bed. Greta had mentioned it once, when she was seven and having a particularly homesick day. "I miss my room at home," she'd said, thinking of her expansive room in her stepfather's house with its frilly daybed and cozy reading nook.

"Well, come visit more and I'll set up a place for you," Paul had said gruffly, as if a seven-year-old had any control over her custody schedule. "It's just for a few days. You'll be fine."

That was Paul's response to everything: *You'll be fine.* When she didn't like the clothes he bought for her to wear at his house or the food he cooked for her or the errands he dragged her on, he insisted that she tough it out anyway. "Just eat the damn meat," he'd snapped at her once after she reminded him for the millionth time that she was a vegetarian. "You'll be fine."

As she surveyed the guest room, largely unchanged except for the gun rack that now hung over the bed, a few guns—rifles or shotguns, she couldn't tell the difference—at the ready in case a burglar or large-racked deer attempted to break in, she could almost hear her father's voice telling her to buck up. "It's not going to kill you to stay at the house for a couple weeks," he would say. "You'll be fine."

Well, she was fine, more than fine actually, but it was despite —not because of—anything her father had done when she was growing up.

The dog trotted into the room, leaping onto the bed and giving Greta a long, serious look before hoisting one leg and proceeding to lick itself. "Well," Greta said. "Looks like I'll be buying a new bedspread tomorrow."

She finished the Luna bar and headed down to the kitchen to throw away the wrapper. As much as she did not want to help her father with work, at least she didn't have to spend the day trapped in this house with her father's grim trophy collection.

Cheered by that thought, she grabbed her suitcase from the car and found her toothbrush, then made her way to the house's only bathroom.

That was where she found the javelina.

Yes, she decided, her eyes fixed on the snarling pig head hanging over the toilet, getting out of this house was going to be quite a relief.

* * *

NICK PULLED INTO HIS GARAGE, parking his car, as he had done for the last two years, diagonally across the space meant for two cars. It made it easier to back out into his driveway. And, just as he had learned with the bed he'd once shared with Lauren, it didn't make sense to leave space for someone who was never coming back.

Flipping on the kitchen light, he dropped his keys on the counter and eyed his stove without enthusiasm. Lauren would have had dinner ready for him when he got home. One of her experiments, most likely, like quiche with mashed cauliflower instead of a crust or some Indonesian rice dish with an egg—somehow both runny and rubbery—sliding off the top. Lauren's aptitude for cooking never quite matched her passion for it.

Her food may have been barely edible, but, for Nick, bad food made by someone else was always preferable to having to cook for himself. Of course, one of the benefits of divorce was that he could slap together a sandwich for dinner and no one would care.

He made himself a turkey sandwich, not bothering with a plate, and carried it downstairs to what Lauren had called his man cave, although he hardly thought an old couch and a TV lived up to that description. There was another TV upstairs in the living room, but with its vaulted ceiling and hardwood floors, the room was too full of echoes, an uncomfortable reminder of just how empty the house was now.

Turning on the TV, Nick considered the impact Paul's daughter might have on the company. She didn't know the first thing about running it—or any company, for that matter. What had she said she did? Right—copywriting. Not exactly the stuff an inspirational leader was made of.

But from what he'd seen of Greta, Nick was fairly certain that her lack of experience and expertise wasn't going to keep her from trying to run the show. And that meant he was going to be a doing a lot of babysitting until Paul got back on his feet.

His phone rang. A glance at the screen made him groan.

As much as he wanted to let the call go to voicemail, he knew that might raise some questions, and the last thing he wanted to do was leave anyone with any sense of uncertainty.

"Hey, Dave," he said. "Kinda late, isn't it?"

"I didn't want to get you at the office."

Of course he didn't. Dave wasn't stupid. "I can tell you no from the office just as easily as I can tell you no from home."

"What makes you so sure you're going to say no? You haven't even heard the latest offer."

Grabbing the remote, Nick flipped through the channels, stopping when he caught a scene from *Die Hard*. Perfect. This was a Bruce Willis kind of night. "I don't need to hear the offer. I just want to make sure you understand one thing: I'm not selling."

Two years ago, Paul had transferred ten percent of King Lures to Nick in recognition of the role he played in the company. Nick had no idea how that information had gotten out, but in an industry that fed on gossip, the news spread quickly. Within months, Dave, who represented a private investment group looking to get involved in the hunting industry, had started calling with offers to buy him out.

There was a sigh on the other end of the phone. "Come on, Nick. We both know Paul's in trouble. How much longer do you think King Lures has? And now that he's had a heart attack—"

"Paul's fine," Nick said, his hand tightening on his cell phone. "And if your clients think King Lures is doing so badly, why the hell would they want to buy my shares?"

Dave cleared his throat. "You know these big investment groups. Sometimes they want a little something that does poorly to offset their gains."

"I'm sure Paul would love having a part-owner with a vested interest in the company not doing well."

"What do you care? You think Paul's sitting up at night worried about your future?"

Yes, Nick did think that Paul was worried about his future. In fact, he *knew* Paul was doing just that because he'd spent many nights sitting with him hammering out ways to keep as many people working for as long as possible, and Nick knew he'd taken a voluntary pay cut in order to keep everyone on the payroll.

"Think about it, okay?" Dave said, and there was an edge to his voice that made Nick wonder how desperate this investment group was to get into the industry.

"I've thought about it. And my final answer is no." Without waiting for Dave's inevitable protests, Nick punched the End Call button and dropped the phone onto the couch beside him. On the screen, Bruce Willis wasted another bad guy.

CHAPTER 6

$\mathcal{I}$n all the ways that mattered, King Lures had been Nick's home for nearly 20 years, ever since that long-ago summer when Paul had finally agreed to hire him. He'd been just 15, and it was the most menial of menial jobs—sweeping the floor for a couple hours a day—but Nick felt like he'd been welcomed into a fraternity. From then on, the unassuming brown brick building that housed King Lures had been his favorite place, far from the cloying potpourri of his grandmother's house, where Nana and Aunt Jeannie spent their afternoons watching soap operas in the family room, the front curtains drawn to keep out the heat. When he came home on college breaks, it was King Lures that drew him, providing a respite from the endless bedside vigils that had accompanied first Aunt Jeannie's and later his grandmother's death. Even when things had been good with Lauren, he'd never fully settled into the house they shared. It was always at work where he could really relax.

And once his marriage had started to crumble, his reluctance to leave work in the evenings to face Lauren's silent, simmering resentment hadn't helped matters. Instead, he'd put long hours in at the office, finding comfort in the predictable ebbs and flows of the business, the photographs from successful customers, the hunting stories traded on the manufacturing floor.

It was the main reason Nick hadn't sold the house after Lauren left town. It was a four-bedroom house on five acres, a house meant for a family. Way too much house for him. But Nick didn't see the point in selling it. He'd bought the place after the real estate bubble had burst and property values had plummeted, so the mortgage was reasonable. Besides, he had to sleep some-where—might as well be there. King was his real home.

He loved the King Lures plant. That's why it hit him like a punch to the gut when he pulled into the parking lot Tuesday morning and, for the first time in awhile, really noticed how much of a toll the years were taking on the building. The metal sign over the door was rusted, the paint that spelled out the company's name chipping. The flowerbeds flanking the front door were beyond overgrown—a small maple tree, a few feet tall and nearly as thick as one of Nick's fingers, was thriving among a tangle of ornamental bushes and weeds.

The building's appearance mirrored the company's health—a long, slow decline.

And that was exactly how Paul's daughter was going to see the place when she arrived. He could imagine her standing in the parking lot in that sad, colorless dress, completely out of place and yet still assessing the building with critical eyes, finding it wanting in so many ways.

The picture didn't get better as he went inside, noting the well-worn carpet in the entryway, the stairs stained with God-only-knew-what, the faint but distinctive odor of mildew perme-ating the second-floor reception area. Helen was already sitting at her desk, her fingers moving clumsily over her keyboard as she hunt-and-pecked her way through an email.

"Morning, Nick," she called without looking up from the keys. "Coffee maker's doing that thing again."

Of course it was. It would be too much to ask to have the

coffee maker behave today so he could at least have a decent cup of coffee before facing Paul's daughter. "I'll take a look at it."

"Kelsey's planning on going down to The Beanery in a few if you want anything."

With money from petty cash, no doubt. Paul didn't care if his employees used company money to buy fancy lattes when the coffee maker was on the fritz, but Nick was keenly aware of how that might look to an outsider bent on fixing the company's financial woes. It would take more than cappuccino money to save King Lures, but Nick wasn't about to give Greta a toehold. "I said I'll take a look at it."

His tone must have been sharper than he'd intended, because Helen looked up at him, her carefully sketched-on eyebrows raised in surprise. "Everything okay this morning, Nick?"

Just then Kelsey appeared in the doorway of her office, and Nick stifled a groan. Kelsey Jenkins had been handling the company's basic accounting for a couple years, and she was great at what she did. But with her jagged hanks of brown-sugar hair, big blue eyes edged in copious amounts of black eyeliner, pale pink lipgloss, over-sized plaid flannel shirt falling to mid-thigh, tiny cut-off denim shorts, and sparkly purple flip-flops, she looked like a little girl playing dress-up.

Normally he found Kelsey's eclectic style amusing. But this morning, between a bookkeeper who looked like she belonged in elementary school, a receptionist who couldn't type, and a coffee maker that wouldn't make coffee, Nick was forced to acknowledge that, at first glance, the company didn't exactly scream professionalism. He rubbed one hand over his face. Hard.

"What's wrong with him?" Kelsey asked.

"He hasn't had his coffee yet," Helen said. "He'll be fine once he gets some caffeine."

"He looks like he needs to get laid."

"That, too."

"Enough," Nick ground out between clenched teeth. "We're going to try to act like professionals today. And that means my love life—"

"Or lack thereof," Kelsey muttered, nibbling on one glittery red thumbnail.

"—is not something we're going to talk about. Okay?"

Helen's index finger hovered in the air inches from her keyboard, circling for a moment before darting down to press a key. "Do we have a customer coming in today? Auggie didn't mention anything."

"No, no customer. Paul asked his daughter to take over running the company until he's back."

Helen's head snapped around to look at him. Kelsey, on the other hand, leaned against the doorframe of her office and smirked. "Wow. Calling in the big guns, huh? What does she do again? Graphic design?"

It was a good thing Kelsey was good at what she did because sometimes she was a real pain in the ass. "She's a copywriter."

"Why does he want her involved?" Helen cocked her head, the beginnings of a frown deepening the divots that ran alongside her mouth. She lowered her voice. "Everything okay with you two?"

"Of course." At least, he thought so. But he had no explanation for why Paul would suddenly turn over control of King Lures to a virtual stranger.

No—not a stranger. His daughter, Nick reminded himself. But from what he could tell, Paul had a closer relationship with the guy who worked the meat counter at Kroger than he did with Greta.

And frankly, while Nick wasn't about to question Paul's judgment, the guy at the meat counter would have been a hell of a lot better choice to run the company.

"When will she be here?" Kelsey asked.

"I'm not sure, but let's assume it's soon." He glanced at the clock on the wall above Helen's head and sighed. It wasn't working, the hands stopped at 3:27, and he had no idea how long it had been that way. He added it to a long mental list of little crap he needed to eventually get around to fixing. But for now he had bigger problems. "Is Auggie here yet? I need to talk to him."

"He got in ten minutes ago." Helen tugged on the sleeves of her lemon-yellow cardigan, pulling them down over her thin wrists. She was a tiny woman, the top of her head barely coming to Nick's elbows, and bird-thin. Her pixie-cut hair was normally impeccably dyed the color of tea, but now, as she lowered her head briefly to pick a piece of lint off one cuff, he realized that the glint of lighter hair at her roots was not blond, as he'd first thought, but gray.

Maybe it was the shock of Paul's heart attack, but Nick was suddenly struck by how vulnerable Helen seemed at that moment. Sweet and cheerfully inefficient and now at the mercy of a woman who didn't know her from Adam. And then there was Kelsey, with those big eyes and even bigger mouth. And Auggie, all of his swagger not quite covering his shrinking sales. And down on the floor there was Ed and Janice and Robbie and everyone else who didn't deserve to lose their jobs thanks to the whims and incompetence of a woman who had nepotism to thank for her temporary rise to power.

If King Lures was his home, then these people were his family. And Nick would do just about anything to protect his family.

* * *

HE FOUND Auggie in his office, his head bent over a report that, judging from the way he was pinching the bridge of his nose between his thumb and forefinger, could not be good.

"Hey," he said, rapping lightly on the open office door. "I need some help."

"Don't we all," Auggie muttered, pushing the report away with disgust and looking up. "Second quarter sales are down fourteen percent from last year."

Obviously, it was not a good news kind of day.

"We can worry about that later. For now, I need to get Paul's office ready for someone."

Auggie rose lightly to his feet and followed him down the hall to Paul's office. They both paused for a moment on the threshold, surveying the chaos from which Paul ruled his empire. They knew what it looked like, of course. But even though he went into that room at some point nearly every day, Nick was always astonished all over again each time he walked in and saw Paul's disaster of an office.

"They say more intelligent people have messy desks," he said. Even to his own ears it sounded defensive.

"Then Paul must be a damned genius." Auggie caught the look Nick shot him. "What? I love the guy, too, Nick, but he certainly has his own way of doing things."

"Yeah, and it works for him."

"Or used to," Auggie muttered under his breath.

Ignoring him, Nick waded into Paul's office. "It shouldn't take too long."

"Seriously?" Auggie gestured to the Leaning Tower of Paperwork threatening to collapse all over Paul's desk.

"Just do your best." He rifled through some folders, trying to put them in some semblance of order. "She'll be here soon."

"Who's coming?" Auggie pulled on the top drawer of a filing cabinet. It didn't budge.

"That's the drawer that sticks, remember?" Nick yanked open a desk drawer and, finding it already filled with several hundred rubber bands and three disposable cameras, promptly closed it again. "Just hit it with your elbow."

Auggie's hands fell to his sides. "You didn't answer my question."

"I'm kind of in a hurry here." Moving to the filing cabinet, Nick rammed his elbow into the middle of the top drawer. It popped open, revealing a three-hole punch and a Fleetwood Mac CD that had never been opened, its case still wrapped in cellophane. It was exactly the kind of thing he should have expected Paul to store in a filing cabinet.

Why file important things away when there were so many horizontal surfaces available on which to stack stuff?

"Why are you being so cagey?" Auggie asked.

That was the problem with working with someone he'd known since they were kids. It had been Auggie who'd first knocked on the door of Nick's grandmother's house to ask if the boy who'd just moved in wanted to play. While Auggie was two years younger than Nick and one of the youngest kids in the neighborhood, he'd always been a natural leader, and his friendship meant that Nick was easily accepted into the group of boys that roamed the neighborhood, something he desperately needed in the wake of his parents' deaths and the loss of his old life.

He filled Auggie in as they worked. Auggie said nothing until he finished. Then he cocked his head and studied Nick with that unnerving intensity that always made Nick feel as if his friend could actually read minds. "You okay?"

With a shrug, Nick flipped open a folder. Vet bills. He set the folder into a pile he was loosely calling "personal stuff." "Sure. Why wouldn't I be?"

"Because you're worried about why Paul decided to put his daughter in charge instead of you."

"I'm sure Paul has his reasons."

Auggie stopped working, hands on his hips. "This isn't working."

"I'm not the one who put her in charge."

"I'm talking about this." Auggie lifted his hands. "There's no way we're going to get this place cleaned up enough for someone to actually work here before she arrives. Maybe you could put her in the conference room."

Nick shuffled a few more folders around. Auggie was right. Paul's office was a disaster. It would take days for someone to sort through everything. Weeks, maybe.

He froze. Everything someone needed to understand the inner workings of King Lures was in this room—buried under a mountain of random crap. Someone needed to go through everything, to sort the important stuff from the stuff that didn't matter.

Like the 1996 Kathy Ireland calendar he uncovered when he lifted a pile of hunting journals.

In fact, it would make perfect sense for the person Paul had placed in charge to go through everything. And if Greta was busy tidying up Paul's office, she wouldn't have time to get herself—or, more importantly, King Lures—into any trouble.

She might even take one look at this mess and decide heading back to Chicago was the wisest course of action.

"You're right," he said, straightening up. "I'll figure it out."

Smiling, he stepped out of Paul's office. All he had to do was keep Greta occupied long enough that he could ensure there was still a King Lures in the future.

And, thanks to Paul's horrendous organization system, he had the perfect way to do it.

Auggie caught up to him in the hallway. "What's she like?"

"It would probably be best for you to keep your distance. She's Paul's daughter, after all."

Auggie glanced up, his wide mouth sliding into a crooked grin. "Is she hot?"

Nick had a flash of two legs sticking out from under Paul's hospital bed, a long run along her calf revealing a glimpse of ridiculously pale skin beneath her stockings. No, she definitely wasn't hot.

"She has a pulse," he said drily.

"That does make her my type." They reached Auggie's office, and he paused just outside. "Don't worry, boss. Strictly hands off."

But as Nick headed for his own office, he found that, for some reason, he couldn't push the thought of that vulnerable white skin out of his mind.

CHAPTER 7

There was a reason, Greta decided as she stood, hands clasped and twisting in front of her, that no one ever said, "Oh, dear. The business is in trouble. Someone call a copywriter!"

She'd searched "running a business" on Pinterest that morning and found a blog on how to be a #girlboss. She didn't want to be a #girlboss; she wanted to be a serious business-woman. Well, no, not even that—she wanted to be a creative director at the Prescott Agency, with her own team working under her. That said, the #girlboss post was an easy read, upbeat and positive, and, as she left her father's house, she felt as if perhaps it wasn't so ridiculous that she handled the company—briefly—after all.

But that confidence had drained away the moment she pulled into the King parking lot. She wasn't sure what she'd expected to find when she arrived. A short pamphlet on how to save a strug-gling business, complete with step-by-step checklist? A file labeled "Mistakes We're Making and How to Correct Them" hidden behind a bookshelf?

Of course, nothing of the sort was anywhere to be found.

Anyway, if the problems at King Lures—or the solutions to said problems—were obvious, her father or the man now watching her darkly would have already identified them.

She blew out a long breath.

"So, um, how many employees does King have?" That seemed like a decent enough question, the kind of thing a #girlboss would want to know.

"Paul keeps all the personnel files in his office." Nick paused in front of a stack of folded cardboard boxes. "This is the shipping department."

She'd thought a quick tour might help familiarize her with the workings of the business, but so far getting anything more than the obvious out of Nick had proved impossible.

"What's the company's annual revenue?" she asked.

"That information is in Paul's office." He was on the move again, heading back toward the stairs that led from the manufacturing floor to the offices on the second floor. Greta had to practically run to keep up.

"Do you know—"

"Look," Nick said as he started up the steps, "everything you need to know is in Paul's office."

Right.

They reached the small reception area on the second floor, and Greta nodded at Helen as Nick led her past the front desk and down a long, gloomy hallway. A couple photos of various King Lures employees with animals they'd killed hung on the walls, but otherwise the place was...uninspiring.

No wonder the company was in trouble.

"Here we are," Nick said as they came to the last door on the right. Stepping back, he swept out one arm in an invitation for her to go in before him.

She stopped short, her mouth dropping open as she surveyed her father's office.

Surely Nick was playing some sort of joke on her. This wasn't an office—it had to be a kid's science fair project proving the existence of the second law of thermodynamics. No one, not even her father, could work in such a...such a...*disaster*.

"As I said," Nick said from behind her, "everything you need to run the company is in there."

"Well, of course it is. I'm pretty sure *everything* is in there. Like, the entirety of the universe." She wouldn't be surprised to find a school bus hidden under some pile of random paperwork. She spun around in time to catch his smirk before he had time to hide it. "You're enjoying this."

"I'm not *not* enjoying this."

Clamping her lips shut to keep from saying what she wanted to say, she turned back to her father's office. It was hopelessly, impossibly disorganized. No wonder the company was in bad shape. How could anyone find anything in this jumble of...whatever was in there?

She froze.

How could someone run a business from this mess? They couldn't, at least not efficiently. And if there was one thing Greta knew she definitely could do, it was organize a space.

Even one as daunting as this one.

"Well, then," she said, stepping over the threshold. She wished she was wearing something different so she had long sleeves to roll up—it felt like that kind of moment—but she would have to make do without them. "I guess I'll get started."

"Are you sure?" Nick sauntered into the office and nudged what appeared to be a pile of dirty socks with the toe of his boot. "Looks like a lot of work."

"I'm not afraid of hard work."

"Right." But he looked her up and down skeptically. Obviously King Lures believed in a casual dress code; Nick was again wearing a plain white T-shirt and jeans, a brown leather belt around his narrow hips. He should have looked unprofessional, but Greta had the uncomfortable realization that he would have looked somehow diminished in a business suit. There was something about the intensely male air of confidence about him that made him look more pulled together in jeans and a T-shirt than Reed Pearson had ever looked in a sports coat and slacks.

Confidence. That was, Greta thought, the difference between men and women in the workplace. Some men had an excess of confidence, often without the competence to back it up, whereas for women it was too frequently the opposite. In this case, Greta knew she didn't have the knowledge or experience to do the job her father had asked her to do, and, faced with the reality of the situation, she wasn't feeling at all confident. But rule number one for being a #girlboss was to fake it 'til you make it, and that seemed like as good a course as any at the moment.

Lifting her chin, she dismissed him with as much self-assurance as she could muster. "Thank you. I don't think I'll need any help with this." She ran her thumb over the tabs on a stack of manila folders, taking in the labels: A/R, BEARS, FOOD PLOT CHARTS.

He shoved his hands in his pocket. "I shouldn't think so. It's not all that hard."

"Give yourself a little credit." She picked up one of the folders. "It must be somewhat hard, or you would have been able to do it yourself."

Nick smiled, a slow, tight smile that didn't come close to touching his eyes. "I have other priorities to take care of."

"You can't be taking care of them very well if my father has asked me to take over."

It was a low blow, but even so Greta was surprised at how hard it struck. His face darkened, his eyes glittering like ice chips. She nearly opened her mouth to apologize, but before she had a chance, the hard line of his shoulders relaxed and he inclined his head toward her. He'd seen right through her, she realized, somehow knew that she was operating based on information from a blog post on how to sell some multi-level marketing product. "You done?" he asked.

"Done?" She pulled out her father's chair and sank into it. "I'm just getting started." She shooed him out of the room with a quick wave of her hand.

His mouth quirked—in amusement or disdain, she wasn't sure. And then he turned away, his shoulders filling the doorway, and was gone.

* * *

TWO HOURS LATER, Greta had a pounding headache that her normal dose of Excedrin hadn't touched. As far as she could tell, none of the labels on the manila folders matched their contents. In a folder marked "INCOME STATEMENTS," she found just one sheet of paper: a receipt for a magazine subscription payment from 1997, and a folder labeled "CABLE BILLS" contained a daily log of how well her father stuck to some diet for two months.

Almost every other day he'd written "cheat day" in his careless handwriting.

At least he'd owned it.

She closed the manila folder in front of her and sighed, massaging her temples in a vain attempt to ease the tightening in her head. She'd moved the room's small trash can next to her chair, and it was already overflowing with papers that were no longer—or had never been—relevant. A light knock on the open door made her look up. The young woman she'd met when she first arrived leaned in, regarding her with a mix of amusement and genuine sympathy. "How you doing?" she asked.

"I'm not sure," Greta said, pulling out a tri-folded sheet of paper. She'd only met Kelsey briefly, but she was grateful for the chance to speak with someone who didn't regard her with suspicion and condescension. "How important do you think this Chinese takeout menu is?"

"Red Dragon or Wok Garden?"

"Wok Garden."

Kelsey slipped into the room and plopped into the chair across from her. "That's a keeper, then."

"But not Red Dragon?"

"Red Dragon closed when I was eleven. And, if I remember correctly, the eggrolls were gross." The young woman leaned back in her chair, studying Greta openly beneath shaggy bangs. "Is there anything I can help with?"

How opposed are you to committing insurance fraud, Greta was tempted to say. Because from what she could see, the easiest way out from under that mountain of useless paperwork was to set fire to it and let the whole place burn to the ground.

It would probably make the company more profitable. Or profitable in the first place.

If only she didn't care about things like ethics and consequences. "You said you did the accounting?"

"Not the complicated stuff. Paul has a CPA for that. I just do the basic bookkeeping, accounts receivable, accounts payable, that sort of thing."

"How's the business doing?"

Kelsey spent several long seconds examining a chip in her nail polish. Then she looked up and met Greta's eyes. "Honestly? It seems to me that we have more money going out than coming in."

Greta didn't need to be a successful #girlboss to know that wasn't good. "What are the company's biggest expenses?"

"Well..." Kelsey brushed her hair back from her face with the back of her hand, revealing a flock of tiny birds, wings outstretched in flight, tattooed on her inner wrist. She chewed on her lower lip. "It's payroll. That's the biggest single expense."

"I see." Pulling out her notebook, Greta made a quick notation.

"Are you here to lay people off?"

Greta froze. She wasn't...was she? Had her father asked her to step in for a few weeks in the hopes that she would do his dirty work for him? After all, she didn't know any of these people, and she'd be gone in a few weeks. If people needed someone to blame besides the great and powerful Paul King, she was a handy scapegoat.

That would also explain why he put her in charge instead of Nick. This way, they could both keep their hands clean while Greta streamlined the company.

Well, her father had underestimated her. Or overestimated. There was no way she was capable of letting people go.

An uncomfortable thought occurred to her. As a copywriter, she'd never been involved in hiring or firing people. But as a creative director, she'd have input into those kinds of decisions.

She drew a sharp line under where she'd written "Payroll" in her notebook and fixed a smile on her face. That was something she could worry about in the future. She hadn't even landed the job yet.

"Of course not," she said. "I'm just here to..." She set her pen down and looked around her at the piles of paperwork. Then she lifted her hands helplessly. "I'm just here to see what I can do to help." There. That was honest.

It also said exactly nothing.

But it had the desired effect on Kelsey, who relaxed visibly. "Great. Everyone will be so relieved to hear that."

She knew she needed to get through at least another stack before she took a lunch break. She'd worked out how much she needed to accomplish per hour in order to finish going through everything in three days; her target goals were written neatly in her notebook. But she just couldn't force herself to open another folder. It struck her that getting to know the employees better would be helpful. Maybe someone in the organization was underutilized or would be better suited to a different position. Perhaps Kelsey, with her youth and probable technological know-how, had some hidden talents that Greta could identify and tap into.

Across the table, Kelsey picked up a sheet of paper from her side of the table, looked over it for a moment, and then absently began folding it into a paper airplane.

Talents besides origami.

"How long have you worked here?" she asked.

Kelsey creased the fold of a wing. "About two years. Since Sarah Bates retired." She added a little flap to the end of the wing and shrugged. "To be honest, I think I got the job because Paul could hire me cheaper than anyone else. I don't have kids, and I still live with my parents, so I don't need to make much. Besides, I'm not working here for the money. I'm here for the eye candy. Auggie Paladino, Nick Campbell, Robbie Montufar..." She sighed.

Just the sound of Nick's name had Greta's heart rate picking up a notch, although she definitely didn't consider him to be eye candy. Eye candy should be uncomplicated. Pleasant to look at, and nothing more. It shouldn't be resentful and difficult.

And it most definitely shouldn't talk back.

She tapped the end of her silver pen against her open notebook, casting about for something to say that would steer the conversation away from Nick Campbell. She'd met Auggie Paladino, the national sales manager, and he was definitely eye candy, with his wide mouth and medium-brown hair touched at the temples with streaks of premature gray. He'd been friendly and warm, but there was something about his eyes, something haunted and wistful, that reminded Greta just a little of James Dean. "I haven't met Robbie Montufar yet. What does he do here?"

"He's in charge of shipping. I went to high school with him."

Her blue eyes grew soft and dreamy. "He played Captain Hook in our school's production of *Peter Pan* senior year. You know how sometimes you don't really notice somebody until they're dressed like a pirate?"

"I can't say that I've had that experience."

Straightening in her chair, Kelsey busied herself with her the second wing of her paper airplane. "Well, I guess a lot of girls had the same reaction I did, because he's pretty much had a girlfriend ever since." She ran her hand along the wing's crease ferociously. "Lots of girlfriends."

Pirates, huh? Greta turned the idea over in her mind. A storm-tossed sea, foam-capped waves battering a wooden ship under the grim eye of a skull and crossbones. A man at the helm, his shirt billowing open to the waist, long hair jeweled with droplets of seawater. And—of course—a cutlass.

A big one.

She flipped back to where she'd made her notes for the Coeurs Sauvages campaign and jotted down a couple thoughts. When she looked back up, Kelsey was regarding her completed paper airplane, her expression gloomy. "I guess if the company goes under, I can always go back to working at my parents' coffee shop. I'll miss seeing Robbie every day, though."

Slowly, Greta closed her notebook. Judging from the tone of Kelsey's voice, she really didn't want to wind up working at her family's business, and that was something Greta understood. "My father and I aren't going to let King Lures go under," she said. "We're going to figure this out. Don't worry."

Kelsey studied her for a moment and, apparently satisfied, nodded sharply. "Thanks." Then she bounced to her feet, looking suddenly years younger. "I better get back to work. Let me know if you need anything."

Greta watched her go, her mind still processing what she'd told Kelsey. My father and I, as if they were a team. Two people working together instead of battling against each other. She wasn't sure she'd ever said those words before.

It felt strange, but as she flipped open the next folder to review the contents, she couldn't help repeating the words silently to herself.

My father and I.

CHAPTER 8

*G*reta left the office shortly after five, marveling at the fact that she had left work while the sun was still up. At Prescott, she would have stayed for several more hours, either because she actually had work to do or because she wanted to look as if she did. But everyone except Nick left the office right on time, and she really didn't want to be alone in that building with him. Besides, she needed to get home to take the dog out before she dropped by the hospital to see her father. Then she planned to spend the rest of the evening working on the Coeurs Sauvages campaign.

As she led the dog down the driveway to the street, she decided having a dog wasn't all that bad. It was nice to have an excuse to go for a walk, although she did wish she had packed more casual clothes when she'd left Chicago. Her heels were comfortable enough for a long day in the office, but they weren't designed for a long walk over asphalt.

Still, it was surprisingly pleasant to meander through her father's neighborhood. A group of kids were playing some complicated version of tag in one yard, gleefully taunting each other about bases and tagbacks and puppy-guarding. Behind another house, a woman hung crisp white sheets on a clothesline, her mouth bristling with clothespins as she battled the flapping sheets into submission. In the distance, a lawnmower hummed, and the wind carried the scent of fresh-cut grass as it tickled Greta's bare arms.

She turned onto a side street, the dog trotting slightly ahead. Although she'd spent time at her father's house as a child, she wasn't really familiar with the neighborhood. She'd suffered through her visits to her father by holing up in the house with an armload of books and pretending that she was already back at home.

As she rounded a bend in the road, an older woman weeding a flowerbed glanced up and saw her. Sitting back on her heels, she pulled off her sunglasses and studied Greta as she approached.

"Well," she said finally. "Aren't you just your father made over?" Then she barked a laugh and hauled herself to her feet. "Don't look so appalled. It was meant as a compliment, even though you obviously didn't take it as such."

"I'm not appalled," Greta said, although she kind of was. She knew she favored her father, but she desperately wished she looked more like her glamorous mother, who had fire-gold hair and fine features and long, elegant fingers.

"You don't remember me," the older woman said.

Greta dredged her memory for any hint as to who this woman was but came up with nothing. She was old enough to be Greta's grandmother, her cheeks paper-thin and sunken above a small, pursed mouth. Her apricot bob was tucked behind her ears and held back with a pink visor that read "Breast Cancer Survivor" in curly script. She was thin, with narrow shoulders inside a baggy Mitchell's Manure Movers T-shirt, but the legs sticking out from her long khaki shorts looked sturdy and her brown eyes were sharp. "I'm sorry. I don't."

The woman shrugged. "I wouldn't expect you to. You never

did care much about mingling with the locals when you came to visit."

It sounded snobbish when put that way, and Greta started to protest when the woman held up a hand to stop her. "Never mind that. It was obviously not an easy situation for you, but you're here now, and that's what counts. I'm Pea Coggshell." The dog sniffed at the older woman's tennis shoes, and she bent down to rub its head. "How are things going so far?"

Greta thought of the mountain of files she still had to go through and how little of what she'd already sorted had made it into the "keep" pile. And that was just the beginning. Somehow she had to figure out a way to turn things around at a company she'd never wanted to be a part of, selling a product that completely mystified her, and doing a job she had no idea how to do.

Oh, and she had to do it all under the watchful eyes of one very suspicious vice president.

"Fine," she said.

Pea's lips quivered. "Don't ever play poker." She turned and began walking away, leaving Greta behind. For a moment, Greta assumed she'd been summarily dismissed, but then Pea, without looking back, waved one hand to indicate she should follow. "Come on. I'll show you my roses."

"Oh, I don't..." But there was no point in saying anything else. Pea was already halfway across her front yard, out of earshot. Reluctantly, Greta led the dog across Pea's yard, noting the riotous jumble of color and scent and swarming pollinators that filled the flowerbeds. Gnomes, too. Pea was obviously fond of gnomes. And fairy houses, and concrete frogs, and little pinwheels that whirred among the flowers.

Pea disappeared around the side of the house, and Greta hurried to keep up. She found the older woman waiting for her by a charmingly classic white picket fence, holding the gate open with one hand. "I keep the best roses this side of the Ohio. That's not bragging, now. That's just the truth."

Greta didn't know much about roses, but as she led the dog through the gate she had a feeling that if Pea was exaggerating, it wasn't by much. The garden was an enchanting place. There were roses of every color—coral and apricot and buttery yellow and ivory and lavender and a deep, secret red. In one corner, a trellis, laden with creamy-pink climbing roses, arched over a barnwood bench. A large statue of an angel, with chubby cheeks and big sausage curls, spread her wings in another corner, and a fountain bubbled peacefully in the center of it all.

Somewhere, an unseen wind chime jingled.

"It's incredible," Greta said.

"Thank you." Pea smiled and sank down onto the bench. She pulled a piece of hard candy from her pocket and held it up. Its gold cellophane wrapper caught the sunlight and sparkled. "Want a butterscotch?"

"No, thank you." She turned in a slow circle, shading her eyes against the late afternoon sun. "It's so beautiful back here."

Pea unwrapped the candy and popped it into her mouth. "A lot of my neighbors come here when they need to think." Her lips pursed even more as she sucked on the candy. "You're welcome to stop by whenever you need to."

Greta nodded, but she couldn't imagine just stopping by a stranger's house to sit in their garden and think. Even with her closest friends back home, she would never dream of dropping in unannounced. She didn't visit her own mother without calling first.

But it was nice to spend a little time there, the dog snuffling at the ground, gently tugging her from bush to bush. It was several minutes before she realized that she'd allowed the silence to stretch out. It should have felt awkward, but it didn't. Looking back at her host, she saw Pea still sitting on the bench, her eye half-closed, not looking at her but not *not* looking at her either. She was just...sitting. Relaxing. Living in the moment.

Unfortunately, Greta had several other moments in which she needed to be living. Turning away from the roses she'd been admiring, she started to walk toward the gate. "Thank you so much, but I really need to—"

The leash went taut.

She pulled a little harder, but the dog wouldn't budge.

From the way Pea's mouth tightened in an amused pucker around her hard candy, Greta had a feeling she knew what she would find when she turned around. But she allowed herself a moment of optimism. *Maybe it's just really interested in these roses,* she thought.

But, no. The dog was squatting, a faraway look on its fuzzy little face as it deposited its own kind of offering at the feet of the stone angel.

Greta stared at the dog. She knew, of course, that this was what dogs did. She should have expected this. She should have been prepared for this eventuality.

But here she was, caught unawares by a dog crapping in a rose garden.

And didn't that just about sum up how her life was going at the moment?

She turned back to Pea, who was still watching her, her eyes twinkling. "You wouldn't happen to have a plastic bag I could use, would you?"

* * *

NICK FLICKED a button on the remote just as the door opened and the uptight vegetarian walked in.

"What the hell are you doing here?" she asked.

Nick took in Greta's wildly curling hair, snapping dark eyes, and heat-flushed skin, which extended from her cheeks down to the tiny V of bare skin exposed by the far-too-modest neckline of her dress, this one an anemic gray. She looked rumpled and hot and, well, almost sexy.

Of course, the bag of what he was pretty sure was dog crap clutched in one hand was kind of a turnoff.

Lazily, he laid one arm over the back of the couch and returned his attention to the TV. "Your dad forgot to record a couple shows. He asked me to come over and take care of it."

"Why didn't he just have me do it?"

"You'll have to ask him." He stretched out his legs, propping one foot over the other. "Maybe he doesn't trust you to get it right."

Work the DVR? Nope. Run the company? Oh, sure.

"But he...Never mind. Do you know where my father keeps his trash can?"

"Yes."

She waited. Out of the corner of his eye, he watched her unclip the leash. The dog bolted toward him, leaping onto the couch and greeting him with joyous sniffs. "Easy, Polly," he said, scratching behind her ears with one hand until she fell onto her side and laid there, gazing up at him adoringly.

"Are you going to tell me where it is?"

"Where what is?"

She sighed. "The trash can."

"When you ask." He flipped the channel. "Nicely."

"Do you ever do anything the easy way?"

"I know your type. You wouldn't be happy if things were too easy." Then he looked up and took pity on her. She had her hands on her hips. Well, one hand anyway. The hand with the dog poop was about as far away from her body as she could manage. "Fine," he conceded. "It's in the cabinet under the sink."

"Not that one. I don't want this—" she wiggled the bag in her hand slightly"—in the house. He must have an outdoor garbage can, right?"

"Shockingly enough, that one is located *outdoors*. You might have found it yourself if you had, I don't know, looked for it."

"I'm not the enemy, you know." She stormed past him, poop bag still held at arm's length, heading for the back door. "Things would go a whole lot smoother if we could just work together."

"Smoother for you." He flipped to one of the outdoor channels and grimaced as he caught a commercial for Hampton Scents, one of King's biggest competitors. Their products weren't as good as King's, but you wouldn't know that from their sales.

He heard the back door open. Giving Polly one last belly rub, he got up. Greta might be perfectly capable of putting the garbage can lid back on properly, but if she wasn't, Paul's backyard would become a raccoon paradise. That would be amusing if it were just Greta, but raccoons could do a number on Polly.

The back door was standing open, so he propped one shoulder against the doorframe and watched through the screen door as Greta tried to maneuver the garbage can lid off with one hand. "You can put that bag down, you know," he called.

She glared at him, which just went to show how much she appreciated it when he actually did try to help.

As it turned out, getting the lid off was just the first hurdle. The moment the lid finally popped off, Greta took one look inside the can and then, with a squeak, leaped back, holding the lid in front of her like a Spartan shield.

"Now what's wrong?" Nick asked.

"There are bees in there."

That there were. He could hear the frenetic buzzing from the door. Clearly, Paul's garbage can had a hole in it somewhere. "So what? They're not going to bother you if you don't bother them."

"And you don't think dropping a bag of poop in there will bother them?" A bee crawled to the top of the trash can and took flight, causing Greta to duck behind the lid, although Nick noticed that she still kept the hand holding the bag well away from her.

As entertainment went, this was far better than badly made scent commercials. "You're not allergic to bees, are you?"

She glanced over her shoulder at him, then jerked her head back around when the bees buzzed ominously within the can. "If I were, would you take care of this bag for me?"

He rocked back on his heels, pretending to consider her question. "Depends on how serious the allergy is. I mean, we're talking about handling a little baggie of dog crap. Honestly, even if it were serious, I'd probably just offer to stand by with your EpiPen."

Greta snorted. "Yeah. Like I'd let you stick anything in me."

"Oh, please. You'd be begging for it."

The arm holding the lid drooped as she turned to stare at him, and Nick wished he hadn't teased her that way. The problem was, at the moment he could kind of picture her begging for it. In the lazy afternoon heat, her hair looked like she'd spent the last hour rolling around in bed, and her skin was flushed and dewy. And then there was her mouth, lush and rosy and just asking to be kissed.

What was that horrible line? *Your mouth says no but your eyes say yes?* In this instance it was exactly the opposite, because, when he finally forced his gaze away from her pretty lips, he discovered that Greta's eyes most definitely said no. And not just a regular, "Oh, thank you, but I must decline." Nope. Her eyes said, "Hell, no, you creep. And stop looking at me like that."

He crossed his arms over his chest and tried to look offended. "I don't know where your dirty little mind went, but I was talking about the EpiPen. If you were deathly allergic to bees and got stung, I'm pretty sure you'd be begging me to use it"—her eyes narrowed—"*the EpiPen* on you."

"Well," she said primly, turning her attention back to the trash can, "I'm not allergic to bees, so you can forget about sticking anything in me."

"Fine. Then you can forget about me helping you with that

little baggie."

"Don't worry about me. I think I'll be fine." And, still brandishing her makeshift shield, she sent the baggie arching toward the trash can—and overshot it by at least two feet.

"Damn it," she muttered, edging around the can with a wary eye fixed on the bees. When she finally reached the fallen bag, she bent down to pick it up, then tossed it toward the can once more.

"Admit it," he said as they watched the bag sail well left of the target. "You went to college on a basketball scholarship."

"If you're not going to help, you can go." Greta started wearily for the bag. "I don't really need an audience for this."

"I wouldn't worry too much about the bees at this point."

"And why is that?"

"Because if they've been paying attention, they're well aware you're not a threat. Unless you plan to make them die laughing, that is."

* * *

IN THE END, it took several tries and more than a few little shrieks, but eventually Greta got the bag into the garbage can and even managed to get the lid back on properly. Nick held the door open for her as she swept into the house, her head held high as if she hadn't just spent an embarrassing amount of time trying to put one tiny bag into one giant can.

"Tell me again why you're here," she said as she headed straight for the bathroom.

He trailed her down the hallway. "Your dad wanted me to DVR a couple shows for him."

"Pretty sure I could have handled that."

Nick watched her flip on the bathroom light switch with her elbow. He shrugged. "Maybe he wanted me to come over and make sure you hadn't stolen anything."

"Right. Because this house has so much worth stealing." Once again using her elbow, she pumped half a bottle's worth of liquid soap into her hand and turned on the hot water faucet.

"Obviously you don't know how valuable taxidermy can be."

Paul's hand soap smelled like coconut, something Nick hadn't noticed until that moment as he stood in the hallway just outside the bathroom and watched Greta rub her hands together under the steaming water, frothy bubbles sliding over her wet skin. She was a thorough hand-washer, taking her time, folding up her fingers to scrub at her fingernails, weaving her fingers together to get between them.

By the time she finally snapped the faucet off, he was beginning to wonder how he'd ever missed just how erotic a woman washing her hands could be.

"Well, I couldn't sell my dad's taxidermy here, now could I? And I seriously doubt there's much of a market for secondhand taxidermy in Chicago." She snatched up a hand towel and turned to face him. Leaning one hip against the vanity, she set about drying her hands with the same tantalizing thoroughness she'd used to wash them.

"Do you? Because I find it hard to believe that Chicago doesn't have plenty of men who'd like to get their hands on some big racks."

She stopped drying her hands and looked up at him. "Well," she said finally. "I think it's safe to say that all the racks under my father's roof will remain untouched tonight." Then she carefully draped the towel over the towel bar and flicked off the light. "I assume you've taken care of the DVR?" she asked as she brushed past him and headed toward the living room.

"Yeah." He followed her back down the hallway, forcing himself to look at Paul's trophy photos lining the walls instead of the gentle sway of Greta's hips.

"Great. Then I don't see a reason for you to still be here."

She stood in the middle of the living room, her hands clasped primly in front of her, the great hulk of Paul's beloved brown bear rising up behind her, and suddenly Nick realized how tired he was of being dismissed. He'd done nothing but be a loyal employee and friend, and now here he was, getting kicked out of Paul's house by the prodigal daughter.

"Let's get one thing straight," he said, advancing on her until he was close enough she had to tilt her head back to look up at him. "I'm here because Paul asked me to be here, and I'm always going to show up if he needs me. That man is like a father to me."

Her lips curled into a humorless smile. "Interesting. Because he actually *is* my father, and I'm pretty sure I can handle taking care of him."

"Really? Because if my father had a heart attack, you can bet I'd be at his side as soon as I could. No way I'd wait three days before moseying on down to see him."

He expected to hear about how important her job was, how he couldn't possibly understand the critical nature of copywriting for some fancy-ass company he'd never heard of. What he hadn't expected was for her to suck in her breath, looking for all the world like he'd just punched her in the stomach.

"What are you talking about? I came as soon as Helen called me."

"Your dad didn't call you over the weekend?"

She stepped back, sinking onto the couch beside a dozing Polly, her eyes fixed on her still-clasped hands. "When did he have the heart attack?"

Suddenly, getting dismissed didn't seem all that bad. He began edging toward the door. "Maybe you should talk to your dad about—"

"When?" She looked up, her eyes blazing in her pale face.

"Friday night."

"Friday night," Greta whispered. "And you know this because?" When Nick didn't say anything, she answered for him. "He called you. Didn't he?"

He nodded. There was no point in denying it. He could still

hear Paul's voice, small and pleading, asking him if he could meet the ambulance at the hospital. The older man would never in a million years have admitted to being afraid, but the fear was obvious. "I'm sure he just didn't want to worry you."

"Yeah." She rubbed her hands together and gave him a tight smile. "Well, I think we've accomplished everything we needed to here, don't you?"

"Sure." And now he was being dismissed again. "Let me know if you need anything," he said as he pulled open the front door.

"I won't need anything, but thanks."

No, he thought as he headed for his car. She wouldn't need anything from him at all.

* * *

AFTER NICK LEFT, Greta slouched on the couch, absently running one hand over Polly's wiry fur as she considered what she'd just learned. Her father had called Nick while he was in the middle of a heart attack.

He'd had his secretary call her three days later.

It wasn't that she was surprised. Thinking back, she wasn't sure she could even remember the last time they'd spoken. She vaguely recalled calling him on Father's Day, but she was almost certain that she just left him a quick voicemail, relieved that he hadn't answered and that she didn't have to waste ten minutes on awkward small talk.

But it did hurt to realize that her father, in what could very well have been his final moments, opted to call an employee instead of reaching out to her. He could have died, and he would have been okay never speaking to her again.

The worst part was, she didn't even have the right to be upset. Had she been the one having a medical emergency, she was sure her father wouldn't be one of the first five people she would contact. Maybe not even the first ten.

Well, she wasn't going to sit there and wallow in the pain of yet another one of her father's rejections. She wasn't a child, and she didn't need to be the first on her father's list of emergency contacts to feel good about herself.

She'd planned on visiting her father, but she decided it was late enough in the evening that it made more sense to wait until tomorrow.

Polly snorted and lifted her head, fixing Greta with an accusing look as if she knew that was just an excuse. "I don't want to hear it," Greta muttered. "It most certainly *is* too late to go now. Besides, I have work to do."

And she did. Because while she was busy organizing King's flotsam and jetsam and boohooing over the fact that Daddy didn't love her, Reed was back in Chicago working his ass off to ensure that he stayed as visible as possible. If Greta was going to compete with that, she needed to have her head in the game.

Focus, she reminded herself as she flipped her notebook open to her ideas page. She needed something spectacular.

Unfortunately, spectacular seemed to be eluding her at the moment. Worse, her headache was back. Rubbing her temples, she popped a couple of Excedrin and chased them down with some tap water from the kitchen sink.

With a sigh, she grabbed her keys from her purse. There was what her father called a home office across from the guest room, although Greta had a feeling it was just her father's way of getting a tax deduction for storing his stuffed mountain goat. Still, the room had a computer, and that's what she needed at the moment. Sticking the flash drive she always carried into a USB port, Greta waited for the icon to appear amidst the jumble of files and folders on her father's desktop, then double-clicked to play the video.

As the music flooded the room, she felt the familiar sense of resolve take over.

CHAPTER 9

*G*reta wasn't in the best mood the next day. A thunderstorm had rolled through during the night, shaking the windows of her father's house with such force that she feared they would shatter. To make matters worse, it turned out that Polly was just as terrified of thunder as she was. The dog had freaked out, pacing and whining and scratching at the closed door of the guest room closet until Greta had gotten up to open it for her.

Then, deciding the dog might know something she didn't, she'd squeezed into the closet too, huddling on the floor with Polly on her lap and the door closed. The closet was stuffed with her father's hunting clothes—she was shocked by how much clothing hunting seemed to require—and the garments dangled around her face and shoulders. It might have been her imagination, but she thought she could smell blood on them.

She was pretty sure that moment in the closet ticked off all the boxes of a decent nightmare: thunderstorm, small spaces, terrified dog, bloody clothes.

So it was understandable that, after two hours of sifting

78

through random papers in her father's office the following morning, she needed a break.

She considered taking an early lunch and heading to the hospital to talk to her father, but she couldn't work up the energy to deal with him yet. Instead, she wandered to the break room, where she found a young man tinkering with an ancient coffee maker.

"Sorry," he said, glancing up as she walked in. "I'll have this up and running in a bit."

Before she could say anything, Kelsey burst into the break room, holding a small booklet, its pages stained and folded. "I found the manual," she said triumphantly. Then she noticed Greta and stopped abruptly. "Oh. Hey."

Today Kelsey had on a pair of camo cargo pants and a tank top that, with its just-this-side-of-sheer fabric and lacy, beribboned neckline, definitely would have been right at home in the lingerie section of a department store. Her messy ponytail revealed an impressive number of earrings—unicorns and hearts and rainbows, Greta noted with amusement—climbing the pale shell of her earlobes, and her face looked like a china doll's: soft mascara emphasizing her long lashes and baby-doll eyes, pale pink lipstick, and high spots of color on her cheeks that, after a moment, Greta realized had nothing to do with artificial blush and everything to do with the young man whose efficient fingers were busy with the coffee maker.

This was Robbie Montufar. She knew this because he was clearly meant to be a pirate. He was still too young and too slight to be truly commanding—he looked like he'd barely grown into his own hands—but he had dark good looks, hooded eyes, and a cruel mouth softened, fortunately, by a glimmer of humor in his eyes. Give the kid a lace cravat and a sword, and a woman didn't stand a chance.

"What's wrong with the coffee maker?" she asked.

"What isn't wrong with the coffee maker?" Robbie said. He twisted a knob and frowned. "Can I see that manual, Kel?"

Kelsey threw Greta a look that made it obvious she knew Robbie's time would best be used elsewhere. "Maybe we should do this later."

"Are you kidding? I'm *this* close to figuring this out. Hand me the manual."

"I just think we should—"

"Just hand it to me."

Clearly torn between her employer and her pirate, Kelsey looked helplessly at the manual in her hands. Edging past Greta, she sidled up to Robbie and whispered something that made him straighten up quickly. "Now that you mention it," he said, "I do have some stuff to take care of down on the floor." He ducked his head in Greta's direction. "It was nice to meet you," he said, although nothing about their brief exchange had involved any sort of introduction. And then he fled the break room, leaving Kelsey standing there alone.

Some pirate.

She held out her hand for the manual, and Kelsey turned it over wordlessly. Greta flipped through it, noting the dog-eared pages and numerous notations in the margins. "How often does the coffee maker go down?"

"Once in awhile." Kelsey was a terrible liar.

"And Robbie fixes it?"

The younger woman scuffed at the carpet with the toe of her flip-flop. "Sometimes Robbie. Sometimes Auggie. Or Nick."

Better and better. The company was struggling, and instead of working on solving the problems, several employees were busy repairing a flaky coffee maker on a regular basis. She handed the manual back to Kelsey. "Well, then. Better put this in a safe place."

There were two people she could discuss this with. She still wasn't ready to face her father, which left her with Nick. Not optimal, but a surge of self-righteous frugality carried her to his office, where she expected to find him doing…well, whatever it was vice presidents did. Maybe making pie charts?

Instead, she found him heading out of his office, keys in hand.

He stiffened as he saw her coming toward him, one hand on the light switch in his office. Greta could almost feel the sharp edges of his steely blue eyes on her.

"How much do Robbie and Kelsey make an hour?" she asked.

"I don't think we should be discussing salaries like this."

She crossed her arms over her chest. "Would you discuss salaries with my father?"

"I would," he conceded. Then he looked pointedly at the open office doors around them. "But I'd probably do it behind closed doors."

"Fine. I don't need to know the exact numbers. I just need to know why it is that we have several employees regularly fixing a cheap coffee maker instead of just buying a new one."

"You'll have to ask your father." He flipped off the light in his office and shoved one hand in his pocket. "That's not my decision to make." He started down the hallway, leaving Greta with little choice but to race to keep up.

"I don't understand. Talk about penny-wise but pound-foolish…" It struck her that he was heading for the exit, and she thought back to his face when he'd seen her coming. He hadn't looked guilty, exactly, but he sure had looked like he wished she hadn't come down the hallway at just that moment. "Wait. Where are you going?"

He hesitated. "I'm visiting one of our suppliers," he said finally.

"And you didn't think that was something I should know?"

A muscle moved in his jaw. "Not really, no."

"My father put me in charge. If you're talking to a supplier, I should be kept in the loop."

They reached the door to the stairs. Turning to face her, he leaned back against the door. "Okay. Well, you're in the loop now. Are we good?"

It didn't matter that he didn't like her. She'd been in the corporate world long enough to know that not everyone was going to like her.

And, frankly, she didn't like him that much either.

But what she couldn't tolerate was that he didn't respect her. So she didn't know much about deer pee, or hunting, or whatever else he assumed she needed to know before she could make a difference. But her father obviously trusted her to handle things in his absence, so why was Nick negotiating with suppliers without her?

He could at least give her the benefit of the doubt.

"No," she heard herself say. "No, we're not good. I'm going with you."

She expected an argument. What she didn't expect was the lazy, appraising look he gave her, those eyes—now not quite as cold—sliding over her careful French twist, her white silk blouse and charcoal-gray pencil skirt, her open-toed black heels.

And she certainly didn't expect to see his lips twitch with amusement.

Drawing herself up to her full five feet, four inches, she lifted her chin to meet his gaze. It must be difficult for a man who worked in a man's world to believe that a woman was capable of handling everything he could, but she wasn't about to be dismissed by this small-minded redneck hunter just because she wasn't wearing camouflage and combat boots.

"I'm going," she repeated firmly.

"I just don't think—" But then he met her eyes. Whatever he saw there must have convinced him that arguing was useless, because he shrugged. "Fine. You want to come? Let's go."

Having been prepared for more of a fight, Greta blinked. Recovering, she nodded curtly, following him down the stairs to the front door. She wished she'd thought to grab her keys so she could insist on driving, but she was afraid that if she went back up to get them he'd drive off without her, thereby making her look like she had no control over anything that happened in her own plant.

No—her father's plant, she reminded herself.

Besides, it was better that Nick drive. He knew his way around, and she didn't exactly trust him to give her easy-to-follow directions.

She expected him to lead her to one of the many giant pickup trucks in the parking lot. Probably one of the lifted ones. Maybe even the immense white one with the metal testicles dangling from the trailer hitch.

That seemed like his speed.

But instead he clicked his key fob and the lights on a silver Prius flashed. "This...this is your car?" she asked.

He was opening the driver's side door, but he stopped to look at her over the roof of the car, the sun at his back so she couldn't quite read his expression. "Yes," he said finally. "Why do you sound surprised?"

"I just..." The truck nuts on the white pickup glinted in the sun. She couldn't explain why she would have felt better if they'd belonged to him.

Nick got into the car and started clearing off the passenger seat for her, tossing a number of baseball caps—all with some mix of camouflage and company logos and deer silhouettes—into the backseat, along with a package of sharp-edged arrowheads and something that looked like a short earth-toned recorder, the kind she used to play in elementary school.

"Sorry," he said. "I wasn't expecting to have anyone else in here."

With the seat cleaned off, Greta slid in. The interior of the car smelled like woodsmoke and musk, with the slightest trace of something warm and sweet under it all. Vanilla, she realized to her surprise.

Buckling her seatbelt, she watched Nick shift the car into reverse, the sun touching the pale gold hairs on his arm. He was wearing a T-shirt again, this one navy blue with a white King Lures logo on the chest, and it was impossible to ignore the way his biceps stretched the edge of his sleeve. Or the way his shoulders filled the shirt, or the way the shirt shifted over his chest whenever he moved, hinting at the muscles beneath.

Really, it was impossible to ignore the way he looked in that shirt. Any woman would have trouble tearing her eyes away from him.

Or at least that's what Greta assured herself. The man might be obnoxious. He might be a chauvinist. He might be a redneck—although the Prius was really throwing her off.

But that didn't mean she couldn't appreciate the strong lines of his torso and arms. In fact, it might be criminal not to.

As her eyes roved upwards, she discovered that he was watching her, his lips quirked in a half-smile. Had he caught her *appreciating* his assets?

The knowing glint in his eyes said yes.

A faint flush came to her cheeks. To cover her embarrassment, she cleared her throat. "Did you grow up around here?"

He turned his attention back to the road, one hand draped over the steering wheel while he flicked on the radio with the other. The discordant strains of some classic rock hit that Greta could never remember the name of filled the car. "I moved here when I was eight."

Judging from the tightening around his eyes, there was a story there. Normally, Greta wouldn't push. But this man had been needling her since she arrived in Bartlett, so she didn't feel bad about prying. "Why'd your family move?"

He was quiet for so long she didn't think he was going to answer at all. But finally he sighed. "My parents were killed in a car accident. My grandmother and her sister took me in."

"Oh." She started to picture the sad, lost little boy he must have been and then stopped herself. She was only going to make herself feel sorry for him. Not only would that put her at a disadvantage when dealing with him, but she was pretty sure he wouldn't appreciate her pity. "I'm sorry."

He inclined his head in acknowledgment and then turned up the music, effectively smothering any chance of conversation.

Eventually, the car slowed, and she realized Nick was turning onto a narrow road—or, rather, something that might have aspired to be a road. It wasn't even quite gravel, although there were enough small white rocks remaining to make the drive unpleasant. The path was so choked with weeds that Greta wondered how Nick could tell where the road stopped and the field surrounding them began.

The sun disappeared as the road wound into the woods and trees pressed so close that some of the longer branches brushed the sideview mirrors. Greta had the sudden realization that if she were going to kill someone and dump the body, this was pretty much the perfect place.

She cast a nervous glance at Nick. He kept his eyes carefully on the road, although she couldn't tell if that was so he didn't reveal his murderous intentions or because he needed to watch closely to keep from driving into the ditch that had appeared alongside the road.

"Where...um, where are we going?"

"To see a supplier. I told you."

The Prius bounced over a particularly deep rut, and Greta grabbed at the handle on her door. Out of the corner of her eye, she saw Nick's lips curve ever so slightly upward.

The bastard.

As the trees began to thin out, Greta spotted a building up ahead. It was a small building, square and stout and white, but at least it meant that Nick was actually taking her somewhere besides the middle of nowhere.

That's when she saw the fencing beside the building, fencing far higher than what was needed for cows or horses. "Wait," she said. "What is this place?"

Nick's voice was carefully expressionless. "It's a deer farm."

Greta looked down at her narrow skirt and high heels. "You're taking me to a deer farm?"

"Actually, it's more accurate to say that you insisted on coming with me to a deer farm." Nick stopped the car, sliding it into park as he let his eyes drift over her once again, this time with a definite look of smug satisfaction.

"Why didn't you tell me we were going to a deer farm?" Greta said, trying hard to keep her voice level.

Nick opened his door. "What is it that you think a supplier might send us?" he asked. "We sell deer urine."

"I don't know. Boxes maybe. Shipping supplies. Bottles." But Nick had already closed his car door and was striding across the uneven ground to the building. She had two choices: sit in the car and look like she couldn't handle this line of work after all, or follow him.

Her heels sank into the spongy ground the moment she stepped out of the car, and she cursed last night's thunderstorm once again. Nick had stopped and was waiting for her, his hands on his hips, his eyes gleaming with amusement. "You coming?" he called as she wiggled her heels free. They weren't even all that high, but on this terrain they acted like spikes, driving into the ground and sticking there.

"This your first visit to a deer farm?" he asked as she finally reached him, his tone light.

Several strands of hair began to rebel, working themselves out of her French twist to fall against her face. Using the back of one hand, she pushed the traitorous locks behind her ear and squinted up at him. "I'm glad you're enjoying yourself."

"I am. Immensely."

She decided then and there that her very first order of business upon arriving back at the office would be to fire Nick Campbell.

Except, of course, she desperately needed him.

She didn't know much about running a business, but she had a pretty good idea that she probably needed at least one person around who knew what the hell was going on.

A shout drew her attention. A young man, probably no older than his mid-twenties, was waving at them from the shadowy interior of the white building. Nick raised his hand in greeting.

"We're here in part to assure the Sandbournes that everything is fine at King Lures, even without Paul in the office," he said, his head bent, his voice low. "Try to look like you know what you're doing."

"What would that look like?"

He gave her a grim smile. "Just let me do the talking."

In the course of her time at Prescott, she'd worked with people from a wide range of industries. Sure, she'd never worked with someone from a deer farm before, but how different could it be from, say, a car manufacturer? The product might be different, but she'd learned that a little flattery and a few good questions worked on pretty much everyone.

They reached the building, which seemed to be a barn of some type. The young man had a big, goofy grin and wispy hair on his chin trying its damnedest—but still failing—to be a beard. His eyes refused to meet Greta's, and his cheeks flamed every time he so much as glanced her way.

"Greta, this is Jake Sandbourne," Nick said. "Jake, this is Greta King."

"It's Greta Tremaine, actually." She held out her hand. Jake stared at it for a moment, then wiped his own hand hard against his jeans before clasping gingerly around her fingertips.

"Nice to meet you," he said in her general direction.

Nick's expression clouded. "I didn't know you were married."

"I'm not." She surveyed the barn before her, then beamed at Jake. "My, this is a lovely place you have here."

For a moment, she thought Jake was going to actually use the word "shucks." Instead, he scraped the ground with his boots and smiled up at her from beneath the brim of his hat. "Thanks."

"I have to admit I've never been to a deer farm before." And wasn't that just the most obvious statement in the world? Because if she had, she would have worn jeans and sneakers and a shirt that wasn't dry clean only. Also, bug spray, because apparently Jake was secretly farming mosquitoes and they were enjoying a banquet on Greta's exposed legs. "Would you mind explaining how you collect the, ah, product?"

Jake stammered and blushed and cleared his throat several times but somehow managed to indicate that she should follow him into the barn.

It took a moment for her eyes to adjust to the dim light inside the building, but soon she could make out the long, narrow interior, lined on one side with what appeared to be sliding plywood panels.

Her nose also needed a moment to adjust to what could only be described as the smell of urine-soaked everything. Pee had happened here.

Jake gathered his courage enough to walk her through the process. The panels, he explained, were the doors to individual stalls with sloping floors inset with a drain. Each drain had its own pipe, which emptied into separate jars. Jake lifted a small trapdoor in the floor just outside the stalls to reveal the ends of the pipes and a collection of jars, all of which were topped with pieces of fabric, which acted as a filter.

To filter what, Greta did not want to know.

"When the time is right," Jake said, "we bring a doe in and keep her in a stall overnight. When she urinates, it all goes into the drain, down the pipe, and into the jar. Now at certain times, we collect what we call the gel, which is this whitish-green—"

"My goodness!" Greta exclaimed. She did not want to hear about a gel-like substance that both came out of a deer and was also any shade of green. "This is really something, isn't it?"

"Yeah." Jake replaced the trap door and rose to his feet, his eyes sliding over Greta's knees and then back to the floor. "My father's been doing this for a long time now."

A muffled version of "Ride of the Valkyries" came from his pocket, and he shifted his weight to one foot as he dug a cell phone out of his jeans. Glancing at the screen, he said, "Sorry. I have to take this." He stepped out of the barn, the glaring sunlight blotting out his silhouette.

"Yeah, Jake seems really hard to impress," she muttered. "I can see why you were worried about me."

"He's going to give a full report to his father later, and Big Jake can read between the lines." Nick toed the edge of the little trap door. "If you're not married, why is your last name Tremaine and not King?"

"It's my stepfather's last name." When he just stared at her blankly, she added, "I legally changed it when I turned 18."

"But...why?" Nick's arms, she noticed, were enviably mosquito free.

"Why does it matter? It's not a big deal."

"Maybe not to you." He rubbed one hand over the back of his neck, the movement doing some annoyingly appealing things to his arm muscles. A photo of him like that could probably sell a lot of perfume. Hell, she was pretty sure she could find a way to sell almost anything to women using a photo of Nick Campbell.

That was a professional assessment, of course. Personally, Greta didn't see the appeal. Her preferences ran toward men who did not take her on surprise trips to deer farms.

"What's that supposed to mean?"

"I mean maybe it was a big deal to your father."

"Trust me. It wasn't." In fact, her father had basically shrugged off her decision to take Don's last name. Had she hoped that he might object, that he would ask her to keep his last name?

Maybe. But he hadn't.

"Look, my stepfather's family is very well-known in…certain circles. Having his last name opened a lot of doors for me. It was the best thing I could do for my future."

"By giving up your past?"

"This was never my past."

He shoved his hands into his pockets and looked at her as if she were whitish-green deer gel. "You don't have to stay, you know."

"You drove."

"I meant in Bartlett."

He wanted her gone. Greta looked away, out into the blinding sunlight that had swallowed Jake up moments ago. She wanted, more than anything, to walk out of that barn, drive back to Chicago, and get back to the perfect life she'd built for herself there. But she'd promised her father that she would help out. And it didn't matter if Nick thought she was useless. A lost cause.

He was wrong.

Footsteps crunched over the sparse gravel outside the barn, and Jake emerged, shoving his phone back into his pocket. "Sorry about that," he said. "Nick, you want to look over our latest inspection report?"

"In a minute," Nick said. He beamed down at Greta, sending sparks of alarm through her.

Anything that made him look happy had to be bad for her.

"Greta was just saying how much she would love to meet some of the deer."

"Oh, no, I don't think Jake has time for that."

But Jake's cheeks flushed with pleasure like she'd just asked if she could page through his baby book. "It really wouldn't be any trouble," he said. He dug a plastic container out of a cabinet near the barn's entrance. Popping the top off, he held it out to her. "You can even give them a few graham crackers. They love 'em."

Her hand hovered above the graham crackers, and she glanced up at Nick. "Aren't deer wild animals?"

"Not these. Anyway, Jake has several does from a local petting zoo that closed down. They're practically as tame as dogs."

Not exactly the reassurance she'd been hoping for.

Jake gave the Tupperware container a little shake. "Go ahead. The ladies are super sweet."

Reluctantly, Greta took a couple of graham crackers from the container and, with one last longing look at the level floor of the barn, stepped outside, following Jake and Nick to where a metal gate broke up the high fence. Above, the sun looked white and washed out, and the air had suddenly become very still. Silence descended upon them. There was no birdsong, no squirrels skittering about in the trees, nothing. Just the line of deer, some snaking their necks toward the ground to watch through the lower bars of the gate, some craning their necks up to watch through the upper bars.

It was too muddy for dust to be swirling around, but otherwise it all felt like a gunfight scene from an old Western.

Several deer were lying in the shade of a large maple tree, but when they saw Jake start to open the gate, they were on their feet in a second, trotting toward him.

"See? Tame," Nick said.

Too tame. The deer were all but stampeding now, and despite Greta's prior belief that they were delicate, fine-boned creatures, these deer looked pretty sturdy.

"Actually," she started to say, stepping back only to bump into Nick, who was standing just behind her. The contact sent little jolts through her and she took an involuntary step forward. Right into the pen. Nick and Jake followed, the gate swinging closed just as the deer swarmed them.

They were everywhere. Bigger than Greta had expected, and

stronger, and all reaching for the graham crackers in her hands. She wasn't even sure what happened to the graham crackers. One minute she was clenching them between her fingers, and the next they were gone, devoured by the churning mass of deer.

"Easy, girls," Jake said.

Shockingly, the deer didn't pay any attention, although in the absence of graham crackers, they soon lost interest in Greta. She stood there, trembling, trying to pretend that everything was cool, that being accosted by a gang of whitetail does was something that happened to her all the time. "What nice deer you have," she said weakly. She looked around for Nick, who was standing apart from the herd, his arms crossed over his chest, his silvery-blue eyes glinting with amusement. "Well, thank you so much for—"

But Nick wasn't quite done. "Hey, is Delores around?"

Greta fervently hoped that Delores was Jake's sister.

No such luck. Jake shaded his eyes and surveyed the area near the woods. "She should be." Then he pointed. "Yeah, there she is. Delores! Hey, girl."

"You'll like Delores," Nick said, which pretty much meant that she would not.

"Yeah, everyone loves Delores," Jake added. "She's not coming in, but we can go out to her."

"I don't think that's—" Greta started to say.

But Jake was already making his way across the yard, and Greta was left with no choice but to follow him, Nick trailing smugly behind.

"Delores is blind," Jake explained. "Can't survive in the wild, and nobody wants her genes in a deer breeding program. They were going to put her down, so I took her. It doesn't matter to me if she's blind. She still makes good deer pee."

"Oh, how nice." Maybe she needed to be more open-minded about a place like this. It was actually a great resource for saving animals that might otherwise be destroyed. Where else would those petting zoo deer have gone if he hadn't taken them? And poor Delores.

She was so preoccupied that she didn't notice what was on the ground in front of her until she stepped in something squishy. Something that squelched over the front of her open-toed shoes, between her toes.

She must have made a sound, because Nick stopped abruptly. His eyes went to the ground, and then, very slowly, climbed over her bare legs and skirt and silk blouse now patchy with sweat until they met hers. He was holding very still, his lips pressed hard together.

"Please," she whispered, "tell me this isn't deer poop."

"I wouldn't call it that," he said.

She relaxed.

"When I'm with a lady, I always refer to it as 'scat.'"

CHAPTER 10

"*I* think that went well, don't you?"

Greta shot him a look. "I'm not talking to you."

He shrugged. "Fine." Turning up the radio, he tapped his thumbs against the steering wheel to the beat of a Red Hot Chile Peppers' song, humming cheerfully.

She snapped the radio off and turned in her seat to face him. "You could have warned me."

"Warned you about what? You were in a pen full of deer. Are you really shocked that there was deer crap on the ground?"

"A 'watch your step' would have been nice."

"Honestly, that seemed like common sense to me."

"I thought deer poop was hard."

"Usually it is. But you get yourself, say, a sick fawn, and you're going to want to be careful."

Slumping back against the seat, she shifted her feet—now mostly clean, thanks to Jake and a handy garden hose. "What am I going to do about these shoes?"

"I don't know…Wash them off?"

"They're rented," she said miserably.

A train was snaking along the railroad tracks on Main Street, which made this day just that much better. He stopped the car a safe distance from the flashing safety arm, rolled the windows down, and shut off the ignition. "You rented a pair of shoes?"

"I rent all my shoes."

He whipped his head around to stare at her. A million questions ran through his mind, but in the end there was only one he could ask: "Why?"

She propped her elbow on the door frame, rested her chin in one hand, and stared out at the train cars creaking softly as they passed. "I need to wear Manolo Blahnik and Christian Louboutin for work, but I can't afford that on my salary."

"You *need* to wear—what the heck did you say?"

"They're designer brands."

"Yeah, I figured you weren't talking about shoes you can find at Walmart. Maybe it would help you to know that they do sell shoes at Walmart and you might be able to actually afford to own them outright."

"Like I could show up at the office in Walmart shoes."

He rested his hands lightly on the steering wheel. "So, they don't pay you enough to afford these fancy shoes, but they tell you that you have to wear them?"

"It's not like they tell me I have to wear them." She turned her head so he could see her profile, her eyelashes nearly black against the faint blue smudges under her eyes as she looked down at her lap. "But you dress for the job you want, not the job you have."

"I assume the job you want requires you to spend a fortune on shoes?"

Greta blew out a long breath. "You wouldn't understand."

"You're right about that." He tried to think about the last time he'd noticed what shoes any of his coworkers were wearing. Sure, he might notice what Kelsey was wearing, but that was only because Kelsey dressed to be noticed. But he couldn't say whether Helen was wearing sneakers that day, or high heels, or sandals. She could be wearing combat boots for all he knew. The idea that there were workplaces where people cared that much about what their coworkers wore on their feet was insane to him.

The last car of the train wobbled by, and he turned the key in the ignition. A thought struck him. "You know, if those shoes are rented, you're going to want to get them cleaned up right away. We're going right by Paul's house. I could just drop you off."

"I don't think that's necessary. Besides, my car's at work. And it's only noon."

"Someone could pick you up tomorrow." He'd ask Helen to do it. "And it's not like we really need you there this afternoon."

He knew the second the words were out of his mouth that he'd made a grave mistake. Greta roused herself for battle. "It doesn't matter whether you think you need me. It's my job to be there, and I'm not going to cut out early on my second day of work."

"Fine." The safety arm rose, and he guided his car onto the railroad tracks. "But can we at least stop at Paul's so you can get cleaned up and change your shoes? We cut the cleaning service down to every two weeks, and it's going to be awhile before they come back to clean the carpets." He glanced meaningfully at her feet.

She settled back against her seat. "Fine," she said. As if she were doing him a favor.

At Paul's house, Greta insisted that Nick come in with her. "How long is this going to take?" he grumbled. All she had to do was wash off her feet and put on another pair of shoes. If it took more than a minute or two, maybe he could head back to the office and just tell her later there'd been an emergency.

"Not long. But I'm not going to risk having you drive off and leave me here without a car."

"Like I would do that," he said, trying to look like he hadn't been considering doing just that.

Her eyes narrowed and she held out one hand. "I want your car keys."

"No."

"If you don't give me your car keys, I'm getting back in the car." When he didn't move, she added, "I'll take off my shoes and wiggle my toes on the floor."

That did it. Muttering under his breath, he handed over his keys and pretended not to notice the look of triumph in her eyes.

Greta took her shoes off on the front steps, balancing on one foot gracefully to pull off each shoe in turn. Leaving them on the front step, she padded quickly to the bathroom, where she closed the door behind her. Nick heard the click of the lock, which, he thought as he dropped onto the couch with an ecstatic Polly to wait, was totally unnecessary.

He found the remote and turned on the TV, flipping through a dozen different talk shows, real-life court dramas, and 24-hour news programs before pushing the power button and dropping the remote. Water was running in the bathroom, and he had a sudden image of Greta peeling off her sweaty clothes, her hair falling loose around her shoulders, the curves and lines of her body softened through the steam of the shower...

Deer crap, he reminded himself forcefully. She was washing off deer crap. If there was anything less sexy, he couldn't think of it.

He pulled out his phone and checked his email, but for once there were no convenient emergencies to distract him. Then, because his brain still couldn't seem to stay out of the bathroom, he called the office. Kelsey answered on the third ring.

"Hey. Where's Helen?"

"She went to see Paul on her lunch break." There was a long silence. "Greta caught Robbie working on the coffee maker."

"I know."

"I haven't seen her since. Do you think she's talking to Paul? You don't think she's going to get us fired, do you?"

"I don't think that's what she's doing at the moment, no." The running water stopped, and he heard the sound of a shower curtain sliding along the curtain rod. She was getting out of the shower, naked and wet and warm, and now that she was clean there was nothing to make the thought of that unsexy. He could imagine her reaching for a towel, her dark hair streaming rivulets of water over her bare back.

Kelsey was talking, he realized belatedly, saying something about Robbie and a truck payment and how much he loved working at King. He tried to focus, but his mind was more interested in what Greta was doing.

And then, as if his mind was actually creating reality, he heard Greta call him. "Nick? I need something."

Okay, focus, he told himself, doing his best to ignore the rush of blood away from his brain. Just because this was how a lot of porn movies started didn't mean that she was going to say what he thought she was about to say. With Kelsey still chattering away in his ear, he moved down the hallway, stopping just outside the bathroom door. "Yeah?" he said.

"I forgot my robe."

His mouth went dry.

"—*really* hard worker, and if you could just *tell* Greta about—"

"Uh, Kelsey, I gotta go." And he pushed the End Call button, cutting off whatever she was going on about. The house was so quiet he could swear he heard Greta breathing lightly on the other side of that thin wooden door. She was standing there, he imagined, wrapped in a towel, her shoulders still glistening with droplets of water from the shower.

"Nick?"

"Yeah?"

"So...can you get it for me?"

His mind was a blank. He couldn't think about anything besides what the skin over her collarbone might taste like just after a shower. "Get what?"

There was an impatient sigh from the bathroom. "My robe. I left it hanging on the back of the door. In the guest bedroom."

Right. Of course. Her robe.

He headed for the guest room, which, as he expected, was impeccably neat. In fact, he was pretty sure it was neater now than it was when no one was staying in it. The bed was made, and if she'd brought a suitcase with her, it was now tucked away behind the closed closet door.

Hanging on the back of the door was a satiny peach robe.

The word "robe" was kind of generous. He'd been expecting something fluffy, something that would make Greta look as round and puffy as a snowman, something that would ease the sharp awareness he had of her in that bathroom, wet and naked. Not this flimsy piece of nothing. It wasn't sheer exactly, but when he grabbed the back of it to take it down from the hook on the door, he could see the dark shape of his fingers right through the fabric. It was short, too, maybe—maybe—reaching to about mid-thigh on Greta.

And it smelled like lavender.

This wasn't helping at all.

He carried it back to the bathroom and, since he wasn't sure he could keep the tension out of his voice, simply knocked on the door. There was the slight snick of the lock being turned, and then Greta cracked the door and stuck one hand through the narrow space between the door and the frame. Wordlessly, Nick placed the robe in her hand and watched it disappear into the bathroom. When the door closed firmly once more, he wasn't sure whether he was relieved or disappointed that he hadn't seen a little more of her.

A wisp of escaped steam hung for a moment in the air outside the bathroom. Like the robe, it smelled of lavender.

"Nick?"

"What?" he snapped.

"Can you go to the living room? Or even outside? Just until I get dressed."

She didn't want him to see her in her robe, he realized. Not that he could blame her.

"Sure," he said, shoving his hands in his pockets and grinding his teeth together as he turned his back on the bathroom and walked away. It wasn't because of frustration. He certainly didn't *want* to see her in her robe. She was Paul's daughter, after all. Not to mention a huge pain in the ass. And she wasn't even pretty, or all that pretty, even if she was soft and sweetly rounded, with big dark eyes that looked like they held all kinds of secrets and creamy skin that he could probably taste right through the flimsy fabric of her robe.

But as he shoved open the storm door to stand in the sweltering heat outside, he still had to firmly remind himself that this was a woman who just minutes ago had deer crap under her toenails.

That helped.

A little.

* * *

"If you liked her, you could have just told me so."

Nick looked up from the email he was reading. Auggie leaned against the doorframe of his office, one eyebrow cocked.

"What are you talking about?" Nick asked.

"I'm talking about the fact that you and Greta went out together this morning." Auggie sauntered in, taking a seat and propping his feet up on Nick's desk. "I heard she took a shower and changed clothes before you two came back. Fast work."

"It's not what it looks like."

"That's usually my line."

Nick closed the email. It was yet another message from Dave, hinting that his client might be willing to increase their mysterious—but, Dave swore, generous—offer. He hit the trash can icon to delete the email. Then he sat back and regarded Auggie. "I took Greta to Sandbourne Farms."

Auggie's mouth slackened. "Why?"

"I wanted to reassure Jake that things were under control here." The visit wasn't exactly a success. Few things made a company look less professional than when a supplier had to literally hose off the acting manager.

"Yeah. I get why you went. But why the hell would you take Greta with you?"

"She insisted on going."

Auggie's eyes narrowed. "So you said, 'Hey, I'm going to go walk around a deer farm,' and she said, 'That sounds like fun.'"

He pretended to be engrossed in his email again. "Hmmm?"

"I see." Auggie studied him for a long moment and then rocked his chair back. "I'm glad it's not what it looks like. It would have been hard to swallow if she preferred your ugly face to what I have to offer."

"Plenty of women would take me over you. I seem to remember Holly DeSantos turning you down so she could go to Homecoming with me."

The chair rocked forward, the front legs hitting the floor hard. "First of all, you had an unfair advantage. I was a sophomore and you were a senior. With a *car*."

"Yeah. Nana's LeSabre. I'm not sure that counts."

"Second of all," he said, leaning forward and setting his elbows on the desk. "Holly wore that awful yellow dress with that sparkly crap all over it. Remember?"

"I believe they're called sequins."

"You would know that."

"You learn a lot from living with a woman. Maybe you should try it sometime."

"Everyone at school called her Banana Bling Barbie for a year after that," Auggie continued. "So her taste is highly suspect."

"Didn't you take her to prom the next year?"

"Clearly her taste improved."

"If it did, it went downhill again. She married Andy Miller." The only time Andy had ever lived away from his mother had been the seven months he spent in the county jail for spray-painting "MARTY SUKS DONKY BALLS" on the side of Mayor Martin Finley's house. Andy had been thirty-two at the time.

A smile played over Auggie's face. "Still a step up from you."

"Yeah, well. We can't all have that legendary Paladino charm."

Nick regretted the words instantly, although Auggie's wince was nearly imperceptible. His father, Steve Paladino, was a notorious ladies' man who'd spent most of his brief marriage to Auggie's mother sleeping with any woman who would have him. The apple hadn't fallen far from the tree, but while Auggie had always been open about not being suited to commitment, Steve was a perpetual optimist. He'd already been married six times, and the seventh future ex-Mrs. Paladino had recently booked the VFW for a September wedding. By now, most people around Bartlett found the whole thing amusing, but Nick knew Auggie didn't see any humor in it. "Listen, I—"

But Auggie obviously didn't want to talk about his father. "I checked in on Greta a little while ago," he said, changing the subject. "She said she'll be done organizing Paul's office in a day or so. What are you going to have her do next?"

"I really haven't had a chance to think about it much." Nor was he planning on devoting much time to it. There was no way Greta could get everything done that quickly. He had days before he had to worry about next steps. Maybe even weeks.

"I'm sure there's some menial task you can find for her." Auggie rubbed his thumb idly over the armrest of his chair. "Maybe she could arrange all the paperclips in the building by size."

"Okay, smartass. You think I should get her more involved in the company?"

"No. I think *Paul* already got her more involved in the company. All you have to do is show her what there is to do and let her do it."

But that was the problem. Nick had no idea what there was to do. For the past two years, King had been in steady decline. The company had come through the recession a decade earlier intact, but it just didn't seem able to compete in a rapidly changing marketplace. In the old days, offering a quality product at a reasonable price had been enough. Now it was blog posts and witty tweets and flashy YouTube videos, and just when they figured out what social media platform everyone was using, it all changed.

And the disaster with the synthetic lure hadn't helped.

"She knows nothing about deer urine. I just don't see how she can help the company," he said flatly.

"You look at that sales report I sent over this morning? I don't see how she could *hurt* the company," Auggie retorted. "Doesn't she work for some fancy ad agency up in Chicago?"

"She's a copywriter."

"Perfect. Ben's coming to town next week. Why not have her work with him on the new campaign?"

Because he didn't want her there in the first place, and he certainly didn't want her mucking around with King's advertising campaign. Nick knew exactly what kind of woman Greta was—he'd married a woman just like her. Lauren had grown up outside Seattle, and she'd been excited at first to move to his hometown with him after college. Everything was an adventure; she found downtown Bartlett charming and adorable. The first time their realtor showed them the house they eventually bought, she ran to the sprawling backyard and twirled in circles, her arms outstretched, her head thrown back, laughing despite the fact that it had started to rain. When she finally came back in, she wrapped her arms around Nick, her damp skin smelling of thunderstorms and fresh-cut grass. "I can't believe how much space there is," she said, city girl that she was. "It's perfect." And in her eyes Nick saw everything he'd ever wanted: Christmas lights strung around the bushes outside the front door, a swingset in the backyard, watching the sun set from the bay window in the kitchen while they drank wine, a welcome mat on the porch and a rag rug by the kitchen sink. Maybe even a big, rangy mutt who let kids tumble all over him with nothing more than benevolent resignation. A home, a real home, and a family they would create together.

It had been perfect.

But it didn't stay perfect, despite all the decorating she did inside the house or the flower gardens she planted outside. Soon nothing made her happy. There weren't enough throw pillows in the world to make up for the fact that she was far from home, stuck in a nothing little town, left home alone for hours on end while Nick worked. He once made the mistake of suggesting she find a job—anything, even something part-time. Not for the money, just so she wouldn't feel so isolated. But Lauren's lack of a career was what allowed her to move to Kentucky, as she quickly pointed out to him. If she wanted to work, she told him, she might as well live somewhere she actually liked.

That had been the beginning of the end.

It would be the same with Greta. After all, she wasn't just disinterested in the company; she'd gone so far as to change her last name legally to separate herself from what Paul had built. Oh, sure, she said she did it because of what her stepfather's name could do for her. But he'd seen the way she was with Paul, and he also knew that a big part of that name change had been an act of rebellion, a rejection of everything Paul King stood for. And Nick knew exactly how much that hurt.

Greta may have handled herself well at Sandbourne. He'd expected her to refuse to get out of the car once she realized where they were, which was what he would have done had she taken him to...well, somewhere comparable. Like a purse factory or a vegan party. But she'd been almost enthusiastic, asking Jake all about the process and, for all Nick could tell, actually listening to the answers.

But it wouldn't take long for her to get bored with Bartlett, with King Lures, with Paul. And the more entangled she was with the business, the harder it was going to be for the people Nick cared about when she fled in disgust.

He sighed. "Yeah. Maybe." Then he turned to look out the window. The grassy field behind the building was sun-parched and yellowing, but the food plot in the distance was lush and vibrant. "She's all upset about the coffee maker not working."

"We all are. If that's an example of her inability to identify the company's big problems, I'd say you don't have much of an argument."

Nick inclined his head. "Touché."

"So, Tracks tonight?" Auggie asked.

But Nick shook his head. He needed to clear his head, and a bar wasn't the place to do it. "I think I'm going to stick around here for a little bit. Get some practice in."

"Sure." Auggie rose to his feet. He started for the door, but stopped before he got there. "Hey," he said, waiting for Nick to look up. "It's all going to work out."

"I know."

But he didn't know that. He didn't know that at all.

GRETA STRETCHED HER ARMS UP, arching her back to loosen the knots that had formed as she hunched over a stack of file folders. The headache she'd banished earlier with Excedrin was back with a vengeance, and she reached around for her purse to get another round of pills. Her hand had just closed around the bottle when a sudden noise made her jump. It was a foreign sound, a hard *thwack* followed quickly by another. With her fingers still wrapped around the Excedrin bottle, she pushed away from her father's desk and crossed the office to the window. Then she sucked in her breath.

Down on the ground, in the wide, flat area next to the King Lures building, someone had set up an archery range, with a number of targets positioned at various distances. And standing alone at one end of the range was Nick, his powerful arms in the process of drawing back a bow.

Thwack!

His back was to her, his burnished gold hair darkening to honey where it met the bronzed skin of his neck, the muscles of his back shifting beneath the T-shirt that clung to his powerful frame as he pulled the string back in one fluid movement. He stood there motionless, so motionless she didn't even realize he'd released the string until she heard the sound of the arrow striking the target. Only after impact did he slowly lower his arms.

She stepped back from the window, the image of all that controlled lethal force burned into her brain. The rattle of her pill bottle reminded her about the headache, and she twisted off the cap and shook two pills into her palm. Normally it took at least three to beat back her headaches, but now that she thought about it, the headache pressing inside her skull wasn't quite as bad as she'd thought.

CHAPTER 11

When Greta walked in, Helen was sitting on the edge of Paul's bed, her head bent over a puzzle on the little tray table situated over his midsection. She was working on it intently, and, much to Greta's surprise, Paul was actually helping.

A lump rose in her throat. As a little girl, she would have loved to do a puzzle with her dad, but he'd never been interested.

"Do you need this piece?" Paul asked, pushing a random piece forward.

"What? No." Helen expertly fitted a couple of pieces together. "Why would I need that piece? We're still working on the edges."

So maybe helping wasn't exactly the right word.

He sighed. "A puzzle she brings me," he said to Greta. "Why can't she bring some of that lemon pound cake I like so much?"

"Oh, you. I got this one just for you. Here, Greta. Look." She held up the box lid, on which was a forest scene, a big buck leaping over a fallen log, various fluffy little animals tucked away in tree hollows and under bushes. "What do you think?"

"Very nice. I would think you would enjoy this, Dad," she said, even though she knew full well that he wasn't a puzzle kind of guy. He was too active, always on the go. Never able to sit still for more than a few minutes.

Which might explain why the company was struggling.

"Looks like a damn Disney movie," Paul grumbled. When Helen made a little mew with her mouth, he added, "Excuse my language."

Helen beamed at him as if he'd done something exceptional. "Do you see any more edge pieces? I'm missing a couple."

Greta watched in amazement as her father scanned the remaining pieces. "Found one."

Then Helen smiled ruefully at Greta. "I'm sure you want some time with your father." To Paul she said, "We'll have to stop here for now."

"Oh, no," Paul said, his tone making it clear that he was anything but sorry.

The older woman gave him a playful swat on the shoulder, so light that it barely rumpled his hospital gown. "Just leave this all here and we can pick up where we left off tomorrow."

"Thanks, Helen," Paul said. But once she'd left, he looked up at Greta. "Where does she expect me to eat with my tray all covered in puzzle pieces?"

Greta slid her handbag strap from her shoulder and settled onto the chair beside her father's bed. "I'm sure you can just put your tray on top of the pieces. It'll be fine."

"Oh, sure. And that will mess up what she's already done. God help me if one of these damn pieces goes missing. Have you seen her desk? I've seen Army barracks that were less organized."

"Probably for the best given your total lack of organizational skills."

Paul flicked a glance in her direction, then picked up the remote control and turned on the tiny television set mounted near the ceiling on the opposite wall. "Nick told me you were messing around in my office."

"I'm not 'messing around' in your office." She sat up a little straighter in her chair and crossed one leg neatly over the other. "I'm reviewing the business's records in order to familiarize myself with the details."

There. Perfect #girlboss response.

As she should have expected, her father merely rolled his eyes. "You're not going to find anything in that mess that will help you. The really important stuff is all in here," he said, tapping his index finger against his temple.

"That's helpful. Considering you almost died of a heart attack and all."

"Don't exaggerate. I didn't almost die." He turned his attention back to the TV.

"It so happens that I did find something I wanted to ask you about." She opened her bag and pulled out a sheaf of papers. "Here. It looks like King Lures owns a patent?"

He regarded the paper warily. "Why do you want to know?"

"Because you put me in charge, and if I'm going to help you, I need to know what I'm dealing with. It looks like the product that came from it cost the company quite a bit of money."

She held the papers out to him, but he waved them away, instead grabbing the remote to change the channel. A TV chef Greta wasn't familiar with was screaming at a harried-looking assistant over a missing bottle of fish sauce. "It's my attempt at a synthetic lure."

She said nothing. The silence stretched uncomfortably until Paul sighed and lowered the TV volume. "One of the issues we're facing at the moment is something called chronic wasting disease in deer. It's always fatal, and we don't really know enough about how it spreads."

He was in full professor mode now, Greta could tell. As a kid, if she ever asked him a question about wildlife—which rarely happened—he would launch into a lengthy lecture that encompassed far more than she needed to know.

"Some researchers were able to show that there may—and I

need to stress the word *may*—be a possibility deer can spread CWD through urine. It's flimsy at best, but the state agencies are under pressure to *do something* to contain the disease. So a handful of states have banned the use of natural deer urine as a lure."

Greta blinked. As she learned on her tour, King Lures had a few attractants for bears and hogs that didn't use urine, but for the most part the company was built on deer pee. Real deer pee. Take that away, and there was no more King Lures.

"A synthetic? Like, fake urine?" she asked.

He nodded. "Yes. The industry's taken some steps to make sure natural deer urines don't pose a risk to wild deer, but I thought it might be wise to have something to sell in states that didn't allow natural urine. We produced the synthetic last year. I thought it worked pretty well, but we just couldn't sell it. Didn't go with the brand. So it was a loser."

Making a notation, she moved on to the next topic on her list. "Did you know the coffee maker keeps breaking?"

"Yeah. So?"

"Dad, it's a crappy little coffee maker. How much could it possibly cost to replace it?"

He spread his fingers wide on the sheets. "We don't need to replace it. We already have a perfectly good coffee maker."

"It's not perfectly good. Today I found Robbie and Kelsey working on repairing it. How many hours of potential work time are your employees wasting on repairing the stupid coffee maker when they could be doing something worthwhile?"

"Your employees."

"What?"

He didn't look at her. "You're in charge. For the time being, they're your employees."

"Well, if I'm in charge, I say we buy a new coffee maker."

"That's the dumbest idea I've ever heard."

There was a pounding in her head that she swore she could hear. "I seriously doubt that."

He crumpled his fingers into fists, his nostrils flaring. "That's the problem with your generation. Something breaks, you just want to replace it without even trying to fix it."

"People have tried to fix it, Dad. It's way past that point."

"It's still worth fixing. If Robbie and Kelsey have time to work on it, then I say let them."

"I thought you said they were my employees, Dad."

"We're done talking about this," Paul said. His cheeks flamed with color, and Greta realized that what she'd thought at first was the sound of a headache was actually her father's heart monitor beeping as his pulse skyrocketed.

She sat back, her shoulders wilting as she grasped how little had changed. Her father might have asked for her help, but it was, as always, on his terms. Why was she even there? Stuffing the papers back into her bag, she ran an assessing eye over him. He looked less gray than he had the last time she'd been there, although perhaps that had just been the result of fatigue. The room seemed colder than it had felt before, and her father had his blankets pulled all the way to his chest, a lightweight camo jacket over his hospital gown.

"When did you have the heart attack?" she heard herself ask.

"I couldn't say for sure. It's kind of hard to keep track of the days in here." Lifting the remote, he clicked through several channels before stopping on one of those movies with explosions and attractive twenty-somethings in tactically tight pants and little else. "Why do you ask?"

"Helen called me on Monday."

"Well, it didn't happen Monday, I know that. A few days ago, I guess."

"Why didn't you call me when it happened?"

On the screen, a woman in a cleavage-baring tank top swore and lifted some kind of automatic weapon to blow away a giant robot. Her father turned up the volume on the TV as if he might miss some brilliantly written piece of dialogue. Greta winced as the sharp staccato bursts of gunfire sliced through her aching head.

"Dad." He didn't even look at her. She tried again. "Dad."

Nothing.

Snatching the remote out of his hand, she punched the power button, plunging the room into merciful silence.

"Hey! I was watching that."

"I came down here to talk to you, and you can't even be bothered to turn off the TV." It was the story of their entire relationship: Greta sitting around waiting for her father to find a way to fit her into his life.

"I didn't ask you to visit me." He fidgeted with one of the puzzle pieces on his tray table. "I'm not really in the mood to talk business."

"I'm sorry if this is an inconvenient time for you, Dad. It's actually not great for me, either. I'm up for a promotion, and I'd really rather be back in the office impressing my boss. But here I am."

"A promotion, huh? Good for you." Her father's hand moved toward the remote. Greta grabbed it from the bed before he could turn the TV back on.

"Why didn't you call me?"

Defeated, her father sank back against the pillows, his eyes fixed on his hands, which lay big and tan against the white sheet. "I didn't know it was a heart attack. Not at first. I didn't want to worry you if it turned out to be nothing."

"You called Nick Campbell."

Her father's hands roamed the sheet, picking at some invisible bits of lint. "Sure, I called Nick. He's here in town. What was I supposed to do? Call you and have you drive down from Chicago just in case something was wrong with me?"

"But then you didn't call me once you knew. And you didn't call me the next day, either. Or the next."

Paul shrugged. "I called you when I needed you."

"*You* didn't call me at all."

"Fine. I had Helen call you when I needed you."

"Right. And not a minute before."

He grabbed the remote back and hit the power button. "What do you want me to do, Greta?" he asked as the room once again filled with contrived grunts and gunfire. "Go back in time and call you the minute I started to feel off?"

"It would have been nice if you had thought to call me before you called your secretary."

"Receptionist," he said. "And believe it or not, not everything is about you. I'm the one stuck in a hospital bed when I really need to be working. You want to feel sorry for someone? Feel sorry for me."

Yeah. Like she would ever feel sorry for Paul King. "I'm trying to help you, Dad, but you won't tell me what exactly you need help with."

"Aren't you supposed to be some big go-getter? I figured out how to run the company on my own. You should be able to do it, too."

She'd forgotten just how frustrating he could be. She was there, wasn't she? Playing the dutiful daughter, risking her own future to make sure her father was okay. She'd gone to a deer farm for this man, and all he could say was that she wasn't doing enough. "Maybe this was a bad idea." Grabbing her bag, she stalked to the door, mentally calculating what time it would be before she could get back to Chicago if she left at that moment.

"I thought you were so good you were up for a promotion," he said behind her. "I guess you'd have to be really exceptional at advertising to figure out a campaign that would save a company."

She froze, the doorknob cool under her palm. She knew what

he was doing, knew she needed to keep right on going, to walk out of this hospital and drive back where she belonged.

She also knew, as much as it pained her to acknowledge it, that she wasn't going to do that.

Because he was just goading her. He didn't really believe that she could do it. And if there was one thing she wanted more than anything, it was to prove her father wrong.

A woman on TV screamed, and Greta sighed. She knew exactly how that woman felt.

She was staying in Bartlett.

* * *

THERE WAS a car parked on the street in front of her father's house when Greta got back. The last time there'd been a car parked in that spot, she'd found Nick sitting on her father's couch.

At least this time it wasn't the white Prius she now knew belonged to Nick. And while she found his vehicle choice surprising, she was pretty sure he didn't also own an adorable yellow Beetle with a suncatcher hanging from the rearview mirror.

Although it would kind of delight her if he did.

Kelsey was in the kitchen dicing an avocado, some jangly not-quite-pop music blaring from her phone. Her face broke into a huge grin when she looked up and saw Greta standing there. "I bet you wonder what I'm doing here," she said.

"I'm actually more wondering how you got in."

"I have a key." The knife made short work of the rest of the avocado. "Paul likes me to come check on Polly when no one's around."

Greta opted not to point out that *someone* was certainly around.

"Anyway," Kelsey continued, "I'm making guacamole." She

glanced up, sympathy etched on her face. "Auggie told me what happened today over at Jake's, so I figured after everything you've been through, you could really use a girls' night."

What Greta could use was a couple hours alone and some amazing ideas for the Coeurs Sauvages campaign. "I appreciate you thinking of me, but I'm actually kind of busy tonight."

Kelsey simply picked up a bottle on the counter and waggled it in Greta's general direction. "I brought wine."

Greta narrowed her eyes. "Are you old enough to drink?"

"Um, of course. I turned 21, like, four months ago."

With a sigh, Greta set down the bag of groceries she had purchased on the way home from the hospital. "There's this ad campaign that could make my career," she explained, as she took Paul's beer out of the refrigerator crisper and put her produce in its place. "I need to do some work on it tonight."

"An ad campaign for what?" The song ended, and a new one—something with a lot of bass—came on. Kelsey shimmied her hips in time to the music, singing along under her breath.

"Perfume."

"Ohmigosh, I would love to work on a perfume commercial."

That wasn't what Greta was doing, but she didn't have a chance to point that out before Kelsey rushed on.

"All you have to do is put a big-time actress in a fancy dress, have her walk around someplace you have to fly to get to, play some cool music, and have her say something in French." The knife stopped moving as she stared off into the distance, her face the picture of concentration. "*Oui*," she said, pouting her lips in an exaggerated French accent. "*Croissant. Café.*"

"I'm not sure—"

"You don't even want it to make sense. People should be like, 'Did her high heel just turn into a boat? What is even happening?' Those are the best perfume commercials."

"Yes, well—"

"You can use that idea if you want. I'm not going to be upset if you take credit for it."

Greta suppressed a smile as she tried to imagine Tamsin's face if she pitched that idea. "Picture this," she would say. "Nicole Kidman in this shimmery turquoise-blue gown, walking along a beach, a gorgeous man racing to catch up. Just as he's about to catch her, she pulls off one shoe and throws it into the ocean. As it touches the water, it's instantly transformed into this luxury yacht. We see champagne, caviar, sophisticated people moving about the deck. And suddenly she's on the ship as it moves away from shore, leaning against the railing watching the gorgeous man on the beach grow smaller and smaller. Then closeup on her face. She touches the side of her throat and whispers, *'Fromage.'*"

It wasn't even the most ridiculous idea Greta had ever heard.

Kelsey set the knife down and wiped her hands on a faded yellow dishtowel. "Did you mean what you said yesterday? About not letting people go?"

"Of course." Having finished with the cold groceries, Greta moved to the cabinet over the microwave that had, up until yesterday, held several bags of potato chips. She'd tossed those. In the interest of her father's health, of course.

If she got any satisfaction out of picturing her father coming home to a house without junk food, that was beside the point.

"So you're not going to fire Robbie?" Kelsey's eyes were fixed on her toenails, which were painted an acid yellow with a diagonal stripe of what looked like grass-green puffy paint.

Greta set a box of nut flour crackers down on the counter. "Why would I fire Robbie?"

"I dunno. Nick said we shouldn't waste time or money when you're around." The operative words seemed to be "when you're around." "And Robbie was afraid that if you knew he could work on the coffee maker because he didn't have any shipments to process at that exact moment, you might start to think the shipping department wasn't busy enough to need a full-time person.

But I told him that you *promised*"—Greta didn't remember necessarily promising anything, but whatever—"you weren't here to get rid of people, and that you'd be impressed that he was, you know, taking initiative. But then I remembered about the wasting time thing and I was nervous that maybe the coffee maker isn't all that important to you and we should have asked you about it first. And then—"

Greta was beginning to need some of that wine. "I'm not going to fire Robbie," she said firmly. "Or anyone else," she added quickly as Kelsey opened her mouth to ask her another question. "It's true that I think constantly repairing the coffee maker is a waste of time, but that's not your fault."

Kelsey looked relieved. "So, we're good, then?"

"Yes, everything is fine."

"Cool." She held up the wine bottle again. "Girls' night?"

"Sorry, but I meant what I said when I—"

"What is that?" Kelsey set the wine bottle down on the chipped laminate of the counter and pointed at the box Greta had just picked up.

She turned the box over in her hands. "Crackers."

"No," Kelsey said, advancing on her. "Those are not crackers." Taking the box from Greta's hands, she pulled open the flap, tore the plastic off one little cellophane tray, and took a small bite of one of the nut flour crackers, all the while regarding Greta suspiciously. "This is sawdust."

"It's just a healthier alternative—"

"Oh, girl. No." She studied Greta as if seeing her for the first time, her eyes raking over the ivory blouse and tan pencil skirt she'd changed into after...well, just *after*. She really didn't want to think about that incident again.

Kelsey's perpetual smile sank into a frown, and she shook her head sadly. "This isn't a cracker. This is, like, the ghost of a cracker. Seriously, Greta, this is not good girls' night food."

"Well, that's because we're not doing—"

"This is worse than I thought." Kelsey dropped the tray back into the box and tossed it onto the counter. Then she put her hands on Greta's shoulders and guided her to the couch in the living room. "You sit down. I'm calling Helen, and then I'm going to finish that guacamole. You need some chips and guac, stat."

"But I—"

"Don't worry about a thing. We're going to have a blast."

* * *

SURPRISINGLY, she did kind of have a blast. Helen showed up with half a bag of Chips Ahoy and stuff to make something she called dressed bananas, which Greta grudgingly admitted weren't as bad as she'd expected when she saw the ingredients. Then Helen bet Kelsey a pedicure that Greta's nut flour crackers would taste better than the pie that Kelsey had brought to the King Lures Christmas party the previous year. The pie must have been pretty bad because Helen won, and then Kelsey ran out to get her nail polish—which, apparently, she kept in her car—so she could pay her debt right away.

While Kelsey painted Helen's toenails a deep shade of midnight blue, Greta explained the importance of the Stella campaign, and they brainstormed ideas for her.

By the end of the evening, Helen, clutching the stem of her wine glass in one fist, announced that the wildest thing she could imagine was *Fifty Shades of Gray*, which made Kelsey snort wine out her nose while Greta hastily jotted down the idea in her notebook.

"Did you just write down 'anal beads'?" Kelsey squealed, wiping her nose with a paper towel.

"It's brainstorming," Helen said. She made a sweeping gesture with her glass, sending the wine inside sloshing dangerously close to the rim. "The first rule of brainstorming is you don't critique any thoughts. Right, Greta?"

She was right, but that wasn't how brainstorming sessions at Prescott normally went. Maybe no one was outwardly critical of any ideas that were proposed, but Greta wasn't an idiot; she knew very well that people kept track of who came up with really dumb ideas. Come up with enough dumb ideas and not enough good ones to balance them out, and your career went into a tailspin.

She tried to remember the last time she'd had a girls' night and came up empty. There was that wine festival a couple years ago, and hadn't she gone out for tapas several months back with Andi and some of the other women from work?

Regardless, she was sure anal beads hadn't come up.

At the end of the evening, after she'd walked Kelsey and Helen to the door and locked it behind them—a completely futile gesture as apparently everyone Paul had ever met had a key to his house—it struck her that she didn't have a single female friend who would offer to paint her toenails. She had plenty of friends, of course, but they weren't the kind of friends she ever, well, *laughed* with.

She collected Helen and Kelsey's wine glasses—she'd stuck with water since it was a work night, much to Kelsey's disgust—and carried them to the sink. It wasn't a bad thing that she and her friends never sat around someone's apartment drinking wine, making homemade guacamole, and discussing whether or not they would sleep with Christian Gray. Her friendships in Chicago were intellectually stimulating. They provided her with great networking opportunities.

They just weren't very fun.

She finished rinsing the wine glasses and set them in the drainer to dry. Fun was something she didn't have much time for. Her career was too demanding; there was too much at stake to lose sight of the brass ring. That had happened once before, and look what the result had been. Failure.

She wasn't going to let that happen again. Spending the

evening with Kelsey and Helen might have been entertaining, but it had been a distraction her career didn't need at the moment. Wiping her hands on the dishtowel, she headed for her father's office, where she quickly pulled up the file she needed.

"Focus," she whispered to herself as the video filled the screen. "You just need to focus."

CHAPTER 12

The next morning, Auggie set a steaming mug of fresh coffee on Nick's desk. "Thanks," Nick said absently, his mind busy calculating how many units they needed to sell this month to make up for the previous month.

"Don't you want to know where that came from?"

He looked at the mug blankly. "I'm assuming from the break room."

"It's from our new coffee maker," Auggie said, lifting his own mug to take a sip. "You should see this thing. It's really nice."

"A new coffee maker?" Sensing danger, Nick pushed his chair back. "I didn't approve that expense."

"Nope. The boss did."

"Paul said we could get a new coffee maker?" That didn't seem like Paul. The man was incredibly generous in some ways, but he was also cheap as hell in others.

"Not that boss." A smile tugged at Auggie's mouth. "The new one. Only it wasn't an expense. She paid for it with her own money."

It took a moment for that to sink in. When it finally did, Nick swore under his breath and stalked out of his office. Sure enough, he found a fancy new coffee maker in the break room, one far more advanced than the basic appliance that had limped along for as long as Nick could remember.

"Can you believe it?" Kelsey asked as he stood in front of that stupid contraption. "It doesn't just make regular coffee. You can use it to make cappuccinos and lattes, too."

"I have never once seen you drink a cappuccino or a latte."

She had the nerve to roll her eyes at him. "It doesn't matter that I prefer regular coffee. What matters is that now I have options."

"Morning, Nick!" Helen sang as she came in. She set a Tupperware container down in the middle of the break room table and removed the lid with a flourish. "I brought homemade spice muffins."

"Ooh, I was wondering when you were going to make those again." Kelsey snagged one. Pulling off the liner, she took a big bite and, with a blissful sigh, closed her eyes. "Spice muffins and a new coffee maker. Could this day get any better?"

"I cannot believe she did this."

"I guess it can get better." Kelsey grinned at Helen. "Nick's upset about the new coffee maker."

"What's there to be upset about? We had a coffee maker that didn't work. Now we have one that does, and the company didn't spend a dime. Seems like a win-win to me."

That it did. In fact, it was such a simple and elegant solution to the problem that Nick should have come up with it himself. And he probably would have if he hadn't been so stuck on following Paul's edict against replacing things that could be repaired.

"I have a feeling this is one of those Freudian things," Kelsey said, leaning back against the break room table and surveying Nick with a self-satisfied smile.

"Huh?" Helen said.

"Sometimes a coffee maker isn't just a coffee maker."

Nick jabbed a finger in her direction. "Don't you have something you could be working on?"

Kelsey popped the last bite of muffin into her mouth and then licked a crumb off one fingertip. "I'll call this my morning break. Want me to call Greta in here? I kinda want to see her handle you."

This wasn't helping. Giving Kelsey a stern look, he stalked out of the break room and headed for Paul's office.

Which was where he got the second shock of the day.

It was empty.

Well, not really empty. But it seemed that way given the absence of files, papers, and books spread across every available horizontal surface.

Greta was sitting behind Paul's desk, the phone pressed against one ear, leaning back in the chair just as Paul always did when he spoke on the phone. The resemblance was uncanny.

But that was where the resemblance stopped. Where Paul generally surrounded himself with chaos, Greta appeared ruthlessly efficient. Except for Paul's computer and a notebook Greta was using to take notes, the surface of the desk was clear, something Nick realized he'd never seen before.

For just a moment, he wondered what it would be like to work for someone as well organized as Greta appeared to be, but the thought felt disloyal, so he pushed it firmly out of his mind.

Spotting him, Greta gave him what looked to Nick to be a triumphant smile and held up one finger to indicate she'd be with him in a moment. "Thank you, Daphne. You've been most helpful. I'll look for that email."

His eyes narrowed. Daphne?

He was well aware that the world was full of women named Daphne, but, judging from the look on her face as she hung up the phone, he had a feeling he knew exactly which Daphne she was talking to.

"Well," she said, jotting something down in her notebook. "That was educational."

He moved to the desk and dropped into the chair across from her. "Who was that?" he asked, straining to keep his tone neutral.

"Daphne Ness. She works for *Outdoor Insider* magazine." She tapped the end of her pen against her notebook. "Maybe you've heard of it?"

"I have." It was the biggest trade magazine in the outdoor industry, and Daphne Ness was the magazine's powerhouse salesperson. She'd been in the industry for nearly as long as Nick had and, while she seemed to make it a point to stay away from gossip, Nick knew there wasn't much that happened in the industry that she didn't know about.

Come to think of it, Greta and Daphne would probably get along like whitetail deer and salt licks.

That couldn't be good.

"I found several old issues of *Outdoor Insider* when I was going through the stuff from my father's office, and I figured someone from the magazine might be a good resource for learning more about what we do here."

He propped one foot on his knee. "You called *Outdoor Insider* to find out about King Lures? Why didn't you just talk to me?"

"You didn't seem especially forthcoming about the company's operations." She drew a single sharp line through something she'd written in her notebook, then looked up at him. "I thought it would expedite things if I found another source of information."

Guilt niggled at him. She was right. He hadn't been forthcoming.

But, then, he hadn't realized she actually wanted to know.

"Anyway, Daphne is emailing over several articles she said I would be interested in. An old cover story on King Lures, several articles on the history of scents, and a couple pieces on the state of the industry today."

Nick remembered that cover story. It had run five years earlier, and in the interview Paul had mentioned all of his employees by name. And then he'd gotten to Nick: *"You know, when you run a business it's not smart to become too dependent on any one employee. Employees leave. They move away, find better opportunities. But even with that in mind, I have to say this: there is no King Lures without Nick Campbell. He's been with me for years, and I honestly don't see how I could run this company without him."*

Greta didn't need to wait for an email to read the article; Nick still had his copy of the issue in his desk. But she looked so pleased with herself that he didn't mention it.

"Where's all Paul's stuff?"

"In here." She waved one hand at the filing cabinets behind her.

"You fit everything in those filing cabinets?"

Greta suddenly became incredibly interested in something she'd written in her notebook.

"Greta."

"Hmmm?"

"What happened to Paul's stuff?"

After a long pause, she set her pen down and folded her hands together as if she were a doctor preparing to deliver bad news. "I sorted through everything."

"And then you put it...?"

"Everything I deemed important has been organized and filed appropriately."

"And everything you did not deem important?"

Greta took a bracing breath. "That was downsized."

He was pretty sure he knew exactly what she meant, but he wanted her to spell it out. "Downsized?"

"I threw it out," she said. "It was just trash. Out-of-date paperwork and phone numbers to companies that went out of business years ago—yes, I checked—and owner's manuals for office equipment we no longer own—much to my surprise, because I didn't think my father was capable of getting rid of anything, judging from that mess."

In growing horror, Nick rose to his feet and moved to the filing cabinets, all the while keeping a wary eye on Greta. Tugging open the top drawer, he stared down at the skinny collection of folders, all labeled neatly in—what else?—ruthlessly efficient handwriting, less feminine than he would have guessed. The next drawer had a similarly skimpy number of files. So did the next, and the next.

He thought of the stacks and stacks of paperwork Paul had kept in his office. There was no telling what this woman might find unimportant. What exactly had she thrown away?

How could he have been so stupid? He'd thought he could distract her with some busy work, and instead she'd taken it upon herself to throw away 90 percent of Paul's stuff. Sure, he might agree with her that most of it was junk just taking up space, but if Paul wanted to work like that, what business of hers was it?

Slowly, he pushed the filing cabinet drawer closed. "How could you throw it all away?"

"I didn't throw it *all* away. Just the stuff that needed to be thrown away."

"But it wasn't your stuff."

She merely shrugged. "You knew I was cleaning out this office. If you'd wanted to review my work, you should have made that clear." Then her eyes narrowed. "No. You know what? My father put me in charge. If he has a problem with what I'm doing, he can address that with me when he gets back. It's not really your concern."

There is no King Lures without Nick Campbell.

"Not my concern? Are you kidding me?" Spinning away from the filing cabinet, he stalked to the window, where he braced his hands against the wall and stared out. Milky-white clouds floated across a brilliant blue sky, casting shifting shadows over the dying grass beyond the office building. Despite the touch of the AC, he could almost feel the golden glow of the sun on his skin.

"I know it's my dad that's the problem," Greta said from the desk behind him, "but, frankly, I think everyone here could stand to learn a little bit about letting go."

He turned slowly. "Letting go?"

"Yes." She leaned back in her chair, settling her clasped hands on the smooth expanse of another drab—probably rented—skirt. "Just think about that stupid coffee maker. I've seen more functional machines at elementary school science fairs, but for some reason my dad insisted on keeping it. What was that about?"

He leaned back against the cool window and crossed his arms over his chest. "What does it matter? Isn't it more ecologically friendly to repair things rather than just tossing them into a landfill?"

He'd assumed she was into ecologically friendly solutions, and judging from the way her mouth tightened, he'd been right. But then she turned back to her notebook, picking up her pen and writing down God-knew-what on the page before her. "If it can be repaired. We both know it can't. Anyway, if my father wants to use the old coffee maker, it's still in the break room. I put it in the cabinet under the sink. Now, I have some articles to read. I'll let you know if I have any questions later."

He was getting really tired of being dismissed by Greta Tremaine. Before he left, he took one last look at the view from Paul's office window.

Home. This was his home. His sleepy rural town, his moldering building, his struggling company, his hard-working coworkers.

At least it always had been. But now, as he thought of that fancy coffee maker in the break room, he wasn't quite so sure about that anymore.

CHAPTER 13

*B*y Friday morning, Greta felt as if she could almost write her own #girlboss blog post. "Step number one," she would write, "remember everyone loves coffee."

Of course, not *everyone* loved coffee, and, she thought as she remembered Nick's thunderous face, not everyone appreciated easy solutions to stupid problems.

There was probably a blog post in *that* somewhere. She'd settle for a great ad idea for the Coeurs Sauvages campaign. Her notebook was filled with ideas, but she didn't have anything that really felt promotion-worthy yet. Of course, Reed had emailed again, all saccharine concern and mansplainy offers to help. "I'm sure this is a tough time for you, and it must be hard to work on such a challenging campaign on top of everything. If you want to run anything by me for the Stella ad, I'm happy to help," he'd written.

Yeah. Said the spider to the fly. Greta wasn't about to fall for that.

She'd learned quite a bit about King's operations from the articles Daphne had sent over and from talking to some of the employees. Occasionally she'd looked up to find Nick watching her from somewhere else in the plant, his expression forbidding.

Good. Despite what she'd said, her father wasn't the only one who had trouble letting go; Nick was clearly having trouble ceding control of the company to her. If he was displeased, that just meant that she was successfully taking over.

She had big plans for the day, so she woke early to go for a morning run through the neighborhood before the heat of the day became too oppressive. On impulse, she took Polly with her, a decision she regretted almost immediately. The little dog clearly had never gone jogging with anyone before; she bounced joyfully around Greta's feet, once in a while darting without warning after a squirrel, barking her head off until the jerk of the leash brought her up short.

Fortunately, by the time Greta reached the cul-de-sac at the end of the neighborhood's meandering main road, Polly was doing moderately better and managed to go the rest of the way home without tripping Greta again. Once the dog was finally inside the house and off the leash, she collapsed in an exhausted heap on the worn couch.

Satisfied that Polly had gotten some exercise, Greta took a quick shower, mentally reviewing her To-Do list. For the first time since the beginning of the week, she finally felt back in control.

That was when her cell phone rang. Even without looking at the number, she had a sinking feeling that her carefully constructed plans were about to be upended.

It was her father. "They're letting me go home this morning," he said, not bothering with a greeting. "I need you to be here at 9 to get me." And then, before Greta could explain that she had a sales meeting planned for that time, he hung up.

"Right." She set her phone down on the bathroom vanity. "Love you, too, Dad."

* * *

IT TURNED out that Paul was the worst patient in the history of the world. Ever.

He started grousing the moment Greta got him settled in the passenger seat of her Civic. "Why didn't you bring my truck?" he asked.

"Because I'm driving and this is my car." Greta pulled her visor down to block the worst of the sun's glare and turned out onto the road.

"It's like a sardine can in here."

"It is not."

"Look. My elbow is touching your elbow," he said, wiggling his elbow where it sat on the center console.

Greta promptly moved her own elbow. "There. Problem solved."

"What if you're in an accident in this thing?" Paul grabbed the door handle and held on as she turned left onto Lafayette.

"It has excellent safety ratings."

"Not if you get plowed into by someone driving a truck like mine."

She sighed as she braked for a red light. There was a good amount of traffic for a small town, and it looked like they might be stuck for more than one light cycle. Which, considering her present company, was just about perfect. "Not a lot of people drive giant trucks in Chicago, Dad."

"Right. But they do here. Which is why you should be driving my truck." He moved his feet restlessly. "Are my legs sticking into the engine? It feels like they are."

Sending a fervent prayer for patience heavenward, Greta cast about looking for something to distract him. "I read the cover story on King Lures in *Outdoor Insider* magazine."

"Yeah?" He shifted his arm on the center console, seizing even more territory. "What'd you think?"

She'd learned more about her father's company in six magazine pages than she had in her previous thirty-two years. "It was interesting."

The light turned green, and the line of cars in front of her began to move forward slowly. It seemed every other car needed to turn right into the numerous gas stations and fast-food joints that lined this section of Lafayette, and apparently drivers in Bartlett had learned to practically come to a full stop before making a right-hand turn.

"Anything else?"

She shrugged. She wasn't going to admit that she'd felt a tiny flicker of pride at the way her father was portrayed in the article, as a straight-talking maverick who did things his way and reaped massive rewards for it.

Anyway, that didn't seem to be the reality any longer.

Just as she'd feared, she didn't make it through the light before it turned red again. Despite the heat, she rolled her window down.

"Talking to you is like pulling teeth, you know that?" Her father turned up the AC and pointed the vents at himself.

"I'm sorry. I'm not used to you wanting to know my opinion."

In response, her father turned on the radio. Static, spliced with the occasional bouncy pop song, filled the car; all of the presets were tuned to Chicago stations. Her father hit Seek until he found a local station and then pushed the button again.

A smile tugged at Greta's mouth. Her father had found a hip hop station, and she was sure he wasn't enjoying the music at all. But there he was, tapping his fingers with the least amount of rhythm possible, pretending to be so lost in the music he was no longer interested in conversation.

She let him pretend.

Finally, he said, "Greta?"

"Yeah?"

"Who listens to this stuff?"

"A lot of people, Dad."

He sighed. "This is why the company is doing so badly. I have no idea what people like anymore."

Greta clicked the radio off. "I agree." The light turned green, and this time she managed to get through it before it changed again. Of course, then she got stopped by the train on Main Street.

"My truck has Sirius radio, you know."

With a groan, she leaned her head forward and rested her forehead against the steering wheel. It was going to be a very long day.

* * *

HOME WASN'T MUCH BETTER. When Greta had envisioned her father's homecoming, she'd imagined herself creating a sea of tranquility in which he could recover. She had straightened up the main areas of the house as best she could, although she would have given quite a bit to be able to make a quick trip to The Container Store. The living room might not be the spa-like retreat she would have loved to create, but she had a feeling a few days with his horrible bear and some TV at home would have a similar effect on her father.

She should have known he wouldn't cooperate.

Polly threw herself into a series of jumps and twists and rolls when she saw him, yipping her head off in uncontrollable joy. "Hey, there, Polly girl," Paul said. To Greta he added, "You used to greet me like this when I came home."

She eyed the frantic dog. "I highly doubt that."

"No, really." He took a shaky step forward, grimacing as she hurried to his side and wrapped one arm around his waist for support. "I don't need any help."

"Humor me." She got him settled in his easy chair, draping a quilt over him and fussing with it until he batted her hands away.

"When you were little, you used to run to the door when I came home from work, just like Polly does now."

She snorted.

"You would spin in circles chanting, 'Daddy's home, Daddy's home, Daddy's home.'"

That was so ludicrous that it didn't merit a response. "You didn't tell me you got a dog." Hands on her hips, she studied Polly, who by now was snorting and rubbing her face, one side at a time, against the carpet. "Not exactly the kind of dog I pictured you choosing."

"I didn't choose Polly. Helen's mother had to move to a nursing home, and she couldn't take her dog. Helen was worried that she wouldn't have time for her what with visiting her mother as much as she was doing, so I took her."

For a moment, there was only the sound of the dog's whiny yelps. Greta wasn't sure why she was so taken aback at this information. Her father wasn't a bad person, although somehow the knowledge that he killed animals for fun had colored her image of him so much that he was the last person she would expect to take in an old woman's dog.

What had she thought he would do? Offer to shoot the dog in exchange for a homemade casserole?

That did kind of sound more like the Paul King in her head.

"Well," she said, breaking the silence that stretched uncomfortably between them, "I'll just take this—" she hefted the overnight bag he'd had with him in the hospital— "to your room."

"Don't bother unpacking it," he called as she left the room. "I don't need you going through my stuff."

Judging from the number of duffel bags she'd found in his closet full of obviously dirty clothes, any bag she left for him to unpack would be left unopened until the next time he needed a bag. She'd only seen her father wear a hospital gown and his camouflage jacket in the hospital, so she assumed he hadn't worn any of the clothes he'd brought with him. That suspicion was confirmed when she unzipped the bag and saw that the clothes inside were still neatly folded.

It was strange that her father had thought to pack an overnight bag in the middle of a heart attack, she thought as she placed the clothes in his dresser, doing her best to bring some order to the drawers as she did so.

And then she realized that her father hadn't packed this bag. It would have been someone else who came to the house once he was stable and knew he would be in the hospital for a few days.

She didn't need two guesses to know who would have handled that for her father.

She was staring balefully down at a stack of stark-white briefs, reminding herself that if Nick Campbell could do it, she too could handle her father's underwear, when a pained roar from the main area of the house had her racing down the hallway. She found her father staring horror-struck into a cabinet in the kitchen, Polly in the process of draping herself over his feet.

"Where the hell are my chips?"

"You're not eating chips anymore, remember?" Greta leaned weakly against the side of the refrigerator, her heart still racing. She'd thought something was terribly, terribly wrong.

Looking at the shock on his face as he surveyed his newly stocked snack cabinet, she imagined that, at least for her father, something was.

His eyes shifting to Greta, he moved slowly to fridge, muttering something under his breath that sounded a bit like a prayer. Opening the door, he disappeared behind it as he ducked inside. "No, no, no," he moaned. He emerged from the fridge, a Tupperware container in one hand. Popping the lid, he took a long look at the contents. "What is this crap?"

It was leftovers from last night, which she'd planned on taking to work for lunch before she'd learned her father was coming home, but he looked so disturbed that she couldn't help herself. "That's your lunch, Dad."

Lifting the container closer to his face, he took a tentative sniff. "That doesn't answer my question. What *is* it?"

"It's a cold lentil salad. You'll love it."

"I certainly will not love it." He replaced the lid and shoved the container back in the fridge. "I don't know what the point of surviving a heart attack was if I have to eat like this."

"It'll be fine, Dad." Greta closed the fridge door and gently turned him toward the living room. This time he didn't push her away when she helped him walk back to his chair.

"Fine? Fine, she says," Paul muttered as he sank into his chair. "When did you get to be such a sadist?"

She thought back to the wild boar spaghetti he'd set in front of her once. When she wouldn't touch it, he'd wrapped her plate in aluminum foil and set it in the fridge. The next morning, he brought it out for breakfast. "When you get hungry enough, you'll eat it," he'd said. It had taken nearly two full days to win that particular battle, and Greta had a sneaking suspicion that Paul gave in only because he was worried about what would happen when she told her mother she'd gone days without food. But eventually Paul had scraped the spaghetti—now rubbery from being reheated several times—into the trash in disgust. "Just like your mother," he said.

Now, she stepped away from the chair, satisfying herself that he was comfortably settled. "I learned from the best," she said. His lips thinned, but he didn't say anything.

Just like your mother.

She'd known even then it wasn't a compliment. Her parents were divorced.

Her father didn't love her mother.

* * *

By THE TIME her father had been home for an hour, Greta had a feeling her blood pressure was high enough that she might be at risk for a heart attack of her own.

Why did everything have to be a battle with her father?

"Why does everything have to be such a battle with you?" Paul snapped.

Greta massaged her temples in a vain attempt to ease the pain throbbing there. She'd maxed out on Excedrin, but she was beginning to consider taking her chances with a couple more pills. What was the worst thing that could happen?

Finally, she fled the house, using Polly as an excuse.

"Sorry, girl," she said as she half-led, half-dragged the dog down the driveway. Polly kept glancing over her shoulder at the house and whimpering. "You'll see him again in a few minutes."

Or a few hours. Greta wondered idly how far she could manage to walk in the midday heat before it was considered animal abuse.

The tension in her head finally began to ease a bit as she breathed in fresh air, sun-warmed though it was. Without thinking, she turned down a side street, a pleasant melodic tinkling sound drawing her along. Before long, she realized she was walking past Pea Coggshell's house, and the sound that was loosening the final grip of pain in her head came from the wind chimes hanging from Pea's front porch.

"Hello, there!" Pea called, her head appearing over her backyard fence. "Didn't expect to see you here in the middle of a workday."

"I took the day off. My dad came home today."

"Ah." Pea's eyes were shaded by a floppy, wide-brimmed cloth hat, but her mouth curved into something of a knowing smile. Unlatching the gate, she pushed it open. "Want to give me a hand back here?"

With a wag of her tail, Polly started toward the gate, Greta trailing reluctantly. "I'm not very good at gardening," she said as she stepped into Pea's backyard.

But Pea was already closing the gate behind her with one hand, her other occupied with a wicked-looking pair of clippers. "Nothing to it." She pushed the brim of her hat up to swipe the back of one hand across her forehead. "You can pull weeds, can't you? I'll show you what to take out, and you just pull it up. Super easy."

Greta glanced down at her cream-colored blouse and camel-colored slacks—basically the most casual outfit she'd brought with her. Oh, who was she kidding? It was the most casual outfit she owned. "I don't know."

"You'll be fine." Pea cupped her elbow with one gloved hand and steered her toward the back door of the house. "Why don't you let Polly off her leash. She'll be fine here. Won't you, Polly? I have some extra gloves and even a mat you can kneel on in the house. Go on in—they're in the top drawer of the gray chest. Can't miss it." Then she turned away and began clipping the branches of an evergreen bush with surgical precision.

Greta had little choice but to open the door of Pea's house and step inside. What she found there made her suck in her breath in wonder.

The interior of Pea's house was dim with the absence of natural light; the house had the same long, ranch-style design and sparsity of windows that Paul's did. Unlike Paul's house, however, Pea's home didn't suffer from the lack of light. Instead, Pea had used the close, intimate shadows to create a magical fairy cottage. All manner of florals were thrown together—cheeky pink cabbage roses on the drapes, spritely daisies on the throw pillows, violet and white ranunculus on the shabby but beautifully curved sofa in the living room. To her left, the kitchen was charmingly outdated with its squat refrigerator and antique stove, a copper teapot on one burner and a tiny wrought-iron table, big enough for only two chairs, tucked in the small eating area. The walls were white, and the cool air inside the house smelled vaguely of honeysuckle.

It was all wrong, and yet it felt so perfect that Greta wished she could just sink into the wicker rocking chair in the corner, wrap herself in the buttery yellow quilt draped over its back, and escape into one of the books stacked haphazardly on the spindly end table.

It was a home, she realized, something she'd spent hours on Pinterest and a fortune with Esme trying desperately—and in vain—to create. Somehow she doubted Pea had spent even a moment worrying about how it would all look in the end.

With a sigh, she found the gray chest of drawers—which was, of course, authentically distressed—and grabbed a pair of faded floral gardening gloves and the kneepad.

Outside, Pea showed her what to look for. As she'd promised, it wasn't hard—the weeds, mostly thistle, were pretty obvious— and soon Greta found herself sinking into the soothing rhythm of the work while Pea puttered nearby and Polly snoozed in the shade of the angel.

The sun baked the back of her neck, and her blouse clung damply to her spine, but there was something gratifying about the growing pile of weeds she pulled from the ground, their roots tangling together like witch's hair. Although silence stretched between Greta and Pea, the music of the garden wove around them: the delicate wind chimes, the drunken buzz of bumblebees, the startled flapping of bird wings, the low bubbling of the fountain, even Polly's gentle snores.

She barely registered the passing of time, and so she was surprised when Pea finally spoke. "You've been working for over an hour. How about we take a break and get some sweet tea?"

Sitting back on her heels, Greta shaded her eyes with one hand and looked up at the older woman. "Thank you, but I try to limit my sugar intake."

Pea chuckled. "Of course you do." She held out one gloved hand to help Greta up. "Well, if you really don't want some tea, I have water, too. But you do need to drink something."

Greta looked around quickly as they walked through the back door, half-expecting to catch one of the wee folk slipping out of the kitchen as they came in. Pea went to the battered fridge and took out a glass pitcher. "You sure you don't want some?" she asked, lifting the pitcher. A lone ray of sunlight slipped in through the small window over the sink and caught the liquid inside, turning it a rich amber.

For a moment, it was possible to believe that calories consumed within these magical walls didn't really count. "You know what? I will have some tea, thank you."

Pea poured two generous glasses and brought them over to the table. "Thanks for your help out there," Pea said, lowering herself into one of the wrought-iron chairs. "It's hard to keep up with everything now that I'm older."

Greta took a sip from her glass, the sweetness almost over-powering after years of seltzer water. But Pea had been right—this was exactly what she needed. "It's a nice break from..." She trailed off, not wanting to say it aloud.

But of course Pea knew what she'd been about to say. She removed her floppy hat, setting it neatly on the table beside her. "The problem is, you and your father are too alike."

Greta choked on her tea. "We're nothing alike. I take after my mother."

"Hardly," Pea said with a snort. "You think Randi Thompson would have spent an hour pulling weeds in my garden? Her hands were so soft a blade of grass could have cut them to pieces."

It took a moment to realize that the older woman was refer-ring to her mother. A small smile played around Greta's lips. Randi? Her mother had been Miranda for as long as she could remember. Greta tried to picture her mother as the kind of person someone might call Randi and failed. "You knew my mother?"

"Of course I did. She grew up not far from here. Kind of a

wild child, if you ask me, though I guess she did grow up just fine in the end."

"My mother, a wild child? I don't think so."

"Oh, but she was. She was always getting your father into trouble, even before they started dating. It was your mother that dared him to sneak in to the county pool after hours, and of course you know how that turned out."

Greta wrapped her hands around the glass in front of her and smiled vaguely as though she had any idea what Pea was talking about. The older woman's gaze sharpened. "The accident? You don't know about it?"

There was no point in lying about it. Greta shook her head.

"Didn't you ever ask how your father got that scar on his leg?"

Something burned at the back of her throat, and she took a sip of tea to ease it. She hadn't known that her father had a scar on his leg.

"Well." Pea rubbed the knuckle of her thumb with her index finger. "Your mother dared him to sneak into the pool." She lowered her voice and leaned closer. "Probably for some skinny-dipping."

Oh, God. Greta took another hasty sip of tea, desperately wishing that image out of her brain.

Leaning back, Pea continued. "Anyway, your father climbed over the fence first. And right on the other side were these hooks that they used to hold the skimmer. Your father went to drop down inside the fence, but he didn't quite clear one of the hooks. It ending up puncturing him about mid-calf and then—"

"Okay, okay," Greta bit out through clenched teeth. She was still adjusting to a world in which her parents went skinny-dipping together. She didn't need any other gory details in her head. "I can imagine."

"Yes. It wasn't pretty. Anyway, the hospital called your grand-mother—your Grandma King, I mean—but she didn't drive at the time, and your grandfather was out of town. So I drove her to the hospital, and there was Randi Thompson in hysterics. She just kept saying, 'It's all my fault. It's all my fault.' And then we got to see him, and he was—well, you know how your father is. He was pale—he'd lost a lot of blood—but he was in there charming the nurses into letting him see Randi. He teased her something awful when they let her in, but he finally got her to smile. I thought your grandmother was going to kill them both once she saw he was okay, but he had her calmed down pretty quick."

Greta didn't recognize the man—boy—Pea had described. *You know how your father is.*

No. No, she didn't.

They finished their tea in silence. Afterwards, Greta collected Polly from the backyard, blinking quickly to acclimate her eyes to the bright sunlight after the pleasantly dim interior of Pea's house.

As she walked home, she tried to imagine her father as a charming teenager whose primary concern after a serious injury was making a girl smile but couldn't do it. Either that young man was gone entirely, or her father had managed to keep a whole chunk of his personality hidden from her for more than three decades.

She wasn't sure which one was sadder.

CHAPTER 14

*N*ick swung into the Arrivals lane at the Louisville Airport a few minutes before ten Monday morning, and a little of the invisible weight he'd been carrying on his shoulders lifted as he caught sight of Ben St. Clair's rangy frame.

Reinforcements had arrived.

Long and lean with a dusky brown backpack slung over one shoulder and a few days' worth of dark scruff on his jaw, Ben looked like a college student home on break. But he had been in the outdoor industry for a long time, and Paul—along with nearly everyone else in the industry—respected the hell out of him. If anyone could get Paul to see how critical it was that he get rid of the reluctant Deer Pee Princess, it was Ben.

Nick pulled alongside the curb. "Hey," he said as Ben slid in and, setting his bag in the backseat, fastened his seatbelt. "Good flight?"

Ben lifted one shoulder in an easy shrug. "Can't complain."

With a quick glance in the rearview mirror, Nick eased away from the curb. Given that he'd never heard Ben complain about a thing, that wasn't saying much.

Of course, considering what Ben was going through at the

moment, a bad flight probably wouldn't even be on his radar when it came to things to complain about.

"How's Carrie?" he asked as he merged onto the highway.

Another shrug. "She's okay," Ben said carefully, which Nick understood to mean that she really wasn't. A longer glance confirmed there were shadows under Ben's eyes, and his face was hollow and etched with pain.

Nick's mouth twisted. "I'm sorry, man."

Ben inclined his head in acknowledgment. "We're still hopeful," he said, although there wasn't a lot of optimism in his tone.

"You want to cancel the trip?" He and Ben were scheduled to head to Colorado together to hunt elk in November. It was part of the reason Ben had flown out instead of just doing the marketing meeting via Skype. They planned to spend a couple of days together looking at Google Earth and doing some pre-hunt scouting.

"No." Ben shook his head. "I asked Carrie that, but she wouldn't hear of it."

Nick was sure Carrie was thinking the same thing he was: Ben could use a few days in the woods. Two years ago, Carrie had been diagnosed with ovarian cancer. While the doctors had initially assured her that they'd caught it early, she didn't seem to be responding to chemo as well as they'd hoped. When Nick had been out to Maryland a few months earlier for a trade show, he'd stayed with Ben and Carrie, and the change in Ben's once incorrigible wife had been shocking.

He'd known then that she was dying. And he was pretty sure Carrie knew it, too.

Only Ben refused to believe the evidence in front of him. As his wife grew weaker, he grew more resolute in his belief that she would pull through, as if his will alone was enough to save her.

But now it seemed that even Ben was starting to realize that love and strength weren't enough to keep someone alive any more than they were enough to keep someone in a marriage.

They drove in silence for several miles until finally Ben cleared his throat. "Auggie tells me Paul's daughter is doing some work at King."

"Yeah." He flicked on his blinker to change lanes. "She's not my biggest fan."

That drew a smile from Ben. "What else is new?"

* * *

GRETA SPENT the morning reviewing King's previous years' marketing campaigns. They were, she had to admit, some of the better ads found in *Outdoor Insider* and the hunting magazines she'd come across in Paul's office. Clean, with a consistent message, appealing images, and strong copy. Most of the ads featured whitetail bucks with big racks; some showed various hunters kneeling respectfully over their downed quarry.

Their target audience probably loved them.

The problem was, there were a lot of other ads that were similar, if not as well done. And while Greta could see the difference in quality between the ads Ben St. Clair had produced for King and the lower-quality ads produced by other companies, she wondered if their target audience saw it.

Probably not.

Nick had gone to the airport to pick up Ben, which had, of course, sparked an argument.

"Why can't he just take an Uber?" she'd asked, trailing Nick down the hallway as he headed out. Clients never picked up any Prescott representatives when they traveled.

"I'm not about to let a friend of mine take an Uber when I can just go get him," he said, one hand already on the door. "Besides, this gives us some extra time to talk about the campaign on the drive."

The unspoken words hung, almost tangibly, in the air. *Without you.*

A headache was forming at her temples, a deep, throbbing one that she could already tell was going to turn into a full-fledged migraine. It was probably too late to head it off, but she rooted through her desk and pulled out her bottle of Excedrin, popping a couple out and washing them down with a swig of seltzer water.

She was glad she'd taken something to dull her headache when, just a few minutes later, the sound of loud voices drew her to the reception area.

That's where she found herself face to face with her father. The same man she'd left settled in his chair at home, a quilt spread over him because, despite every argument about climate change and high electricity bills and the risks of going from one temperature extreme to another, Paul liked to keep the AC on 55 while he was home. She'd handed him the remote. She'd arranged a stack of magazines near his chair—hunting magazines, too. The ones he actually read. She'd even portioned out healthy snacks in plastic containers and left a note on the fridge as to what time to eat each one.

She'd done everything to ensure he would be comfortable at home. And yet here he was.

Behind him, Helen, her cheeks all aglow, was in the middle of saying something about how much everyone had missed him. Robbie and a handful of guys from downstairs were standing near the door, grinning like idiots at him.

"Dad," she said, her hands finding her hips. "We talked about this."

He held up one hand. "You said I couldn't come in to work. And I didn't. I'm just here to visit everyone."

"You're not even cleared to drive yet!"

"Robbie came and got me."

Greta turned her ire on Robbie, who pretended to be suddenly very interested in something on Helen's desk. "Robbie," she admonished. "I can't believe you left work to get him."

"Don't worry. She can't fire you," Paul said, although Robbie was looking between the two of them as if he wasn't exactly sure.

"I had to get out of the house. There was nothing to do there. And nothing to eat."

"I left you snacks, Dad."

His eyes blazed. "Nothing to eat," he repeated in a tone that Greta could only assume was meant to sum up his feelings for the cold beet salad with goat cheese and mint she'd left him.

Well, to be fair, that had been kind of a low blow on her part. One she'd taken a perverse pleasure in delivering.

He braced one hip against the reception desk. "Helen, did you bring in those muffins I like so much this morning?"

"No, but there's some homemade pound cake with cream cheese frosting." As Paul straightened and made a beeline for the break room, Helen's mouth sagged. She met Greta's eyes. "Should he be eating that?"

"I'll handle it," Greta said, steeling herself for a fight. Over pound cake. With a grown man.

As she had expected, her father was busy slicing himself a piece of pound cake roughly the size of Montana. "Dad," she scolded, hurrying forward to grab the cake.

He didn't even have the decency to look ashamed. Instead, he hefted the piece and shoved as much as he could into his mouth before Greta snatched it away from him. Crumbs dribbled down his shirt, rolling onto the break room table. "What?" he mumbled around the mouthful of cake.

Trying to ignore the feeling of moist cake and thick frosting squishing between her fingers, Greta gave him her sternest look. "You have to start eating better."

Paul's gaze trailed down to the ruined cake in her hand. "You waste a lot of food, do you know that?"

"Sorry." She turned on her heel and walked over to the trash can. Scraping the cake off her hand as best she could, she added, "I'm trying to save your life."

"Run my life, you mean." Paul sank into a chair. His shoulders slumped, whether from discouragement or exhaustion, Greta couldn't tell. She opened her mouth to ask if he was okay, but then she stopped herself. It was clear he didn't want her fussing over him, and he probably wouldn't tell her the truth, anyway.

"Speaking of that…" She stepped to the sink and turned on the hot water, rinsing the frosting from her fingers as she let the water warm up. "It would be really helpful if you didn't under-mine me in front of your employees. Telling Robbie he doesn't have to listen to me because I can't fire him? That doesn't make me look much like a leader."

Paul was staring at the fallen cake crumbs so hard Greta was a little worried he was on the brink of licking the table. "You can't fire him."

Greta scrubbed at some stubborn frosting around the cuticle of her index finger. "You put me in charge. How am I supposed to help you if you tell the employees that I have no real authority?" She turned the water off a little harder than necessary.

Paul's lips twisted, and she thought perhaps she'd made her point. But before he could say anything, Nick walked in, his face breaking into a relieved grin as he saw Paul.

"Hey," he said, gently clapping Paul on the back. "I didn't expect you back so soon."

"Don't get too excited. He's only here for a visit," Greta said.

Nick shot her a look. "Still, it's good to see you back on your feet again. We were all worried."

"It's going to take more than a heart attack to keep me down."

"Don't I know it," Nick said, smiling fondly down at him.

It took everything Greta had not to roll her eyes. Paul and Nick were practically glowing at each other, basking in their mutual masculine admiration, enjoying what would have been described as a bromance if they were the same age. This was more of a father-son relationship. So…sonmance? Dadmance?

She shook her head as if that might jog something clever

loose. Obviously, she needed more coffee if she was going to have to deal with both Paul and Nick at the same time. She had just starting filling her mug when the male banter behind her stopped abruptly.

"What the hell is that?"

She turned to find Paul's eyes fixed on the new coffee maker. Nick stood beside him, one hand still resting lightly on his shoulder, a deer-in-the-headlights look on his face.

Taking a sip of her perfectly brewed coffee, Greta considered how best to respond. On the one hand, her father was recovering from a heart attack and should be handled as gently as possible. On the other hand, he was at work against her—and his doctor's—orders, and the answer to his question was so glaringly obvious that he deserved whatever he got.

She was still trying to come up with a response that expressed her current frustration with her father without raising his blood pressure when Nick jumped in. "Greta bought a coffee maker as a gift for the staff. I know how you feel about repairing appliances, but—"

Paul cut off whatever defense Nick was going to mount on Greta's behalf. Or, rather, the new coffee maker's behalf.

"So you just tossed the old coffee maker in the trash?" Paul struggled to his feet, his hands braced on the tabletop.

"Of course not," Nick said. "We just moved it."

Paul's eyes scanned the counter. "Where?"

Nick hesitated.

"It's under the sink, Dad." Greta took another long sip of coffee.

"Under the sink," Paul repeated, tripping over the words as if he were reading a deadly curse off the wall of a crypt. He turned to Nick, who was suddenly preoccupied with wiping the crumbs off the table.

"Hey, Nick, I've got everything set up if you're ready..." The newcomer, a tall, dark-haired man with a worn, gaunt look that hinted at recent weight loss and sleepless nights, trailed off as he walked full force into the tension in the break room. His eyes moved from Nick to Paul to Greta, taking everything in. And then his lips twisted into a barely suppressed grin as though he knew exactly what was happening in that room.

Greta liked him immediately.

"Hi," he said, his dark green eyes finding her. "I'm Ben St. Clair. You must be Greta."

She could only imagine what he'd heard. "Guilty." She set her mug down on the counter. "Can I get you anything? A cup of coffee?"

Paul muttered something under his breath.

Ben may have found the situation amusing, but he clearly wasn't about to step in the middle of it. "No, thank you," he said. "I had coffee on the plane."

"Well, we should probably get started," Nick said, edging out of the break room.

"I happen to have a marketing background myself," Greta said to Ben. "I'd like to sit in, if that's okay with you." Out of the corner of her eye, she caught the way Nick's face tightened.

But Ben flashed her an easy smile. "I would love that."

"Let me just get my notebook."

"I'll sit in, too," Paul said gruffly.

Nick glanced at the ceiling as if searching for divine intervention. "Great."

* * *

GRETA HAD QUESTIONS. About nine thousand of them.

She wanted to know all about hunting demographics—how many hunters bowhunted vs. gun hunted, how old the average hunter was, what the household income was of the average hunter. She asked how old the average hunter was when they were introduced to the sport. She needed to know what TV shows they liked to watch when they weren't hunting, what restaurants they liked to eat at, what kind of cars they drove.

It was maddening. Ben was unbelievably patient, but Nick had to restrain himself from—well, he didn't know what he could do to turn off that endless river of questions. Instead, he opted for pacing the conference room, walking back and forth in the narrow space between the long fake mahogany table and the far wall.

Greta would occasionally spare him a glance as she launched into yet another series of questions, listening avidly to Ben's responses and recording them in her infernal notebook.

Nick would never have believed how infuriating watching a woman write stuff down could be.

He waited for Paul to intervene, but the older man just sat back, his eyelids half-lowered so that Nick couldn't tell what he was thinking—or if he was even fully awake. Finally, he could take no more of it. "It's getting late," he said abruptly, cutting Greta off in mid-question. "If we're going to look at the new ad materials, we need to get started."

Ben gave him an unreadable look, but he clicked a few keys on his computer. On the large screen at one end of the conference room, the first slide of a projected PowerPoint presentation appeared. It had the King Lures logo on it, big and bright yellow.

"Great idea," Greta said smoothly, turning to a clean page in her notebook. "Nick, could you get the lights please?"

His head was going to explode. Seeing her sitting there, pen tip poised just over the blank page, her legs elegantly crossed at the knee, swinging one ivory-sandal-clad foot ever so slightly back and forth...It was like she owned the place.

And that's when it hit him: if anything happened to Paul King, she would.

Mechanically, he walked across the room and flipped off the light as the reality of that washed over him. Paul would leave the company to his daughter. He'd never specifically said as much, but what had happened when he was sick? He'd put Greta Tremaine, Chicago princess, in charge.

Dropping into a chair, Nick took a steadying breath. What had he expected? That Paul would leave King Lures to him? No, of course not.

He'd just expected Paul to live forever.

Maybe Paul would live another twenty, thirty years. Maybe more.

But if something did happen to him—and, let's face it, the man was currently pushing his limits while recovering from a heart attack—then the woman sitting across the table would be Nick's boss.

"Well, that's…interesting." Greta cocked her head to one side as she stared up at the screen.

It was one of the ads for the campaign Ben and Nick had worked out. This one featured a husband and wife kneeling on either side of a recently downed whitetail buck, a brightly colored King Lures scent wick dangling from a nearby branch. The wife's face was beaming with excitement as the husband gripped the buck's massive rack in his hands. At the bottom, clean white text read, "King Lures: For all of your happy endings."

It was a great buck, a great photo, a great concept.

"It's amazing, buddy," he said.

Paul leaned forward in his chair, his forearms resting on the table. "I like it."

"There are some other ads in the campaign?" Greta asked, her tone making it clear that she hoped the answer was yes.

In response, Ben advanced to the next slide. This one was of a father and son dousing a scent drag with King Lures Royal Estrus Doe. Greta made a noncommittal noise, and Ben showed her the third ad. A bowhunter at full draw in a treestand, the straps of his safety harness visible against the camouflage of his coat.

Greta didn't say much as they went through the remaining

ads. She didn't even write much, having set down her pen. But when Ben reached the end of the slide show, she said, "What about non-hunters?"

"What about non-hunters?" Ben asked in a tone that was far more polite than what Nick would have gone with.

"These ads are all aimed at people who are already active hunters. What are we doing to reach non-hunters?"

Ben sent Nick a confused look, and Paul shifted uncomfortably in his chair. Trying to keep his expression neutral, Nick said, "Greta, this may surprise you, but non-hunters buy remarkably little deer urine. As in, zero. They make up exactly zero percent of our customer base."

Greta picked up her pen and tapped it against her open notebook. "But you have an aging customer base. As they stop hunting, who's replacing them?"

Nick clenched his teeth. "Ben, can we see that second ad again?" He waited until Ben had clicked back to the ad with the kid and his dad. "There," he said, pointing at the kid. "That's who's replacing them."

"Sure, some of their kids will take up hunting. But not all of them end up enjoying it. If you don't reach outside of this small target market, you're missing out on a lot of sales."

Nick studied her. She'd been in the office for less than a week, and she was already speaking to him like he had no idea what he was talking about.

"I've been doing some research," Greta said, flipping around in her notebook. "This says that one of the fastest growing markets in bowhunting is women. Is that true?"

Ben shot a quick glance at Nick and then nodded. "A number of surveys find that female participation is growing, yes."

"But you don't have any ads aimed at women."

"What are you talking about?" Nick said, leaning back in his chair and shoving his fists into his jeans pocket. "What about the married couple?"

"Ben, can we see that one again?" Greta was on her feet, moving closer to the screen. "This woman," she said, pointing, "is not married to this man. Unless we're living in this man's dream world, of course."

Standing, Nick joined her in front of the screen. "And why not?"

"Look at her. Then look at him."

Nick studied the woman. She was young, mid-twenties, with long blond hair gathered together and pulled over one shoulder, and she was gazing at her ad-world husband like he hung the moon. Or, in this case, maybe just a couple of treestands.

His eyes shifted to the husband, and he let out his breath in a soft hiss. So the guy was a little older than the female model. That happened, right? And he was a little thicker around the waist— Ben had specifically been looking for an average hunter, not some beefy male model. And, okay, the guy wasn't going to win any beauty contests any time soon. And the woman...Nick sighed. She probably had quite a few beauty pageants under her belt.

He didn't say anything, but Greta was watching him triumphantly. "This," she said, moving her hand between the man and woman on the screen, "is nothing but a male fantasy. And a tired one at that. No woman looks at this ad and thinks, 'Ooh, just what I've always wanted. Deer pee and a husband twenty years my senior.'"

"Maybe she's not as shallow as you are," Nick drawled, rocking back on his heels. "Maybe their mutual love of hunting has drawn them together, and she loves the qualities he has. Look at him. He's a good outdoorsman. He's a good provider." He studied the screen, casting about for something else to say. "He has good taste in deer urine."

"Sure." Greta nodded, but that triumphant gleam only intensified. "They both love hunting so much they fell in love and got married. Tell me, though, why isn't this a photo of an older woman with a much younger and hotter man?"

"Because that's not..." Nick realized he was trapped. He tossed a desperate look Ben's way, getting zero help from that quarter. Stuffing his hands in his pockets again, he turned back to the screen, deliberately keeping his gaze from wandering Greta's way. He really wasn't in the mood to see her gloat.

"Because this is an ad for men, that's why," Greta said. "All of these are ads for men."

"Men still make up the bulk of hunters," Nick retorted.

"You're missing out on a growing market because you're not advertising to them. You're advertising to yourself. What you want. What your hopes and dreams are." She walked back to her chair and sat down, tucking her legs beneath her chair. "But if you want to ignore a sizable segment of the market because the company is doing so well with your current strategy, be my guest."

Nick's jaw practically turned to stone. "So, women. Got it. But non-hunters?"

Greta turned a few more pages in her notebook, bending her head to scan her notes. The light from the screen shone blue on her dark hair. "I read an article that said urban consumers were starting to embrace hunting as part of the locavore movement. How are you communicating your message to them?"

Rubbing a hand over his face, Nick said, "We haven't seen a big push from that type of consumer. Marketing to them would be kind of a waste of money. And it doesn't really go with the brand message."

"You haven't seen a big push because you don't know how to talk to them. And it may not go with the brand message, but neither does bankruptcy."

That was it. He'd spent nearly twenty years with the company, and she had the nerve to talk to him like he was an idiot. He turned back toward the table, where Ben and Paul were both sitting stiffly as if they could become invisible by remaining motionless. Nick's gaze went to Paul, to his now grayish skin and the sloped shoulders and the way Paul wouldn't quite meet Nick's eye.

He wasn't going to stand up for Nick. Not for Nick, not for himself, and not for the company.

He was going to sit there while this woman said ludicrous things, insulting his management and embarrassing them in front of Ben.

"Right." He turned to Ben. "I've got some things I need to take care of. Why don't you and Greta discuss her ideas, and you can grab me when you're done?" Without waiting for a response, he strode from the room, taking deep breaths to calm himself down as he walked to his office.

Instead of sitting down right away, he moved to the window, bracing his arms against the window frame and leaning against the glass. Below was the archery range where he often burned off a little steam. But at the moment even archery wasn't enough to calm him down.

There was nothing he could do. This was Paul's company, and Paul didn't seem all that concerned about the havoc Greta was wreaking in the conference room. The heart attack seemed to have done something to him. The old Paul King, the man who'd hired Nick, would never have put someone so inexperienced and just plain wrong for the position in charge of his company.

And then there was the niggling fear that Paul could have another heart attack. Then where would they be?

It would have been bad enough if Nick were just an employee. But he wasn't. He was part-owner of King Lures, and he had a vested interest in the well-being of the company.

Turning from the window, Nick sat down in front of his computer, staring at the screen as he contemplated the situation. He owned a tiny amount of a company that, at the moment, was still worth something, but his shares didn't give him any voice whatsoever in how the company was run. That had never bothered him in the past—it was Paul's company, and he'd never expected to have Paul gift him part of it. But now that Greta had arrived and seemed to be making herself comfortable, it did bother him.

A lot.

Without actually formulating a plan, he picked up his cell phone. Then he scrolled through his recent calls. Selecting the one he wanted, he pushed the call button.

"Dave," he said. "Do you have a few minutes?"

CHAPTER 15

*G*reta sank into the chair behind her father's desk and closed her eyes, rubbing her temples with her middle fingers. The meeting had gone pretty well. Her father had even nodded once or twice at something she'd said, which was more approval than he'd ever shown her before. Ben had been incredibly helpful, and they'd had a decent brainstorming session for a new ad concept.

But instead of feeling like a total #girlboss, Greta just felt drained. No matter how hard she worked or how much she accomplished, it seemed like all she managed to do was piss Nick Campbell off more.

She leaned back in her chair and let her head fall into her hands. Maybe she should have been gentler in how she approached him during the meeting. Should she have to handle him with kid gloves? No. They were both adults, and he should be able to admit when he was wrong.

Especially given how frequently he seemed to be wrong.

Her phone dinged with an incoming text message. It was Andi. "Anything for Stella ready for me yet?" the text read,

157

followed by about thirty-two emojis because, Greta knew, Andi didn't want to come off as nagging.

Her gaze fell on her notebook, to a tiny note she'd jotted in the margin about the Stella campaign. So far, she was pretty sure the best idea she had was still anal beads.

So, no.

"Close," she texted back. No emojis, because she was already lying enough. With the marketing meeting out of the way, she had time to hit the Stella campaign hard. If she just got a good hour or two in...

For a moment, she allowed herself to fantasize about how much better her life would be if she got the promotion. Her clients wouldn't be anything like Nick. They would be smart and polished, eager for a new direction and pleased with her initiative in developing one.

But then...She thought back to some of the client meetings she'd sat in on. There had been plenty of clients who wanted to stick with an idea that wasn't very good. Argumentative clients. Hard-to-please clients. Impossible to deal with clients.

But it would be different, she assured herself. She'd seen Tamsin handle some difficult clients before, and it was nothing short of masterful. Like Tamsin, she would guide her clients to reach her conclusions on their own, allowing them to believe they were the ones coming up with the ideas.

Reaching out, she grabbed her silver pen and tapped it on the desk in front of her. There was another big difference between Nick and her future clients—her clients would choose her. They'd come to Prescott because they wanted to benefit from the agency's renowned reputation for splashy campaigns. The Prescott Agency wasn't cheap, and it didn't attract penny-pinching clients. It was for companies that wanted the very best.

But Nick hadn't chosen Greta, and maybe that was the problem. He wasn't open to her ideas because he had no idea what she could do.

She could do this. She could come up with a brilliant idea for Stella and develop a new campaign for King, and she could manage a grumpy vice president at the same time. She wasn't going to fail.

Taking a deep breath, Greta pulled her flash drive from her purse. Plugging it into her father's computer, she clicked on the file. Then she turned the volume down so that only she would be able to hear the music and watched the shaky video fill the screen.

There she was. Seventeen, a senior in high school. Dressed in one of those ridiculous dance costumes she hated so much, but so confident. So self-assured. So sure that she could do anything. That she would never fail.

And then...She closed her eyes, although this was the part she was watching for. When she opened her eyes again, the video was even shakier. She clicked on the screen to stop the video.

She'd seen enough.

* * *

AN HOUR LATER, she gathered the portfolio she'd printed out and headed down to Nick's office. "I was wondering if I could have a few minutes."

He quickly closed a folder in front of him, sliding it into the top drawer of his desk and then closing the drawer firmly. "Sure," he said, in a tone that made it clear he didn't think he had a choice.

She had something of a speech that she'd carefully composed, and as she settled into a chair across from him she smiled coolly.

"You want to talk about what happened at the meeting, right?" he asked, leaning back in his chair and tossing a small foam basketball through the hoop on the wall to his left.

"Yes," she said, quickly running through her speech to see what she no longer needed to say and where she could pick it up.

"Well, I'm sorry about that." But he didn't look sorry. Not at all. Instead he pulled a second foam basketball out of his desk and launched it through the hoop as well. Then he turned to face Greta, his eyebrows arched. "So...we done here?"

"No, we're not done." Greta placed the folder with her portfolio in it on the desk and pushed it toward him. "I wanted you to see this."

Slowly, he opened the folder and looked down at the top sheet, which was an ad for Lumiere perfume. It was one of her favorite campaigns—classic and elegant, with a little touch of whimsy. Perfect for the client. And perfect for Greta's career— that had been the campaign that put her on the path to creative director.

She didn't expect him to appreciate everything that went into that one ad. But she was sure if he just looked through her portfolio, if he just saw the breadth and depth of her experience, he would understand that maybe she could help the company.

But he just raised his head, boredom written all over his face. "What is this?"

"It's a sample from my portfolio. I wanted you to see—"

He closed the folder and slid it back across the desk to her. "I've already seen it."

Flustered, Greta said the only thing that came to mind. "How?"

"Your company's website." He pushed his chair back, propping an ankle on his knee. The T-shirt he was wearing fit him so well it might have been a wetsuit. "When Paul put you in charge, I did a little research. I like to know who I'm working with."

Greta held her portfolio against her chest, crossing her arms over it to hug it to her. "So you've seen my work." He nodded. "And you know what I can do." Another nod. "And you still don't think I can handle this."

This time he shrugged. "Look, it's nothing personal. I'm sure you're a nice person, and I'm sure you're very good at what you do. But you have no idea what hunters want. How can you market to them if you don't know who they are, what their dreams are, what it is that drives them?"

"The same way I know what any consumer wants. By doing research. Do you think I just happen to know what a luxury car buyer's priorities are? No. I drive a Civic, not an Audi. But I do my research, and I learn."

"We don't have that kind of time. And I don't need you bumbling around here while you figure it out."

She straightened her spine, folding her hands primly in her lap. "I do not bumble," she said. "Ever."

"The thing is, deep down, you don't like hunters. That's the real problem. You might not drive a luxury car, but you don't feel disdain for those who choose to. And that's what you feel for hunters, isn't it? Disdain. You think we're ignorant rednecks who just like killing things." He placed his elbows on the desk, hands fisted, knuckles together. "And that's why you can't sell to us. Because you look down on us."

"That's not..." *true.* But that was mostly a lie. Because while she didn't look down on hunters—exactly—she certainly didn't like them as a group. "Why would you think that?"

"Because it's written all over your face when you look around this place. When you see the taxidermy on the walls. When you tell me that changing your name to your stepfather's name opened up doors for you."

Greta froze, her mouth slightly open. Maybe there was some truth to what Nick was saying. It wasn't that she had a problem with hunters, per se. It was just that hunting was such a barbaric pastime. What was the point in going out and shooting a beautiful wild animal? Sure, some people ate what they killed, and that, she supposed, was probably better for the environment and animal well-being than buying factory-farmed meat at the grocery store.

But who actually needed to eat meat? No one, unless they

lived in the Arctic or some other place where agriculture was impossible. A vegetarian diet was far healthier than a meat-heavy one—just look at what had happened to her father.

So did she look down on hunters? Not exactly. She merely thought that their choices and attitudes were...unenlightened.

Which wasn't the same thing as looking down on them at all.

Very carefully, she set the folder containing her portfolio down on the desk, neatly aligning it so that it was perfectly perpendicular to the front edge of the desk. "You know," she said softly, "from the moment I arrived here, you have had it in for me. You could have offered to help me learn what I need to know, but you didn't. You see me as someone who could never understand what you do. And maybe I can't. But you never gave me the chance. If anyone is close-minded here, it's you."

Outside, a cloud passed over the sun, momentarily casting a shadow across his office. "None of this matters. The sooner you realize that you have nothing to offer this company and get back to whatever it is you might actually be good at, the better for everyone. You want to stay here and play at running a business? Fine. Be my guest. But stay out of my way. I have too much to do to take precious time to teach you the difference between a deer and an antelope."

With that, he flipped open a folder on his desk and busied himself studying its contents. When she didn't move, he said, without looking up, "Are we done here?"

No. No, they weren't done at all. He had just spoken to her as if she were a lazy subordinate, not his superior. Which, of course, she wasn't. Not technically. But she was Paul King's daughter, and she would have expected him to speak to her with more respect if only for that reason.

She needed to say something, to put Nick in his place. But to her horror, she felt her cheeks burn as embarrassed color crept over them, and she was sure that if she managed to find her voice at all, it would tremble and break. So she did the only sensible thing left to her: she retreated. As she walked down the hallway, she considered her future. She had assumed that managing her own team would be fairly easy—after all, everyone she worked with was a professional. But what if someone on her team pulled what Nick had just pulled? That thought stopped her dead in her tracks. What was she going to do when someone else treated her as if she were incompetent or stupid? Because there was no guarantee that wouldn't happen in the future.

Was she going to walk away as she'd just done? Slink off to lick her wounds in private? If that was the case, maybe she didn't deserve to be creative director after all. Maybe she would be terrible at it.

Her hands began to shake, and she wondered if perhaps her blood sugar were low. And then she realized that her shaking fingers had nothing to do with hypoglycemia.

She was furious. Absolutely furious at Nick. He'd made her feel stupid, made her doubt herself, made her question her own abilities.

Spinning on her heel, she looked back at the wedge of light that was all that was visible of Nick's office from this angle. He was in there, feeling so smug. What she wanted to do was march back into his office and let him have it. Unfortunately, she was having a very hard time figuring out what she could say that wasn't totally unprofessional.

What would a #girlboss do in this situation? Greta had no idea.

Worse, she wasn't even sure what search terms to use on Pinterest.

CHAPTER 16

*A*fter work, Greta wanted nothing more than to go back to her father's house and focus on what really mattered —the Stella campaign. Emojis aside, Andi was getting impatient, and she had every reason to be. It had been a week since Tamsin had given her the assignment. She needed to focus.

But Kelsey had other plans. "You can't just sit at home all night," she said, following Greta out of the building that evening. "It's $2 Margarita Night at Tracks."

"I need to get some work done." Greta pushed her key fob to unlock her car door. "Maybe some other time."

"If you work too much, your brain never has time to recharge. You're operating on suboptimal brain waves."

The problem was, of course, that Greta wasn't working too much. Not on what she needed to be working on. Not on anything that actually made a difference.

"Come on. It'll be fun, I promise."

Greta was about to say no. It was on the tip of her tongue. And then she heard Nick's voice. "Give it up, Kelsey," he drawled. "She doesn't want to go to Tracks." He put a slight emphasis on the last word. *Tracks*. As if Greta thought she was too good for someplace like that.

Turning, Greta saw Nick and Ben standing near Nick's Prius. Ben flashed her a friendly grin, but Nick's gaze glittered with ice. She had a vivid flash of that scene in his office earlier where he had accused her of looking down on King's customers. He thought he knew her so well. He thought he knew what she would do.

Well, he didn't. She opened the door to her car and set her bag down on the driver's seat. "You know what, Kelsey? I'd love to go."

Kelsey smiled. "Great. I'll come by and pick you up in an hour."

* * *

THE DOOR to Paul's bedroom was closed when she got home. Tiptoeing close, Greta put her ear against the door. Silence. She knocked as softly as she could, waited a moment, and then eased the door open just far enough to peer in.

He was asleep on his back, the thin blue bedspread stretched over his chest rising and falling as he breathed. His face looked drawn, his lips too pale. Greta felt a pang of worry. He'd over-done it at the office.

Well, she thought as she closed the door again, hadn't she told him to stay home?

She took Polly for a short walk, then threw together a quick dinner for him and put it in the fridge for when he woke up. Then she went to her room, opened the door of the closet, and surveyed her options. Everything was tasteful, classic, impeccably tailored.

And it was all wrong.

She sank onto the bed, still eyeing the lackluster array of beige, gray, and ivory garments. It might be the ideal wardrobe for her life in Chicago, but none of it looked like it would fit in at $2 Margarita Night.

Probably because Greta wouldn't fit in at $2 Margarita Night.

Back home, her clothes made her feel more confident. They were part of her carefully crafted image, a uniform of sorts. In them, she blended in with the kind of people she wanted so desperately to approve of her.

But here, in Bartlett, all her clothes did was make her stand out, and not in a good way. They made her look out of touch. Pretentious. Stiff. Like she didn't even want to fit in.

And, okay, maybe she hadn't. Maybe she hadn't really thought much about it until Nick had pointed out how little she understood their customers. Not that he was right, of course. Market research could tell her everything she needed to know about the people who bought deer urine.

She just needed to find clothes that said, "Why, yes, I do know a bit about deer pee and the people who need it."

Or something like that.

She was still perusing her choices—or lack thereof—when she heard a knock at the front door, and Polly barked joyfully.

Shushing Polly so she wouldn't wake Paul, Greta hurried to the door to find Kelsey standing on the front porch. "Has it already been an hour?"

"Sure has. Hey, Polly girl." Kelsey bent down to scratch behind the dog's silky ears. Straightening up, she surveyed Greta's work-wrinkled skirt and blouse, her blue eyes dubious. "You ready?"

"I was just deciding what to wear." She held the door open so Kelsey could come in.

"Oh, good. Not that you don't look great the way you are. It's just so…beige."

"It's ecru." Greta headed back toward her room, fairly certain that Kelsey wasn't going to be a fan of any of her options. Kelsey, of course, looked like she would fit in perfectly at $2 Margarita Night in a grape-colored corset top, a shimmery gold shrug, faded denim capris, and strappy gold sandals that showed off her sea-green toenails.

Kelsey followed her down the hallway to her room. "Sorry," the younger woman said. "Ecru."

"Now *this* is beige." Greta pulled a dress out her closet and held it up in front of her.

Kelsey nodded slowly.

She tossed the beige dress onto the bed, then grabbed another one. "And this is taupe." The second dress followed the first. "This one is sand." The dress landed on the bed with the other two as she turned back to her closet. "Camel. Buff. Ivory." More garments joined the growing pile. "It's all so...*boring*."

And that was the real problem, wasn't it? Somehow she had ended up with a closet full of boring clothes. She could blame it on the fact that she'd only packed a few outfits when she left for Bartlett, but her clothes back in Chicago weren't more interesting.

"They're not boring," Kelsey said, picking up a couple of the discarded garments and holding them up for a better look, her face impressively devoid of expression.

"Liar," Greta said. She held up her hands in defeat. "I guess what I'm wearing is as good as anything."

But Kelsey wasn't about to give up. "I think we can do better," she said. "I'll call Helen."

"Helen?" Visions of sherbet-colored cardigans danced in her head. "Wait. I think I can actually—"

But Kelsey already had her phone to her ear and held up one hand to silence her. "Hey, Helen. Did you get over to Goodwill yet? No? Perfect. I'm with Greta, and we have a bit of an emergency."

"I wouldn't call it an emergency," Greta grumbled.

"I would," Kelsey said, glancing meaningfully at the bed. Then, into the phone she added, "Oh, no, he's fine. It's a fashion emergency." She listened for a moment, then gave Greta a thumbs up that was not the least bit reassuring. "Yes, exactly. That's why I called. Yes. Perfect. We'll see you in a few." Then she headed for the front door, Greta trailing after her.

"Where are you going?"

Kelsey flashed her a grin. "To get my makeup. Don't worry, Greta. We'll get you taken care of." The storm door snapped shut behind her.

Helplessly, Greta turned, her gaze catching on the giant stuffed bear in the corner. "What have I done?" she said aloud.

It might have been her imagination, but she thought the bear, even in mid-roar, had a sympathetic glint in his glass eyes.

APPARENTLY, Helen's youngest daughter had recently moved to Nashville for a new job, leaving behind several Hefty bags of clothes she no longer wanted. Greta learned this as Helen was in the process of upending two overstuffed trash bags onto her bed, their contents spilling out in a riot of color and texture and sparkle.

Helen's daughter was clearly a big fan of sequins.

Kelsey, having returned with a makeup tote that looked suspiciously like a fishing tackle box, dragged one of the chairs from the kitchen into Greta's room and made herself comfortable as she rifled through her cosmetics while Helen sifted through the mountain of clothes on the bed.

"Oh, look at this one," Helen said, holding up a slinky black thing that, with the addition of a few more yards of fabric, might have been dress. "Isn't this cute?" She ran an appraising eye over Greta. "But maybe a little small. Tonya's about your size but not quite so..." She trailed off.

"Not quite so what?"

"You know." Helen held her hands out in front of her, a generous gap between them. "Curvy."

"Right." Greta wished fervently that she hadn't accepted Kelsey's invitation. She could have spent the evening getting some actual work done, but no. Instead she was being insulted by a 50-year-old woman currently oohing over a turquoise romper.

"Oh, don't take it that way, honey," Helen said. "You have a very nice figure. You just need to add some color to your wardrobe if you want to get men to notice you." She pulled a one-shouldered tank top from the pile. "Do you like pink?"

Greta crossed her arms over her chest. "This isn't about getting men to notice me."

Helen studied her for a moment. "Oh, I'm sorry, honey. You're probably a feminist, aren't you?" She dropped the pink top and fished around in the pile for a moment before she found what she wanted. "So maybe something in blue, then?" she said, brandishing a spangled halter top.

"What I think Helen is trying to say," Kelsey said, jumping to her feet and shooting the older woman a warning look, "is that you should wear what makes you feel comfortable." She took the halter top from Helen's hands and held it up in front of Greta. "We just want you to feel good about yourself. Do you feel comfortable in what you're wearing right now?"

Greta looked at the shimmery blue top in Kelsey's hands. It was a pretty robin's egg blue and covered all over with big, iridescent sequins that winked and flirted every time they caught the light. It looked like how she imagined a mermaid's tail might look, the sequins overlapping like fish scales.

It was a ridiculous choice for a woman in her thirties. It was the tackiest thing she'd ever seen.

And she loved it.

"I...guess not," she said finally, and Kelsey's baby-doll mouth kicked up at the corners in the tiniest smile of triumph.

"Why don't you just try this on? And, Helen, can you find something to go with it? Maybe a pair of shorts or something?"

"On it." Helen dove back into the mass of clothing. She

emerged a minute later waving a pair of white shorts like a flag. "Will these work?"

Greta locked herself in the bathroom. She felt like an idiot. But once she had the halter top on, she had to admit that maybe her neutrals weren't doing as much for her as she'd thought. The cheerful blue of the shirt gave her skin a little color, and the lines of the top emphasized the curves of her breasts without making her look wide all over.

The shorts were a different story. Helen wasn't kidding when she said her daughter wasn't as curvy as Greta. She managed to squeeze into them, and was even able to battle the zipper into the fully zipped position, but there was no way she was going to leave the house wearing those shorts. On Greta, they looked more like a bathing suit bottom than a pair of shorts.

And not even in a sexy way.

"The shorts don't fit," she called to Kelsey, who was waiting outside the door.

"Let me see them."

Greta looked at herself in the mirror. "Uh, I don't think so."

"Oh, come on. They can't be that bad."

With a sigh, Greta opened the door. "Can't they?"

"Oh." Kelsey struggled to keep a straight face. "Okay, so they're a little snug. Helen, we're going to need something a little bigger."

"How about these?" Helen walked into the hallway, snapping the waistband of a pair of black capris. "They have a little more give."

Greta glared at her but took the pants anyway. Closing the bathroom door, she struggled out of the white shorts and managed to slide into the black capris. They were still a little snug but in a more flattering way. "Much better," Kelsey said when she opened the door to show her the outfit. "Now, for makeup."

Before she knew it, Greta was perched on the edge of the

chair Kelsey had brought to her room while the younger woman rubbed her hands together over the tackle box of makeup. "Um, I usually go for a certain look," she said. "Understated elegance."

Kelsey didn't look up. Instead, she grabbed a fresh makeup sponge. "I don't know the meaning of the word 'understated.'"

"That's what I was afraid of."

* * *

TRACKS WAS NOT YET busy when Nick and Ben got there, and Brenda, the owner, greeted them at the door. With her hatchet face and bottle-red hair, Brenda was an intimidating figure.

Her personality didn't help.

"You look terrible," Brenda said while looking Nick up and down.

"And you always know how to charm your customers," Nick said.

"No one ever complains." No one would dare, and they both knew it.

"Hey, sweetcheeks," Brenda said to Ben, offering him a rare genuine smile. Her face seemed to crack in several places from the unpracticed movement. "Good to see you again. How's your wife?"

"She's..." Ben hesitated for a moment, his gaze sliding past Brenda to the exposed brick wall behind the bar as if he were making up his mind about something. "She's dying."

The smile faded from Brenda's face. "I'm sorry to hear that." She jammed her thumb in Nick's direction. "You want me to find you someone better to hang out with than this guy?"

Ben chuckled. "No, that's okay, Brenda."

"Well, just say the word." Impulsively, she reached forward and patted Ben's shoulder. Then she nodded toward a table in the back where Auggie sat waiting for them and whispered to Ben, "You can do better than that one, too."

"Never change, Brenda," Nick said as they headed toward where Auggie sat.

"Who said anything about changing?" she muttered.

The bar was dimly lit and poorly air conditioned, the walls covered in railroad ephemera Brenda had collected over time: vintage railroad crossing signs, old timetables in beat-up frames, awkwardly proportioned watercolor paintings of trains by local artists. The building had once been a crematorium, and Brenda claimed that in the beginning she'd had a few troublesome spirits hanging around. It was hard to picture anyone—even the undead —messing with Brenda, but it had been a smart marketing strategy. Tracks was now the last stop on the ghost tours that ran on the weekends throughout the fall, and few things made tourists thirstier than a good ghost story.

But at just after five on a Monday, only a handful of people sat at the bar, and the banter of some sports analysts on ESPN was the only sound besides the occasional clink of glasses on the scarred, pale-honey wood of the bar top.

Dropping into the chair next to Ben, Nick opened his menu.

"So," Auggie said, his expression suspiciously innocent. "How'd the marketing meeting go?"

Obviously, Ben had already filled Auggie in on Greta's suggestions. Flicking Auggie a quelling look, Nick made a show of studying the menu. "I've had better." Then he turned to Ben. "Sorry you had to put up with that."

Ben shrugged. "She had some good suggestions."

"What—marketing to people who don't hunt? Yeah, there's a winning strategy."

"The industry is changing. We can't keep fighting over pieces from the same shrinking pie. We need a bigger pie."

Brenda appeared with a round of beers. "You ready to order?"

Auggie ran one finger over the appetizer section of his menu. "You guys want to split—"

"Split? What are you, grown men or Girl Scouts? Order your

own damn appetizer." She set a glass in front of Auggie. "I recommend the fried pickles."

After they'd ordered, Nick drummed his fingers on the table. "If you think that Greta has some secret formula for making money off a bunch of hipster locavores, you're out of your mind."

"I don't think you're in a place to be objective at the moment," Ben said, carefully focusing on unrolling his silverware and spreading his napkin over his lap.

Nick's eyebrows shot up. "And what's that supposed to mean?"

"It means that your feelings for Greta are complicating your take on the situation."

Nick nearly choked on his beer. "My feelings for Greta? What kind of feelings do you think I have for that woman?"

"Umm…" Ben was suddenly very busy smoothing every last wrinkle out of his napkin.

"He took her to a deer farm last week," Auggie said. "They had to stop by Paul's house on the way back to the office so she could shower." He tilted his head. "That's his story, anyway."

"Interesting." Ben rubbed one hand over the dark scruff on his chin.

Fortunately for Nick, Brenda chose that moment to return with their appetizers, distracting Auggie and Ben from that line of thought. The whole situation seemed to be getting away from him. All he wanted was for Greta to leave, and if he wasn't mistaken, that's what she had originally wanted, too. But she was still there, inserting herself into meetings and offering input where none was needed.

And then there was the other thing. The thing he didn't even want to think about.

He was contemplating his nachos morosely when there was a small clunk beside him. He looked up to find Brenda, a sympathetic expression on her face, setting another beer down next to him. "This one's on the house," she said softly. "Looks like you had a bad day."

"Thanks, Brenda."

Auggie started working on his mozzarella sticks. "I don't think she's as bad as you think she is."

"No," Nick said, watching Brenda head back to the bar.

"Dude, I meant Greta."

All of his anger—well, most of it, anyway—had faded by now, and he was left feeling just tired. Tired of dealing with Greta, tired of shouldering the burden of the company, tired of worrying about Paul. Changing the subject, he turned to Ben. "What's the plan for the campaign?"

Ben wiped his mouth with his napkin. "Depends on what kind of changes you guys want to make. Greta had some...extensive suggestions."

"One way or the other, we need to do something different," Auggie said, dipping a mozzarella stick in marinara sauce. "Two of the retailers I spoke with today were lukewarm about their future with us."

They ate the rest of their appetizers in silence while that sunk in. It wasn't hard to see why retailers were suddenly pulling back. At least not when even Nick was feeling lukewarm about the company's future.

* * *

TRACKS DIDN'T STAY quiet for long. Bartlett didn't have much in the way of night life—there weren't enough single people in a town best known for its slow pace and excellent school system— but cheap margaritas have a way of bringing people together. By the time Nick finished his burger, the bar was filling up. Robbie and a few other guys from the plant filtered in, raising a hand in greeting before settling in at the bar. Two women, clearly mother and daughter, walked in. Tourists, obviously, loaded down with bags from the antique shops and little boutiques that made up Main Street. Auggie sat up a little straighter when he spotted them.

"Excuse me," he said, setting down his beer and pushing back his chair. Nick watched his friend approach the two women, saw their initial wariness fade until they were beaming up at him, blushing a bit as they responded to something he'd said. Both women were attractive. The mother was only in her forties, with expensively cut champagne hair that brushed her shoulders. The daughter was tall and leggy in short shorts, and she practically bounced on her toes as she spoke, her long caramel hair gleaming as it swished back and forth. Nick wasn't sure which one Auggie was hoping to take home with him.

He wasn't sure Auggie knew, either.

He wasn't jealous of Auggie. Both of those women looked to be fairly high maintenance, which most definitely wasn't his type. Not that Auggie planned to have a woman stick around long enough that he would have to do any maintaining.

Brenda swung by, raising her eyebrows in a silent question. He lifted his still half-full beer and shook his head. As fun as it was to sit around and watch Auggie pick up women—by now, the mother was trailing one hand up his arm—he really just wanted to get home and put this day behind him. He was still edgy from his phone call with Dave, and everything was beginning to annoy him. Someone by the bar laughed, a thunder clap of a laugh that made Nick wince. A woman in overly high heels jostled their table as she walked past on her way to the bathroom, giggling as she turned over-heated eyes on him.

"You okay, man?"

"Yeah. Why?"

Ben gestured to the table, and Nick realized he'd been shredding a paper napkin, the remains spread out in front of him like the aftermath of a sudden snowstorm.

He needed to leave, but he had to wait for Ben, who was

crashing in his guest room. "I'm good. Just tired. You almost ready to go?"

Ben nodded. "Let me finish my beer, and we can go."

And that was when Greta walked in.

He almost didn't recognize her, not when he was used to seeing her in those drab colors she liked. What she had on tonight was most definitely not drab. Shimmery blue fabric clung to her breasts, dipping down to reveal the barest hint of cleavage. Her hair, normally pinned back in some severe knot, waved around her face like fronds of seaweed, and her lips were stained a pale pink, like the delicate interior of a seashell.

He realized he'd never seen her in color before.

Ben leaned forward, resting his elbows on the table and following Nick's gaze. "I like her," he said.

"I don't." Nick stacked his silverware on top of his empty plate. When he glanced up, he saw Greta at the bar, Kelsey standing near her. As he watched, Kelsey put one arm around Greta's shoulders and gave a quick squeeze. Apparently, he was the only person at King Lures who felt that way. "What could you possibly like about her?"

Ben shrugged. "She's smart. And she cares. She doesn't have to, you know."

It was a fair point. Running the company was something that had been thrust on her, and she could put in far less effort, sitting in Paul's office playing Solitaire all day and leaving things up to Nick.

The fact that she didn't said worlds about her. Annoying worlds, but worlds all the same. He took a contemplative sip of his beer.

"Plus," Ben continued, "I think she's good for you."

Nick nearly did a spit-take. "Good for me?"

"I haven't seen you feel anything for a woman since Lauren left."

"I don't have feelings for Greta."

"You do. They may be feelings of strong dislike, but given how you've been, I take that as a good sign."

The area around the bar was getting crowded, and the noise level had risen to a steady buzz. The talking heads on ESPN were arguing about something, but Nick could no longer hear them. Kelsey spotted Robbie and dragged him over to where Greta was sipping a margarita. She flashed him a friendly smile.

He couldn't help but remember how she'd looked when she stalked out of his office earlier. It seemed the stiff, frozen expression she'd worn then was reserved just for him.

Gritting his teeth, he said, "I guess I just haven't been able to dislike a woman so much because I haven't found one this annoying before."

Ben chuckled, but it was a knowing chuckle. Nick ignored him. This was what marriage—happy marriage, anyway—did to men. It made them want to fix everybody up, to force the whole world into blissful coupledom.

Unhappy marriage did the exact opposite, or at least it had for Nick. The last thing he wanted to do was get involved with another woman. Especially one as different from him as Greta. That had been his mistake with Lauren. He'd thought he could make her happy, thought that he would be enough to hold her in Bartlett despite how foreign it all was to her.

But he hadn't been enough.

If he were ever to get married again, it would be to a woman who wanted exactly what he had to offer—a quiet life in Bartlett, plenty of organic venison in the freezer, and a couple of kids climbing trees in the backyard. Since there didn't seem to be many of those women available, he felt he was pretty safe.

"If this is your attempt at matchmaking, you're terrible at it. Most people believe that mutual dislike is a bad sign for a potential relationship."

"You're right," Ben said, wrapping his hands around his beer bottle. "What do I know?"

Across the room, Kelsey had wandered off to talk to some guys Nick recognized as lifeguards from the county pool. Greta leaned back against the bar, bracing herself on her elbows. Neon light from the Blue Moon sign behind the bar washed over her as Robbie leaned closer to say something. The sequins on her top winked up at him, and her bare shoulders gleamed like pearls as she slanted him a smile as if he were the only man in the room. She took a sip of her margarita, her eyes never leaving Robbie's face. And then she ran her tongue over her bottom lip, perhaps to lick off a bit of salt left from her glass.

Or perhaps she was thinking about all the things she wanted to do to Robbie later.

Ben cleared his throat. "It's just for someone who dislikes her so much, you sure have spent a lot of time watching her this evening."

"I'm not watching her," Nick said, setting his beer bottle down on the table a bit harder than he'd planned.

Ben merely raised an eyebrow.

At the bar, Greta nodded at something Robbie said. What could they possibly be talking about? It wasn't like they had anything in common, and the kid was half her age. Or not half, exactly, but certainly far too young for her to be paying this much attention to. When Greta threw back her head and laughed, exposing the smooth column of her throat, Nick's hands balled into fists.

There was no way Robbie was *that* funny. This was a guy who, when asked what five movies he'd want if he were stuck on a desert island, had immediately said he'd take five of the *Transformers* movies.

And then Greta touched Robbie's arm, and Nick was on his feet headed toward the bar before he knew what he was doing.

Greta saw him first, the soft smile she had for Robbie hardening and turning brittle as he got closer. "Nick," she said. "Surprised to see me here?"

"Surprised to see you in this," he said, gesturing to her outfit. "What happened? Is it laundry day?"

"It's blue. Because I'm a feminist."

Nick was still trying to puzzle that out when Robbie turned to him, clapping him on the shoulder and leaning close so he could speak without Greta overhearing. "Hey, could you keep an eye on her for a bit? She seems a little tipsy, and I don't like the way those guys in the corner are looking at her."

"Sure." He ran an eye over Greta's flushed face. "How many margaritas has she had?"

Robbie shook his head. "Dude, that's her second." With a shrug, he made his escape, heading over to where Kelsey and the lifeguards were feeding quarters into a jukebox.

So, the Deer Pee Princess was a lightweight. Well, that explained why she found Robbie so riveting.

Resting his hip against an empty barstool, he turned to find her studying him with narrowed eyes. Obviously, she was still sober enough to hate his guts.

Which, given the way he'd spoken to her earlier, he could understand. "Listen, Greta, I—"

But before he had a chance to apologize, she cut him off. "You hate feminists, don't you?"

"I...what?"

"You hate feminists."

Robbie was right. She *was* tipsy. "That's a pretty big assumption."

She toyed with the stem of her margarita glass. "And yet you had no problem assuming that I hated hunters."

"I didn't say you hated them. I said you looked down on them. There's a difference."

"Fine." Greta's eyes glittered. "You look down on feminists, then."

"Define 'feminists.'"

"Gloria Steinem said a feminist is a woman who has sex

before marriage and a job after." She plucked the lime wedge garnish from the rim of her glass and set it between her teeth, sucking gently on the fruit.

Heat shot through him. It was a bad idea to talk about women who have sex before marriage with Greta, especially when he couldn't pull his eyes away from where her lips met the green rind of the lime. "Oh, no. I have no problem with those women. In fact, I like those women. A lot." He watched her set the lime wedge down on a cocktail napkin. "But that's not what Gloria Steinem said."

She blinked. "What?"

"Nope. That's her definition of a liberated woman, not a feminist." At her sharp stare, he shrugged. "What? I read."

"That's a surprise," she muttered.

So much for apologizing. "That's what I'm talking about, Greta. You think you know me because I hunt, and you have this idea of who a hunter is. But you have no idea who I am."

"I know exactly who you are." She gestured toward him with her margarita glass, the remaining icy green liquid sloshing wildly. "You're arrogant and close-minded."

"*I'm* close-minded?"

"Yes." She leaned forward a little too far and would have toppled off her stool had Nick not grabbed her elbow to steady her. He had a fleeting impression of smooth, warm skin before she tugged her arm free. "You think you know everything there is to know about this industry, and you can't imagine that someone else might have an idea that could help."

When she was sober, Greta's buttons were easy enough to push. Tipsy, she was one great big red button with a sign overhead that read, "For a good time, press here." There was no way he could resist.

"Oh, I know for a fact that there are plenty of people who are smarter than me and could do a better job for King Lures." He propped his foot on the rung of the stool and smiled at her, one elbow resting on the edge of the bar. "I also know that you're not one of them."

The effect on her was immediate. Her eyes sparked like chocolate diamonds, and she flushed all the way to the tempting little shadow between her breasts. "You know what you are?" she said, her voice rising. "You're a...a...a *Bambi-killer.*"

Several people nearby turned to look at her, and Nick realized he needed to get her out of there before she said anything worse. As amusing as a drunk, riled-up Greta might be to him, it wasn't going to be good for the company if she went off on some boozed-up rant about what awful people hunters were.

"Come on," he said, jumping to his feet and putting one hand on her bare back to guide her outside. Her top was held up by two thin strips of fabric that tied around her neck. Judging from the lack of visible straps and the way the fabric hugged her breasts, she wasn't wearing a bra.

Something to think about. Later. After he'd saved her from being tarred and feathered by an angry mob of outdoorsmen.

Metaphorically speaking, of course.

But Greta had little interest in self-preservation. She leaned away from him, nearly upsetting her glass. "What the hell are you doing?"

"Getting you out of here before you get yourself in trouble."

She looked around. "You just don't want people to hear about what kind of a coward you are."

Now she was pushing it. Wrapping an arm firmly around her shoulder, he forced her to her feet. "You're not even making sense now."

"Sure I am." She tilted her head to look up at him, allowing silky threads of her mink-dark hair to slide against his jawline. "You think you're such a big man, killing innocent little animals."

He'd never understood it when other men said a woman looked beautiful when she was angry. Lauren certainly had never been particularly attractive when she was angry, although she would just freeze him out, drawing more into herself. But Greta, with her wide, sparking eyes, slightly parted lips, and the flickering blue flame of a shirt licking up her torso, looked like wildfire, hot and furious beneath the weight of his arm. She was mesmerizing.

Unfortunately, she was also still talking loudly enough for the people around them to hear, and those guys did not look better when angry. One guy, a Realtree camo cap fitted over his shorn hair, gave Nick a tight look. "Hey, buddy," he said. "You better get your girlfriend out of here."

"I'm not his girlfriend," Greta said, dragging her feet as Nick attempted to do just that.

The guy's eyes flicked from Greta to Nick. "Lucky for him."

It took a good amount of wrangling, but Nick finally managed to get Greta through the front door out into the bruised twilight. She flung his arm off her shoulder and whirled on him. "What the hell is wrong with you?"

"I'm just watching out for you."

"Well, let me tell you something." She tried to jam her hands on her hips, but in her inebriated state the movement threw her off-balance and it took her a moment to recover. "I don't need you to watch out for me."

"I see that."

She advanced on him, carrying the scent of limes and salt and some unidentifiable laundry detergent, and underneath it all, the now-familiar spiky notes of lavender. "I don't need your help. Not here, not now, and definitely not at work. I'm going to save King Lures whether you like it or not."

"Well, I'd definitely like it if you did. I mean, it's my livelihood, so…" She was standing very close to him, her lush breasts in that half-liquid, half-fire shirt just inches from his chest.

"No. You'd rather see me fail than admit that someone else could do your job better than you. You need to be the one that saves the day."

She was wrong, of course. He didn't want her to fail.

It just wasn't possible that she could succeed where others hadn't.

"This is how you prove yourself, isn't it?" She took another step. She was so close now that she had to tip her head back to look up at him. The rich tangle of her hair fell back over her shoulders, exposing the vulnerable curve of her neck, the clean lines of her collarbones, the gentle swell of her breasts. "It's the same reason you hunt. You prance around the woods slaughtering Bambi so you can prove that you're a real man."

That's when he snapped.

* * *

SHE KNEW she'd crossed a line—again. Those damn margaritas—she'd never been able to hold her liquor. She needed to apologize, to thank him for getting her out of the bar before she said something that jeopardized both their futures. But her head was swimming and the streetlight behind him threw his face into a stark half-shadow that made him look even more imposing than normal and suddenly she couldn't even remember why she'd been so angry with him in the first place. She just stood there, breathing harder than anything she'd done that night warranted.

He was the one who broke the silence. "Is that so?" And then he wrapped his arms around her and drew her hard against him, crushing his lips against hers in a punishing kiss.

Nothing about this moment makes sense, she thought, even as her eyes drifted shut. She wasn't even supposed to be there—not in Bartlett, not standing outside a bar that had $2 Margarita Nights, not pressed against the man who'd been pushing her away since she met him. She knew she needed to break this off. She even brought her hands up, sliding them over his chest so she could stop him.

But her hands kept going, running over his shoulders, slipping into his hair.

Urging him closer.

With a muffled groan, he traced the swell of her bottom lip with his tongue, teasing her until her lips parted for him. And then he was everywhere—his hands, big and hot; the solid wall of his chest; the wild, woodsy scent of him; lips and teeth and tongue, hot and malty from his beer. Claiming her. And all she had to do was let him take what he wanted.

Suddenly, he broke the kiss off. Cool air rushed over her abandoned mouth as he raised his head, gazing down at her for several beats, his face once again impassive. His harsh breathing and smoke-filled eyes were the only signs that he had been at all affected by what had just happened.

His hands gripped her hips. She was so close she could feel the hard, insistent length of him beneath his jeans. He bent his head until his lips were just inches from hers. But he didn't kiss her. Instead, he said in a low voice, "I don't have anything to prove."

And with that, he released her and turned away, pulling open the door and disappearing into the noisy mass of people inside Tracks. Greta was left standing alone on the red-brick sidewalk, weak-kneed and wanting, the twilight darkening around her.

CHAPTER 17

*W*ater. Greta needed water—a lot of it—and some Excedrin and maybe two or three days locked in her room to think about what she'd done.

She was going to have a horrific hangover in the morning. In fact, she was pretty sure it was already starting, although that might just be a reaction to what happened outside Tracks.

Afterwards, she'd gone back inside only as long as necessary to ask Kelsey to drive her home. The younger woman had taken one look at her face and grabbed her keys. Greta had been dreading some kind of interrogation in the car, but aside from asking if she was okay, Kelsey left her alone.

Of course, Greta had been doing her best to keep from vomiting all over the interior of Kelsey's obnoxiously cheerful Beetle, which might explain her friend's uncharacteristic restraint.

When they pulled into the driveway, Kelsey put the car in park. "So, Robbie told me a little bit ago that he broke up with his latest girlfriend, and I think he kind of wanted to talk about it. Do you mind if I head back, or do you need me to come in with you?"

"No, I'm fine."

"Because I'll *totally* hang out if you need me to," Kelsey said, although she'd already shifted the car into reverse.

Greta managed a tiny smile. "Have a good night."

Kelsey's answering smile had a wicked edge. "I plan to."

The bathroom door was closed when she went inside, the water running in the shower, and Greta was grateful that she wouldn't have to face her father at the moment. After filling a glass with water from the kitchen tap, she went to her room, locked the door, and tried to extricate herself from her borrowed shirt. When she couldn't manage to undo the knot Kelsey had tied for her, she gave up and flopped down on the bed, fully dressed. Squeezing her eyes shut, she tried hard to ignore the fact that the room was spinning.

Stupid cheap tequila.

At least she had water. She'd need to drink more than one glass if she wanted to be able to function in the morning, but she'd deal with that later. For now, all she wanted to do was pretend the whole ridiculous night had never happened.

Why hadn't she stayed home? She needed to be working on the Stella campaign. It was the most important opportunity she'd been given since she was first hired at Prescott.

And she was blowing it by allowing herself to get distracted.

It was happening all over again.

Her head pounding in earnest, she grabbed her flash drive and stumbled across the hall to her father's home office, where she once again locked the door behind her.

There was a burning sensation somewhere in the neighborhood of her heart as the shaky video filled the screen. She'd just wasted hours embarrassing herself when she should have been here seizing the incredible chance that had landed in her lap. She knew better. Getting distracted was exactly what led to failure.

And she couldn't fail. Not at coming up with a killer

campaign. And not at saving her father's company. She could still succeed at both.

All she had to do was stay focused.

On the screen, the lithe ballerina that was a young Greta stumbled and fell.

* * *

"How are you feeling this morning?"

"Fine." Nick glanced at the passenger seat, where Ben was busy adding creamer to his coffee. They'd stopped at Bartlett Coffee Roasters because, as Nick explained on the way, he was really trying to patronize local businesses these days. If Ben suspected the real reason was because he was trying to avoid the coffee maker at work—which reminded him too much of a certain incredibly appealing pain in the ass—he wisely kept his mouth shut. "Why do you ask?"

"No reason." Carefully, Ben snapped the top back on his cup and took a thoughtful sip. "It's just you missed the turn into the office."

Crap. "Well," he said, pulling into the parking lot of a septic company to turn around, "that's what I get for driving before I've had my coffee."

"Right. *Coffee* is what you need."

Nick waited for a blue pickup to rattle past before pulling out on Main Street. "You're really annoying in the morning, you know that?"

Ben chuckled. "So Carrie tells me."

It didn't take long before they were approaching the King Lures building, and Nick's fingers tightened on the steering wheel. He didn't want to turn in to the parking lot. He didn't want to go inside the building. He didn't want to face Greta.

Not after what he'd done the night before.

He still couldn't quite wrap his mind around it. He'd kissed Greta. Paul's daughter. His temporary boss.

And, frankly, he'd probably do it again if given a little encouragement.

That was what worried him the most. He had no idea how Greta was going to react. She might fire him. Or, worse, she might assume that last night was the start of something. And that wasn't how Nick operated.

He wasn't nearly as good at starting things as he was at ending them.

"You sure you're okay?" Ben said as Nick shut off the car and looked wistfully at his coffee cup. It would be nice if he had something a bit stronger to help him get through the day.

"I'm fine." And he would be. As long as he could stay away from Greta.

But, as usual, luck was not on his side. When he and Ben walked in, he found Greta right there, sitting on the edge of Helen's desk. Kelsey stood nearby, her hair braided into twin pigtails of all things, regaling the other two women with some story about Robbie and lifeguards and a runaway cow. Helen laughed so hard she had to wipe her eyes, but Greta's smile looked forced and edgy, and it faded completely when she looked up and saw him.

Gone was the bedazzled shirt from the night before. She was back to her old self in a slim black skirt and a pinstriped white blouse, her hair once again pulled back from her face. But while he'd never found her clothing all that attractive before, Nick found that she suddenly had this whole sexy librarian thing going on.

He nodded at the three women and then started to make his escape. He wasn't fast enough.

"Nick, I need to speak with you," Greta said, rising to her feet.

"Could it wait until this afternoon? Ben has limited time here, and I'd like to—"

"No," she said. "It can't wait."

"Right." He turned to Ben, who, to his credit, was maintaining a strict poker face. "Why don't you get set up in the conference room? I'll be there in a minute."

"Let's go down to my office." Greta led the way to Paul's office, her hips shifting back and forth as she moved.

Like a cobra preparing to strike a snake charmer.

Of course, snake charmers milked their cobras of venom before they performed, rendering them mostly harmless. The same could not be said for Greta.

Nick sank into the closest chair and pondered all the ways he'd wronged this woman as she closed the door behind them, thereby ensuring there would be no witnesses for whatever it was she had planned. Then she turned, poised almost on tiptoe as if she were about to take flight, her hands unconsciously smoothing over her skirt, and smiled.

His heart dropped. This was what he'd feared—Greta assuming that last night was a step toward...something.

"Greta, I—"

"I need to apologize to you."

"—need to explain some—What?"

A wash of pink swept over the creamy skin of her cheeks. "I was way out of line last night, and I want to apologize."

"*You* were out of line?"

"Yes." She settled into her own chair and placed her hands, fingers linked, on the desk in front of her. "It was entirely inappropriate for me to engage in a...a physical encounter with a subordinate."

A subordinate? This was one heck of an apology. "I wouldn't exactly call myself a subordinate."

"Oh?" Her voice sharpened, and her fingers, still clasped together on the desk, tensed visibly. "And just what would you call someone who answers to someone else?"

He blinked. "I don't answer to you. You're just here temporarily until Paul gets back."

"Happily, this is temporary. But until he gets back, I'm in charge." She looked awfully pleased with herself, and Nick had the feeling she had practiced this. He wondered if she had a little script written out somewhere, one of those choose-your-own-adventure-type things telemarketers used: *If he threatens to quit, gracefully accept his resignation. If he says you're not the boss of him, tell him you're rubber and he's glue.*

If he kisses you again, shove everything off the desk and just go for it.

Nick took a deep breath. It was damned frustrating to be attracted to a woman he didn't even like.

"Anyway," she continued, "I bought you this." She pulled a small white box with a gold ribbon around it out of her purse. "To make it up to you."

For a moment, Nick was speechless. If she had pulled a gun from her purse, he would have been less surprised. Mutely, he took the offering from her. It was a box of Bette's Kentucky Proud Bourbon Balls, which were sold by the cash register at the Shell station. When he could finally speak, he said, "You bought me gas station bourbon balls?"

"My dad says everyone loves them."

Paul certainly did. Paul had never met a bourbon ball he didn't like. "I kissed you, and you bought me gas station bourbon balls as an apology?"

"I feel like you're putting unnecessary emphasis on the gas station part. That just happens to be where they sell them. And it's not just because of the..." She trailed off. "...the *thing* that happened. It's also to apologize for the whole Bambi-killer thing. And to thank you for getting me out of the bar when I started to go off about that."

He stared down at the little white box, coils of gold ribbon springing from it like Rapunzel's hair, just waiting for a prince to come along and climb right up. This was the most disconcerting response to a kiss he'd ever encountered. He'd expected...Well, he wasn't quite sure what he'd expected. Was it so ridiculous to think that she might have been just as affected by what happened last night as he was? Not that it could go anywhere, but it would have been nice to know that it had gotten under her skin. That she had laid awake in bed last night replaying the whole thing in her mind the way that he had.

Instead, she'd stopped by the Shell station on her way to work and impulse-bought a box of candy.

It...*cheapened* it.

Pushing back his chair, he tossed the box onto the desk and stood up. "You know what? It's fine. We're good. Don't worry about it." And wheeling on his heel, he strode out of the office.

Just down the hall, Robbie and a few guys from the plant were milling around outside Auggie's office. Nick slowed his pace, nodding his head at them as he got closer. "Hey, guys."

They nodded absently in response. And then their eyes shifted to focus on something behind him, and Nick realized that Greta must have just walked out of her office as well. He kept walking, hoping against hope that she wouldn't say anything.

"If you don't want your balls, that's fine with me," he heard from behind him.

Nick froze. The guys from the plant froze. Auggie, who had just stepped into the hallway, froze.

The other guys shifted, their faces all wearing identical gleeful smirks. Not wanting to meet their eyes, Nick turned to face Greta instead.

And saw instantly that she knew exactly what she was doing.

Her hands were on her hips, which had the rather distracting effect of pushing her breasts out, and there were two stains of pink on her cheeks. Those deep brown eyes of hers were snapping with irritation, but there was something about the set of her mouth that made Nick pretty sure she was going to keep saying

191

the word "balls" until he dropped to his knees and groveled for forgiveness.

For what, he didn't know. What he did know was that at the moment, Greta had him by the, well, balls. And she knew it.

"I'm going to get back to Ben now," he said, and she nodded.

"Right." But as Nick started to flee the scene, she fired one last parting shot. "I'll just keep your balls in my purse until you want them."

The guys were snickering in earnest now. "She's talking about bourbon balls," Nick called to them as he made it to the relative safety of the conference room.

"Whatever you say, boss," one of the guys said.

BY MIDAFTERNOON, Greta was wishing she had called in to work sick. Pain was chewing away at the edges of her brain, and the company's mystifying financials weren't helping. Nothing made sense. If the sales figures she'd managed to pull together for the previous two years were correct, King Lures should be bankrupt by now. There was no way the company could even make payroll given the numbers Greta had compiled.

Which meant the numbers she'd compiled weren't right.

Just the thought of going through everything again made her feel nauseated. No one should have to puzzle through that many numbers while suffering through a hangover.

But indulging herself wasn't going to get the job done.

At least she wasn't going to run into Nick, who had taken Ben to the airport. There was no telling what kind of retribution he would exact for her little stunt this morning.

It had been completely worth it.

She knocked on Auggie's open door and stepped into his office as he looked up, his quick smile chasing the shadows from his eyes. "Hey, Greta. What can I do for you?"

Auggie's office was what Greta thought of as a professional man cave. A large whitetail deer head with wide, spreading antlers was mounted on the wall behind his desk, which was a large, solid-wood piece, dark and heavy. The only object in the room that didn't fit into the perfectly masculine image was a small pink teddy bear propped up against a brass desk lamp. "Could you please run the sales reports for me one more time?"

A line appeared over the bridge of his nose. "Sure. Is there a problem?"

"No, no problem." A total lie. "I think I may have some outdated information from somewhere and I just wanted to rule out the sales reports first."

He smiled easily, but his eyes were sharp on her face. He was, she reminded herself, the consummate salesman—telling her what he wanted her to know while gleaning things she wasn't willing to share just from her body language.

Auggie would make a hell of a poker player.

Nodding at him, she went back to her office, sinking into her chair and opening the folder where she'd been keeping everything she could get her hands on regarding the financial state of the business.

Her head throbbed, and the numbers swam before her eyes. She closed the folder with a sigh. It was no use. She wasn't going to get to the bottom of this muddle, not without the new reports, and not now, when she felt like her head might cave in at any moment.

Standing, she moved to the window, shading her eyes against the wash of sunlight. It wasn't terribly hot out, and she was filled with a sudden longing to be anywhere but in that overly air-conditioned office. Her eyes fell on the archery targets lined up beside the building.

The air conditioning didn't feel quite so chilly as the memory of Nick shooting on that range rose up unbidden. He'd looked so powerful, so in control.

What she wouldn't give to feel in control of anything at the moment.

Her hands gripped the windowsill. She'd never shot a bow before, but it didn't seem all that difficult. Pull the string back and let go, right? And, given that she was charged with marketing to people who liked to shoot a bow, actually shooting a bow herself might give her some insight into who they were. There were, she knew, several bows in a little cabinet in the warehouse, along with arrows.

On her father's desk, the mangled reports waited. Outside, a little puff of a breeze stirred the trees in the distance.

It wasn't a very hard decision.

NICK DROVE BACK from the airport under a robust blue sky, the clouds white and thick over the vibrant green landscape. The road wound past farms heavy with corn and cows, tidy brick-red barns perched on slight hills. Under a sky like that, it was possible to believe that Bartlett was immune from tragedy, that here there could be no cancer or heart attacks, no unhappy wives who left without warning, no companies that went bankrupt and dumped a dozen people into unemployment.

In other words, the sky was a big, fat liar.

He almost didn't go back to the office. It was after three already. Who would care if he cut out a little early? But the thought of his depressingly empty house kept him driving past his turn. Work might not be the refuge it once was, but it was still better than his sad, haunted house.

Movement caught his eye when he pulled into the parking lot. There was someone on the archery range. Auggie, most likely, or Paul if his doctor had cleared him. His mood lightened. An hour of target practice with one of the guys was exactly what he needed at the moment.

But as he neared the range, he slowed, then stopped altogether. It wasn't Auggie, or Paul.

It was Greta.

Shooting just about as badly as he'd ever seen someone shoot.

The bow's draw weight was too heavy for her to pull back, but that didn't seem to stop her from trying. She fought the string back, her arms shaking as she pulled. Finally reaching letoff, where the cams took over and held most of the weight for her, she stood awkwardly, staring at the target twenty yards away, holding the bow too low. Then she released the string, her arms dropping almost before the arrow had a chance to clear the rest.

Unsurprisingly, the arrow embedded in the grass, nowhere near the target.

It looked like the Deer Pee Princess was learning that archery was a little harder than she'd assumed.

He expected her to head back into the office, but she didn't. Instead, she reached down, grabbed an arrow from the ground beside her—it looked like she didn't realize the vertical tubes spaced along the line were meant to hold arrows—and popped the nock onto the string. Then, staring down the target, she fought the bow back to full draw once again.

What the hell was she doing? She couldn't possibly enjoy shooting a bow that way—her arms were shaking so hard he worried she might end up hurting herself, and she definitely wasn't going to feel good tomorrow. And for a woman like Greta, a woman obsessed with success, seeing the arrow fly wide every time had to be downright painful.

But she wouldn't give up. After her second arrow flew far left, skipping between targets to slide under the grass forty yards out, she picked up another arrow and started the whole miserable process all over again.

How could Paul let her shoot like that? Hadn't he shown her how to shoot a bow? It had been Paul who'd taught Nick to shoot, more than twenty years ago when Nick had been a lonely 12-year-old desperate for a way to escape his grandmother's fussy house. Surely he'd taken the time to teach Greta, as well.

But judging from the way Greta held a bow, he hadn't.

Well, it wasn't any of his business whether Greta pulled a muscle. And what did it matter if her shooting form was terrible? It wasn't like she was going to develop poor shooting habits. Once she was back in Chicago, she'd never pick up a bow again. He turned, intending to slip away unnoticed and get back to work.

But...this was archery. The sport he loved. And while he wasn't Greta's biggest fan at the moment, he couldn't let her shoot like that. Maybe she would go home and forget all about her time in Bartlett. But maybe, if she had a proper introduction to archery, she might fall in love with the sport. There were archery ranges in Chicago, and plenty of people enjoyed recreational shooting. Maybe Greta could introduce her friends back home to the sport, and they'd go shooting together, and the sport of archery would gain several new converts.

He might be able to turn his back on Greta, but he could never turn his back on archery.

With a sigh, he walked over to the range and waited for her to release the string—as much as he loved archery, he wasn't about to startle a woman with a bow at full draw. "I see you're as good at archery as you are at basketball," he said, moving closer.

She looked over her shoulder at him, her expression wary. "What do you want?"

"Nothing. I just thought you might like some pointers."

"From you? No, I'm good. Thanks." Grabbing another arrow, she lifted the bow once more.

"Oh, sorry. I was under the impression you liked to do things well."

She paused. "I'll get it eventually."

"Not like that, you won't," he said as she began battling the

196

bow back. "I know this is going to shock you, but there are some things you can't just will yourself to be good at."

For another heartbeat, she continued trying to pull the bow back. But then her arms drooped, her head bent in defeat. "I know I can't just will myself to be good at everything," she said softly.

He read the tension in her neck and shoulders, took in the tightness around her mouth, and wondered how long she'd been shooting that damn bow. How many shots had she struggled through? He'd seen her take three, but he had a feeling she'd been out there for awhile. And she hadn't given up.

Just like she hadn't given up on King Lures, despite knowing nothing about how to run a company in general, or the products King sold in particular. She showed up, day after day, even though everything she'd done so far business-wise looked pretty much the same as her audacious shooting form.

It was hard not to respect a woman who tried that hard.

Gently, he took the bow from her. "The first problem is this bow," he said. "It's too heavy for you."

She didn't look at him. "I know. Robbie said it was the lightest bow we had."

"It is." The bow was Kelsey's bow, set lighter than what all the guys pulled but still a legal hunting weight. "Some of the muscles you use to draw a bow don't get used much in everyday life, so it's normal to have trouble the first few times. I'm sure we can find you a lighter bow for next time."

She nodded curtly. "Great. Thanks." She started to walk back to the building.

He took a quick step sideways to block her. "Whoa, you can still shoot. I just have to help you. But we're going to do things a little differently."

He had her wait while he went inside to grab a release aid. "Here," he said, holding it out to her. "This will make for a smoother release."

Then he made the mistake of helping her put it on.

The bones of her wrist were light and delicate, the skin over her pulse point soft and silky and surprisingly cool. It took forever for him to buckle the release properly, her nearness making his fingers clumsy. When his pinky grazed the spot just below her palm, she exhaled, her breath skittering over his skin.

She looked up, her eyes warm and wide as they met his. He'd thought they were merely dark brown, but now he saw sparks of gold and amber and bronze in their chocolate depths.

He realized he was just standing there, holding her wrist in his own frozen hand. "Okay," he said, stepping back and dropping her hand. "That will help."

She took a shaky breath. "I'm sure it will." She started to move back to the firing line.

"Actually, we're going to try something else. Come on." Grabbing a handful of arrows, he walked closer to the line of targets, stopping just five yards away. "We're going to shoot from here."

She nibbled her bottom lip. "Here? We're almost on top of the target."

"That's the point." He moved to the target, turning it so that a big white square faced Greta instead of the colorful bull's-eye. "You're too worried about aiming. Don't worry about hitting the target." He grinned. "From five yards, it'd be pretty hard to miss."

"This feels too easy."

"Sure, hitting the target from here is easy. It's getting your form and process down that takes some work."

He showed her how to stand, positioning her shoulders correctly, sliding one foot between her legs to nudge them shoulder-width apart. Then, when she had the proper stance, he had her nock an arrow. "I'll help you draw," he said, putting his arms around her from behind, one hand covering hers on the bow grip, the other settling on the string. "Ready?" he asked. She nodded.

He raised the bow to shooting level, holding it a bit

awkwardly to allow her to be able to look at the sight picture. "Keep this arm straight," he murmured, squeezing her bow hand. "And make sure you keep your finger behind the release trigger." He pulled on the bowstring, slowly drawing the bow back to full draw, the scent of lavender making it hard to concentrate on anything besides the dark silk of Greta's hair just beneath his chin.

"There you go," he said, gently adjusting her elbow. She was utterly still, and he realized she was holding her breath. "Try to remember to breathe," he added, smiling against her hair as she let out her breath in a rush. With the bow at full draw, she was holding a manageable weight, but he couldn't bring himself to step away. Instead, he moved his right hand to where her fingers were still tucked carefully behind the release trigger. "Okay, go ahead and shoot."

But she didn't. The tip of the arrow wavered against the white expanse before it. And still she stood there, her fingers clenched in a tight fist.

He didn't need to ask her what was wrong. He might not understand everything about her, but he understood this. "Greta," he said, his voice low. "It's okay. You can't miss."

She nodded jerkily, her index finger inching forward to wrap around the release. And a moment later, the *thwack* of an arrow hitting the target made her jump.

"I...I did it."

"You certainly did." She was still inside the circle of his arms, and he was reluctant to let her go. "Want to try again?"

"Yes." But she didn't seem eager to move, either. He could practically feel the tension fading from her shoulders. She turned her head and looked up at him, an impish grin on her face. "I'm sorry about what happened earlier."

"I see how sorry you are." But he couldn't help but smile back.

"No, really. And those bourbon balls are really still in my purse if you want them."

"Oh, sure. Now you throw in the 'bourbon' part."

She shrugged, briefly stepping away from him to grab another arrow. "What can I say? I have the maturity of a 12-year-old boy. So...truce?"

He placed his hands over hers once more, his arms just barely not touching her. "I don't have much of a choice, do I? You've got my balls in your purse and a weapon in your hands. Common sense dictates I agree to anything you ask."

That made her laugh. As they reached full draw—when she was supposed to be concentrating on her form—she looked up at him once more. "I really am sorry about the Bambi-killer thing."

"I know," he said. "Now make sure your elbow is pointed back straight. Like this."

They stood there, his chest brushing lightly against her back, their hands connected on the bow, and he had the sudden impression of being poised on the edge of something big. It was the same feeling he got when he drew back on a big buck, that feeling of infinite possibilities quickly whittling themselves down to the one possibility that would become reality, the feeling that he shouldn't miss but that maybe he would anyway. The bow practically vibrated with the potential energy stored in its cams, and then suddenly Greta touched the trigger, loosing the arrow, sending it on its now sealed path.

It struck the target, hard, shivering for a moment before it finally stilled.

And Nick had the uncomfortable realization that now he wasn't just attracted to Greta. Now he kind of liked her, too.

CHAPTER 18

*G*reta went into the office even earlier than usual the next morning. She'd promised Andi a great idea, and that was exactly what she was going to deliver.

Just as soon as she thought of one.

She leafed through her notebook, considering the ideas she'd already written down.

Nothing. At least nothing that she felt confident about.

Flipping to a blank page, she wrote Coeurs Sauvages in big, dark letters across the top of the page and then underlined the words with a quick slash of her pen. Coeurs Sauvages. Wild Hearts. The possibilities were endless.

But now when she thought of the word *wild*, the only thing she could think of was the way her heart had pounded when Nick had buckled the worn leather release strap around her wrist the day before. And that hardly seemed like a universally wild moment.

She threw her pen down in disgust. This was exactly what she worked so hard to avoid in her regular life. She didn't need distractions, even if one of them was particularly delicious looking. Especially when he shot a bow. Or helped her shoot a bow.

Basically, whenever his muscles were doing something.

Greta turned on her computer with a snap and forced any visions of Nick and his muscles out of her mind. She needed to focus.

But her mind kept recalling the way his sun-warmed arms had felt around her, how his hands had covered hers. She'd dated her share of men over the years, all other urban professionals short on time but long on class and money. In other words, ideal partners. But she'd never had someone get under her skin the way Nick had. She'd never felt so overwhelmed by a man before, as if she could lose herself in his arms.

Even in the full blast of the AC, she was starting to get warm. The pinstriped blouse and navy pencil skirt that had felt thin earlier suddenly felt suffocating.

She needed to get her mind off Nick. Gritting her teeth, she inserted her flash drive into the computer and clicked the file she wanted. She wasn't going to lose sight of what mattered. She just needed to focus.

The video opened, bathing her face in a blue-white light.

That was what she was doing when Nick walked in.

* * *

IT WAS the music that piqued his interest.

When he got to work that morning, Nick was determined to put whatever had happened on the archery range behind him. So she had grit, and soft skin, and hair that smelled like a whole field of French lavender. She also lived in Chicago. And she thought tofu was an acceptable form of protein and wore rented shoes.

And lived in Chicago.

He had no idea how long the music had been playing before he finally noticed it. It sounded like something classical, delicate notes that made him think of lace and shortbread cookies, and it was coming from Paul's office.

It stopped suddenly, cut off mid-note. Nick dropped into his chair, switched on his computer, and took a shot at his basketball hoop while he waited for the computer to start up. And then the music started again, but not from where it left off. From what he assumed was the beginning of the song.

As he opened Microsoft Outlook to check his email, it happened again—the music stopping and restarting. In the same place in the song, too.

He clicked through his email, but it was mostly junk mail— how was it that junk mail always seemed to arrive in bulk around five in the morning? He skimmed over the email subjects, quickly deleting the promises of profit-boosting business secrets, greater stamina, and romance—the last purporting to be from a Russian woman longing for "the long and the strong love," which may or may not have been intended as a euphemism. Regardless, it did not improve his mood.

Maybe because he'd spent the night thinking about sharing "the long and the strong love" with Greta. Euphemistically speaking, of course.

The music stopped and restarted again next door, and it occurred to Nick that Greta might be having trouble with something. Computer problems he could handle.

She was staring at her computer screen, her face tight. Then she winced.

"Are you okay?" He moved to her side so quickly she barely had time to pause the video she'd been watching. Nick's gaze moved from her face to the screen, where a blurry woman in a white tutu was halfway through what looked to Nick's untrained eye to be a very ungraceful fall. "What are you doing?"

She rushed to minimize the window, but instead she accidentally maximized it. The falling woman was now large enough that, despite the blurred features, he was able to recognize her.

"That's you," he said as she frantically clicked on the window in an attempt to close it. But she was moving too quickly, and instead all she managed to do was start the video again.

On the screen, the blurry woman that was Greta fell in an ungainly heap. There was the sound of a collective gasp from the audience, and the music stopped abruptly.

Defeated, Greta sat back in her chair, her hands dropping to her sides. "I know," she said. "It's awful, isn't it?"

Nick looked from the screen to Greta's face. "What is this?"

Her face was very white. "It's the one time I failed."

"The one time you failed to do what?"

"The one time I failed period. This is it." She lifted one hand and gestured toward the screen. The video had cut off by now, the little play triangle appearing over what must be a still image from the very beginning of it—Greta standing onstage, her hands held out to her sides, her face turned in profile. With her dark hair pulled back in a gleaming bun and her lowered lashes black against her pale cheek, she looked like something out of a fairy tale. Something ethereal, something out of reach.

Although that fall sure did help bring her back down to earth.

Suppressing a grin, he tried to understand why Greta was sitting in her office at 6:30 in the morning watching an old video of herself messing up at some ballet recital. "Try again. And this time use more words."

She stood up, moving to the window, her hands twisting restlessly in front of her. "It was my junior year. I wanted to stop taking ballet, but my mother insisted I do it for just one more year. She thought it was good for my confidence." She shot him a rueful grin. "Look how that turned out."

"And what's that have to do with that video?"

"I was in this competition. I knew my routine was challenging. I knew I needed to push myself harder. Practice more. But I got distracted. My friends were always calling me to see if I wanted to go out for ice cream or a movie and I…" Her voice trailed off. She lifted her hands and stared at them as if she were

Lady Macbeth and there'd just been a murder. "I thought I could get by with the bare minimum. It turned out I couldn't."

"You went out for ice cream instead of practicing ballet? And none of this appeared on a background check for your current job?"

"You don't understand."

"Not even the tiniest bit." He sat down on a corner of her desk. "So explain it to me."

"My mother was so angry," she whispered, turning so she could gesture once more to the computer. "She accused me of doing it deliberately to sabotage my dancing career. Who knows? Maybe I did."

"Ah. So you never wound up going pro?"

"It's not funny. That was when she finally gave up on the idea of me attending Julliard."

He supposed she was right. It was a lot of things—neurotic, crazy, sad—but funny wasn't one of them. "Don't take this the wrong way—"

"I definitely will."

"—but you don't exactly strike me as the dancer type. You're just not all that..." He cast about for the right word. "Uh...*graceful*."

"Maybe I wasn't a natural at it, but if you put your mind to something and work hard, you can accomplish anything." She ejected the flash drive from her computer, setting it carefully on the desk beside her stupid notebook and a bottle of Excedrin. No wonder she practically lived on headache medicine if this was how she pumped herself up.

"You are really wound tight, you know that?"

Her chin came up sharply, her eyes burning. "There's nothing wrong with being driven."

"Does everyone you work with do this? Do you all sit around your office every morning reliving every misspelled word at a spelling bee or imperfect cello performance? Or do you lock yourself in your office so no one knows you're doing this?"

She looked away, and her fingers twisted together. "It was a turning point in my life."

"It was a stupid dance competition. It wasn't like you set the cure for cancer on fire or ripped the brakes out of a speeding train."

She nodded, but he could tell she wasn't really listening to him. "And here I thought I was screwed up." He made a quick decision. "Okay, let's go."

She blinked up at him. "Go where?"

"We're getting out of here for a little while."

"I can't. I have too much work."

"What are you going to do? Call up a bunch of hunters and convince them to buy gallons of our products? Contact all the retailers who've dropped us and sweet-talk them into taking us back? Because if you're not going to do either of those things, then whatever it is you have to do can wait."

She hesitated, looking uncertainly at her desk.

"Fine. You want to stay here. I'll sit right here until you're ready to go." He dropped into one of the two chairs by her desk, one ankle propped on his knee.

"Whatever," she said finally. "I can take a few minutes."

"Good. Leave your purse here," he said when she reached for it. Then he glanced at her feet. "We'll stop at your house so you can change. You're definitely not going to want to wear heels. Or," he added, his eyes skimming over the pencil skirt that hugged her luscious hips, "a skirt."

She was instantly wary. "We're not going to the deer farm again?"

He chuckled. "No, not the deer farm." When she didn't look reassured, he said, "Come on. I promise you'll like this place."

* * *

GRETA STILL FELT hollow and bruised as Nick backed out of her father's driveway. Paul wasn't awake yet when she crept back into the house to change, which was good because she really didn't feel like explaining to her father that Nick was taking her to an unknown location because he'd discovered just how messed up she really was.

"Something casual," Nick told her in the car.

She'd had to raid the bag of clothes Helen had left behind for her, which meant a lot of trying on and discarding of clothes. When she finally emerged from the house wearing a pair of black slacks, a sleeveless coral blouse, and black ballet flats, Nick shook his head. "Is that the best you could do?"

"The only thing I have more casual than this is my pajamas," she told him tartly.

He pressed his lips together and said nothing more.

She expected to head back for Main Street, but instead Nick turned the other way, driving deeper into the neighborhood. They passed Pea's house, and Greta caught a glimpse of roses glowing like jewels in the thick dawn. He turned down one street, and then another, until Greta was hopelessly turned around. Finally, Nick pulled to the curb and stopped the car. "Here we are."

The house before them had butter-yellow curtains tied back in the front windows, and in the front flowerbed there was a small two-dimensional wooden swing with two smiling ragdolls —a boy and girl—painted on it. She turned to him slowly. "Is this where you live?"

"No." He pulled the keys from the ignition and opened his door. "But I grew up a couple houses down."

"Really?" Greta slid out of the car, surprisingly curious about where Nick had lived as a kid. "Which house?"

He pointed to a small house farther down the road. "That one. And Auggie lived right next door."

It was strange to think that he and Auggie had grown up

together. She kept in touch with a few college friends on Facebook, but she had no high school friends in her life, let alone friends from her childhood.

She followed Nick as he walked through the yard of the house they'd parked in front of. "Whose house is this?" she whispered, catching up to him and grabbing his arm. "Should we be here?"

"Don't worry. It's Mrs. Harrison's house, and she's used to it."

Before she could ask what he meant, a woman stepped out of the side door. She was older, with gentle puffs of smoke-gray hair and cat's-eye glasses with multi-colored rhinestones set in the corners. She wore a champagne-colored velour track suit, the kind that Greta had seen sold in places like Victoria's Secret and Forever 21 a few years earlier. "Isn't it a little early, Nicky?" she called. Then her eyes fell on Greta, and her face creased in obvious disapproval. "Nicholas," she said, folding her arms over her chest and sounding so disappointed in Nick that Greta felt guilty. For what, she didn't know. "Do I need to get the hose again?"

"It's not what it looks like, Mrs. Harrison," Nick said, a smile playing about his lips. "This is Paul King's daughter. I'm just showing her the treehouse."

Mrs. Harrison sniffed, apparently still unconvinced. "Just make sure that's all you show her." Then she turned to go back inside her house.

The word JUICY was spelled out in glittery letters across her rear end.

"Oh," Greta said softly.

"She shops at thrift stores a lot." Nick inclined his head toward the woods behind Mrs. Harrison's house. "Come on."

A well-worn dirt path wound its way through the trees. Beneath the canopy of branches, it was still nearly as dark as night, and all around them were the sounds of small creatures waking up or returning to their beds for the day. A spider had spun an intricate web across the path; only the fact that the silken strands were dotted with dew kept Greta from walking face-first into it. She wasn't crazy about spiders, but even she had to admit that the web, which sparkled like diamonds in a lonely ray of sunshine, was breathtaking. Nick ducked beneath it, and she followed suit, although afterwards she ran her hands over the back of her neck to make sure no spiders had fallen on her.

Nick led the way as the path twisted up a hill, becoming rockier and harder to follow. At one point he reached back to help her up a particularly steep stretch, but she grabbed hold of a couple straggly saplings for balance instead.

Finally he stopped and pointed at a small house tucked in among the trees. As she got closer, Greta realized that it wasn't just among the trees—it was *in* one, built several feet off the ground around a sturdy trunk. "Oh," she breathed. "When you said treehouse, I assumed..."

"Yeah," Nick said, and there was an unmistakable note of pride in his voice. "It's something, isn't it?"

Something wasn't the right word. It was, as treehouses go, magnificent. It appeared to be two stories tall, with a small transom window on the second floor and steps leading up to a real front door. Two windows flanked the door, window boxes full of cheery red geraniums under them. The whole thing was painted bisque, with a bright blue door and a gray roof.

"Want to see the inside?" Nick asked. She could only nod.

They climbed the stairs, Greta holding onto the sturdy handrail. Nick knocked loudly, then pressed one ear to the door. "Expecting someone to be here?" Greta asked.

Nick smiled. "I'm not the only person who comes here. Just want to make sure we don't stumble upon anyone who needs Mrs. Harrison's hose." Then he twisted the doorknob and pushed the door open.

If the outside had surprised her, the inside left her totally speechless. It was a real house, complete with a tiny kitchenette and a tiny living room and a ladder that she imagined led to a tiny bedroom upstairs. The floors were a cottage-gray fake-wood vinyl tile, and overhead fluorescent lights cast a stark white glow over the leopard-print area rug and bean bag chairs in varying gumball colors—blue, green, red—when Nick flipped the switch by the door.

"What is this place?" Greta asked when she could finally speak.

"It's our treehouse."

"Our?"

Nick flopped down on one of the blue bean bag chairs. "Mine. Auggie's. The other kids from the neighborhood."

Greta gazed around in astonishment. "But it can't be that old. This floor looks new."

He shrugged. "We still maintain it. It's good for kids to have a secret place where they can get away from adults. We decided it was a good idea if that secret place was somewhere all the adults around here know about, too."

There was a sliding glass door along the back wall of the tree-house, and Greta walked over to peer out. Outside was a deck, held up with a number of sturdy support beams. "Who built this?"

"We did." When she turned to look at him, he added, "Auggie's dad is an engineer. He helped with a lot of the more advanced stuff."

"Did you have to get permits for the electricity?"

Nick chuckled and set his wrists on his knees, his big hands dangling. "Oh, no. This place is totally illegal. Think any of this is built to code? Nope."

"Don't you worry about getting sued? If some kid got hurt here…"

"Sure, I guess someone could sue. But considering that this place is pretty much an open secret, it's not something I worry about. Hell, our current mayor was the one who figured out how to run the lines to get electricity in, and the sheriff's kids play here all the time."

"But—"

"Sometimes breaking the rules makes life a whole lot richer."

Something she knew nothing about. She'd never so much as parked in a no parking zone. Sinking into the green bean bag chair, she rubbed her upper arms against the early morning chill.

"So tell me how you end up becoming the kind of person who tortures herself over one bad ballet performance."

She couldn't bring herself to look at him. "I know it looks a little crazy…"

"I would say a lot crazy, but whatever."

"It reminds me not to lose sight of what's important."

"A ballet competition?"

She skimmed a hand over the ankles of her pants, wiping away some damp bits of leaves that clung to them. "No. Just whatever's important at the moment."

"But that recital was never important to you."

"Competition. And it was important to my mother."

"Then maybe she should have been the one dancing in it."

She caught her bottom lip between her teeth, worrying it as she tried to think of a way to make him understand. "I know you think it's stupid," she said finally. "But I should have practiced more. Look what happened. It was humiliating. All those people saw…" A shaft of sunlight played over the floor. "It was the only time my dad came to see one of my performances."

"Tell me," he said, settling deeper into the chair, "how many of those people do you think are still talking about it? Think there's anyone who's sitting around today telling their coworkers about a teenaged girl who tripped during a ballet recital twenty years ago? Think your dad has ever mentioned it to anyone?"

No, of course not. But, then, he wouldn't have mentioned it to anyone had it gone well, either. "It was fifteen years ago, thank you." But he had a point.

"What's important now?" His voice was soft.

Her eyes found his, the blue-gray not quite as steely as she remembered. "What if I can't help my father's company? What happens to all those people?"

Rising, Nick moved to where she sat and knelt down in front of her so they were eye to eye. "Hey," he said softly, placing his hands on her knees. The warmth of his palms burned through the fabric of her slacks. "Everyone will be okay. And while we all appreciate the work you're putting in, in the end this is our battle to fight." He smiled. "Why don't you let me and Auggie and your dad take on some responsibility?"

Just having him so close made it hard for Greta to remember exactly what they were discussing. The irises of his eyes were outlined in midnight blue, and his shoulders looked impossibly broad in his white T-shirt. It was all she could do not to reach out and run her hands over them.

Then she remembered something Mrs. Harrison had said.

"Get the hose again?" she repeated.

He grinned and sat back on his heels. "Yeah, she caught me bringing a girl up here once. Diana McNally. I thought we'd gone far enough into the woods that no one could see us, but I guess Mrs. Harrison was watching."

Greta had a feeling she knew the answer, but she had to ask anyway. "Watching you do what?"

"You know how teenagers are. We couldn't keep our hands off each other. The goal was to get to the treehouse so we could have a little privacy, but once we got into the woods…"

No, Greta did not know how teenagers were. She'd never been in any situation where someone was unable to keep his hands off her, and vice versa. But she nodded anyway.

"Mrs. Harrison saw us and got her hose. But it all turned out for the best. I guess Mrs. Harrison didn't consider what happens to a girl's white T-shirt when she gets soaking wet. We made it to the treehouse, and then we were so wet and cold we had no choice but to take off all our clothes." His smile turned decidedly wicked. "In a way, Mrs. Harrison was responsible for the first time I got laid."

"Mrs. Harrison didn't come after you when you ran off?"

"She put a lot of faith in that hose to cool a couple of kids down. Besides, I don't think she knew where this place was."

"I guess that means we're safe from the hose, then." Just thinking about that made Greta's face grow warm.

"Are you kidding?" Nick stood up. "She knows now. Who do you think planted those geraniums in the window boxes? Come on. I want to show you one more thing."

He led her out of the treehouse, clattering easily down the stairs. Then he walked around the charming little house to where the ground dropped away. A small creek chugged along at the bottom of a shallow embankment. "This is what you need," he said.

"A creek?"

"Yes. I'm not sure a few minutes of playing in a creek can make up for whatever the hell made you feel like the whole world is your responsibility, but it can't hurt."

She looked doubtfully at the murky water. "I don't think—"

"Good." He grinned down at her. "This isn't about thinking. This is about experiencing."

He started down the embankment, walking sideways to keep from sliding out of control down to the bottom. This time when he held out his hand, Greta took it.

On the banks of the creek, Nick pulled off his shoes and socks and rolled up his jeans. Then he straightened up, hands on his hips, waiting for Greta to do the same.

She gestured toward the water. "I'm not going in there barefoot. There could be anything in there. Broken glass or rusted fishhooks or hypodermic needles or—"

"You're right. There could be anything in there." But he didn't look worried. In fact, he looked like the endless possibilities were a good thing. "Come on. If you step on something bad, I'll pay for the tetanus shot, okay?"

"With an offer like that, how can I refuse?" she said drily. Slowly, she slipped off her shoes, the feeling of the moist leaves and the water-worn rocks and the silty mud of the creek bank strange beneath her feet.

She let him guide her into the water one step at a time. The water was surprisingly cold as it lapped over her feet, and the rocks on the bottom of the creek bit into her skin. She moved gingerly, letting her feet grow accustomed to the unstable layer of thin rocks. "How is this helping again?"

"I'm giving you a taste of what childhood should be like."

"Right." She was careful to keep her tone light, but beneath it she felt a stab of pain. Her father had constantly nagged her to get outside when she stayed with him. Was this what he meant? If she had listened to him, would he have brought her to this treehouse to play with the ragtag group of children that frequented it? They would have been ragtag, she knew, in cutoff shorts and mud-encrusted flip-flops and T-shirts drenched in sweat and creek water.

And she'd missed it. She'd holed up with her books, refusing to even entertain the notion of going outside to play. Although she was fairly certain that even if she had gone to the treehouse to play, she would have still been an outsider, kept on the fringes by her own inability to fit in and by the fierce bonds that formed among people in small towns, effectively keeping outsiders out.

A light breeze lifted the leaves on the trees stretching over the creek. "Did you play here a lot?" she asked Nick.

He took several steps through the water, stirring up lazy tendrils of mud with each step. "When I could." He stared into the water, where little silvery streaks darted here and there. Minnows, Greta thought, or some other tiny fish. She knew so little about creeks and what might live in them. "I wasn't really supposed to."

"Why not?"

The sun fell through the leaves, dappling his face with shadow. "My grandmother didn't like it. She didn't want me getting muddy."

"I thought getting muddy was the state sport of Kentucky."

He chuckled. "It wasn't the mud she was really worried about." He was silent for a moment. "By the time I moved in, she'd buried almost everyone she loved—two husbands, a stillborn baby girl, her only living son. All she had left was her sister and me. So she was understandably a bit overprotective."

There was something about the way the breeze was ruffling his hair that made him look boyish and vulnerable, and she didn't want to think about that bereaved little boy anymore. Changing the subject, she asked, "Were you and Auggie friends growing up?"

"We were all friends. Course, Auggie was a couple years younger than me. But I let him hang around." His head tilted back, a calculating look in his eyes. "He's always looked up to me."

She tried to imagine a much younger Auggie tagging along with Nick, gazing adoringly up at him, and failed miserably. "I can see that." She splashed through a particularly deep section of the creek, wincing as the water soaked into the rolled cuffs of her pants. "So this is your definition of childhood?"

"Almost." A glint developed in his blue-gray eyes. "Wading in a creek is fun and all, but to really recapture your youth, you have to embrace immaturity. And that means..."

Bending down, he thrust one hand into the water and sent an arc of water droplets in her direction. For a moment, they seemed to be suspended in midair, and Greta was reminded of the dew-jeweled spiderweb. The water fell over her like raindrops, and she squealed, stepping backward into a still-deeper part of the creek. Her pants were wet to her knees. Water dripped from her hair, and she found herself grinning. "That's how we're going to play it, huh?"

Her splash wasn't as effective as his, but she did get the satisfaction of watching him step sideways into a fairly deep pool, the water coming to above his knees. He laughed, the shadows gone from his face.

Later, as Greta was standing as still as possible to catch glimpses of the tiny fish, Nick waded closer to her. "Close your eyes," he said, one hand held behind his back.

"I don't—"

"—trust me, I know. Close them anyway."

He was smiling, his hair falling over his forehead, his T-shirt clinging to the hard planes of his chest, and slowly Greta obeyed. Her heart thudded as she waited for whatever it was he wanted to give—or do—to her. She was already imagining the warmth of his lips on hers when he said, his voice low and husky in her ear, "Hold out your hands."

She was sure it was a mistake, but she put her hands together, cupping them in front of her. Water dripped into them as he moved his hands over hers, and then there was something cool and light and delicate in her hands.

Whatever it was moved.

Startled, she opened her eyes. In her cupped hands was a baby lobster, scuttling around her palms, wielding his tiny claws like daggers. "What...?"

"It's a crawfish."

So it was. As she watched, it tried to pinch her thumb, but it was so small, its claws so tiny, that it didn't actually hurt. She looked up at Nick, and he grinned at the look on her face. "That's a little one," he said. "The big ones will get you if you don't pick them up right."

After a few minutes of marveling over the little crustacean, Nick plucked it carefully from her hand, showing her how to place her fingers on the body just behind the claws. Then he gently set the crawfish back in the creek, where it promptly scurried beneath a rock, blending in with all the small pebbles and decaying wood that littered the creekbed.

"Thank you," she said as Nick straightened up. His eyes were fixed on her face, and she felt the color rising under his gaze.

And then his hand came up, slowly reaching for her. She closed her eyes, expecting to feel his hand on her face.

But once again he surprised her. His hand bypassed her face, instead moving to her hair. She felt his fingers smoothing over her French twist, locating the pins she used to hold it back. And then he was pulling the pins from her hair, one by one, her hair sliding from its restraints to fall around her shoulders. Her pulse quickened.

When all the pins were out of her hair, he ran his fingers through it, loosening it, playing with the dark strands. "I've wanted to do that ever since I met you," he whispered.

Only then did she open her eyes, and immediately she wished she hadn't. There was something raw in the way he looked at her that stole her breath, that made something deep in her stomach start to uncoil.

Now his hands did move to her face, his thumb skimming over her cheekbone, tracing her jawline. "Greta."

"Yes," she said, and she wasn't sure whether it was a statement or a question.

That was all he needed. His mouth dipped down to meet hers, his hand tilting her face up to meet him. He tasted of sun and secrets and something warm and musky. His tongue slid into her mouth, and Greta's arms went around him, wrapping around his neck.

The creek water played around her calves, and the strengthening sun grew warm on her bare shoulders. Nick made an impatient sound deep in his throat and pulled her against him. The friction of his chest against her breasts was almost painful, and she felt the hard length of him against her stomach.

KELLY MCKERRAS

Still he kissed her, his mouth demanding, taking, plundering. All the while his hand cradled her cheek, as if she were something precious and delicate. As if she were made of glass. His other hand wandered, first stroking her back, then running over her hips, pulling her closer still.

And then he was tugging her toward the bank of the creek, and she was letting him. Keeping one hand firmly in his own, he led her up the embankment, pausing to pull her against him, his lips going to her throat as they stood beneath the cool shade of the oak trees. She felt his mouth on the tender skin beneath her jaw, felt the graze of his teeth along her shoulder, before he grabbed her hand once again.

She followed him up the steps of the treehouse, followed him to the base of the ladder that led to the second floor.

And then she followed him up.

He reached a hand down, helping her onto the second floor. She got only the barest impression of a small, open room—pale blue walls, gold area rug, inflatable palm tree, more bean bag chairs, and a cheap plastic table—before Nick bent his head back to hers, taking her mouth, filling her with his warm, masculine scent. His hands moved over the row of pearl buttons holding her shirt closed. He made short work of them, letting her blouse fall open. Then he drew back to look down at what he'd uncovered.

She was wearing a little gossamer slip of a bra, a warm apricot color. "Tell me," he murmured. "Is this rented too?"

She managed to suppress a giggle. "No, I buy my underwear."

"Good to know." His mouth dropped to the upper curve of her breast, moving slowly over the gentle swell. Pushing the blouse from her shoulders, he knelt before her, his lips capturing her budding nipple right through the filmy lace of her bra. She gasped at the gentle suction, her hands threading through his golden hair.

His hands went to the straps of her bra, drawing them down

218

over her upper arms so that he could push the fabric of her bra down, and then his mouth once more closed over her.

She let his tongue work its magic until she was panting with need. Sinking to her knees, she pushed her hands beneath his T-shirt, skimming her palms over the rigid ripples of his abdomen, over the sleek muscles of his chest, over his shoulders, all the while bringing his shirt with them. He obliged by drawing back from her breasts long enough that she could drag his shirt over his head.

She feasted her eyes on the hard expanse of his chest, his broad shoulders, the strong column of his throat. "I've been such an idiot," she muttered as his mouth found its way to the sensitive spot just beneath her ear.

"Not that I don't agree," he said against her skin. "But could you clarify why you think that?"

"I'm just thinking about how much time I wasted not looking at you shirtless."

He chuckled low in his throat. Then he sank down onto the floor, pulling her down with him. Undoing the button at her waist, he slid the short zipper down achingly slowly, parting it one tooth at a time. She raised her hips to let him slide her pants down her legs, leaving her clad only in a pair of silky panties that matched her bra. He wore only a faded pair of jeans, the denim bulging in the front where his arousal was in full evidence.

She measured the breadth of his shoulders with her hands, loving the way the muscles she'd admired so much felt as they shifted beneath her hands. His eyes were smoky with desire, his face hard-edged as he gazed down at her. He lifted one of her arms, kissing the sensitive skin of her inner wrist, inside her elbow, her upper arm, as he looped it over his neck.

His hands, meanwhile, were stroking their way up her legs, drifting slowly from her ankles to the apex of her thighs. Watching her intently, he slipped one finger inside her panties, stroking over her. Greta gasped at the sweet invasion.

Her hands reached for the button of his jeans. He let her undo it and drag the zipper down, but then he shifted so that she could no longer reach him. Instead, he kept stroking her with his finger, over and over until she was practically begging for relief.

That's when her phone rang. Not just any ring. A very particular ringtone. Vivaldi's "Winter." Greta had assigned that ringtone to only one person.

Tamsin.

Nick's mouth moved to the junction of her neck and shoulder. "Ignore it," he murmured, his tongue coaxing little shivers from her.

She wanted to, wanted to close her eyes and lose herself in whatever it was he had planned. But the phone rang again, and before she could think, she was rolling away from him, sifting through the discarded clothes on the floor in search of her slacks.

"I have to take this," she said, the music of the ringtone building inexorably. "It's my boss."

Nick sat up. "So what? What could she possibly need from you that you can't handle in an hour?" His eyes grew heated as they ran over her body. "Or maybe two?"

"It could be important." She located her pants and dug her phone out of one pocket.

"More important than this?"

She paused, the phone vibrating in her hand. Nick's back was hunched, his arms draped over his knees, and he watching her with a resigned expression. He already knew what she was going to do.

"This is my life," she said helplessly.

"I see that." And with that he got to his feet, reaching down to grab his shirt, all lean grace and pent-up frustration. Greta's fingers itched to touch his sun-warmed skin again, and for just a moment she almost hit "Ignore" on her phone. But then Nick pulled his shirt on and gave her a jerky nod, his face shuttered, before turning away. She heard his footsteps descending the ladder as she answered the call.

"Tamsin, hello," she said, forcing her mouth into a smile. She'd read somewhere that people could hear a smile over the phone.

"Greta." Tamsin's voice was as cool and crisp as ever, and Greta wondered what color suit she was wearing. Lemon? Clementine? Kiwi? "I wanted to check in with you on the Stella proposal."

The Stella proposal. Right. She thought of her notebook, of all the stupid ideas she had noted down there.

"It's going really well. I can't wait to show you what I've come up with."

"I'm glad to hear it. Reed has found some time to develop some rough ideas, and I have to say, they're very impressive."

Greta was in her underwear, she realized, sitting on the floor of a treehouse in the shadow of an inflatable palm tree, listening to her boss talk about Reed's amazing ideas.

And it wasn't even eight in the morning.

"I'm sure he's come up with some really great suggestions," she said, her voice bright and tinny. "And I'm glad for the competition. That just drives us all to be better, and in the end, that means better service for our clients. That's what really matters, isn't it?" There. That almost sounded like something she believed.

"That's a very positive way of looking at it," and Tamsin, too, almost sounded like she believed it. "There's still time, of course. We have a couple more weeks before we need to finalize the pitch. I just wanted to see if I could still count on you."

"Of course. I won't let you down."

"I know that." Although the fact that she'd felt compelled to call pretty much said she did not know that. "Oh—how's your father?"

Greta fixed her eyes on her toes. They were streaked with a light film of mud from the creek. "He's doing much better, thank you."

"Good. I'm looking forward to seeing your proposal."

So was Greta.

Nick was waiting when she climbed down the ladder, fully dressed but for her shoes, which she'd left beside the creek. He stood at the base of the treehouse's front steps, his hands jammed in his pockets, his back facing her. "Sorry," she said.

He didn't turn around. "Everything okay?"

No. Reed was going to get the promotion and Tamsin had said she was counting on Greta and now Nick wouldn't even look at her. Just a couple weeks ago, everything had been so perfect. Now it was all tilting wildly, and she couldn't seem to get control of her own life.

But she couldn't say any of that. She padded slowly down the steps, wincing as her feet found every splinter. Somehow she hadn't noticed how rough the steps were on her way in. "Yes."

He glanced at her as she reached the bottom of the steps, his expression unreadable. "We'd better be heading back then."

She thought once again of that notebook on her desk. Three hundred miles away, Reed was probably already in the office, drinking his third cup of coffee and smiling that smug smile he always wore when things were going well for him, all while Greta's perfect cubicle was empty.

Which was where she belonged. Not throwing caution to the wind on the floor of a children's treehouse.

She nodded. "Yes."

Nick retrieved her shoes for her, but he didn't offer her a hand when they got to the tricky spots along the path back to the car. Greta wasn't sure if that was because he didn't want to touch her, or because he knew she would refuse to take it.

They were almost to the car when Mrs. Harrison slid open one of her front windows, her face grainy behind the window screen. "There you are, Nicky. I was just about to go looking for you." Her voice was one part disapproval, one part avid curiosity. "With my hose."

Nick laughed. "That's okay, Mrs. Harrison," he said, his voice admirably even. "You wouldn't have been interrupting anything."

No, Greta thought as she slipped into Nick's sunbaked car. Beside her, Nick started the engine, his long, capable fingers closing over the gearshift to put the car in drive. She wouldn't have interrupted anything.

More's the pity.

$\mathcal{N}$ick made the mistake of assuming his day couldn't get much worse.

Then he got back to the office and walked in to find Helen, Kelsey, and Auggie chatting it up by the front desk like they had nothing better to do than wait for something interesting to happen to them.

And didn't Nick deliver? He and Greta walked in, not quite together, but close enough. And if that wasn't bad enough, Greta's hair was a disaster, all tumbled around her shoulders like...well, like she'd had sex on the floor of a treehouse.

Which she hadn't. Technically.

With a stiff nod, Greta—the coward—fled to the relative safety of Paul's office, leaving him to handle any questions alone. Judging from the looks on their faces, there were going to be questions.

The worst part was, Nick didn't like the answers. A surge of frustration shot through him. "You guys need something to do?" he said, his tone sharper than he expected.

Not that it did any good. Some employees might be afraid of their bosses. These weren't that kind of employee.

"I'm on my break," Kelsey said, leaning back against Helen's desk, her long legs, encased in red-and-gold striped tights, stretched lazily out before her. "Although it looks like your break was a lot more interesting than mine."

"Whatever you think happened is wrong."

"I'm sure it is." Kelsey flicked a glance at Helen. "He's way too surly to have gotten laid this morning."

"He's got mud on his shoes," Helen said.

"Not sure how having sex would get his shoes muddy."

"It would if he had to go somewhere muddy to have the sex," Helen pointed out, cocking her bird-like head to one side.

"Where would he go to have sex that's all muddy?" Kelsey drew a lock of her hair through her fingers and examined the ends as she considered.

Auggie grinned. "Dude, you're either doing it all wrong or you're doing it all right."

"I didn't have sex!" Nick snapped.

"All wrong, then," Kelsey said, nodding solemnly.

"I don't know about the rest of you, but I have work to do." Gritting his teeth, Nick headed for his office. Just before he reached it, he heard Kelsey say, "Auggie, go give him some pointers. He's even grumpier than usual."

And it wasn't even nine in the morning.

* * *

LATE THAT AFTERNOON, Greta set down her pen. Thankfully, it was almost five, which meant this nightmarish day could finally end. In addition to passing up what had promised to be mind-blowing sex in a treehouse and discovering that Reed had already wowed Tamsin, she'd spent a good chunk of time listening to Kelsey deliver a play-by-play account of her night with Robbie.

"He didn't *exactly* kiss me," the younger woman had said, lounging in the chair across from Greta, her back pressed against one arm rest, her legs draped over the other. "But there was a *look*. You know what I'm talking about?"

Yes, Greta knew what she was talking about, and just the memory of Nick's face in the moment before he kissed her had her insides feeling all shivery with longing and regret.

"Maybe he's done playing the field. Maybe he's looking for one woman that can meet all his needs." Kelsey, one foot swinging idly, turned her head to grin at Greta. "Obviously, that one woman is me."

It was so simple for Kelsey, Greta reflected now. She and Robbie had so much in common—same hometown, same friends, same workplace. They made sense in a way that she and Nick never would.

And wasn't that depressing?

So she wasn't in the best mood when she found Paul in the factory when she went down just before quitting time. He was engaged in a packing race with one of the new packers, hurriedly filling boxes to see who was the fastest.

Which was most definitely not Greta's definition of resting.

"Dad," she said, raising her voice to be heard over the din of the machines. "We talked about this."

"Hold on a sec, honey. I'm showing this kid how it's done."

Greta sighed. She was going to have her hands full trying to keep him alive until she left for Chicago.

On the way home, he was infuriatingly quiet, occupying himself with a cheap little game that involved navigating silver balls through a maze. She had no idea where he'd gotten it.

"I don't know what you were thinking by showing up at work today," she said finally, unable to stand the silence.

"I was bored. There's nothing to do at home."

"You're not supposed to be doing anything. And you're definitely not supposed to be engaging in stupid competitions with your employees."

"It's not a stupid competition." Paul kept his eyes on the little maze in his hands. "It's a way to make training fun. 'Course, normally I win. I would have won this time, too, if it hadn't been for that damn heart surgery. It's limiting my mobility."

"The heart surgery kept you from winning a pointless competition? I wonder if we can sue for malpractice."

"Sarcasm isn't as cute as you think it is."

"You're not supposed to be lifting boxes. You're supposed to be at home resting. You had surgery a little over a week ago. You're going to hurt yourself pushing too hard."

He tilted the maze away, watching as the ball zipped around a narrow arc. "If you don't push yourself, you end up staying exactly where you are."

She'd always assumed she'd gotten her drive from her mother, but now, watching her father frown over a stupid plastic maze, determined to succeed, she realized she might have more in common with him than she'd initially believed.

She thought of Nick's surprise when he caught her watching the ballet video. He was wrong, she knew. She didn't need to relax. She needed to work harder.

"I wish you'd take this seriously," she said as she turned into her father's neighborhood. "I'm up for a promotion, you know. I should be at my office right now impressing my bosses with my work ethic and creative brilliance. Instead, I'm here."

Paul set the maze down on his knee, his gaze fixed on something outside his window. "You wouldn't need to worry about promotions if you'd just stayed here and worked for me."

She laughed a hard, bitter laugh. "No, I guess I wouldn't. But I never wanted to work for you. I never wanted to work in the hunting industry. And most of all I never wanted to work someplace where everyone would think I had the job just because I was the boss's kid. I wanted to prove to myself that I could make it on my own."

"Well, you did." But he didn't sound proud. He just sounded tired. "Congratulations."

She pulled into her father's driveway, and the memories of all the times she'd arrived at this house, homesick and lonely, during her childhood washed over her. She'd almost gotten past that, but her father's disapproval brought it all back. Her hands tightened reflexively on the steering wheel, and it was all she could do not to throw the car in reverse and flee to Chicago.

Besides, it wouldn't do any good. Her father was still in the car.

Neither of them moved. Finally, her father picked up the maze, tilting it randomly back and forth, the little ball inside making tiny clacking sounds as it bounced around its little plastic prison. Clearing his throat, he turned his face in her direction, although his eyes were fixed on the maze.

And then, without speaking, he got out of the car and closed the door softly behind him.

Greta watched him through the windshield as he made his way to the front door, greeting Polly with abrasive cheer as she bounced around him.

She wanted to leave. It would make everything easier—with her father, with her job, with Nick. In a few days she would be back to her old routine as if she'd never been gone.

As if none of this had ever happened.

But when she closed her eyes she could still see the scattering of jeweled water on that spiderweb and she could still feel the tickling scuttle of the crawfish over her palm and she could still smell that wild, secret scent that belonged only to Nick.

She slipped the keys from the ignition. Yes, it would be a lot easier if she left now. But when had she ever done something just because it was easier?

That said, she was too jangled up to sit on the couch watching some hunting show with her dad. Instead, she snapped Polly's leash on. "I'm taking the dog for a walk," she said.

He didn't look up. "Take a bag with you."

Like she hadn't learned that the first time.

She hadn't planned on visiting Pea, but her feet found their way there anyway. Pea was visible over the fence, her pink visor shading her face as she surveyed something Greta couldn't see.

"Hey," Greta said, leading Polly across Pea's yard to the gate. "Need some help?"

"Always," the older woman said, walking over to open the gate. Pushing back her visor with one gloved hand, she ran an assessing eye over Greta as she bent to let Polly off the leash. "Rough day?"

Greta fumbled with the leash. "What makes you think that?"

"No reason. It's just that your dad always shows up whenever he's had a bad day and needs to think things over." Instead of pushing further, she turned away, her flip-flops whispering against her sun-browned feet as she walked across the yard. "Why don't you go on in and grab yourself a pair of gloves?"

Just entering Pea's fairy cottage of a home did wonders for Greta's nerves. She breathed in the cool, sweet, honeysuckle-scented air, and the tension of the day began to seep out of her muscles.

She found the kneepad and floral gloves she'd worn last time and stepped back out into the rapidly mellowing sunlight. Once again, it was so easy to lose herself in the mindless work of identifying and pulling weeds. They were everywhere, the ground shaggy with them, and it felt good to set the world to order, even if it was just the tiny world of Pea's garden.

This was what she lived for—hard work, the sense of satisfaction she got from seeing a task through. The knowledge that she'd taken on something and *won*. That didn't make her "wound tight," as Nick had said. That made her successful.

But she couldn't expect him to understand that kind of drive. After all, he was happy working at a struggling company, maintaining the status quo, never pushing for growth.

And he had the nerve to think she was the one with issues.

Gritting her teeth, she ripped a plucky little thistle plant out of the ground with more force than necessary. Tiny clumps of dirt, shaken from between the plant's roots, spattered her bare arms.

"Everything okay?"

Greta sat back on her heels and looked up. Pea stood with the sun to her back, her face in shadow, her outline gilded by the weakening light. "You have to work hard to maintain all this, don't you?"

"I wouldn't quite call it work," the older woman said. "I enjoy being out here. Gives me a sense of purpose."

"Yes, exactly." Although it wasn't as hot as it had been earlier in the day, Greta could feel a thin sheen of sweat on her face. "A sense of purpose."

Pea leaned down to collect the growing pile of weeds beside Greta. "Are you interested in starting a garden?"

"What? Oh—no." She flexed her fingers inside the stiff fabric of the gloves. "I just got into an argument with…someone."

"I see." Straightening, Pea dropped the weeds into a large black plastic bag. "Would you like to talk about it?"

Greta cringed. She didn't want to relive her day at all, let alone tell this sweet old woman about it. "No."

"Okay." Pea hefted the bag and walked away, heading for a sunny corner of the garden.

Greta's shoulders slumped. She *did* want to talk about it. Not everything, of course. Just the part where Nick made her feel crazy. Pushing herself to her feet, she hurried after Pea.

"Do you think I'm wound tight?"

The older woman dropped the bag and turned to survey her, her lips clamped together. Finally, she said, "Do you think you're wound tight?"

"No." She stared down at her hands, still encased in the rough floral gloves. The fabric over one knuckle was starting to wear; she imagined it wouldn't be long before a hole appeared and the gloves would become useless. "Maybe."

"Ah."

"But the thing is, I *have* to be wound this tight. This is what it takes to make it in my business. If you don't work hard, if you allow yourself to slack off, you're not going to make it."

"I suppose."

"Look at this place." Greta spun in a slow circle, holding her arms out to encompass the entirety of the garden. "People see something perfect like this, and they think it just happens. But it doesn't. If you weren't out here every day weeding and pruning and fertilizing, what would happen? Chaos, right?"

She expected Pea to nod in agreement, but instead the older woman's eyes glinted with something that looked suspiciously like amusement. "Can I show you my favorite part of this garden?" she asked.

It felt like a trap, but Greta had no choice but to nod. She followed Pea over to the back fence, which separated Pea's lovely garden from a tangle of weeds beyond. "Here," Pea said. "This is my favorite part."

"The fence?" As symbols went, it made perfect sense. This was exactly what Greta had been trying to explain—the fence kept the flora of the outside world from encroaching on the well-maintained garden. It was, metaphorically speaking, Greta's video, a reminder of what happened when she failed to put in the necessary work, a stark barrier between success and failure.

But Pea chuckled. "No, not the fence." She gestured with one gloved hand to the plant life beyond. "That. That's my property, too, you know. And it's the very best part."

Greta stood on her tiptoes to get a better look at the mangy patch of overgrown vegetation. It didn't look like the best part of anyone's garden, let alone Pea's. It looked like an abandoned lot. "I don't understand."

"Look closer."

"I still don't—"

"Look." Pea rested her arms on the top of the fence. "It's alive."

It took several seconds for Greta to realize what Pea meant. And then she saw it. Where she initially saw only the straggly green shoots, she now saw the flowers: tiny purple ones that resembled chenille, lacy white ones, scrawny yellow ones. Nothing like Pea's magnificent garden. But while Pea's garden attracted its share of pollinators, this patch of overgrowth was literally crawling with bees, butterflies, and other insects.

It was, as Pea had said, alive.

"They're all native plants. I don't do a thing to care for them besides leave them alone. And this is what I get from it." Pea turned away from the fence. "I love my garden. But I have to remember that what I do here, I do for me. That, back there? That's what really matters to the world. And it takes no effort at all on my part."

Greta stood at the fence, staring at what she was sure were the full-grown versions of the weeds she'd just a few minutes ago been tugging from the ground. "Are you saying I shouldn't work so hard?"

"Nope," Pea called as she walked away, her flip-flops scuffing over the worn garden path. "I'm just showing you what I love best about my garden. You're the one trying to make that connection."

Obviously, the garden was a poor metaphor for the work she did in her career. Because while butterflies might like native weeds, no one wanted to hire someone who didn't work hard. And why would she want to work someplace where success wasn't valued? She wanted to be on a winning team, and that wasn't something she was going to apologize for.

But...what if the work she was doing wasn't the work she was supposed to be doing? She considered what Pea had said about her garden being what she did for herself. Was Greta's own work something she did for herself, and only herself? She took pride in it; she even enjoyed it. But was she doing anything truly worthwhile?

A smile tugged at her lips. Coming up with endless synonyms for convenient, or luxurious, or attractive, or whatever descriptive adjective she was using? No, probably not all that worthwhile.

She returned to her weeding, ignoring the ache that developed in her lower back as she eliminated the little invaders mechanically. When Pea offered her a glass of sweet tea, she glanced at the sun, glimmering in rose gold and violet clouds. "It's late," she said, snapping her fingers for Polly. "I should probably get back. Dad will be hungry."

"Tell him I said hi," Pea said as she opened the gate to let Greta out.

"I will." Greta made it halfway to the street before she turned to look back. Pea was still standing by the gate, the setting sun turning everything about her soft and pink. "And thank you."

It was silly to find meaning in a patch of weeds, she thought as she led Polly down the street. Seeing a bee perched on a thistle flower should not impact her life in the slightest. And it wouldn't. She knew who she was, and she couldn't just change that. But Pea had given her something to think about, and an hour in which to think.

And that was a start.

CHAPTER 20

$\mathcal{G}$reta did her best to avoid Nick at work the next day. It wasn't all that hard—he seemed every bit as interested in avoiding her.

And she had plenty to do without contending with him. The company's finances still didn't add up, the Stella proposal still needed some spark of inspiration, and her father still refused to cooperate with even the most basic medical advice, somehow managing to show up at the office every day.

By late afternoon, she was tired and headachy and frustrated, and it seemed like it didn't matter how hard she worked—she was destined to end up with a patch of weeds regardless.

"Greta?"

She looked up to find Auggie standing in her doorway, a manila folder in one hand, his other hand balled inside his pocket, jingling some coins together.

"Everything okay?"

"Of course." More jingling. "Well, not really. I just talked to two more retailers who want to cancel their programmed orders for third quarter."

She held out her hand for the file. Flipping it open, she found information on the two accounts in question. They were both good accounts, located in what Auggie had explained were good states for hunting. Losing them was going to hurt.

Not that this was an anomaly. From the reports she'd seen, King products were in fewer and fewer retailers every year.

"Thanks, Auggie," she said, picking up her pen and underlining a figure on the top sheet at random. It didn't help her feel any more in control of the situation, but she hoped it looked purposeful to Auggie.

Always look like you know what you're doing. That was a #girlboss tip.

After Auggie left, she pushed the file away, leaning back in her chair and turning so she could see out the window. Two days ago, when she'd been overwhelmed with everything, she'd found some comfort on the archery range outside.

Of course, it might not have been archery that had made her feel better. She had several warm memories of Nick's arms around her as he gently helped her draw the bow back.

He'd promised he would set the bow to a lower poundage, one she could draw by herself, and Greta wondered if she would find the same comfort on the range shooting without him.

Well, there was only one way to find out.

Downstairs, she grabbed the bow, some arrows, and a release aid, and headed outside.

The sun felt good after the air conditioning, and she tilted her chin up to let the late afternoon rays fall on her face. Then she stood at the firing line, walking herself through the steps Nick had laid out for her. He may have had her stand so close to the targets she couldn't miss, but what was the point in that? She wanted to practice from the proper firing line.

But after sending two arrows flying off in two very different directions, she thought better of it. She couldn't aim—her arrow kept jumping around whenever she tried to hold it still. Her palms felt sweaty, and she shifted her feet anxiously. Moving closer to the target, she turned it around so that the back was facing her. Now there was nothing to aim at.

No distractions.

It was incredibly freeing.

She drew back the bow, holding it as steady as she could while she settled into what Nick had called her anchor point. The lighter bow helped tremendously since she wasn't fighting to draw it back or struggling to stay at full draw. Instead, she felt open and strong. She felt like she could breathe.

When she was ready, she let go. The arrow jumped from her bow in one split second, hitting the target with a heavy thud.

She nocked a second arrow and came to full draw again. It was nice to have the steps to walk through, a checklist to keep her mind from wandering. She shot arrow after arrow, the tension leaving her body as the arrows leaped from her bowstring. She still had no idea how she was going to fix her father's company, or what she was going to submit to Tamsin for her proposal. And she had no idea how to deal with whatever had developed between her and Nick. But for now, all she needed to do was point the arrow at the target and let go.

* * *

HER FATHER HAD GOTTEN a ride home with Robbie by the time she finished shooting, and he was already home when she pulled up.

She was walking to her room to change when she heard him swear.

"Everything okay?" she asked, hurrying back to the living room.

"Yeah." He pulled a file from the camouflage backpack that he used instead of a briefcase and looked at it with a mulish expression. "It's just I thought I gave this to Nick and I guess I didn't."

Greta's pulse quickened. "Is it important?"

He glanced up at her. "Kind of. I guess it can wait 'til tomorrow. I just really wanted him to be able to review it tonight so we could discuss it in the morning."

Her keys were still in her hand. The smart thing to do would be to put her keys on her nightstand and change into yoga pants. Her father had just said the file could wait until tomorrow. It wasn't like Nick needed it right this minute.

But then she heard herself say, "I can run it over to his house if you'd like."

Which was most definitely not the smart thing to do. She didn't even know if he was home or not. Not that he needed to be home—she could just stick the folder in his mailbox or something. In fact, it would be far better if he were not home.

Paul frowned, but there was a glint in his eye that made her suddenly wary. "You don't have to do that."

That was that. She should agree with him, put the file in her car so she could give it to Nick when she saw him the next day at the office, and get started on the tofu and soba noodle dish she had planned for dinner.

What she said, however, was, "Oh, I don't mind."

Because, apparently, she was an idiot.

Paul smiled, capitulating way too easily. If he hadn't wanted her to go, he would have argued until he was blue in the face. But, no—he handed her the file and just said, "That would really help me out. Thank you."

"What are you going to do for dinner?"

"Don't worry about me. I'll be fine." He put one hand on her upper back and started walking to the front door, the gentle pressure all but forcing her to go along with him. Greta looked over her shoulder. And that's when she saw it.

A package of hot dogs peeking out from a plastic grocery bag.

"Did you and Robbie stop at the grocery store?"

"I don't know what you're talking about."

"Dad, you know you're not supposed—"

"I really appreciate this, honey," Paul said, giving her a gentle shove out the door. "Thanks."

Then he closed the door in her face, and she heard the snick of the lock.

It looked like dumb choices all around.

* * *

NICK LIVED a few miles outside of town in a sprawling subdivision Greta had never been to before. It was an older neighborhood, the houses an eclectic mix of Victorian and modern, with the slanting roofs and wood siding in green and blue that was so popular in the '70s and '80s. The lots were large, several acres at least, and a number of his neighbors had horses grazing in small, fenced pastures.

Not Nick, though. His grass was freshly mowed, but the yard had minimal landscaping. There were a few sad-looking rose bushes in the flowerbed in front of the house, but other than that, there wasn't much besides a huge expanse of grass.

Holding the file in front of her like a shield, Greta made her way along the front walk to the door. The house was bigger than she would have expected, maybe three or four bedrooms, two stories, with a big stone chimney rising from one side of the roof.

She lifted the brass knocker and rapped twice, then stood on the front porch, her heart pounding, wondering how long she needed to stand there before she could just do what was the wisest course of action, which was to leave.

But there were footsteps inside, and then the door opened. Nick just looked at her for a moment, not smiling. She held out the file. "My dad meant to give this to you today," she said. "I thought you might want it."

He took it from her without saying anything, his eyes dropping to the label on the file. For a moment, Greta was afraid that he was going to just thank her and close the door, leaving her standing on his front porch like an idiot. That would, after all, be the smart thing for him to do. But he seemed to be an idiot as well, because the next thing she knew he was opening the door a little wider.

Letting her in.

She stepped into a decent-sized foyer, the kind of foyer that used to be impressive before McMansions decreed a foyer should have the highest ceiling in the house. The walls of the foyer were, surprisingly, painted teal, and from what she could see of the adjacent living room, its walls were painted a bright pumpkin orange. Not what she had expected from Nick.

"Thanks for bringing this over." He hesitated before he seemed to come to a decision. "You want something to drink?" He walked past her through a door to her left, and she followed him into a spacious kitchen. The walls here were a cheery yellow, and the cabinets, which formed a U-shape on the left side of the room, were dark and heavy, adorned with tarnished brass handles. The white laminate counter held only a coffee maker and a toaster. To the right side of the room there was an eating area that looked over the backyard through a bay window. A small round oak table was surrounded by four chairs, only three of which matched.

Nick opened the refrigerator. "I've got beer. And water. Milk, if you don't mind living dangerously." He closed the fridge. "Or I could make coffee if you'd like some."

"Water's fine, thank you."

There were no personal touches in the room. No framed prints on the wall, no family photos, not even a magnet on the fridge. Against that stark backdrop, the curtains on the bay window—creamy sheers embroidered with delicate pink rose-buds—looked incredibly out of place.

It felt like Nick had simply moved into someone else's aban-doned house.

He handed her a glass of water and, grabbing a beer for himself, said, "We can sit in the living room, if you'd like."

Her feet clicked over the hardwood floors as she took in the living room, which was also empty of anything that looked remotely like it belonged to Nick. Against one of the bold orange walls was a white couch, its cushions so perfectly straight that Greta knew at once no one ever used it. Two chairs, upholstered in robin's egg blue, were situated facing the couch in a neat conversational group. Nick settled on the couch, one arm slung over its back. "What are you doing here, Greta?"

She felt awkward standing there, her water glass slowly dripping condensation onto her hand, so she sat down in one of the chairs and took a long sip. "I told you. I brought you that file."

"So you said."

She glanced at the door. If she'd thought this was a bad idea before she left her father's house, she now knew exactly what a terrible idea it was. She needed to leave. This was just a dedicated manager making sure her employee had everything he needed. It had nothing to do with what happened the day before in the treehouse.

But Nick was watching her, his face still. Swallowing hard, she said, "The truth is, I've been thinking."

His eyes were suddenly watchful. "Yeah?"

"And…and I don't want to anymore."

"Don't want to what?"

"Think."

Carefully, he set his beer down on a pale yellow end table. His eyes were gleaming silver, the shadows over his lean cheeks making him look dangerous, like the predator he was. "What don't you want to think about, Greta?"

Anything. Everything. "Whatever…whatever this is," she said as he stood, easing closer, inch by inch, those smoky eyes fixed on her face.

He knelt down before her, just inches away, so close she could feel the heat rolling off his body. "I'm going to need something more official than that."

She knew what he was asking for. Her voice dropped to a whisper. "I want this." He reached out, wrapping his hands around her upper arms, stroking the sensitive skin with his thumbs.

"Be more specific."

She closed her eyes. "I want you."

That was all it took. She felt Nick's lips roll over hers, a gossamer whisper of a kiss, and something inside of her stirred, something long dormant, and suddenly everything seemed right. Raising one hand, she threaded her fingers though his hair. Then she let her fingers trace over the back of his neck.

He made a low sound deep in his throat and pulled her closer, his kiss suddenly hard and demanding, his lips tasting of citrus-spiked beer. Moving her hands down to his waist, she slipped them under his shirt and then slid them back up again, taking her time, reveling in the hard ridges of his abdominal muscles, the planes of his chest beneath a light covering of chest hair.

His mouth moved down the column of her throat as his fingers found the buttons of her blouse. One by one he flicked them open, spreading the panels of her shirt so that it framed her breasts, covered only by her shell-pink bra.

He slid his thumb inside her bra, brushing against her nipple and making her cry out. His agile thumb made another sweep, circling with the lightest possible touch. Then again. And again. And then he was pushing aside the thin fabric of her bra, laying her breast bare for his mouth. She sucked in her breath and plunged her fingers into his hair, pulling him closer as he worked his magic on first one breast and then the other.

And just when she was sure she couldn't take another moment of that slow, sweet torture, he slid his hands under her skirt, tracing them up her thighs and taking her skirt with them. He hooked the waist of her pale pink panties, lifting her so he could slide them down, over her thighs, over her calves, over her ankles. Then he settled between her thighs.

His fingers parted the slick flesh at the apex of her thighs, stroking her, finding the secret places that made the fire burn even hotter. She felt the slow slide of his finger inside her, and then there was a delicious warmth on the skin of her inner thigh just above her knee. His mouth, she realized, tasting the taut skin there, his tongue making small circles on her already inflamed flesh. His mouth crept ever higher while his hands kept exploring, his fingers now wet and honeyed. She shivered as his lips touched a spot at her upper thigh just as his thumb stroked over the very center of her. Her eyes drifted shut as his mouth settled over the place where his thumb had just been. Teasing. Suckling.

Torturing.

And with one last skillful flick of his tongue, he sent her over the edge.

She cried out, the stars in front of her closed eyelids scattering any remaining ability to think. Now all she wanted was Nick, on her, inside her, all over her. She was speaking, she realized, begging him, pleading with him, tugging at him to cover her, to slide inside her, to make love to her.

And there was Nick, taking his own sweet time, his face hard-edged with desire, enjoying the words that rose, unbidden, to her lips. He was still fully dressed, while she was in a decided state of disarray, and she knew her face was flushed from what he'd just done. He was breathing hard but still very much in control, and, as he rose to his feet, it looked like he thought this might be a bad idea.

But just for tonight, thinking was bad. Tonight, there was no room for second thoughts. Tonight was all about feeling. And since Greta had managed to figure that out so well, perhaps it was time for her to teach Nick that.

She pulled herself together as best she could, smoothing her skirt down so that it covered her to mid-thigh. She left her shirt gaping open, though, as she liked the way Nick's gaze kept dropping to her exposed breasts. Then she hooked one finger under his belt and pulled him closer. She undid his belt, letting the two ends dangle against his hips, and then unbuttoned his jeans. She heard him let out a breath in a low hiss as she pulled down his zipper and her fingers closed around the hot, hard length of him.

And then he groaned as she took him into her mouth.

It was payback time for all the torture and torment he'd put her through. She stroked her tongue over him, loving him with her mouth while he gripped her shoulders hard, swaying with the effort of remaining upright under her assault.

She felt him tense, his whole body going rigid, and then he pulled away from her. "Not yet," he whispered, scooping her up in one easy movement and laying her down on the couch. He came down on top of her, his mouth leaving a trail of fire down her neck. His hands found the growing ache between her thighs and then he slid inside her, burying himself deeply in her, making her gasp at the sudden fullness.

He dropped soft little kisses on her jaw, her cheek, her temples, murmuring words she couldn't quite understand into her hair. She squirmed against him, and he froze, the limits of his control reached. With a muffled curse, he pressed his face into the curve between her shoulder and throat, thrusting into her over and over again, taking them both to the edge of the cliff.

And then over it.

Greta lay with her heart pounding, Nick's weight pressing her into the couch cushions, her limbs loose and heavy. It felt good to have his body over hers. It felt, in fact, right.

Then he lifted his head and looked down at her, his steely eyes cool and assessing, and, despite her best efforts, she started thinking again. Thinking about all the reasons why she shouldn't get involved with anyone at the moment, let alone Nick. Thinking about how hard it was going to be to say goodbye to him when it came time to go back to Chicago. Thinking about all the ripples in her life this one moment of not thinking was going to leave her with.

He was thinking again, too. She could see it in the way his face slowly shuttered, feel it in the coolness that settled over her bare skin as he pulled away from her, rolling onto his side. He was still there, his lips quirked in a half-smile, one hand sliding back and forth over her hip. But at the same time he was gone.

She should get dressed. She should head home. Her father was probably wondering where she was, might even have called while she was…indisposed.

That, she realized, was what Nick was waiting for her to do. To get up and walk out.

And that was what she was going to do. Eventually.

Because tonight she was here, in Nick's house, on Nick's couch, in Nick's arms, and tonight, at least for a little while, she was going to enjoy it.

In for a penny, in for a pound.

She stretched lazily, relishing the way Nick's hand tightened on her hip. Then she looked up at him through her lashes. "So," she said. "Are you going to show me the rest of your house?"

* * *

LATER, when Nick had given her a very, *very* thorough tour of his master bedroom, Greta laid her cheek on Nick's bare chest and gazed around her. The bedroom was pink. Not one of those shades of white that takes on a pinkish cast in some lights—it was pink. Not a bright pink or a pale pink, but something in between. A shade of pink that reminded her of the plastic baby doll furniture she used to see in toy stores when she was a child.

Nick's eyes were closed, but even so he knew exactly what she was thinking. "I didn't choose the paint color," he said.

"I assumed that." She thought of his ex-wife, who must have

loved color. The yellow kitchen, the teal foyer, the orange family room. "So why don't you change it?"

He shrugged. "There hasn't been a need to change it."

"Not even that you don't like it?"

At that he opened one eye and grinned. "What makes you think I don't like it?"

She lifted her head, waving one hand at the closest wall. "You like this color?"

"Just because I'm a guy doesn't mean I can't like pink. Isn't that what all you feminists are always saying?"

"Oh, yes. I believe that's covered in the second chapter of the feminist handbook."

"I'm glad to see you received a handbook."

"They handed them out in college." She lowered her head again, feeling the gentle rise and fall of his chest as he breathed. "Seriously, though, you never wanted to repaint?"

"Painting is a lot of work. Didn't seem to be worth it just because it's not the color I would have chosen."

"Fair enough. But what about the curtains?" Her gaze went to the ruffled pink curtains covering the bedroom windows. They might have been bridesmaid dresses in a former life.

Another shrug. "Just not something I pay much attention to."

She pushed herself to a sitting position. Nick opened his eyes, letting his gaze linger on her bare breasts. "It just seems like this whole house—"

Before she could finish, he pounced on her, rolling her over onto her back and looking down at her with a wolfish smile. "You're awfully worried about how my house is decorated. Maybe you need a distraction."

His fingers trailed up the curved side of one breast, and Greta felt a thrill shoot through her. Not that he needed to know that's how he affected her. "I don't know," she said, doing her best to look thoughtful. "That pink is awfully distracting."

"Then I'd better make it a good distraction," he said, lowering his mouth to the underside of her jaw.

And he did.

* * *

THE SUN SET, but they didn't get up to turn on a light. Instead, Greta lay snuggled against Nick's side in the dark bedroom. Under her cheek the skin of his shoulder felt smooth, his chest under her hand textured with hair.

But it was the way he smelled that made her feel like home. It was that wild, outdoorsy smell, like the woods and an icy mountain stream and a sweet, sun-bathed hayfield all at one time.

This was what she was going to miss most. Oh, she'd miss the way his eyes went from cold steel to lightning hot depending on his mood, and she'd miss that rough-timbered voice that she could practically feel reverberating in her chest. And his fingers. She'd definitely miss those.

But the way he smelled was something she knew she'd never find anywhere else. No cologne manufacturer could ever replicate the way he smelled, not in a million years. She wished she could bottle it up and keep some for later.

Her thumb rubbed over one of his nipples, and she felt the muscles beneath his skin tense up. He began making languid circles on her back, on her hip, and the warmth she always felt at his touch pulsed through her.

The way he smelled...She would know that smell anywhere, she realized.

She sat bolt upright.

"Greta?" Nick's voice was even and soothing, like he was trying to comfort a frightened horse. "You okay?"

"Yeah." She pressed her hands together, trying to tamp down her growing excitement. "I'm fine, but I need to go."

Nick was still stretched out on the bed, his impressive body completely naked, and it was clear that he had other ideas for what they should do next. Sparing him a quick look of regret— why did she have to start thinking again *now*?—she pushed aside the sheets and started looking around on the floor for her clothes. Her skirt was hopelessly crumpled, and she couldn't find her underwear anywhere.

"Wait," Nick said, sitting up. "You're really leaving?"

"Yes." She dropped to her knees, crawling over the floor, feeling for her lost underwear with her hands. "Sorry. It's really important."

"It must be." Nick's tone was dry.

She searched around under the bed, lying flat on her stomach so she could reach as far as possible. "I think if this works out, you're going to be pretty happy."

"I think I would have been pretty happy with what I had planned for the next ten minutes."

She lifted her head to grin at him through the darkness. "Ten minutes, huh? Wow, that sounds really enticing."

"Ten minutes was just what I had planned for your left breast."

Both of her breasts tightened at that. "Save it for next time, cowboy."

"Ah. You're assuming there will be a next time."

This was where she was supposed to say that, sadly, no, there would not be a next time. They'd had one beautiful night, but they both knew that it couldn't last. They were two very different people. They didn't even live in the same timezone.

But what she heard herself saying instead was, "Maybe. If you play your cards right."

He swung his legs off the bed. With the dim light coming from the window behind him, she couldn't make out his expression, but his entire body radiated a tense stillness. "Greta…"

But she didn't want to talk about the realities of their situation, and whatever he was going to say looked to have "cold, hard truth" written all over it. "I just really need to find my underwear at the moment."

"Huh." He was quiet for a long minute. "You know, we could turn on a light."

"Oh." She sat back on her heels. "That would help."

"Yeah." He stood, opening the dresser and taking something out—boxers, she realized as he stepped into them. "Course, it would help more if your underwear were in this room."

That's when she remembered Nick pulling her underwear off while she was in the chair downstairs. "You sure waited long enough to tell me that."

He flipped on the light, and she sucked in her breath as the full impact of his boxer-clad body hit her. He was lean and well muscled, his skin bronzed and taut, and he surveyed her with a hint of amusement in his flinty eyes. She wanted to run her hands all over him. But, no. She had to get to Walmart.

And wasn't that a first—her running out on a gorgeous man because she needed to go to Walmart.

She straightened out her skirt as best she could. "I'll see you tomorrow at work?" she said, hating the way it came out as a question.

"You could stay," he said, hands on his hips.

"No," she said, and she couldn't help the little smile playing about her lips. "Being with you has made me realize I really need to buy some deer pee."

And then she padded downstairs to find her underwear, leaving Nick standing there speechless.

Just as she was heading for the front door, keys in hand, she heard him say from upstairs, "What?"

CHAPTER 21

*B*en called mid-morning. "Hey," he said. "Daphne Ness called me. She wants to know if you've seen her ad proposal for *Outdoor Insider*. Have you had a chance to look at it yet?"

"No, not yet." He tried to focus on the numbers of his computer screen, but he was having trouble banishing the image of Greta's pleasure-flushed cheeks and kiss-swollen lips from his mind.

"Well, look at it soon. You know Daphne. She's going to keep pushing for an answer until she gets one."

"I'll look at it this afternoon," he said. "Of course, I'll need to run it by Greta first."

And didn't that have the possibility of getting interesting? He imagined locking the door of her office, sweeping that notebook of hers from her desk to place her on it, parting her thighs as he pushed up her skirt...

"Greta, huh?" There was something in Ben's voice that made Nick afraid he'd just described that fantasy aloud. "I heard you had a good night last night."

He broke out in a cold sweat. Had Greta talked to Ben about

what happened last night? But, no—why would she do that? "What makes you think that?" he asked, trying to sound cool.

"A little bird told me you had a visitor."

"And what little bird might that be?"

Ben chuckled. "All right, fine. Auggie said he drove by your place on his way home." There was only one plausible explanation for why Auggie would pass Nick's place on his way home, and her name was Renee Worth, a single mother of three who lived two doors down. "I guess there was a car parked in the driveway. A Civic."

Although Ben couldn't see him, Nick shrugged. "She came over to drop off a file I needed. That's all."

"Right. Because I'm sure it wasn't possible to email said file."

"It was important, and I needed it right away." But Ben had a point, and Nick smiled into the phone. She probably could have emailed the information to him, but instead she'd driven it over herself. It was a warming thought.

But then he remembered that Greta would be heading back to Chicago in a few weeks. She might have enjoyed last night, but she wasn't about to sacrifice everything she'd worked for. "Look, it's complicated," he said, drumming his fingers on his desk.

"Maybe it's not as complicated as you think it is."

"And maybe it is." Nick dug the *Outdoor Insider* ad proposal out from a stack of paper on his desk and looked it over. "I'll get back to you on the proposal this afternoon."

He set his phone down. He wasn't sure how Greta was feeling this morning, or if she wanted to see him. But the proposal gave him as good an excuse as any to see her.

She was in her office, smiling and satisfied. She looked exactly like what any man would want his woman to look like the morning after.

Unfortunately, Nick got the feeling that her satisfied smile was due more to the clear plastic cups of deer urine on her desk than from anything he'd done the night before.

Which didn't exactly say much about his performance.

She glanced up, her smile turning uncertain when she saw him. "Hi," she said.

"Hey." He nodded at the cups in front of her. "Is this why you left last night?"

She beckoned him closer. "Yes. Come smell."

"Come...smell?" He approached haltingly, wondering if perhaps this was what happened to Greta after sex.

"Yes." Picking up the first cup, she offered it to him. "This is our Royal Doe in Heat. Dad had a bottle in the freezer at home." She sat back in her chair. "And let me tell you how delighted I was to learn I was storing my frozen edamame next to Dad's deer pee."

He held up a hand to decline the cup. "I'm familiar with Royal Doe."

"Yes, well." She lifted another cup, this one full of a much darker liquid. "Now, this is one of our competitors' hot doe urines."

Even from a distance, he could detect the teeth-clenching scent of ammonia. "Okay, so they're different. So what?"

"So, if you can tell the difference, a deer most definitely can. This one—" she pointed at the cup of Royal Hot Doe—"is dated to ensure consumers know when the urine they're buying was bottled. They know how fresh it is. This other urine could be from a previous season. It's not as fresh, which is why it smells so strong."

"Right." He settled into the chair opposite her, stretching his legs out and crossing one ankle over the other. "We stress the fact that our bottles are all dated in our advertising. I think most people just assume it's kind of a gimmick. It's hard to understand unless you actually see the difference for yourself."

"I'm glad you said that." Her smile turned almost smug. "Have you ever heard of experiential marketing?"

"Not really."

"We do some experiential marketing at the Prescott Agency. It's where you create an experience that engages your target audience directly. You get consumers to participate. I thought we could create something like that for King Lures. Something that gets people involved with the brand while demonstrating the difference between King's products and other, inferior urines."

Nick sat up straighter. "We don't have a very big marketing budget left at the moment. And we don't have a ton of time to right this ship."

"I know." She tapped her pen against a page in her open notebook. "I've been thinking of how we could do this quickly and cheaply. I'd like to introduce King Lures to an entirely new audience, have some new conversations."

He wasn't sure where this was going, but the gleam in her dark eyes had a prickle of excitement running down his spine—and not just because it reminded him of how she'd looked up at him when he was on top of her last night. "What exactly are you proposing?"

"There's a farmer's market in Louisville that has some space available. We could do it almost like a game show." Her eyes took on a faraway look as she thought. "We ask people if they can pick out the freshest deer urine—a smell test, if you will—and give them prizes when they get it right. Gift certificates—to local businesses, maybe. Do we have any King Lures branded items? Hats, shirts, decals?"

"We have some left over from the trade show we did in January."

"Ooh—we'll get a prize wheel." Bending her head, she started taking notes, her pen moving over the paper in rapid jerks. "Hopefully we can get some of it on video to post on Facebook and Twitter. That will let us reach the rest of our consumer base. We just need a catchy name." The pen jiggled in her hand. "What if we call it Whiz Wiz?"

"I don't know about—"

"People like catchy names."

He studied her. She had dark circles under her eyes, and he wondered what exactly she'd done after she left his house the night before. Given the evidence before him, she'd bought deer pee from a few rival companies, thawed out a bottle of Royal Doe in Heat, and spent a good amount of time coming up with some outlandish idea to make urban residents smell deer urine.

And while she'd been doing that, he'd gone to bed.

She didn't even really work for King, and still she was the one doing all the work. Sure, he and Paul and Auggie were doing their best to keep the company afloat. But Greta was willing to go a step beyond that, pushing the envelope to try something different.

If she said people like catchy names, that's what they were going to go with.

"All right, then. I think it's a good idea."

She dropped her pen. It hit her notebook with a surprisingly heavy thud. "I'm sorry. What was that?"

She'd been expecting him to put up more of an argument, he realized. He couldn't blame her—he'd objected to everything she'd come up with so far. "I said, it's a good idea."

"I don't think I've ever heard you say those words to me before."

"There's a first time for everything." He steepled his fingers. "Now, since we're doing it as a game show, I assume we'll get a couple attractive female assistants to help out?" He couldn't help it. As much as he liked making her smile, he also liked that obstinate expression she got when he was being difficult. "What? You saw Ben's ads. People like looking at attractive women. Maybe they could wear camouflage bikinis, something like that?"

Her eyes narrowed. "We don't have the budget to hire anyone."

"No?" He rested his chin on his knuckles and regarded her

thoughtfully. "Would it be possible to convince you to wear a camouflage bikini?"

"No one is wearing a camouflage bikini." She stood, gathering her notebook and pen. "Let's loop Auggie in. I'd like to hear his thoughts."

But Nick stopped her. Lowering his voice, he said, "Spoiler alert: he's going to be all for you wearing a bikini of any kind." He touched the pad of his thumb to her bottom lip, watching her eyes darken and melt as he slowly traced the seductive curve of her mouth. Her lips parted on a soft sigh. And then, even though they were in her office and anyone—even her father—could come along at any moment, he lowered his head and kissed her, slowly, thoroughly, gathering her gently against him. The notebook slipped from her hands and hit the floor between them.

He wanted her, yes, but more than that he wanted just this: the chance to feel her tremble in his arms, to taste her sweet mouth, to believe, just for a moment, that they were different people, people who could make the most of whatever was developing between them.

But they weren't. With great effort, he managed to raise his head, although his arms were still around her. She laid her cheek against his chest.

"Nick?" she said softly.

"Yes?"

"No bikinis."

With a chuckle, he bent to retrieve her notebook.

* * *

IT WAS A LONG DAY, filled with meetings and phone calls and calculations. Paul showed up about noon, having gotten a ride from a neighbor. Greta was afraid that he'd be skeptical of the idea—she could practically hear him saying, "In all the years I've been doing this, I've never had to do something silly like this."

But he merely listened as she outlined the idea, nodding and asking questions. When she was finished, he looked at her for several seconds without speaking, and she thought he had something he wanted to tell her. But then, with a slight shake of his head, he just said, "I think we should do it."

And that was that.

By the time she was in her car driving back to her father's house, she was mentally exhausted. But it was the good kind of mentally exhausted, the way she used to feel after a long day of working on a campaign for a client.

It was strange to realize it had been a long time since she'd felt that way. Her work at Prescott had become far less about delivering a really amazing campaign to the client and more about winning, about being the best. About putting in more hours and doing more work than anyone else. She hadn't had fun at work in a very long time.

It was even stranger to realize that spending a day talking about deer urine and hashing out the details had been fun. Actually fun.

Paul was already home when she walked into the house, sprawled out in his chair, the quilt wrapped around him. The bear looming in the corner no longer startled her. In fact, she was starting to kind of like him just a little bit. If it didn't involve killing an animal, she might have wanted one for her apartment in Chicago. No one was going to casually break into a house with an enormous brown bear rising up from behind a piece of furniture.

As usual, it was freezing in the house, and goosebumps broke out over Greta's bare upper arms. "Dad, this can't be good for you," she said, rubbing her arms vigorously to keep warm.

"I can't sleep if it's hot," he said without looking away from the TV. "And not sleeping can't be good for me, either."

There wasn't much she could say to that, but she did stop in front of the thermostat and raise the temperature a couple of degrees. "I saw that," her father said.

"I wasn't trying to hide it." She leaned one shoulder against the wall and studied her father. His color was better, but he still didn't look like the Paul King she remembered from her childhood. He looked smaller. More vulnerable, even if she couldn't put her finger on exactly why. "Hey, Dad, do you remember that ballet performance you came to?"

He briefly tore his eyes from the game show he was watching. "What ballet performance?"

"It was my junior year, remember? You came up to watch me dance." She hadn't really expected him to come, even though he'd told her mother he planned on it weeks in advance. It wouldn't have been the first time something more important came up.

"Oh, yeah. That one." He pushed the quilt from his shoulders. "You did great. Can you turn up the AC? It's getting hot again."

The AC had just shut off moments earlier. "I didn't do great, Dad. I fell."

"Yeah, you had a rocky start. But after that you did great."

After that...

She didn't remember anything after the fall. Her mother had stopped filming then, so that was where her video ended. She remembered the sickening realization that her footing was off, her balance all wrong, the world tilting around her. She remembered the sharp intake of breath that was the audience's collective response. She remembered the hot light washing over her, ensuring that no one missed the moment. And then...nothing. Not until after everything was over, when her mother let her have it in a whispery hiss, so quiet none of the other parents would hear, while Don stood off to the side and slipped his business card to some older gentleman in an Armani suit.

In the middle of it all, Paul King had appeared. She hadn't known he had actually come, not until the moment he came striding through the crowd toward her, somehow making everything worse. That he was there at all, stiff and awkward and so out of place even in his perfectly normal, perfectly non-camouflage navy blue sweater. That his presence made her mother's nerves go so taut Greta could practically hear them twanging. That he had driven all that way—finally—just to watch that miserable performance.

That she had let down not only her mother and Don, but her father too.

He stood there, gazing down at her for a moment before nodding curtly. "Good job, kid." And then he turned and walked out.

Greta had assumed he was being sarcastic, and that had rankled her more than her mother's open fuming. But now, looking at him, she wondered if maybe she'd gotten it wrong.

"What happened after I fell?"

He stared at her blankly. "You got back up, you shook yourself off, and you went right on dancing." He looked back at the TV, but a smile spread from his mouth to his eyes, and Greta was surprised by the pride in his voice when he added, "You always did have grit."

Grit. That was what he'd seen on the stage that day. "Mom was furious," she said softly.

"Well, yeah." Now her father's smile turned into a full-blown grin. "That was just icing on the cake."

It was Greta's turn to smile, but before she could say anything, her cell phone rang. Her heart fluttered as she saw the call was from Nick. Glancing up at her father, she said, "I need to take this. Give me a minute?"

"Sure." He waved his hand to indicate she should take her time as he turned his attention back to the TV.

Wistfulness curled inside her. She wanted to finish this conversation. It felt like something important was happening. But there would be time for that later.

She and Nick had anything but time.

"Hey," she said, closing her bedroom door behind her as she answered the phone.

"Hi." There was a short pause. "Listen, I was thinking about grabbing some dinner over at Tracks. I thought you might like to join me. I had a couple thoughts about the campaign I'd like to run by you."

Not a date. More like two coworkers having dinner after work. Practically a business meeting.

Between two people who'd had sex the night before.

"Sure. Sounds like fun," she said. She glanced in the mirror over the dresser, smoothing back a stray lock of hair.

"Great. I'll pick you up. Twenty minutes work for you?"

"That would be great."

After she got off the phone, she moved to her closet to figure out what to wear. She wanted to look date-like enough that Nick wouldn't think she hadn't made any effort, but not so date-like that he thought she'd put in too much effort.

Sadly, even Pinterest wasn't much help.

In the end, she turned once again to the clothes Helen had left, choosing a short-sleeved top crafted so that it shifted from dusky red to almost black depending on the light and a pair of denim capri pants that had, as Helen would say, a bit of stretch. Then she went to the living room to tell Paul he was on his own for dinner.

* * *

WHEN NICK GOT to Paul's house, he stood awkwardly in front of the door for several moments, unsure of what to do. He hadn't knocked on Paul's door in years. They'd gotten to the point where Paul considered him family, and family never has to knock.

But Nick wasn't going over just to shoot the breeze with Paul. He wasn't going to be watching a game or grilling hot dogs or arguing about whether a head shot was the only ethical shot on a wild turkey.

He was going to pick up Paul's daughter. Who, if things went well, he hoped to be having sex with later on.

From that perspective, knocking and waiting to be let in seemed like the polite thing to do.

But Paul would be weirded out if Nick knocked, and as much as Nick enjoyed being with Greta, he also wanted to preserve his easy relationship with Paul. So, taking a deep breath, he grabbed the doorknob and let himself in.

Paul was watching TV alone in the living room. He gave Nick an absent-minded smile, his eyes glued to the television set, where a woman in a Christmas sweater was nervously answering a question that could win her a quarter of a million dollars. Nick waited, wincing as the woman guessed that the animal pictured on the screen—a Cape buffalo—was a wildebeest.

"You need something, Nick?" Paul asked. On screen, the studio audience groaned as the woman's guess was revealed to be incorrect.

"I just came to get Greta. I thought she might like to get out of the house for a little bit, maybe grab a bite at Tracks." He tried to keep his tone casual. He'd considered taking her somewhere nicer, but the thought of having to tell Paul he was taking his daughter to anything more formal than Tracks made his palms sweat.

Paul nodded, but his gaze turned assessing. After what seemed like an eternity, he said, "Well, I hope you two have fun."

Nick had known Paul for more than half his life, and the two of them had always understood each other. Now, Nick realized that Paul was giving him his blessing to take Greta out, and the realization humbled him. He certainly didn't have noble intentions when it came to Paul's daughter, at least not given the realities of their relationship—or non-relationship, as the case may be. Paul had to know that whatever went on between Nick and

Greta was only short-term. But he relaxed back against his chair and said, "Want a beer?"

"No, I'm good." Nick sat down on the couch and watched as a new contestant struggled to come up with the year of the Louisiana Purchase. "Think this experiential marketing thing is going to make a big difference?"

Paul's mouth curved in a faint smile. "Can't hurt, can it?"

Just then, Greta walked into the room, her hair loose around her shoulders, her dark eyes sparkling. "Hey." Then, to Paul she added, "There are falafels in the fridge for you to reheat."

"Can't wait to try those." Paul gave Nick a long-suffering look.

"I'd better not find any more hot dog wrappers in the trash when I get home."

"Take out the trash. Got it."

Greta shook her head. "I don't know why I'm so worried about keeping you alive when you don't seem to care much."

But Paul just smiled. "Life just doesn't mean as much if you can only eat falafels."

* * *

"ARE you making him eat healthier because of the heart attack, or would you expect him to eat like that anyway?" Nick asked in the car.

Greta fiddled with her seatbelt, undoing a twist before buckling it. "What do you mean?"

"If he hadn't had a heart attack and you were staying with him for awhile, would you try to improve his diet?"

"I wouldn't be staying here for awhile if he hadn't had a heart attack."

"I know." It was weird to him that she had a loving father she never came to visit, but that wasn't what he was worried about at the moment. He couldn't imagine a life eating the kinds of food Greta preferred, either. And although he knew there was no future with her, it still bothered him that in a Venn diagram of foods they both liked, there wouldn't be very many items in the middle. "I just mean, is this how you would normally cook? Falafels?"

She gave him an unreadable look. "Sure. Why not?"

Right. Why not?

Suddenly, Tracks seemed like a terrible idea.

But Greta reviewed the menu Brenda handed her (with a pointed—but fortunately silent—look at Nick) without complaint. Then she closed her menu and settled against the back of the booth. "Why are you looking at me like that?" she asked him.

"I wasn't sure you were going to find something you could eat here."

At that she grinned. "Nick, I've been a vegetarian for half my life. You think I haven't had to figure out how to navigate a meat-eater's world by now? This may be my first time eating at Tracks, but I've eaten in a hundred places just like this one."

Of course she had. "Sorry. It's just Paul has been telling me about the kind of food you make him eat and…"

"And it sounds awful?" she finished for him. She unrolled the napkin from her silverware and spread it over her lap. "You know, my father was always complaining about what a picky eater I was when I was little. Now I eat a ton of things he won't even try, but he would blow up if I ever called him a picky eater. Makes me think that a 'picky eater' is just someone who doesn't like the food you're used to."

Brenda stopped by, order pad in hand, smiling in what Nick knew was her attempt to look like a real waitress. It was all for Greta's benefit; he'd seen her acting that way in front of strangers before. "Good evening," she said. "What can I get for you folks?"

"Relax, Brenda. This is Paul King's daughter, and she's been here once before, so she already knows all about what a dump this place is."

"Considering what a dump it is, you sure do come here often."

"I only come here for the service."

That forced a gravelly laugh out of her. "You gonna order, or am I going to have to guess at what you want tonight?"

Greta ordered a salad. Nick assumed she would have a number of special requests—no croutons, extra tomatoes, substitute avocado for the cheese, dressing on the side. That was the sort of thing Lauren would have done. But Greta just ordered and handed her menu back to Brenda. "Thank you," she said with a smile.

Brenda turned to Nick. "She's far too pretty to be with you. What's going on here?"

"Oh, I don't know," Greta said, looking at Nick warmly. "I think Nick is awfully pretty himself."

"Exactly." Brenda made another note on her pad. "He usually doesn't like to compete with his dates. Makes him self-conscious to date a woman prettier than he is."

"I like her," Greta said to Nick as Brenda walked off. "She really has you pegged."

"You only think that because she called you pretty."

"She called you pretty, too," Greta pointed out.

"Hey, Nick." He looked up to find Auggie approaching the booth. "I thought you said you had plans to—Oh." He stopped short when he realized Greta was there too. "Sorry. Didn't mean to interrupt. I just had a couple thoughts about this new campaign I wanted to go over with you."

Greta hesitated. And then she slid over in the booth, making room for Auggie beside her. "Why don't you join us? We can talk about it over dinner."

Auggie shot Nick a cautious glance. Nick shrugged. Sure, he'd envisioned a more intimate meal with Greta, but he should have known better than to bring her to Tracks for that. To get away from everyone he knew, he should have taken her somewhere outside of Bartlett.

By the time Brenda brought food for the three of them, they'd reviewed some additional details for the Whiz Wiz event and had moved on to discussing football, which Greta was surprisingly well versed in. "We have a fantasy football pool at work," she said. She speared a piece of lettuce with her fork and brought it to her lips. "I don't like to lose," she added before taking the lettuce between her teeth.

"What a surprise."

Nick was glad that Auggie was there because it gave him the opportunity to watch her eat, something that he was quickly discovering he enjoyed very much. He liked the way her mouth closed over her fork. He liked the way she held her fork as she cut her salad into smaller, more manageable pieces. He liked the way she gestured with her silverware as she talked.

Basically, if she was doing something with her hands or mouth, he liked watching it.

The other thing he noticed about the way Greta ate was that she really seemed to enjoy her food. There was nothing mechanical about the way she ate. Instead she savored every bite she put into her mouth—especially the French fries she stole from his plate.

He didn't want to keep comparing Greta to Lauren, although they had seemed so similar at first that it was impossible not to. But by the time Brenda dropped off their check, he realized that there was a very important difference between the two women. Lauren had never once seemed to belong in Bartlett. Greta didn't seem like she should fit in, either, and yet there she was, joking around with Brenda and teasing Auggie while wolfing down a Tracks salad like it was something from a Michelin-rated restaurant.

And maybe, just maybe, that meant something.

* * *

IT WAS A GOOD DINNER, Greta thought as they left Tracks. They'd gotten a lot of work done. So much work, in fact, that they certainly didn't need to extend the evening by driving back to Nick's house.

And yet that was exactly what they did.

Nick poured two glasses of wine, something sweet and dark that he said came from a local winery, and led her out the back-door onto a screened-in porch. The floor was tile, and the porch had a wrought-iron table with four chairs beneath a lazily spinning ceiling fan. The evenings were starting to get cool, but the fan still felt good on her overheated skin. Nick hadn't bothered turning on the light, and so they sat in the dim half-light that came through the backdoor.

The night air was alive with sounds. There was the steady chirp of crickets, the raspy song of the katydids, and the occasional deep croak of a bullfrog. And then in the distance came the eerie wail of a lone coyote, followed by a chuckling sound that gave her goosebumps.

"Just more coyotes," Nick said. "They make a lot of noise. They say if it sounds like there are ten of them out there, you probably only have two."

She nodded and took a sip of her wine, suddenly grateful for the protection of the screen—and Nick. She didn't like the idea of killing animals, but that didn't mean she wasn't glad to be with a man who knew more about coyotes than she did. "Do you ever hunt them?" she asked. She knew her father had killed several over the years.

But to her surprise, he shook his head. "No, I can't kill coyotes. They remind me too much of dogs."

She must have looked doubtful, because he shook his head. "Contrary to what you might think, I'm not some bloodthirsty killer. All hunters have their own personal ethics that they follow in addition to the laws. Some hunters won't kill does with fawns. Some hunters won't take a shot over a certain distance. Some hunters won't use bait even in places that allow it." He shrugged. "I can't bring myself to shoot an animal that reminds me of dogs. Doesn't mean I'm not okay with other hunters doing it. I just can't do it myself."

She took another sip of wine and struggled to fit this new information with the picture of Nick she was developing in her head. It would have been easier if he were just a mindless killer, a guy who killed for the sheer joy of killing. Then it would have been as black and white as she wanted it to be. This was too many shades of gray, too nuanced for her to come to easy conclusions.

She remembered Nick saying that she looked down on hunters. The thing was, it was totally acceptable to look down on people when everything was black and white, when she knew that they were bad people. "Bloodthirsty monsters," as Nick had put it. But when she opened herself to seeing more shades of gray, suddenly it wasn't so acceptable to dismiss people like Nick as simply bad people.

The big problem, of course, was that she was sleeping with Nick, which was a situation made for black and white. They were two very different people living two very different lives in two very different places. They had no future.

They barely had a present.

Her phone chimed, and she pulled up the new text message. It was a picture of a blank computer screen. "Really coming along on the stuff you gave me for the Stella campaign," Andi wrote.

Her father was right. Sarcasm wasn't as cute as people thought.

Nick was watching her, his eyes gleaming in the half-light of the porch. As lovely as the evening had been, it was time to go. She would just tell Nick she needed to leave, and he would drive her back to her father's house, and she could spend a few hours working on the Stella campaign.

But instead, she carefully set her glass down on the table. "You know, I don't think I made fun of your pink bedroom walls enough last night."

His glass followed hers, clinking on the surface of the table. "Oh? That's a shame."

"I know."

He stood up and reached down to help her up. "Should we rectify that?"

"Yes," she said, grasping his hands and letting him pull her to her feet. "We should."

CHAPTER 22

She had two weeks to pull off the experiential marketing campaign, but by the morning of the event, Greta had a major problem: she still had no idea what she was going to wear. She plugged an endless number of search terms into Pinterest —"professional outdoorsy outfits," "bowhunting chic"—but there just didn't seem to be any help for deciding what a #girlboss should wear to run a urine smell test at a farmer's market.

"Nothing I wear is going to be right," she despaired as she stood in front of her closet.

But, then, there was no right for something like this. This wasn't an event with a dress code. So if there wasn't a right...

Maybe there wasn't a wrong, either.

She thought of Kelsey, who seemed to wear whatever the hell she wanted. People still viewed her as competent, despite the sometimes outrageous outfits. It was almost as if what she wore didn't really matter at all.

Was that even possible?

Logically, she knew it was. But having spent so much of her life investing in a very particular image, it was hard to believe that maybe people viewed her as good at her job because she was, in fact, good at her job and not just because she dressed like her own Platonic ideal of a copywriter at an advertising agency.

Maybe instead of worrying about what outfit would present the right image at this event, she could just wear something she felt comfortable in.

It was such a revolutionary thought—such a freeing idea— that she sat down heavily on her bed and spent a full two minutes just letting it sink in.

She decided on the pair of denim capris she'd worn to Tracks a couple weeks earlier because they were comfortable, and her sleeveless ivory blouse because it was her favorite.

Surveying herself in the mirror, she decided she wasn't going to win any Best Dressed awards anytime soon—not that she'd won any before. But she felt better than she had in a long time. Happier. More relaxed.

In fact, she realized, it had been several days since she'd needed to take an Excedrin. Her headaches, once almost constant, had tapered off. Maybe it was all the fresh air and sunshine she was getting on the archery range, or maybe it was the challenge of working with a team to save her dad's company instead of working alone to advance her career. Or maybe it had something to do with Nick.

Whatever it was, she wasn't complaining.

* * *

THE FIRST TIME Greta asked a stranger to smell deer urine, they declined. No surprise there.

What was surprising was that the second time she asked someone, they actually said yes.

Chalk it up to Midwestern politeness and the lure of the prize wheel.

After that, the constant *clack, clack, clack* of the prize wheel and the squeals of people winning even small gift certificates attracted enough attention that the King Lures table was a happening place. Robbie recorded the whole thing, capturing the reactions of people as they caught a whiff of stale deer urine. "Whoa," one comfortably plump middle-aged woman said, jerking back from a cup of rival pee. "That doesn't smell fresh at all."

Greta caught Auggie's eye, and, grabbing one of the releases they'd printed up, he turned on the charm. If he could get the woman to sign the release, they could use that video on social media.

Judging from the way the woman beamed at Auggie, that wouldn't be a problem.

It wasn't just the prize wheel that had Greta and Kelsey busy offering cups to people to sniff. The presence of Robbie, Auggie, and Nick ensured a steady stream of female consumers eager to get close.

It seemed King Lures had booth babes, after all.

Of course, she reminded herself, booth babes were, strictly speaking, only there to look pretty. The guys understood the product and could speak about it with authority, so it wasn't like she was exploiting them for their looks.

Not that Auggie or Robbie appeared to mind.

Beside her, Kelsey grew increasingly brittle as Robbie flashed his pirate smile at pretty much every woman that walked by. After one woman brushed a bit of lint off his sleeve, practically drooling on him as she did so, Greta decided it best to take the cup Kelsey was holding away. No point leaving her armed with urine.

"You okay?" she asked when they had a quick break between Whiz Wiz contestants.

"Look at him," Kelsey said miserably. "I thought he was ready to settle down, but…"

But obviously he wasn't. An older man in a pale yellow button-up shirt stepped up to the table, and Greta could do nothing more than give Kelsey a sympathetic pat on the shoulder. As the man sniffed tentatively at the sample cups, Greta looked around for Nick, spotting him crouched down beside a little boy, showing him something on his phone. Trail camera photos of deer, she realized as the boy held a photo up for his mother, standing nearby, to see. The boy smiled, delighted with the photos. Nick grinned back at him, and Greta felt her heart turn over in her chest.

She was falling in love with Nick Campbell.

The realization was staggering. It was such an utterly stupid thing to let happen. They had so little in common, starting with the most important fact—they lived 300 miles apart, and Greta couldn't imagine Nick ever moving to Chicago. That meant that any relationship they could have would be a long distance thing, which couldn't possibly work.

But what if it could? Greta nodded absently as the latest Whiz Wiz contestant guessed correctly. She considered the possibilities. Three hundred miles. A five-hour drive, six with stops. A 45-minute flight. An obstacle, sure, but people overcame relationship obstacles all the time. They could take turns visiting each other, or maybe they could meet halfway in Indianapolis.

If they did that, they might be able to see each other at least a couple times a month. Given Greta's long hours in the office, that was about as much as she saw any of the guys she'd dated so far.

Her fingers twitched. It was...possible. She smiled as the man spun the prize wheel, its bright colors flashing quickly past.

With regular visits, they could maintain a relationship, maybe date for a couple years, and then...

And then what? A long-distance marriage? Long-distance parenting?

Well. There was no point in worrying about that just yet. She didn't even know if Nick wanted children. Although, recalling the look on his face as he talked to that little boy, Greta realized she did know. What's more, she realized she wanted children, too, as long as she had them with a man who would take time to show them pictures of wildlife, a man who would take them down to a little creek and let crawfish skitter over their palms, who would let them feed graham crackers to semi-tame whitetail deer at Jake's deer farm.

Provided he hosed them off before bringing them home, of course.

The fact that all of that happened here in Bartlett when her future was shaping up perfectly in Chicago was something she didn't want to think about.

"Having fun?"

She glanced up to find Nick standing on the other side of the table, giving her the lazy smile that made her insides melt. Fun? Of course not. She was in Kentucky, on a hot July day, asking strangers if they wanted to smell deer urine. It was like a nightmare come to life.

But as she looked at Nick, Greta realized she was having one of the best days she'd ever had.

Not that he needed to know that. "I think we're accomplishing our goals," she said primly.

"Good." He leaned closer. "I have some goals I'd like to accomplish later. Some of them might involve you. Think you might have some time to get together tonight?"

She flushed. "I do believe in setting goals."

"I know. So, 6 o'clock?"

But then she caught sight of Kelsey, who was overseeing a contestant's smell test with a look of grim determination on her face. "Do you think we could meet up later? I think someone might need a girls' night."

He followed her gaze, his lips curving in a knowing smile. "Sure."

She watched him walk over to help Paul answer questions from a guy in a camouflage hat, enjoying the contrast between Nick's broad shoulders and lean hips. Then she turned her attention back to the waiting contestants while making a mental note to look for guacamole recipes on Pinterest afterwards.

* * *

GRETA WAS FEELING PRETTY good about everything as she drove Paul back home. She'd done it. She'd taken something from idea to reality, and she'd made it a success. It didn't even bother her that Paul kept fiddling with the radio—if there was any music he actually liked, she wouldn't know it as he changed the station about two-thirds of the way through every song—and even when he started bellowing at her Google Maps app—"What the—? That's the stupidest thing I ever heard."—she couldn't muster any irritation.

"I'm starting to see why you had a heart attack," she said as he erupted in his second outburst in as many miles.

"It wants you to take 71? That's stupid. I know a much faster way."

Never mind that Google Maps automatically compared all possible routes to find the fastest one. "We can take whatever way you want. I just don't understand why you have to yell. It's an inanimate object, Dad. It's not listening to you."

"You are."

"Then why can't you just tell me what you want at a normal volume? You know, when you talk to me, you're usually either yelling or muttering. You never just talk to me."

There was a long moment of silence. Glancing over, Greta saw his hands opening and closing reflexively in his lap. Finally, he said, so quietly she almost didn't hear him, "You did a great job today."

"This is exactly what I mean. I wish you would…" She trailed off as the words hit her. "What did you say?"

"I said you did a great job today." He turned to look out at the

272

strip malls and gas stations sliding past the car window. "I appreciate the work you put in."

She couldn't remember ever hearing her father praise her before, and she wasn't quite sure how she felt about it. Somewhere deep inside, the wounded little girl that she had once been was enraptured at having finally won her father's approval.

But the grown up that she now was couldn't help but feel it was too little, too late.

"It's what I do," she said finally.

"I didn't know how talented you are."

"How could you know that?" she asked, and she was pleased that she was able to keep most of the bitterness out of her voice. "You never ask me about work."

He inclined his head, acknowledging the truth of that. But then he added, "You never ask about my work, either."

There was truth there, too. After all, she hadn't known the company was in such dire straits. Would he have told her about that if they had a closer relationship, or was he the kind of father who wouldn't want to worry her? She had no idea.

"Dad, what will you do if things with the company don't work out?"

Beside her, he stiffened. "What do you mean?" he asked carefully.

"I mean if—"

"Take a right at this next light."

She slowed and pulled into the right turn lane. "I just hope you have a plan if—"

"In 400 feet, make a U-turn," the disembodied voice of Google Maps broke in abruptly. It still wanted her to take the highway, and she'd turned away from it.

"Wrong!" Paul snapped in the phone's direction. "Don't listen to it."

"I really hope we can turn the ship around for your company, Dad, but if we can't and everything ends up—"

"In 100 feet, turn left on Fox Hollow Road." Google Maps again, in another attempt at returning her to the most efficient route.

"I don't think so. Just keep going straight."

"In half a mile—"

"Dad, just turn it off!" she yelled.

"I don't know how!"

Greta angrily reached for the phone to shut off the app while keeping an eye on the road.

"I have some money saved for retirement, you know," her father said, not looking at her again.

It was a relief to know, although "some money" was fairly vague. Her father was still young, so if he stopped working then he'd need a lot of money saved to ensure he didn't outlive it. Health insurance alone...But asking him about the size of his investments felt too intrusive for their tentative relationship, so all she said was, "I'm glad to hear that."

"And it's not like I can't work again. I'm not so old that I can't do something else."

The light turned green. "I didn't think you were."

"I'm not going to ask to move into your spare bedroom, if that's what you're worried about."

It was, but it felt churlish to say it. "That's good," she said finally. "Because I don't have a spare bedroom."

They approached another red light—the highway would definitely have been faster. Bright orange cones separated the lanes close to the intersection, and older men in funny hats walked between the cars collecting money. Shriners, she realized.

There was movement beside her, and then Paul thrust a twenty-dollar bill at her, waving at the closest Shriner as he did so. Obediently, Greta took the twenty and rolled down her window. A blast of warm air hit her. "How you doing today?" Paul called, leaning over Greta as the man approached the car.

"Oh, pretty good," the Shriner replied, holding out a red bucket for Greta to drop the money into.

"Thanks for all you do. And try to stay cool out there."

"Appreciate it. Thank you." The man moved on to the next car, and Greta rolled up her window.

"That was nice of you." She wasn't sure why she was surprised. For all she knew, her father handed out twenty-dollar bills like they were candy.

Paul shifted in his seat so he could slip his wallet back in his pocket. "They do good work for kids." He pushed a button on the radio, cutting Pink off mid-syllable and scrolling through the stations in search of something else. "What would it be like if I had to move into your apartment?"

She whipped her head around to look at him. "What? I thought you just said—"

"I know, I know. I was just wondering—"

Behind them, a car honked, and Greta realized the light had turned green. Taking a deep breath, she tried to remember what she'd learned about mindfulness from the three yoga classes she'd taken.

It didn't help.

"Dad, I don't have room for you in my apartment. Seriously. It's tiny." It wasn't that small, but it certainly wasn't big enough for Paul. And Polly. And his giant bear.

Just the thought of Paul's bear standing next to her perfect couch and her perfect coffee table with her perfect bowl of décor balls made her feel lightheaded.

"I'm not asking you to make room for me." His voice was so quiet that she could barely hear him over the Van Halen song he'd settled on for the moment, and there was something in his tone that made her feel almost sad. "I was just wondering what kinds of things we would do if I was in Chicago. If we did the kinds of things you normally do, I mean."

It took her a moment, but then she understood: he was asking what her life in Chicago was like. Why her father couldn't just ask like any reasonable person would, she didn't know. Nibbling her bottom lip, she realized it felt kind of good that he wanted to know.

So she told him. She told him about her pretty apartment and her commute to work and how she liked to buy fresh flowers for her cubicle. And then, because he seemed to be listening—really listening—she talked about the vegan cooking class she took over the winter, and the gym she joined three years ago but never seemed to have time to use, and the Thai place a block from her apartment that she liked to order takeout from. She told him about her friends, although even as she described them to her father she realized that they weren't so much friends as great dinner party guests. They weren't people who would insist on making guacamole for a girls' night, or who would bring over a bag of extra clothes and try to make her feel like…

Like she could be herself.

She lapsed into silence, contemplating that thought. Was it possible that here, in the middle of nowhere Kentucky, she actually felt more like herself than she had in…well, years? Maybe ever?

Her father cleared his throat. "You know, there's a really great Thai place on Lafayette. Maybe we could have lunch there tomorrow."

"You've eaten Thai food?"

"You say that like it's a surprise."

"I've just never heard of a Thai place that serves venison jerky."

He chuckled, but it was a brittle chuckle. "Maybe you don't know me as well as you think you do."

Maybe she didn't. He looked unnaturally stiff, his hands resting on his knees and his face turned slightly toward the window. He looked…*hurt*. Greta tightened her grip on the steering wheel. She'd spent so many years focused on how painful his lack of interest in her life was, but she'd never considered the fact that her apathy toward him might be equally as painful.

But she had enough to think about already, and she just didn't have the mental energy to parse her relationship with her father at the moment. She'd get to that later. Instead, she said, "Lunch sounds good. What do you recommend there?"

"I really like the pineapple chicken curry." He paused. "They have several vegetarian options, although I've never tried them."

She turned into her father's neighborhood and caught sight of his house. It reminded her, as it always did, of all those lonely summers she'd spent here as a child. But instead of the cold, suffocating feeling she normally had when she thought back on those visits, she felt a tad...wistful. Like maybe she had overlooked something important and was only now able to see what it was.

CHAPTER 23

*S*he didn't show up at his place until after ten, but Nick didn't mind. Judging from the way Kelsey had been moping around the Whiz Wiz, she needed some time with a friend, and though he didn't want to think about it too much, it made Nick happy that Greta wanted to be that friend.

Maybe she was putting down roots.

"Sorry. I should have called to see if we were still on," she said when he opened the door. "But I—"

He kissed her, drawing her into his arms, into his home, as he did. When he lifted his head, he was pleased to find her cheeks flushed, her eyes dark. "Oh, we're still on."

"Thank God." She nuzzled her cheek against his chest and sighed. "I was told there were goals to meet?"

Her hair, loose and wavy, brushed his chin. "I definitely have some goals. But first, I thought we should open some champagne. Celebrate a successful day of getting strangers to tell us our pee is the freshest."

"There's a statement I never imagined I would want to hear." She followed him into the kitchen, where he grabbed a bottle of champagne from the fridge, two Yeti tumblers, and a flashlight. "Classy."

"Make fun all you want, but this is more practical for what I have in mind. Come on." He led her out through the screened-in porch to the backyard. Switching on the flashlight, he used the narrow beam of light to make his way across the yard to where it met the woods that covered the back two acres of his property.

"We're going in there?" Greta pressed close against him as he stepped into the deeper shadows of the trees.

"This would have been a heck of a lot more romantic at sunset, but I think I can still make it work." He glanced up at where the branches of the trees blocked the nearly full moon. Yes. He could definitely make it work.

It said a great deal about how far they'd come that she followed him, one hand clinging to his arm. "This is a game trail," he said softly as they walked. "The deer come up through here in the evenings. You can see tracks here and there." He shone the flashlight on a part of the trail where a handful of cloven impressions marked the soft ground, then smiled to himself as she knelt down to see the tracks more clearly.

"Where are we going?" she whispered.

"It's just up here." The terrain got steeper, and Greta's hand tightened on his arm as something unseen crashed through the woods ahead of them, moving away. "Just a raccoon," he said. "We startled it."

"The feeling is mutual."

And then they reached the little clearing where Nick already had a blanket—and, more importantly, bug spray—waiting. Moonlight turned the leaves on the trees to silver and made the mushrooms that grew on the edge of the clearing glow like opals. Maybe it wasn't a Michelin-starred restaurant or a luxury Caribbean resort, but by Bartlett standards, it was pretty damn romantic.

"Oh," Greta said, taking it all in. "It's beautiful."

He risked ruining the moment a little by insisting on spraying them both down with bug spray—there was nothing romantic about mosquito bites—and then he uncorked the champagne, the sudden pop extra loud in the still of the night. "Congratulations on a job well done," he said, handing her a tumbler.

She slipped off her shoes and settled onto the blanket, tucking her feet under her. "You really think it went well?"

"That one video Kelsey posted on Instagram has already gotten more response than we've ever seen on the platform before." He stretched out beside her. "I don't know if it will translate to sales, but you definitely got us some buzz."

"Good." She rubbed a finger along the lip of her tumbler, her eyes fixed on her hand. Then she took a deep breath. "You know that I'm going back to Chicago in a couple weeks," she began.

And there it was. Her break-up speech, or what would have been a break-up speech had there been something there to end in the first place. But he'd always known where he stood with her, where Bartlett and King Lures stood. He didn't need to hear what she had to say. Not now. Not tonight on a blanket beneath a heavy moon.

So instead of letting her go on, he set his tumbler down on the grass beside the blanket and pulled her against him, his mouth finding the little place below her ear that always made her sigh. "We don't have to talk about that now," he murmured against her skin, sharp with the lemon eucalyptus bug spray he'd used. "We can talk about it later."

She hesitated as if she didn't want to let it go, but his hand skimmed up her ribs to the side of her breast. "I do have something I really need to ask you," he added.

She turned her head to meet his lips with her own. "What's that?" she asked.

He drew back just a fraction. "Have you ever made love outside?"

"I can't say that I have."

"I'd say that's a pretty important goal to set."

She smiled, her teeth a flash of white in the wash of moon-light. "I just wonder if it's an achievable goal."

"I think we can make it happen." And then he rolled on top of her, letting her feel just how achievable it was.

* * *

"WELL," Greta said, still working to catch her breath. "I guess I can cross having sex outdoors off my bucket list."

Beside her, Nick rolled onto his side, propped up on his elbow so he could look down at her. "You could. Of course, 'outdoors' is pretty broad. You've only done it in the woods on a summer night. You haven't done it in, say, a meadow on a cool spring morning. Or the desert under the stars." His eyes twinkled in the moonlight. "Or on the side of a mountain in the middle of a blizzard."

"You can't have sex in a blizzard."

The corners of his lips twitched. "Shows how unimaginative and unadventurous you are."

"You'd get frostbite in very interesting places."

"Sweetheart, you haven't lived until you've gotten frostbite in very interesting places."

"You're saying I've only experienced a small sliver of what sex in the outdoors can be."

He dropped a kiss on her temple. "Exactly." His hand slid idly over her hip. "I am a little uncomfortable about everything that raccoon just saw."

She jerked into a sitting position and glanced around. "What raccoon?"

"That little guy hunkered down in that tree over there." He shook his head slowly. "Poor traumatized little guy. Just a baby, too. Way too young to see that. Especially that thing you did at the end."

She swatted his shoulder lightly. "There's no raccoon."

"Whatever makes you feel better."

He flopped down onto his back, tugging her down so that her head was pillowed on his chest. Around her, the woods was alive with chirps and clicks and whirs as the little creatures of the night called to each other. And just beneath her ear, Nick's heartbeat thrummed as if it, too, were calling to something. Someone. Her.

She knew he was teasing her about the blizzard, but she couldn't keep her mind from imagining what it would be like to make love to Nick in a meadow, or the desert, or whatever other wild places he could show her. Maybe she would like camping more than she'd first thought. Maybe—

Her breath caught in her throat as the idea hit her, nearly fully formed. She could practically see the ad in her mind, the colors, the image, the neat lines of text, the graceful curve of the trademarked Stella "S." It was so perfect, so *right*, that she could scarcely breathe.

And it was all because of Nick.

"I have to go back to the house," she said, sitting up once again and scanning the area for her clothes.

"What? Everything okay?"

"Yes, it's…" Her stomach was fluttery with excitement. "Everything is perfect. You'll see. I just need to…" She made tiny movements in the air with her hands, wishing she had her notebook with her. She needed to outline, to plan, to get everything down before she forgot something. "I need to make a quick phone call."

* * *

GRETA LOCKED herself in Nick's guest room and pulled out her cell phone. She didn't want Nick to overhear this conversation. It would be so much better to surprise him with the end result.

Scrolling through her contacts, she found Andi's number and hit the call button.

"Do you know what time it is?" Andi griped when she picked up.

"Sorry. Were you sleeping?"

"No. But I was enjoying a piece of cheesecake that's better than sex."

Maybe some sex, Greta thought, her mind flashing back to the clearing. "Sorry to get in the middle of that, but I have an idea for the Stella campaign."

And because no matter what the time or how good the cheesecake was, Andi was Andi and that was all it took. "I'm listening."

CHAPTER 24

*M*onday morning, Greta arrived at the King office earlier than usual. She was nearly vibrating with adrenaline, a result of the success of the Whiz Wiz, finally coming up with what she hoped was a winning idea for the Stella campaign, and the tentative hope that maybe she and Nick might be able to hammer out some sort of dating arrangement.

Didn't that just sound romantic?

So maybe "dating arrangement" wasn't the term she was looking for. She'd work on that later.

First, she had to fine-tune the copy for the Stella ad. The ad was heavily dependent on the image, so Andi's work would be the most important part, but she wanted the copy to be perfect.

Once she felt good about the text, she sent it over to Andi and turned her attention back to King, reviewing the posts, comments, and retweets about the Whiz Wiz.

She was on the phone with Ben when Helen appeared in the doorway of her office, her face flushed. "Greta?"

Greta held up a finger to indicate that she'd just be a minute.

But Helen hastened into the room. "It's an emergency," she hissed.

Without taking her eyes off Helen, Greta said, "Ben, I'll call you back."

"There's a man on the phone looking for Paul," Helen said as soon as she'd set her phone down. "I told him Paul wasn't here, and he said it was urgent that he speak to him." She lowered her voice. "He said some things that really confused me."

Greta looked at her office phone, where the red light was blinking on and off indicating a call on hold.

There was no reason why she should have felt the strong sense of foreboding that swept over her. But something about the way Helen's fingers were twisting together had her reaching for the phone warily. It was just someone for her dad. She would just see what the caller needed.

It was fine. Everything was fine.

"I'm sorry. Paul is not in the office at the moment," she said smoothly. "This is his daughter, Greta. Can I help you with something?"

As the caller told her why he was calling, she began to understand what Helen had meant by him saying some things that confused her. Because what this man was saying made no sense.

And yet something about it made such total and complete sense that she wondered why she hadn't seen it before.

Helen stood by the desk, her eyes fixed on Greta's face, wringing her hands so vigorously that Greta worried she'd wear the skin off by the time she finished the call.

Finally, Greta managed to get the caller off the phone, promising that either she or her father would get right back to him. Then she met Helen's eyes grimly. "I need to speak to my father."

* * *

IT TOOK Helen twenty minutes to track down Paul, who had gone to Tracks for lunch with Nick and Auggie. By the time he got back to the building, Greta was pacing the office, her hands clasped firmly together. *Breathe*, she reminded herself. It was all going to be okay.

Except if what the man on the phone had said was true, it was most definitely not going to be okay. And there was nothing she could do.

"Helen said you wanted to see me?" Paul said, leaning into the office. He took in her wild eyes and clenched hands. "Something wrong?"

"I just got a phone call from someone at Whitetail Sports Co. Do you know it?"

"Sure. One of those big conglomerates run by suits in New York."

She nodded curtly. That's what she'd gathered from her internet research. Backed by a private investment group, the company was busy gobbling up small, family-owned businesses around the hunting industry.

Companies exactly like King Lures.

"Dad, he said they have majority ownership of King Lures."

She hadn't expected him to look so shocked. After all, there was only one way WSC could have gotten ownership of King—if Paul had sold it to them.

But Paul gasped, one hand shooting out to grasp the door-frame as his knees threatened to buckle. Greta rushed forward, slipping an arm around his waist to help him to the closest chair. "Dad," she said softly, "how could you?"

He shook his head. "No. They don't own a majority share. It's not possible. I made sure I didn't sell them more than 45 percent. And then the only other person who owns shares is Nick."

Nick. Greta felt her heart lurch. "Excuse me for a minute," she said stiffly, striding from the room.

"Greta, come back. I need to tell you something."

But she didn't even look back. She homed in on Nick's office door. Walking into his office, she closed the door behind her.

He looked up at her and smiled, that familiar crooked smile that made something in the vicinity of her heart ache. How could he have done this to her father? To her?

There was only one way to find out.

"Why'd you do it?" she asked.

That crooked smile vanished, replaced with instant wariness. "Why'd I do what?"

"You sold your shares of the company to Whitetail Sports Co."

"What? Of course not." But his shoulders stiffened, and she knew he was lying.

"They own a majority share now. My father has lost his company."

Nick froze, his eyes widening. Like her, he must be going through the mental calculations—the spreadsheets that never balanced, the payroll that continued even as sales fell—and coming to the same conclusion she'd reached: Paul had gotten money from an outside source. "I only owned 10 percent of the company," he said.

"It was enough."

"I didn't sell to Whitetail, though. I would never do that to Paul."

"Then whoever you sold to turned around and sold to Whitetail." She could feel the press of tears behind her eyes. "How much did you get?"

"Greta—"

"*How much?*"

He slumped back and stared at his desk. "$350,000."

It was more than she'd expected. And that's when it hit her. She thought he'd embraced the Whiz Wiz because he supported her. But he'd been doing it to show the company making changes, moving in a positive direction. Becoming more profitable, which would make his ten percent worth more.

It was never about his feelings for her.

"I hope it was worth it," she said. "They want to consolidate."

He stared at her, comprehension dawning in his eyes. "Hampton Scents."

She nodded. Hampton Scents was a competing attractant company already owned by Whitetail. The plan, according to the man who'd called her, was to shut down the King Lures facility and produce everything in the Hampton facility.

Everyone who worked at King would lose their jobs.

"I can't believe how stupid I've been," she said. "This whole time you've been acting like you actually cared about this company. About my father. About—" But she broke off. She couldn't say it: about *me*. Because what had he done when she tried to raise the possibility of seeing each other in the future?

He had brushed her off, told her they could deal with that later. He didn't care about her at all.

For a moment, he looked like he was on the verge of saying something. She wanted him to, she realized. She wanted him to find a way to make this better, to say whatever it was that he could say that would redeem himself. Tell me I'm wrong, she nearly begged him. She wanted so badly to believe that.

But he simply studied her, his face gradually hardening. And then he stood, slowly, unfolding his big, lean body until he loomed over his desk. "You think I don't care about this company?" he asked, his voice lethally soft.

"How can you argue that you do? You *sold* your share of it to the competition. We've lost everything."

He moved around the desk, his blue-gray eyes so flinty that she had to will herself not to flinch away from him. "'We?' What exactly have you lost, Greta? Because from where I'm standing, it's your father who's lost everything. You father and everyone who works here. You're going back to Chicago soon, remember?"

She lifted her chin. "I've spent the last few weeks on FMLA leave from a job I love just so I could help out around here. And to have that all be for nothing..."

He sank down on the corner of his desk and crossed his arms over his chest. "Is this about your dad losing the company, or is this about you not winning?"

"Not winning?" she repeated slowly. "What does that have to do with anything?"

"Oh, come on, Greta. Saving King Lures has never been about helping anyone here. It's always been about your ego—you hate to lose."

"How can you say that after everything I've done for this company?"

"Don't forget—I've caught you obsessing over a mistake you made *in high school*. You talk a big game about letting stuff go, but you've held on awful tight to the one time you didn't live up to your own expectations."

The video. She felt a prickle of pain on her hands and realized she'd balled her hands into fists, her nails digging into her palms. The unfairness of him throwing the video in her face was staggering. "Look who's talking."

"What's that supposed to mean?"

"You're the one living in a pink bedroom."

"That's nothing like whatever neurotic drive makes you watch that video," he scoffed.

"No?" She paced to the window, then whirled and paced back. "You don't think you've kept the walls pink as a reminder of your failed marriage?"

He blinked. "Of course not."

"You hate the color of your bedroom."

"I don't love it, but that doesn't mean I've kept it as a reminder of my marriage."

"Then why haven't you repainted?" She held up one hand, not letting him answer. "It takes a couple hours to paint a room. If you wanted to change it, you would have done so long ago."

"It's not that simple."

"It is that simple."

"You don't understand anything."

No, she didn't. She didn't understand how he could have betrayed her father like this. She didn't understand why he couldn't at least bring himself to apologize. And she didn't understand how it was that she had actually let herself fall in love with this man.

But she did understand one thing: it was time to go home. King Lures was gone, and so was any chance of a future with the man who'd let it all go.

"You're right," she said. And then she spun around and walked out of his office just in time. The tears that had been threatening welled up in earnest. She made a quick stop in her father's office to grab her purse, relieved to find the room empty. She could deal with her father later. Blindly, she staggered down the hallway, almost running head first into Auggie. "Greta? Are you okay?" she heard him ask. His voice sounded far away, as if he were at the other end of a long tunnel.

And then she was pushing through the metal door at the top of the stairway, ignoring Helen's questions. She hurried down the stairs and burst out into the bright sunlight of the parking lot.

* * *

SHE NEEDED to get out of Bartlett, but there was one person she couldn't leave without saying goodbye to. After a quick stop to pack up her clothes, she drove down to Pea's house, unsurprised to see the older woman working away in her front flowerbed.

Pea glanced up. "Greta," she said, ambling over to the car. "What a pleasant surprise. I haven't seen you in a little while."

It took every ounce of control Greta had not to launch herself into Pea's arms and start sobbing like a kid with a popped balloon. Instead, she smiled wanly. "I'm heading back to Chicago and just wanted to thank you for letting me spend time here when I needed it."

Pea's mouth drooped, and she glanced past Greta to the car, where a suitcase stuffed with the world's drabbest clothing was visible in the back seat. For just a moment, Greta had considered taking a few of the items Helen had left for her. She'd even had her hand on the sparkly blue top she'd worn to Tracks. But where would she wear any of those clothes? No, she was going back to her old life, and all she needed was her old wardrobe.

"Leaving? Now? I thought you were staying a little longer," Pea said.

"So did I." But she couldn't form the words to explain any further, so she simply stepped forward and wrapped her arms around the older woman, being careful not to squeeze the fragile shoulders too hard even as something suspiciously like home-sickness squeezed her heart. Pea smelled like fresh, sun warmed earth and rose petals and sweet tea. "I'll miss you."

"Oh, honey." Pea patted her back with one gloved hand, almost certainly leaving behind a bit of dirt. Greta realized she didn't care. "Before you go, I have something for you." Stepping back, Pea turned and bustled into her house. She was back a moment later with a potted plant, something lush and green, with heart-shaped leaves snaking over the side of the pot.

"It's a philodendron," Pea said, thrusting the pot at her. "It reminds me of you."

Greta eyed the messy tangle of leaves. "I'm not sure what to make of that."

"It's hard to kill." Pea smiled. "It's very adaptable, so it can thrive in a number of places."

"Well, thank you, Pea. That's very thoughtful."

She knew what Pea was trying to tell her, of course. But as she backed out of Pea's driveway, the messy-looking plant settled onto the passenger side floorboard, she knew that for once the older woman was wrong. Maybe a philodendron could grow just as well in an ugly ranch house in Bartlett, Kentucky, as it could in a one-bedroom apartment in Chicago. But Greta wasn't a house-plant. She'd put a lot of hard work into building her life. Maybe she'd gotten a bit distracted over the last few weeks, but that was over now.

It was time to go home.

CHAPTER 25

*G*reta Tremaine had the perfect life. She was in the running for a creative director position at the Prescott Agency, a position that she'd spent years working toward. Her cubicle was perfectly decorated, although she no longer had room for fresh-cut apricot roses thanks to the philodendron that now lived on her desk. She had a gorgeous apartment, and if she stood all the way to one side of her window and peered out, she had what some would describe as a spectacular view. And her bedroom had restful taupe walls and a bed that might have stepped right out of a Pottery Barn catalog (which it had).

There was not a pink wall to be found.

She did not have to sleep on camo sheets, her bathroom was certifiably javelina-free, and there were no bears lurking in corners.

In short, she'd never been happier.

If only she could convince herself that was really true.

She knew that, with time, the pain of Nick's betrayal would pass. It helped that he had turned out to be such a snake, although her heart was still grieving for the person she had thought him to be.

Also, she kind of missed the bear.

* * *

HER FATHER CALLED her one night to see if she wanted the coffee maker she'd purchased for the office.

"That's okay," she said, stirring the lentil stew she was making for dinner. "You keep it."

"I don't need it. I have the old one."

"The one that keeps breaking? Dad, that's ridiculous. Just keep the new one."

There was a weighty silence. "I don't need it."

Lifting the spoon to her mouth, Greta took a tentative taste of her stew, scalding her tongue in the process. "Damn it," she whispered. Then she set the spoon down a bit harder than necessary. It was all too much. Her headaches were back and it turned out the man she'd fallen in love with didn't really exist and her father was refusing to use a perfectly good coffee maker and her stew was too hot. What else could go wrong? "Why are you being so stubborn about the stupid coffee maker, Dad?"

"I just don't agree with throwing things out when you don't see a use for them anymore."

"But that's exactly why you throw things out. That's how I do it, and I don't have all the crap you do cluttering up my life."

"I know."

And there was something about his tone that made Greta understand there was more to this than she realized. "Why do I get the feeling you're not really talking about the coffee maker?"

"Of course I'm talking about the coffee maker. What else would I be talking about?"

She turned down the heat on the stove. "I don't know, Dad. Why don't you tell me?"

She heard a rustling sound and imagined him adjusting the quilt around himself. Briefly, she remembered the frigid temperature he always kept his house at, and the worry over his health came back. Then she pushed it firmly away. He hadn't listened to her when she was right there. He certainly wasn't going to jump up and adjust the thermostat because she was fretting about it from Chicago.

Finally, he sighed. "It's always been obvious there wasn't room in your life for two fathers. I know you wish you could have shoved me under the sink. Not literally, of course."

"That's not…" That's not true, she wanted to say. Except maybe it was. A little.

"I understood when you were little. You lived with him. He was the one who ate breakfast with you every morning and listened to you talk about your day every night. I knew that. I told myself how lucky I was that my little girl had a loving stepfather. Heck, even I like the guy.

"But then the more you were around Don, the less you wanted to be around me. Suddenly I was an embarrassment to you. It was like you and your mother had traded in for a better model. You even changed your name as soon as you were old enough."

So that had bothered him. Greta worried her bottom lip with her teeth. She hadn't known that.

"I know what's going to happen—when you get married, you'll want Don to walk you down the aisle. And when you have kids, Don will be Gampy or Gramps or PooPah, and I'll be Grandpa Paul."

"Dad, I—What the hell is a PooPah?"

"It's a PooPah. You know. A PooPah sneaks his grandkids ice cream for dinner and lets them stay up past their bedtime and surprises them with dead snakes so they can make their own snakeskin belts."

For the first time in weeks, she laughed. She couldn't help it.

She could just imagine her father showing up wielding handfuls of dead snakes for the grandkids.

Don, on the other hand, wouldn't be the kind of grandfather to amp his grandchildren up on sugary treats or set up a tent in the living room to watch movies late at night. In fact, Greta had a hard time picturing Miranda and Don Tremaine as grandparents at all. If she ever did have children, she supposed Miranda and Don would be the kind of grandparents who exposed their grandchildren to artisanal cheese and took them to the theater and recommended the best piano instructors. No PooPah here— Don would probably prefer being called Grand-pere.

Not that there would be any grandchildren. Greta glanced at the clock. It was 9:30, and she was making dinner. She'd worked late and gotten home late, and none of that lent itself to dating, let alone marriage and children. And if that realization made her feel a little hollow inside, she could take comfort in the fact that she had a career she loved.

You can't have everything, she told herself firmly. But still she suddenly heard herself say something that surprised even her: "You'd make a good PooPah, Dad."

"Damn right I would."

"I'm sorry about the coffee maker."

And because he was her father and they were so much alike and he hated to say certain things too, he understood. "That's okay. I'm sorry I lied to you about the company."

She paused in the middle of ladling lentil stew into a bowl. "Lied to me?"

"I knew the company was done for. You could never have saved it."

That was something she'd started to suspect. If her father had already sold 45 percent of the company and it was still struggling, he had to know the chances of pulling it through were infinitesimal. "So why'd you let me invest so much effort in trying to save it?"

There was a long silence. Finally, Paul said, "I just wanted to fix things with you."

Carefully, she set the ladle down on the spoon rest and wiped her hands on an ivory dishtowel. "Fix things?"

"I know I should have just told you the truth. But you hadn't come down to visit me in so long. I knew I wasn't going to need much help at home, and I knew as soon as I didn't need you anymore, you'd go back to Chicago."

Her heart squeezed with loss for what they'd never had. What they'd been so close to reaching before she left. "Maybe if you'd just asked me to stay..." She trailed off. Not even she believed that.

"Before my heart attack, I was so afraid of losing the company. It was the one thing I'd really done in my life." He sighed. "But once I realized what was happening and the ambulance was coming to my house, I realized it was just a business. It was a big part of me, sure, and it was important to a lot of people. But you're the best part of me, Greta. You're what really matters."

She blinked away the moisture in her eyes. "Why didn't you just say that when I first showed up at the hospital?"

"Because you wouldn't have believed me. And..." He paused. "And because I was afraid I'd mess up my one chance to fix this. You and me. If I messed this up, I didn't think you'd ever give me another chance."

Greta rested her forehead against her hand, her elbow propped up on the table. Things with Nick hadn't worked out. But maybe she'd found love down in Bartlett after all. "I guess...I guess it was better this way."

"Yeah." He was quiet for several beats. "Maybe you can come down and visit again sometime. Maybe Christmas?"

The last place in the world she wanted to be was Bartlett, Kentucky. But maybe by December, she'd be over Nick enough to be able to visit. "Maybe."

"Okay." He wasn't going to push her for a hard commitment, which she appreciated.

"Or maybe…" She took a deep breath. "Or maybe you could come up here. We could get some Thai food and I could show you the city."

There was a long pause. Then Paul said, "Yeah. That would be nice."

After she got off the phone with her father, she ladled up a bowl of lentil stew and sat alone at her table for two, eating it slowly. She forced herself to think about how happy she was. About how perfect her life was. About how much better she was starting to feel.

And then she decided that her high school ballet performance wasn't her worst failure after all.

* * *

THE HOUSE SEEMED to be closing in on him. He spent his nights in a state of semi-wakefulness. He thought about calling Greta, but there didn't seem to be much point in that. Even if she forgave him, he didn't have much to offer her. Hell, he didn't even have a job anymore. Whitetail had come in and closed the factory down. They'd extended offers to a few members of management, but none of them had accepted.

So, no, he didn't really feel that Greta would be happy to hear from him.

Auggie stopped by one Tuesday, pushing past Nick when he cracked the door and shoving a handful of papers at him.

Nick glared down at the papers. "What the hell is this?"

"Figures you wouldn't recognize them, seeing as you've never had to apply for a job in your life. Those are job postings. I printed a few out that looked up your alley." Auggie crossed his arms and studied him critically. "Have you left the house in, oh, I don't know, the last week?"

He hadn't just printed out a few job postings. Auggie had highlighted a few critical points on each sheet of paper, often making notes about specific hiring managers in the margins. Nick glanced up. "I've been out to check the mail every day." Almost every day, at least.

"That's what I thought. Well, get ready. We're going to Dairy Queen."

"I'm busy."

"Watching 'The Price is Right' does not count as being busy."

"I wasn't watching 'The Price is Right.'"

"If I go down to your basement right now, you're telling me I'm not going to see anyone spinning a giant wheel or playing Plinko?"

"I'll get my shoes."

"I thought so."

As they reached Auggie's 1998 Camaro, Nick regarded him over the top of the car. "I really wasn't watching 'The Price is Right.'"

"Whatever you say, dude."

Nick slid into the car, waiting for Auggie to turn the music down before speaking again. "I was actually watching a murder show."

"Cool."

"It was about a guy who killed a particularly annoying coworker." He drummed his fingers on his knee. "Gave me some good ideas."

Auggie slipped on his sunglasses and grinned at him. "Good thing we don't work together anymore, isn't it?"

Every cloud has a silver lining, he almost said. But he couldn't even joke about it yet. "Why are you doing this?"

"We're friends, dude." Auggie had one elbow propped on the doorframe just inside the closed window, his hand resting against his head.

This, despite the fact that Nick had single-handedly destroyed the company that had been home and family to him since he was a sophomore in high school. He fixed his gaze on the blinking red light of a distant radio tower. "Thanks."

"Yeah, well." Auggie cleared his throat. "Anyway, you look so bad at the moment, it's going to do wonders for my game to be seen next to you."

Good to know Auggie would always be Auggie. "Happy to be of service."

His phone chimed, and he pulled it out of his pocket. It was a text message from Ben. He stared at the words, understanding them but simultaneously unable to comprehend exactly what he was reading.

"What is it?" Auggie asked.

Slowly, Nick raised his head to look at him. "It's Carrie."

* * *

GRETA'S CELL phone rang around two in the afternoon, and she was surprised to see her father come up on the caller ID. "Dad," she said. "Everything okay?"

"Honey, Ben's wife died this morning. I thought you'd want to know."

Greta sagged back against her chair. Oh, poor Ben. She'd known that his wife wasn't doing well, of course, but somehow it was still a shock.

It looked like she'd been hoping for a miracle.

"When's the funeral?" she asked, her throat tight.

"Saturday at 10." He paused. "Nick's going."

Of course he was. Greta nodded, although her father couldn't see her. "Thanks for letting me know."

When she hung up, she pushed her chair away from her desk, staring blankly at the bustle of her coworkers going about their day. Life was going on as usual, the mutter of voices, the hum of a laser printer a few cubicles down, the brush of the AC on the leaves of her philodendron, the endless stream of people—some she knew, some she didn't—walking past her. That was the most infuriating and beautiful thing about life—it went on. Sure, it paused every now and then, took a breath when something particularly tragic happened. But then it resumed, adjusting to a world in which even this particular tragedy was possible.

It didn't matter to life that hearts got broken along the way. It just kept going.

CHAPTER 26

The morning of Carrie's funeral dawned soft and muted, the pearlescent bowl of the sky glowing with milky color. Nick knew it was exactly the kind of sky Carrie would have nagged everyone around her into noticing.

"Quick, Ben, take a picture," she would say.

"It never turns out right in pictures," he'd grumble.

"I don't care. I'll remember it right in my head. Just take the photo as a reminder."

Nick was still thinking about the sky when he and Auggie pulled into the church parking lot. Beyond the quaint white church where the service was being held, a trail of crisp white clouds spread out like an angel's breath.

"You go on in," he told Auggie. "I'll be there in a sec."

As he stepped around the side of the church, phone in hand to take a quick picture, he saw that he wasn't the only one with that idea. Ben was leaning against the side of the church, eyes fixed on the horizon, pain and grief radiating from every line of his body.

"Hey," Nick said.

Ben glanced up and shot him a ghost of a smile. "Hey. You get in last night?"

"Yeah." Looking up at that blue, blue sky, he thought of the last time he'd visited Ben's small Maryland town. Carrie insisted on baking her famous chocolate chip walnut cookies for him because she remembered how much he liked them. "How's Savannah doing?"

Ben rubbed his fingers together absently. "She's confused, and she keeps asking when her mama will come home from heaven. To be honest, I keep thinking the same thing."

"I think that's natural."

"Is anything going to feel normal ever again?" Ben looked up at him. His eyes were red-rimmed, his hair tousled. "Because right now I just don't see how that's possible."

Nick thought of the sharp, hot scent of his grandmother's iron as she attacked the wrinkles in her freshly done laundry, the TV blaring a soap opera in the drape-darkened living room. Swallowing hard past a lump in his throat, he realized he missed moments like that. "No," he said honestly. "But eventually you create a new normal."

"A new normal." Ben tilted his head back, studying the sky that would have so delighted Carrie. "God, I would give anything for a cigarette right now. I chose a hell of a time to quit."

"You quit when Savannah was born."

"I still should have waited."

"Well, you can't have a cigarette. I'm not going through you quitting again." Despite the tragic circumstances, the corner of Nick's lip kicked up in something of a smile. "You were a real jackass the whole time."

Ben grinned, red-rimmed eyes and all. "I was, wasn't I? I'm still not sure how she resisted killing me when I told her—at 39 weeks pregnant—that she couldn't understand what I was going through." He stared down at his hands, his fingers still mechanically rubbing together. "I don't know what I did to deserve her."

They stood in silence as the clouds scattered across the sky.

Finally Ben straightened up and sighed. "Speaking of women we probably don't deserve, did Greta come with you?"

Nick squinted against the sun's glare. Ben knew that they'd lost control over King Lures, but it looked like the gossip mill hadn't gotten around to telling him what had happened with Greta. "No."

Although he tried to sound neutral, Ben must have heard something in his voice. He looked at him sharply. "Why not?"

This didn't seem to be the right time, but Ben had asked. Nick's shoulders slumped. "I messed everything up."

"Yeah, I could have told you that you would. But then what?"

"Then what what?"

"Then what did you do to try to fix it?" When Nick just stared at him, Ben shook his head. "Nick, tell me you tried to fix it."

"Dude, we don't need to talk about this now. I mean, you just…" He couldn't go on. He couldn't bring himself to put Ben's loss into words.

"I know. But that's the point. If I could bring Carrie back, I would in a heartbeat. You can still get Greta back."

"I don't think I can." He thought of Greta's face when she realized he'd been the one to sell the company out from under her. There was no coming back from that. Besides, there was also the fact that she had a life in Chicago—one that certainly wouldn't translate well to Bartlett. "I can't make her happy."

"Jesus Christ." Ben raked one hand through his hair. "Is that why you're such an idiot? You think you have to make her happy?"

Nick wasn't sure how to explain it more clearly. "Look at what happened with Lauren," he said. "She was so happy before we got married and moved to Bartlett. And at first she really threw herself into decorating the house, but once she had finished that and was just stuck with me…" He shrugged.

Ben stared at him. "You think Greta is anything like Lauren?"

"Neither of them wants to live in Bartlett."

But Ben shook his head. "Lauren was...Look, I know you loved her, and I'm sure she had her positive traits. But she was never going to be happy. And that wasn't because of you. That was because Lauren didn't want to be happy."

"Of course she wanted to be happy. That's why she left."

"Lauren was only happy when she was complaining. Trust me, everyone else saw it. There was no way you could have made that woman happy. Maybe she didn't like Bartlett. But did she ever come to you and tell you she'd rather live somewhere else?"

No, she hadn't. She'd just grown increasingly moody, prone to outbursts and then long periods of chilly silence. The only time she'd actually said she wasn't happy in Bartlett was when she announced that she was leaving him. She'd thrown her misery in his face, her mouth twisted with bitterness.

"Greta's not Lauren, Nick. And you know what? It's not your job to make someone else happy, not even in a relationship. Do you think I made Carrie happy?"

Nick thought of Carrie, always laughing, her cheeks perpetually flushed with her zest for life. "Of course."

Ben shook his head. "No. Carrie was happy because that was who she was. I supported her in all of the things that made her happy, of course. I cared about whether or not she was happy. But I didn't *make* her happy. Do you see?"

Not at all. Nick studied his hands.

"That's a lot of responsibility to put on someone, Nick. People don't make each other happy. You have to make yourself happy." He paused. "It just happens to work out sometimes that two people are happier together than alone."

Clapping a hand on Nick's shoulder, he said, "I need to get back to Savannah. Just think about it, okay?"

By Monday morning, Nick was feeling restless. He went for a

run through his neighborhood, returning dripping with sweat and still edgy. It wasn't until he turned the light on in the master bathroom that he suddenly understood what Ben had been saying.

Like his bedroom, his bathroom was pink. Very, very pink. Lauren had taken some of the décor items, but she'd left quite a few things behind. On the vanity, which offered a wide middle section stretched between two sinks, was a collection of apothecary jars on a thin silver tray—not genuine silver, surely, or Lauren would have taken it with her. One of the apothecary jars held cotton balls. The other three were empty.

He had four apothecary jars on a silver tray in his pink bathroom, and he'd never wanted any of it.

Still sweaty, he went down to the garage and found a cardboard box and some newspaper. Then he carefully packed the apothecary jars away, filling them with newspaper and stuffing crumpled newspaper between them. He stuck the silver tray into the box as well.

Looking around the bathroom, he saw more and more things Lauren had left behind. A framed print of a finch. A soap dish shaped like an owl. A half-dozen woven baskets under the sink that held absolutely nothing. He packed everything into the box. When it was full, he got a second box and began filling that one, too.

Once the bathroom was clear of all of Lauren's things, he took a quick break to shower and pull on a pair of gym shorts and a T-shirt. Then he moved to the bedroom.

By lunchtime, he had the master bathroom and master bedroom emptied of all traces of Lauren. Stepping back, he already felt lighter.

And the more he put everything Lauren had brought into his life in one place, the more he realized the truth in what Ben had said. Lauren had never made him happy. He'd enjoyed his life while they were married, but that wasn't because Lauren had made his life better. He'd had his job. He'd had his hunting. He'd had his friends. And while he'd tried to involve Lauren as much as he could, she had wanted no part of it. He'd loved her, and he believed even now that at one point she'd loved him, too. But that hadn't been enough for her.

Hands on his hips, he stood back and surveyed the pink walls. What was it Greta had said?—he'd kept the walls pink because they reminded him of his failed marriage.

Just thinking of Greta brought a sharp stab of heartache. She wasn't like Lauren at all. Maybe she wouldn't want to live in Bartlett. But while she was there, she'd made the best of it. She'd become friends with her coworkers. She'd learned to shoot a bow. She'd thrown everything she had into saving a company she didn't care about. Because that was how she lived life. She went all-in on whatever she did.

It was how she would be in a relationship, too.

Nick sank down onto the bed. Greta wasn't like Lauren at all.

He'd let Lauren go without a fight, and that had been the right thing to do.

Letting Greta go was another story entirely.

He wasn't sure how he was going to fix this. He'd lost her father's company for her, and while he wasn't guilty of doing it for the money like she thought, in some ways it was worse: he'd sold out because he didn't believe in her vision. Of course, that was before he knew her, before he understood what she was capable of. After seeing how hard she worked, even for a cause as hopeless as King, he had no doubt she could make a success out of anything she put her mind to. In fact, if they'd had Greta on their team a couple years earlier, things might have been differ-ent. He thought back, trying to pinpoint exactly when things had gone sideways. The synthetic lure project, he decided. They'd taken a bath on that whole thing, and for what? A useless product.

Not quite useless, though. It had been a pretty solid product, actually. In fact, it was hard to tell the difference between King's Royal Doe in Heat and the synthetic estrous lure they'd developed. It wasn't the product.

It was the marketing.

He stared at the pink walls, considering. Maybe Greta was right. Maybe it was time for a change.

Besides, he needed time to think. And what better way to occupy his hands while he figured some things out than a paint roller?

CHAPTER 27

"I'm excited to see what you have," Tamsin said, her hands folded primly on her desk. Her suit today was a bold orange, as rich and tart as a kumquat.

Greta slanted a glance at Andi, who was perched on the chair beside her. It was a sign of how important this moment was that Andi was sitting up straight; normally she had the sitting posture of a sulky sixteen-year-old.

"I'm excited to show it to you," Greta said. Sliding the final mockups from a large manila envelope, she set them in front of her boss.

Tamsin's eyes narrowed, and she lifted the top sheet to study it more closely.

On the right side of the page was an urban scene, all grays with just the barest hint of color, with a skyscraper jutting up from the jumble of streets and sidewalks and pedestrians. There was an open window on the top floor of the skyscraper, and a woman leaned out in a Rapunzel-esque pose. On the left side of the page was a forest, all cool greens and rich browns and flashes of brightly colored birds. Out of that forest strode a man, his face lifted toward the woman in the tower. Calling her, wordlessly.

And he was bringing the wild with him. Wherever the man stepped, the bleak city sidewalk bloomed with grass and moss and wildflowers. Andi had done brilliant work, capturing the man's innate confidence, the woman's longing for something different. Something fresh and breathtaking and utterly untamed.

It was good work. And she could barely look at it. All she saw was Nick's face, Nick's shoulders, Nick's big, capable hands.

She should have known better than to use him as inspiration for the ad. But he'd just been so damn *inspiring*.

While she waited for Tamsin's feedback, she pulled out her bottle of Excedrin.

"You okay?" Andi mouthed.

She nodded and shook a couple pills onto her open palm. Then she rattled out one more. This was a three-Excedrin headache.

Tamsin set the mockups down and cleared her throat. She looked from Greta to Andi, her expression unreadable. "I'm impressed," she said finally.

It should have been the best moment of her life. Instead, Greta found her mind wandering back to a moonlit clearing that reeked of lemon eucalyptus bug spray. "Thank you."

"I think you have a really solid concept here. I do have a couple suggestions. First—"

The door of her office swung open and Marion poked her head in. "Greta," she said, her face pale.

For a moment Greta flashed back to the day she'd learned about her father's heart attack. Her heart jumped into her throat, and she started to rise from her chair. Then Marion said, "There's a man here and he insists on seeing you. I told him you were busy, but…" Her voice trailed off, implying a whole host of problems this mysterious man might cause if he weren't seen right away.

Tamsin started to say something pointed about meetings and

interruptions and the value of their time, but she broke off abruptly as a man stepped into the room, his big body dwarfing Marion where she stood just inside the doorway.

It felt like all the air had been sucked out of the room, and Greta sat down again as her knees gave out.

It was Nick.

Nick in a suit.

She'd been utterly wrong about how he would look in a suit, she saw. He should have looked ridiculous, like a child playing dress-up in his father's closet. Instead, the smartly tailored blue suit emphasized his lean grace, the cut of the jacket drawing the eye up to his broad shoulders, the color making his hair and skin glow golden and bronze, respectively. But his civilized attire couldn't hide the predator beneath. He was still obviously a wolf. And the way he was looking at Greta made it clear he was on the hunt.

Marion's eyes were wide as they met Greta's, and she mouthed one word— "Wow"—before closing the door behind her.

Clearly, he hadn't expected to find her in a meeting. But he didn't let the presence of the other women intimidate him. Squaring his shoulders, he tossed out one of his crooked grins. "Hello, Greta."

Finally tearing her eyes away from Nick, Greta caught sight of Tamsin's and Andi's faces, which were avid with appreciation and curiosity. She considered pretending not to know who he was, but it would be patently obvious that wasn't true. Even if he hadn't called her by name, she wasn't that talented an actress. She pasted a bland smile on her face. "Ladies, this is Nick Campbell."

"Hello," Tamsin said, just as Andi said, "Wow."

It was too much. It was one thing to betray her, but to show up at her workplace unannounced when she was in the middle of one of the most important projects of her career was just unforgivable.

Well, she would make him pay.

"He's gorgeous, isn't he?" Greta said. Then she twisted her mouth in a little moue. "Sadly, he's gay."

Nick's gaze shot to hers, and she could see the gathering storm in those cloudy blue-gray eyes. But all he said was, "That's right. Very gay."

"What a waste," Andi breathed.

"His boyfriend doesn't think so." Greta was starting to enjoy herself despite—or maybe because of—the sharp look Nick threw her.

"What's he doing here?" Tamsin asked.

Sabotaging her career at Prescott was Greta's best guess. "He's just leaving."

"I repainted my bedroom," he said, taking a step closer to her desk. "Beige."

"That's disappointing," Andi said. When Tamsin and Greta turned to stare at her, she added, "What? I was hoping he was going to have some insight on the latest hot new paint color. Like Nate Berkus."

Tamsin's lips tightened. "Not all gay men are like Nate Berkus."

"But it would have been cool if this one were."

Ignoring them, Nick reached into his pocket. "And I brought you something." Eating up the space between them in three deliberate steps, Nick carefully set something on the desk in front of her as if he were presenting her with a rare bottle of wine.

Or, she thought, like a cat proudly laying a decapitated vole at its owner's feet.

It was a glass bottle, small enough that it fit neatly into his palm. And it contained something that looked suspiciously familiar.

"Is this...*urine*?" she asked in growing horror. This was a nightmare. It had to be. There was no other explanation for why the man she couldn't forget would suddenly show up at her work to put a bottle of pee on her boss's desk.

Oh, God. She was going to become the Deer Pee Princess at Prescott, too.

"Kind of."

"This is weird," Andi said in a mock whisper. "Should we call security?"

"Yes," Greta said.

"No." Nick leaned forward, bracing his arms on the side of the desk. She met his eyes and found determination there. Determination, and fear. Something twisted in the region of her heart, and she firmly pushed the feeling aside. "Greta, look, I know I messed up, but I'm going to fix it for you. Do you see this?" He lifted the bottle of amber liquid. "It's synthetic urine. And it's ours."

"Gross," Andi said.

Greta stared at the bottle in his hand. "What are you talking about?"

"I bought the patent for King's synthetic back. Whitetail wasn't going to use it, so they were glad to make some money off it."

The room froze. She knew Tamsin and Andi were still there, taking in the entire exchange with wide eyes, but for just a moment all that mattered was Nick. Nick, and that little bottle clutched in his hand. "How much?" she whispered.

"$250,000."

"Wait. He spent a quarter of a million dollars on pee?" Andi asked.

"Shhh," Tamsin hissed, her eyes fixed on Greta's face.

"That means I have enough left over for startup costs," Nick continued. He set the bottle back down in front of her. The surface of the liquid shivered.

"I thought the concept was a loser."

"No. The product's good. We just never could market it well enough for it to take off." He crouched down beside her chair.

She was overwhelmed by him. By his sheer size, by the glint of molten gold stubble over his jaw, by the knife-edge shimmer of hope in his eyes, by the outside-brought-in scent of him. She wanted so badly to touch him, for him to touch her. But even as his hands reached out as if to grab hers, he stopped, his arms dropping to his sides.

He wasn't there to take, she realized. He wanted her to give.

"What do you want from me?" she said.

"I painted my bedroom," he repeated. "You were right. I was hanging onto my failed marriage by leaving the house the way it was. Not because I was still in love with my wife, but as a reminder that I hadn't been able to make her happy."

Greta drew in a breath. "Well, I'm glad that you can get a fresh start."

"I don't think I can make you happy, either."

She had left him, but that admission still hurt. What had she expected? That he would show up to fight for her? That he was there to win her back?

"But I think maybe you might be able to be happy in Bartlett. With me."

Her shoulders slumped in surprise even as she began to form an objection. Her? In Bartlett? It wasn't happening. There was nothing for her in Kentucky.

Except a treehouse along a creek. And her father. And Nick.

"We don't have to live in Bartlett," he said, his voice low. "We could stay here. I'm not sure how I'll do living in a city, but if it's important to you to stay, I'll give it a chance."

She imagined all that was wild in Nick trying to adapt to city life. "You would hate it."

"Then we'll talk about it. I know we're different people, but I don't think we're so different that we can never be happy together. Because the truth is…" He glanced at Tamsin and Andi, then shook his head and blundered on. "The truth is, I've fallen in love with you. And not being with you definitely will not make me happy."

The room whirled around her for a moment, and she closed her eyes to steady herself. Dimly, she heard Andi say, "I'm confused. What about his boyfriend?" Maybe she'd been right before; maybe this was a nightmare. Because only a bad dream could be this cruel, offering her all she'd ever wanted just when she'd decided she no longer wanted it.

"Greta," he said, and his voice was so soft, so close that she could have been back in his pink bedroom, tangled with him in his bedsheets, his lips buried in her hair.

But his bedroom was no longer pink. And she was no longer the woman who needed him to say those words.

"I'm sorry," she said, steeling herself to open her eyes. When she did, she found him rocked back on his heels, his beautiful face slowly turning to stone. The stupid part of her, the part that believed in ridiculous notions like fairy tales and true love and happy endings, ached with sorrow at his pain.

Fortunately, the sane, smart part of her won out. "I appreciate the gesture," she said, and was amazed at how brisk and businesslike her voice sounded. Maybe she was a better actress than she thought. "But we are under a very tight deadline here, and I need to get back to work." With that, she grabbed the bottle, ignoring the lingering warmth from Nick's hand, and handed it back to him. "Thank you."

Then she turned to Tamsin and Andi, who were staring at her with rapt attention. "Where were we?"

She felt more than saw Nick slowly get to his feet, felt the air around her grow cooler as he stepped back. "Okay, then. I'll show myself out." He inclined his head toward Tamsin and Andi. "Ladies."

Even with the smart side of herself running the show, Greta couldn't keep herself from watching him leave, his shoulders heavy with defeat. Well, what had he expected? He suddenly needed her for a little side venture, and she was supposed to give up everything to take a chance on fake deer pee?

He took a chance on it, the stupid side of her whispered. On fake deer pee, and on her.

The door clicked behind him, and the light in the office seemed to flare, haloing painfully inside Greta's brain. Absently, she reached for her Excedrin bottle.

"Greta," Andi said.

"Yeah?"

"You just took some of that."

She paused, her hand on the cap, blinking at her coworkers. Had it only been a few minutes earlier that she'd taken those three pills? It felt like a lifetime ago. "Right." She dropped the bottle back into her bag and smiled. It probably looked a bit grim around the edges, but she was damned if she was going to let Nick Campbell ruin her chance of landing the creative director position. "Now, Tamsin, you said you had some suggestions?"

The other two women just stared at her. Finally, Tamsin said, "Andi, give us a minute, would you please?"

Andi groaned. "Come on. Don't make me leave now. Whatever you're going to say has to be good."

Tamsin's lips compressed into a managerial frown, and Andi sighed. "Fine. But promise me you'll tell me everything later." Her eyes darted from Tamsin to Greta, making it unclear who she was speaking to.

"Just go. Now." Tamsin rolled her eyes as a grumbling Andi closed the door behind herself. "She's lucky she's a genius at graphic design."

"I think you're being a little generous with the word *genius*, but okay."

Leaning back in her chair, Tamsin folded her hands together. "You want to talk about it?"

"Not even a little bit." She glanced down at the desk, where the ad she'd dreamed up mocked her.

"Greta, do you remember the roses you got for Valentine's Day last year?"

Roses? Greta massaged her temples as she tried to bring up the memory. Finally, it came to her. "The accountant."

"I guess."

James. Never Jim—that she remembered. He'd been the perfect boyfriend, respectful of her career, ambitious in his own. Attractive. At least, she though he'd been attractive, although she couldn't quite call up the details of his face anymore. For Valentine's Day, he sent her seven red roses, one for every month they'd been dating. It was supposed to be romantic, and she'd thought it was more romantic than, say, a generic and thoughtless dozen, until she realized that seven was also the number of dates they'd been on. Between her schedule and his, they only had time to get together about once a month. Which was fine, but that in itself was the problem. Should it really be fine to not care that she couldn't see him more than a couple hours a month?

But that had been over a year ago. She barely remembered the roses, and she sure as hell didn't understand why Tamsin was bringing them up now.

"I didn't realize you noticed them."

"Observation is a pretty critical part of my job." A tiny gold wishbone glittered from the hollow of Tamsin's collarbone. "When those roses arrived at the office, you oohed and ahhed over them. You said you couldn't believe how sweet it was of your accountant to send them to you. You displayed them in your office. You did everything you'd expect a woman would do when her boyfriend sends roses."

"So?"

"As soon as those roses started to wilt, you threw them out."

Greta was sure her boss had a point, but she sure did wish she would get there quicker. "Isn't that what people do with dead flowers?"

"Some people. But some people leave the flowers out a little past their prime, because they're a reminder of the person who sent them. Not you, though. And it wasn't just the flowers you threw away, was it?"

No, it wasn't. She broke things off with James a few days later. Probably about the time the flowers started to shrivel and droop.

"You had to know things weren't working out when you got those roses, but you acted like everything was perfect. Because that's how you are—everything is always perfect on the outside no matter what's going on on the inside."

"I still don't understand—"

Tamsin smiled. "Everything is always perfect with you. Except for today."

Greta winced. "I'm sorry you had to see that, but it's over. I'd like to focus on this campaign now."

"Greta, that man brought you a bottle of—am I understanding this correctly?—*fake urine*, and it nearly brought you to tears. Honestly, before today, I didn't know you were capable of an emotion besides suck-upness."

That one stung. "That's not an emotion. Or a word."

"You know what I mean," Tamsin said with a wave of her hand. "You have feelings for that man, and yet you're sitting here talking to me instead of doing what you should be doing."

"And that is...?"

"Go after him. Yell at him. Cry, if that's what you feel like doing. Kiss him, which is what I would do if I were you and that man brought me—well, I don't get the urine thing, but it seems to mean something to you. But figure this out. Because if a man can get you this shook up, that means you have something you need to figure out."

"I can't do that. Not now." She gazed past her boss to where a big window let in natural light. If she made creative director, she would get an office, maybe one with a window, too. "I'm not giving up a chance at a promotion for a man."

Tamsin surprised her by chuckling. "Greta, do you know why I work?"

"Because..." She faltered. "People have to work."

"My husband is a VP of finance at Decuir Price. I don't need the money."

Greta blinked. She hadn't realized Tamsin was married, although it wasn't like she and her boss spent any time together outside of work.

"I work because I love what I do. And you might have noticed that this job requires long hours. There's no punching out and going home for the night—part of me is always working. If I didn't have a supportive partner at home, there's no way I could keep doing this.

"Look, if I thought you were happy to see that man go, then I would give you a high five and tell you that you did the right thing. Well," she added with a shudder, "not a literal high five. I don't high five.

"But you're not happy. In fact, you look like you're barely holding yourself together." She tapped one perfectly manicured finger on the desktop. "That man didn't bring you roses, Greta. He brought you a challenge. I'd say he understands you pretty well."

Greta stared at her. Tamsin was right. Maybe it *was* possible to have it all—a meaningful career and the man she loved.

The man who'd spent a quarter of a million dollars on a patent and then came all the way to Chicago to tell her he loved her.

"Oh my God," she whispered.

She'd let him walk out the door.

As if she could read her mind, Tamsin said, "I'm sure you can still catch him. You know how the elevators are after lunch—he might even still be waiting for one."

"I—" She jumped to her feet. Of course it was ridiculous to think she would find him just outside the office waiting by the inadequate bank of elevators. But...maybe. She had to get to him before...

Well, just before.

"I have to go." She glanced at the ad on her desk, then looked up at Tamsin. "Can you...?"

"I've got this covered. Go." Tamsin swept the ad from Greta's desk. "You do good work. I'm looking forward to seeing what you come up with to sell fake urine. Now get out of here."

Every day, Greta moved gracefully through the warren of hallways and open spaces and sound-eating offices that made up the Prescott Agency, smiling sedately at all the right people, nodding at important people as if they should know who she was.

But not today. Today she ran.

It wasn't a good run, either. It was an awkward, high-heeled, elbows flying, I-just-let-the-love-of-my-life-walk-away-and-have-to-find-him-before-he-meets-a-less-obtuse-woman kind of run. Reed stepped out of an office at the end of the hall, all mediocre-male swagger and arrogance. Seeing Greta careening toward him, he jumped back, plastering himself against the wall.

Greta didn't even have time to enjoy the look of shock on his face. One minute she was blowing by him, and the next she was dodging surprised visitors in the Prescott reception area.

And then she was out the door and headed for the elevators. Her heart sank. Nick wasn't there.

But an elevator was, its doors starting to close, a handful of people in drab business suits inside. "Hold the elevator, hold the elevator, hold the elevator," she cried, running full tilt for the narrowing gap between the doors.

It was like an Indiana Jones movie, she decided. If she ran fast enough, she could slide into the elevator just as the doors closed behind her. She could—

—bounce off the polished brass elevator doors as they closed before she got there. "Oof," she said, her breath stolen by the impact. She looked at the closed doors. It would take forever for another elevator to arrive. There were stairs, but she was never going to catch up with Nick if she had to climb down 15 flights of stairs. "No," she whispered. "No, no, no."

And then, very slowly, the doors magically slid open. "Sorry," a short man with a graying beard said. "It took me a second to find the Door Open button."

She wanted to hug him. "Thank you," she said.

And then she burst into tears. Which meant that nobody bothered her for the entire elevator ride down to the lobby. Even better, by silent agreement, everybody let her off the elevator first.

Apparently, not looking perfect had some advantages.

She couldn't quite run through the crowded lobby, especially not with its polished marble floor, but she did her best, making it to the front door without spraining an ankle or taking out an old lady. On the sidewalk in front of the building, she realized exactly how crazy this whole thing was. She had no idea which direction Nick had gone. She didn't even know how he'd gotten there. Had he driven himself to Chicago? Or had he flown and grabbed a cab at the airport?

She was turning to go back inside the building when she caught sight of a tall man in a navy suit walking down the sidewalk to her right. He was almost to the end of the block, but there was no mistaking those broad shoulders and dark gold hair.

It was Nick.

"Nick!" she called, her high heels pounding the sidewalk as she ran. "Nick!"

It was hard going, trying to avoid running into anyone else

while still keeping one eye on Nick's retreating back to make sure he didn't disappear on her. Not now. Not when she was so close.

At the end of the block, Nick stopped, probably to wait for the light to turn. If he crossed the street before she got there and she got stuck by traffic, she might lose him again. Gathering her flagging energy, she put on a burst of speed.

She saw the dogwalker too late. It was a young woman, clearly out of her league with nearly a half-dozen dogs churning around her ankles. They moved like a low-hanging cloud of dogs, their leashes tangling and untangling as she stood, lost and confused, in their midst.

Greta juked to the right to avoid the main mass of dogs. "Nick!" she yelled, waving one hand frantically as if he might somehow hear it moving through the air.

That's when she saw the cocker spaniel, which was squatting a little apart from the rest of the dogs to do its business in the relative peace of the pedestrian traffic moving up and down the sidewalk. Finishing, the spaniel moved off to the left, while oncoming pedestrian traffic shifted to the right and the hapless dog walker, bag in hand, tried desperately to corral her charges in that general direction.

Up ahead, the traffic light changed.

"Nick!"

There was no help for it. With the dogs on one side and a mass of people on the other, Greta had no choice but to take the clear path down the middle. Right over the dog poop.

She was running too hard to do more than halfheartedly attempt to avoid stepping directly in the pile.

Which was exactly what she did.

Just as Nick turned his head and caught sight of her racing down the sidewalk. His whole body stiffened. "Greta?" he said.

She reached him, finally, flinging her arms around him, her

hair tumbling every which way, her chest heaving as she tried to catch her breath.

He studied her, his eyes cautiously hopeful even as his arms went around her. Then he looked over her shoulder at the jumble of dogs and the flattened pile of poop. "Did you just step in—"

"Yes," she said, still breathless. "Urban scat."

And then she kissed him, loving the way he pulled her hungrily against him, the way his fingers shook just a little as they tenderly traced the curve of her cheek. When she finally came up for a gulp of much-needed air, he moved his lips to her temple and whispered her name over and over until she felt dizzy with how much she'd missed him.

Pulling back, she gripped the lapels of his suit in both hands as if holding on might keep him from getting away again. "I love you," she said. "I want to go back to Bartlett with you and sell synthetic deer urine."

"Are you sure?" Nick's gaze was warm on her face. "We can do anything you want. We can live here, or somewhere in-between, or wherever. I just want to make a life with you."

She pressed her face against his chest and nodded. "I'm sure, Nick." He smelled like the woods, even in the middle of a busy Chicago street. "Let's go home."

"Okay. But would you mind terribly if we stopped at your place so you can change shoes?"

She glanced down at her shoes, her nose wrinkling as she caught a whiff of dog poop. The shoe rental company was not going to be pleased with her. Again. "That's probably a good idea. I kind of want to take a shower now, too." She cocked her head to the side. "You know, I could probably use some help in the shower. If you're available for that sort of thing."

Nick gave her a lazy, wolfish smile. "I think I just became a very big fan of urban scat."

And when he kissed her again, she decided she had, too.

EPILOGUE

*S*ix Months Later

"I don't need your help drawing the bow anymore," Greta grumbled as Nick's hands settled over hers. But she leaned back against him, enjoying the way his body felt against her own.

"I don't know about that. You were shaking pretty hard that last time."

"That's because I'm freezing. Why are we doing this outside, anyway?"

"If I'm ever going to make a bowhunter out of you, you're going to have to get used to the cold. There's nothing better than a crisp, cold November morning in a treestand."

"Bad news, buddy. You're never going to make a bowhunter out of me." She eyed the target, where Nick had pinned up some brightly colored balloons for her to aim at. She'd already popped two, and she had just three left. "Now, are you going to let me shoot or are you going to keep getting in the way?"

His lips found the skin under her ear, and she drew in a

breath. "Oh, I'm going to keep getting in the way," he said, his voice low and seductive. But then he sighed and straightened away from her. "Think you can hit that green one next?"

"Maybe." But she knew she could. Lately she'd been practicing more than Nick had, which was understandable given the amount of time Nick was spending getting the new Bartlett Attractions up and running. The company had debuted at the annual industry trade show the previous month. There was still a lot of work to do, but sales had already exceeded their initial projections.

They'd gotten lucky in that Whitetail Sports Co. was only too happy to divest itself of a factory in Kentucky it no longer needed, along with some of the equipment. Paul had hired a chemist to help tweak the formula, and most former King employees were once again working for him.

For her part, Greta was busy, too, working with Ben on a campaign for some new products Paul had dreamed up. But she made time every day to shoot her bow. As she explained to Nick, it kept her in touch with her customers.

She aimed her bow at the green balloon, walking through the shot sequence steps she'd gone through over and over again. Then she touched the release, and the green balloon exploded with a satisfying pop.

"Nice shot," Nick said.

"Thanks," she said. But something wasn't quite right about the target. The balloon had popped, but there was still something hanging from the pin it had been stuck up with. "What...?"

"You should probably take a closer look," Nick suggested.

Setting down her bow, she moved closer to the target. Yes, there was something hanging from the pin—a red ribbon. And dangling from the end of the ribbon was—"Oh, my God."

She spun around to find Nick down on one knee, cold grass and all. "What are you doing?" she asked.

"Trying to remember the speech I wrote about how much I loved you, but this cold is kind of getting to me."

"Was it a long speech?"

"Terribly."

She gave an exaggerated shiver. "Seems like something best done inside."

"I guess I should have planned it a little better. We'll have to classify this as a marriage proposal fail."

She walked to the target and drew the ribbon through her fingers until she reached the glittering ring at the end. She was certainly not the kind of woman who got weak-kneed over a sparkly diamond, but, as it turned out, she wasn't completely unaffected by it, either.

Especially not when it was from one of the sexiest men she'd ever met.

"I don't know that I'd classify it as a fail," she said slowly. "I think I'd have to say no to calling it a total failure."

Nick got to his feet and pulled her against him, his hands rubbing her upper arms. "I know how much you hate failure."

"That's true. I do," she said, admiring the way the ring caught the sunlight. It wasn't exactly what she'd call understated elegance. It was a little more on the bling side.

She loved it.

"Of course, I have been getting more used to the idea that failure isn't the end of the world," she said.

In response, Nick tightened his grip on her arms, hauling her up for a long, passionate kiss. When he finally broke away, he rested his forehead against hers and said, "In this case, failure would definitely feel like the end of the world to me."

"Well, we can't have that, can we?" And she slid the ring over her finger and lifted her face to kiss him again.

"I love you," he whispered against her ear as she nestled into his chest.

"I love you, too."

Her life was no longer perfect—she had a job she'd never known she wanted and lived in a town she'd once sworn never to return to and was now engaged to a perfectly imperfect man.

She'd never been happier.

Or colder.

"Can we go inside now?" she asked.

His eyes crinkled at the corners. "You don't want to pop the rest of the balloons?" he teased.

"Is there more jewelry in them?"

"Nope."

She studied the remaining balloons where they bounced gently against the target. "You know what," she said, walking over to her bow. "As it turns out, I do want to pop them."

"I figured."

Yes, she thought as she took aim with her bow. This was exactly the life she wanted.

THANK YOU!

Thanks so much for reading! If you enjoyed Greta and Nick's story and want to leave a review on Amazon—well, you've probably read enough of these requests to know how helpful reviews can be to an author.

If you'd like to find out when the next book (which will have significantly less deer urine in it) will be available, find me on Facebook at www.facebook.com/KellyMcKerrasAuthor or sign up for my newsletter at www.kellymckerras.com.

ACKNOWLEDGEMENTS

There is a Tracy Lawrence song called "Find Out Who Your Friends Are" that posits you learn a lot about who your true friends are when the going gets tough. Though it's not mentioned in the song, the process of writing a book was similarly illuminating. There's no better way to test the strength of your friendships than to spend an entire dinner ruminating aloud on a minor plot point or send messages to people during the work day asking questions about their thoughts on deer urine.

In that regard, I am immensely fortunate.

My amazing husband puts up with a lot and still supports me. My children have generously agreed not to kill each other/superglue their fingers together/shave the cat while I'm writing—and mostly followed through. And my parents, sister, and in-laws are generally awesome.

I'm so lucky to be a member of the Second Draft writers' group. I could not have made it through this book without Julia, Eric, Erv,

ACKNOWLEDGEMENTS

John, Navin, Elise, Kay, and Greg. And though we lost him too soon, it would feel strange not to mention Brian, who, I have to assume, is amusing and confounding the angels as I write this.

I am grateful for the wealth of knowledge I've gotten from my work with Shadow Alley Press. Though we work in different genres, I have learned so much from Jeanette, James, Nick, Aaron, Jess, eden, D.J., Nathaniel, Mark, Zack, Jake, and Emily. I could not have asked for a more supportive place to work. Also, their gif game is on point.

This book would not exist without Tony Peterson, who basically nagged it into existence and then edited the heck out of it. (Apparently, I cannot spell the word ~~refridgerator~~ ~~refrige~~—oh, you know what I mean—to save my life.) Whitney Beatty of LongPlay Communication provided creative direction when I was blithely heading down the wrong path. Red Leaf Book Design created this beautiful cover. And Jody Gilbert did the final proofread (and caught some pretty embarrassing typos).

Last but not least, Margaret, Christy, Jessica, and Mark provided emotional support and cheerleading to an extent I probably do not deserve. I'm so grateful to have friends like you in my life.